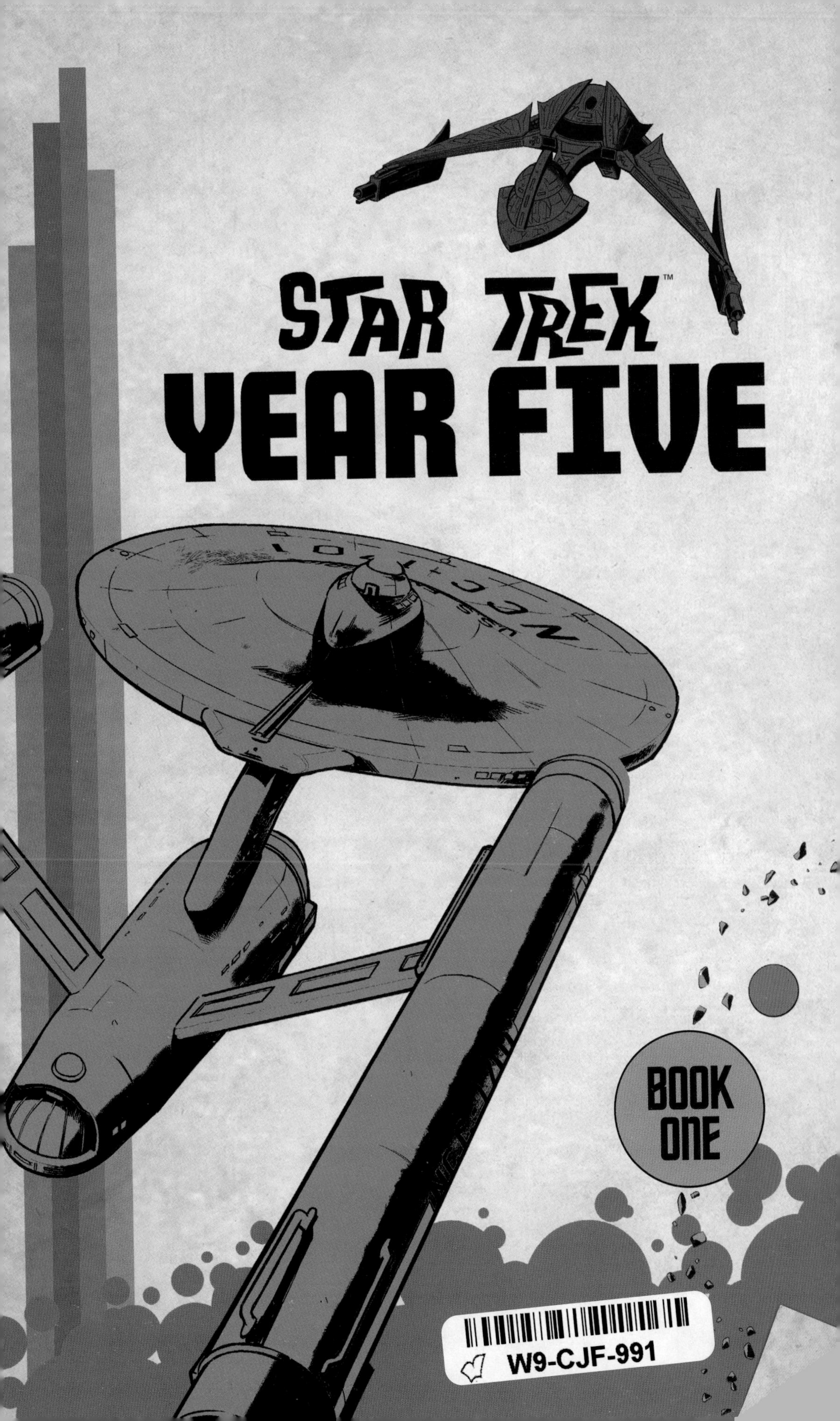
STAR TREK™
YEAR FIVE
BOOK ONE

STAR TREK
YEAR FIVE

Become our fan on Facebook **facebook.com/idwpublishing**
Follow us on Twitter **@idwpublishing**
Subscribe to us on YouTube **youtube.com/idwpublishing**
See what's new on Tumblr **tumblr.idwpublishing.com**
Check us out on Instagram **instagram.com/idwpublishing**

IDW
www.IDWPUBLISHING.com

COVER ARTIST
J.J. LENDL

COLLECTION EDITORS
JUSTIN EISINGER
AND **ALONZO SIMON**

COLLECTION DESIGNER
CLAUDIA CHONG

Chris Ryall, President, Publisher, & CCO
John Barber, Editor-In-Chief
Cara Morrison, Chief Financial Officer
Matthew Ruzicka, Chief Accounting Officer
David Hedgecock, Associate Publisher
Jerry Bennington, VP of New Product Development
Lorelei Bunjes, VP of Digital Services
Justin Eisinger, Editorial Director, Graphic Novels & Collections
Eric Moss, Sr. Director, Licensing & Business Development

Ted Adams and Robbie Robbins, IDW Founder

ISBN: 978-1-68405-568-5   23 22 21 20   1 2 3 4

Originally published as STAR TREK: YEAR FIVE issues #1–6.

Special thanks to Risa Kessler, Marian Cordry, Dayton Ward, and John Van
Citters of CBS Consumer Products for their invaluable assistance.

For international rights, contact licensing@idwpublishing.com

EPISODE ONE: ODYSSEY'S END

WRITERS: JACKSON LANZING & COLLIN KELLY
ARTIST: STEPHEN THOMPSON
COLORIST: CHARLIE KIRCHOFF

EPISODE TWO: COMMUNICATION BREAKDOWN

WRITER: BRANDON EASTON
ARTIST: MARTIN COCCOLO
COLORIST: FRAN GAMBOA

EPISODE THREE: THE TRUTH ARTIFACT

WRITER: JODY HOUSER
ARTIST: SILVIA CALIFANO
COLORIST: THOMAS DEER

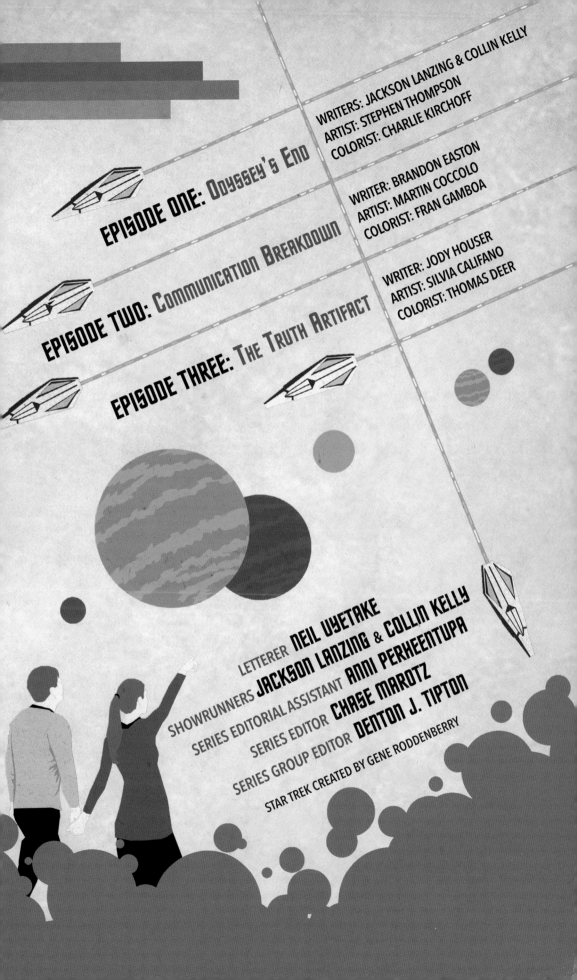

LETTERER NEIL UYETAKE
SHOWRUNNERS JACKSON LANZING & COLLIN KELLY
SERIES EDITORIAL ASSISTANT ANNI PERHEENTUPA
SERIES EDITOR CHASE MAROTZ
SERIES GROUP EDITOR DENTON J. TIPTON

STAR TREK CREATED BY GENE RODDENBERRY

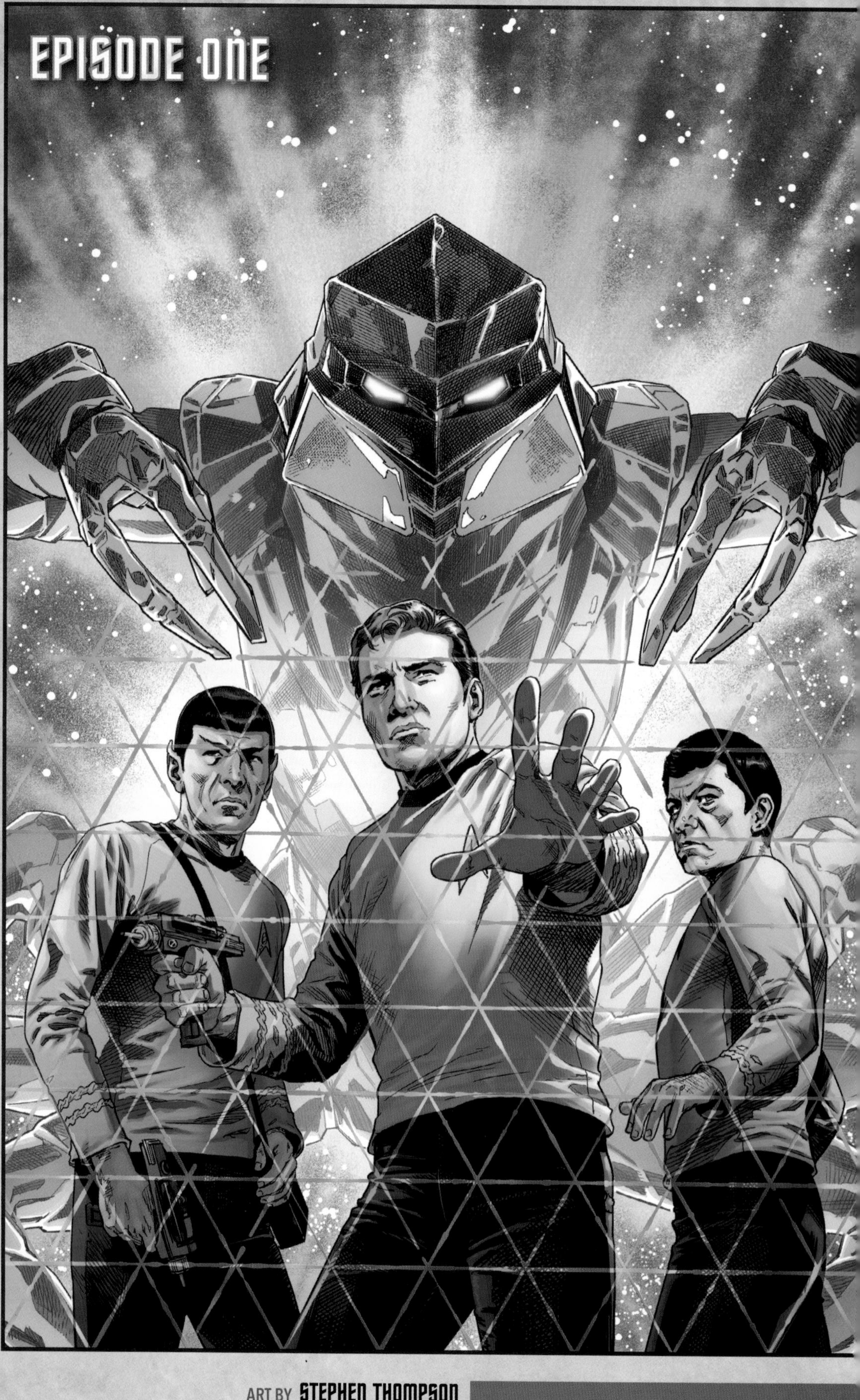
EPISODE ONE

ART BY STEPHEN THOMPSON
COLORS BY CHARLIE KIRCHOFF

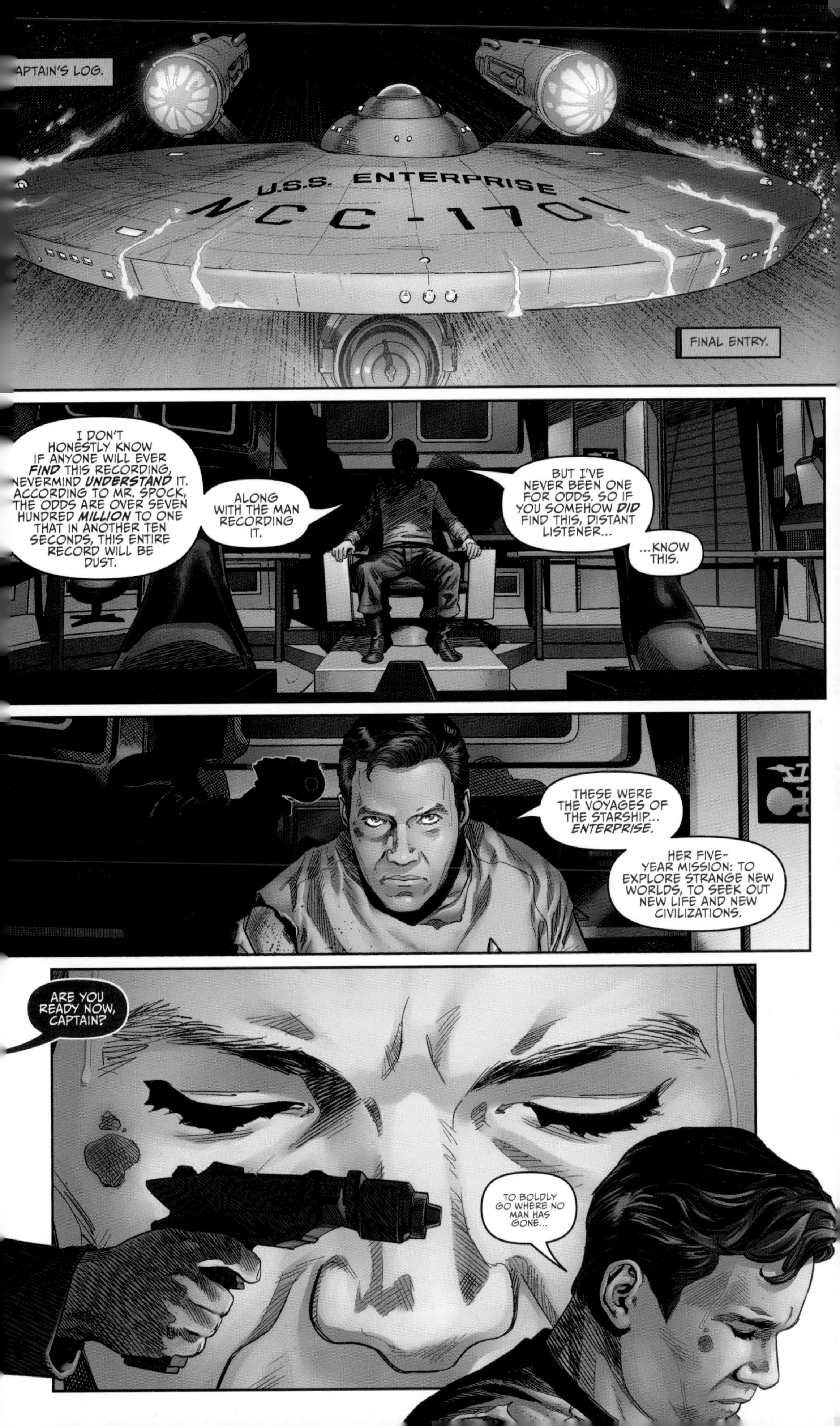
APTAIN'S LOG.
U.S.S. ENTERPRISE
NCC-1701
FINAL ENTRY.
I DON'T HONESTLY KNOW IF ANYONE WILL EVER FIND THIS RECORDING, NEVERMIND UNDERSTAND IT. ACCORDING TO MR. SPOCK, THE ODDS ARE OVER SEVEN HUNDRED MILLION TO ONE THAT IN ANOTHER TEN SECONDS, THIS ENTIRE RECORD WILL BE DUST.
ALONG WITH THE MAN RECORDING IT.
BUT I'VE NEVER BEEN ONE FOR ODDS. SO IF YOU SOMEHOW DID FIND THIS, DISTANT LISTENER...
...KNOW THIS.
THESE WERE THE VOYAGES OF THE STARSHIP... ENTERPRISE.
HER FIVE-YEAR MISSION: TO EXPLORE STRANGE NEW WORLDS, TO SEEK OUT NEW LIFE AND NEW CIVILIZATIONS.
ARE YOU READY NOW, CAPTAIN?
TO BOLDLY GO WHERE NO MAN HAS GONE...

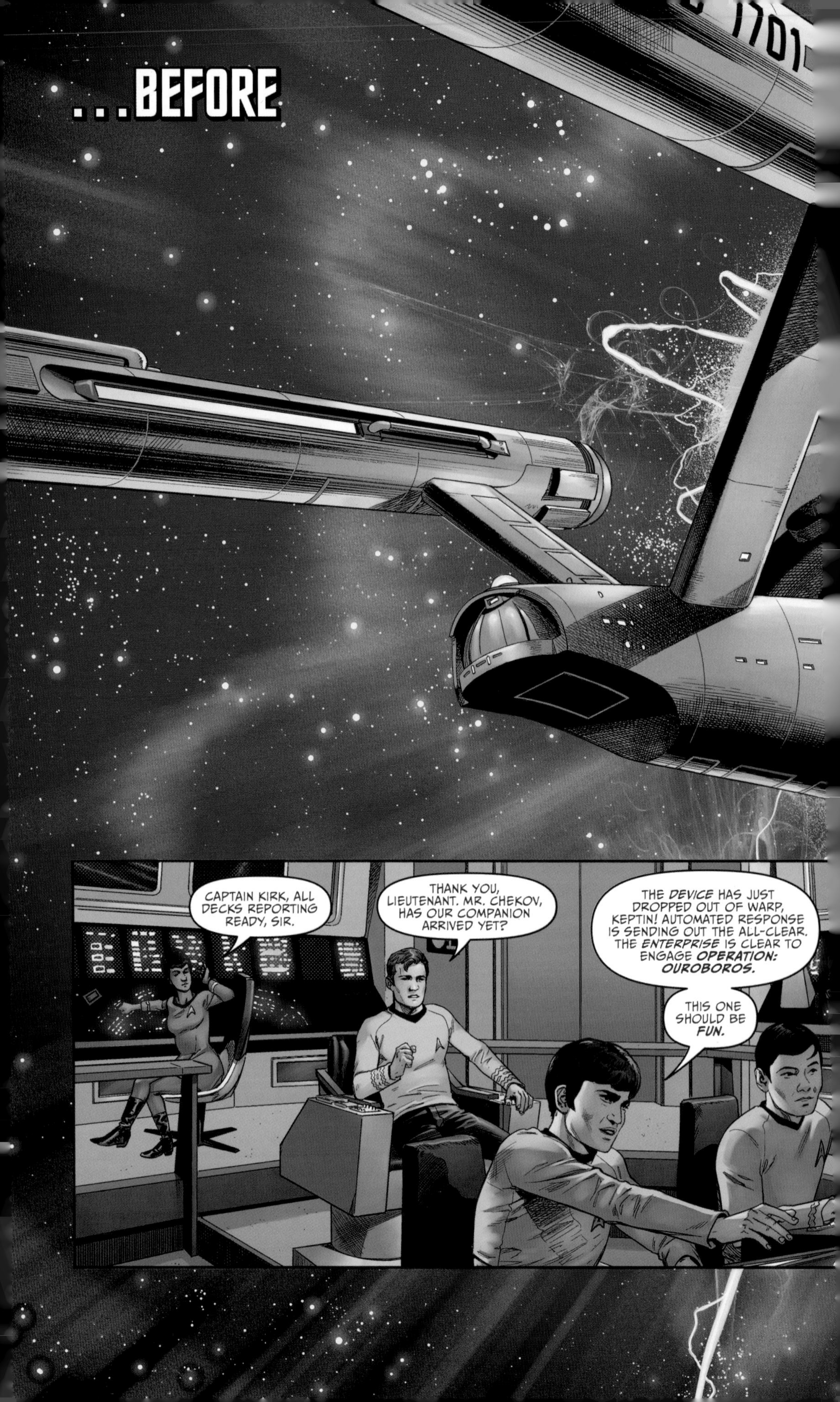
...BEFORE
1701
CAPTAIN KIRK, ALL DECKS REPORTING READY, SIR.
THANK YOU, LIEUTENANT. MR. CHEKOV, HAS OUR COMPANION ARRIVED YET?
THE DEVICE HAS JUST DROPPED OUT OF WARP, KEPTIN! AUTOMATED RESPONSE IS SENDING OUT THE ALL-CLEAR. THE ENTERPRISE IS CLEAR TO ENGAGE OPERATION: OUROBOROS.
THIS ONE SHOULD BE FUN.

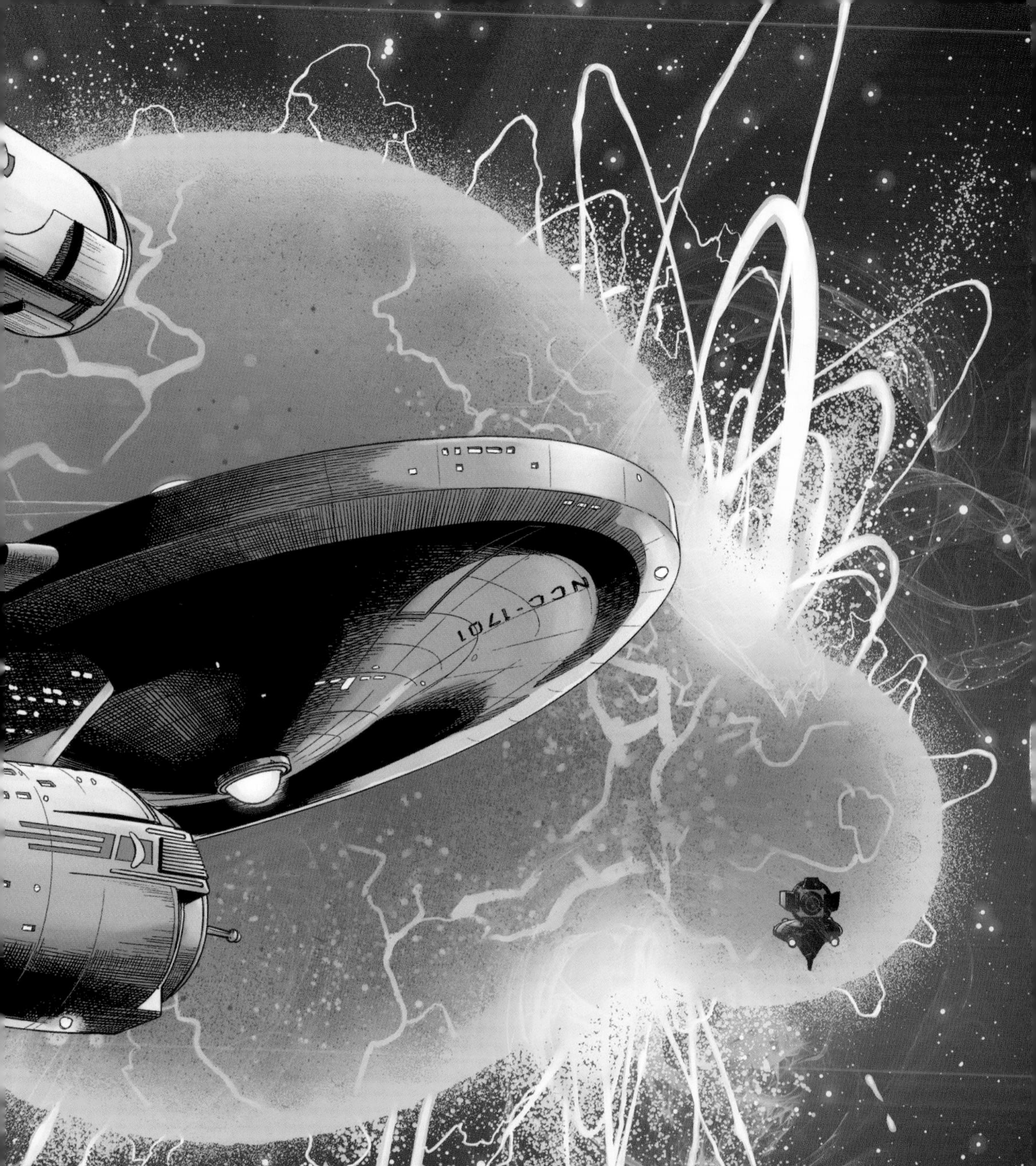
NCC-1701

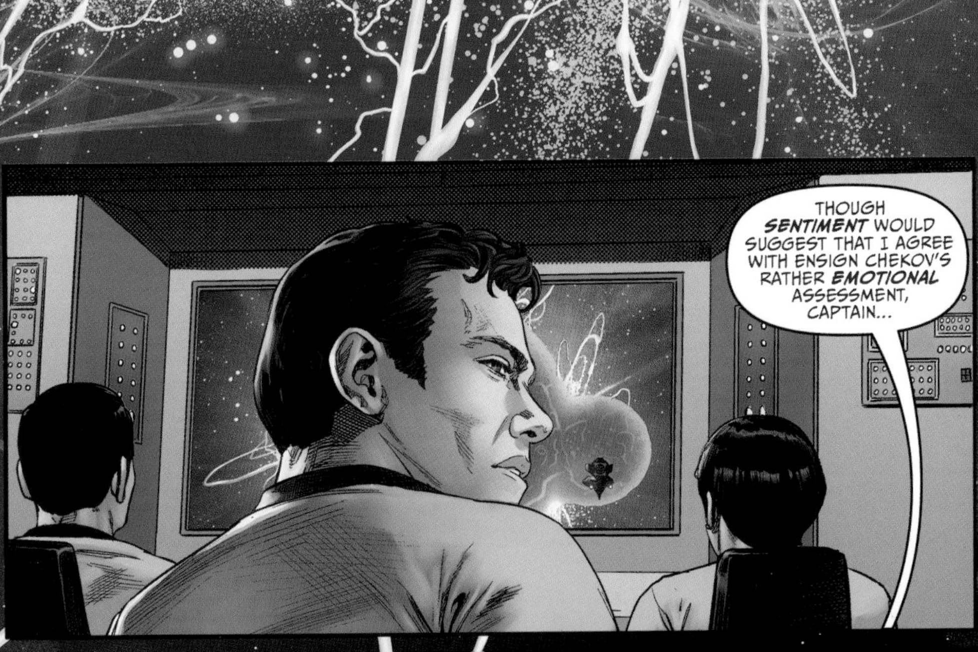
THOUGH **SENTIMENT** WOULD SUGGEST THAT I AGREE WITH ENSIGN CHEKOV'S RATHER **EMOTIONAL** ASSESSMENT, CAPTAIN...

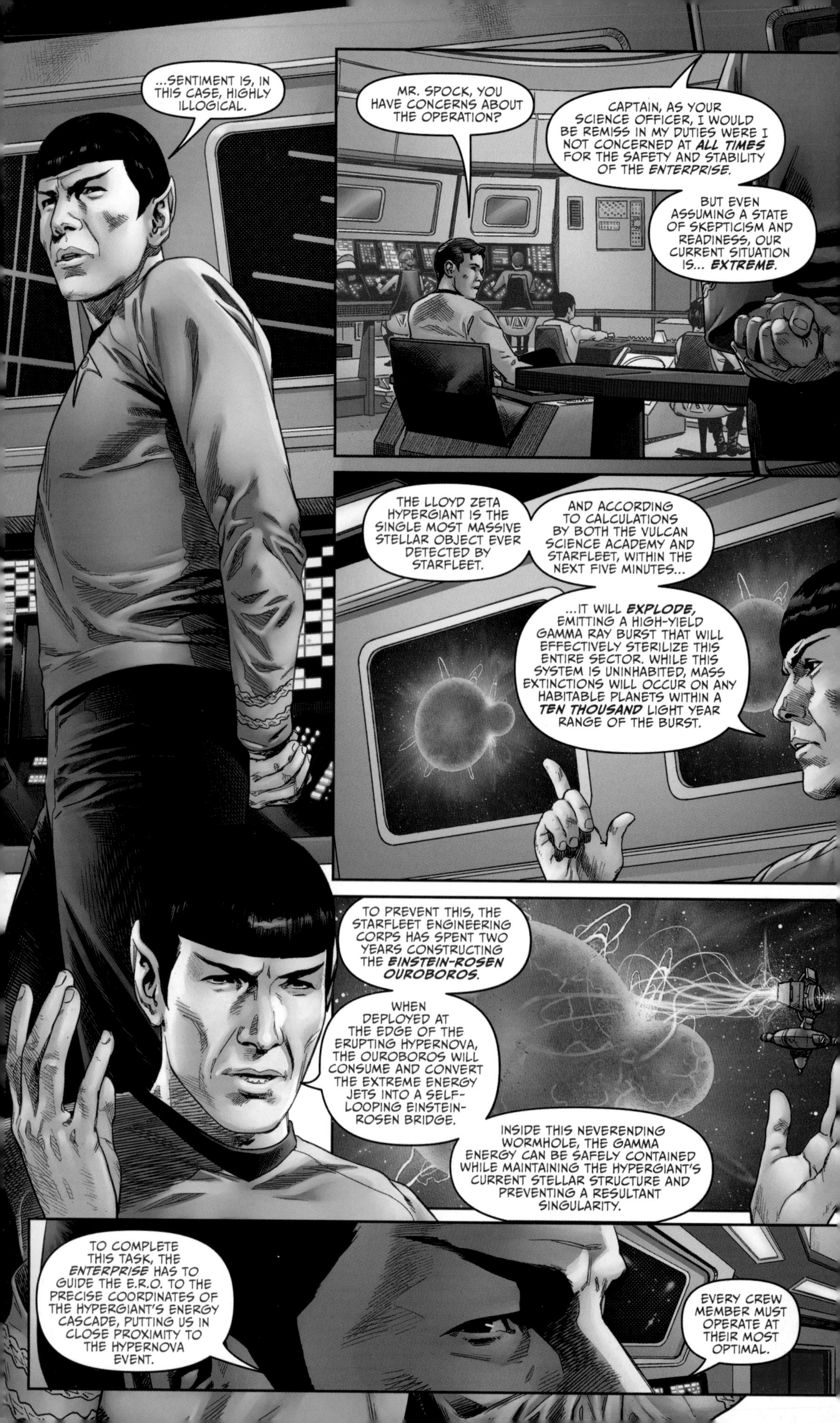
...SENTIMENT IS, IN THIS CASE, HIGHLY ILLOGICAL.
MR. SPOCK, YOU HAVE CONCERNS ABOUT THE OPERATION?
CAPTAIN, AS YOUR SCIENCE OFFICER, I WOULD BE REMISS IN MY DUTIES WERE I NOT CONCERNED AT ALL TIMES FOR THE SAFETY AND STABILITY OF THE ENTERPRISE.
BUT EVEN ASSUMING A STATE OF SKEPTICISM AND READINESS, OUR CURRENT SITUATION IS... EXTREME.
THE LLOYD ZETA HYPERGIANT IS THE SINGLE MOST MASSIVE STELLAR OBJECT EVER DETECTED BY STARFLEET.
AND ACCORDING TO CALCULATIONS BY BOTH THE VULCAN SCIENCE ACADEMY AND STARFLEET, WITHIN THE NEXT FIVE MINUTES...
...IT WILL EXPLODE, EMITTING A HIGH-YIELD GAMMA RAY BURST THAT WILL EFFECTIVELY STERILIZE THIS ENTIRE SECTOR. WHILE THIS SYSTEM IS UNINHABITED, MASS EXTINCTIONS WILL OCCUR ON ANY HABITABLE PLANETS WITHIN A TEN THOUSAND LIGHT YEAR RANGE OF THE BURST.
TO PREVENT THIS, THE STARFLEET ENGINEERING CORPS HAS SPENT TWO YEARS CONSTRUCTING THE EINSTEIN-ROSEN OUROBOROS.
WHEN DEPLOYED AT THE EDGE OF THE ERUPTING HYPERNOVA, THE OUROBOROS WILL CONSUME AND CONVERT THE EXTREME ENERGY JETS INTO A SELF-LOOPING EINSTEIN-ROSEN BRIDGE.
INSIDE THIS NEVERENDING WORMHOLE, THE GAMMA ENERGY CAN BE SAFELY CONTAINED WHILE MAINTAINING THE HYPERGIANT'S CURRENT STELLAR STRUCTURE AND PREVENTING A RESULTANT SINGULARITY.
TO COMPLETE THIS TASK, THE ENTERPRISE HAS TO GUIDE THE E.R.O. TO THE PRECISE COORDINATES OF THE HYPERGIANT'S ENERGY CASCADE, PUTTING US IN CLOSE PROXIMITY TO THE HYPERNOVA EVENT.
EVERY CREW MEMBER MUST OPERATE AT THEIR MOST OPTIMAL.

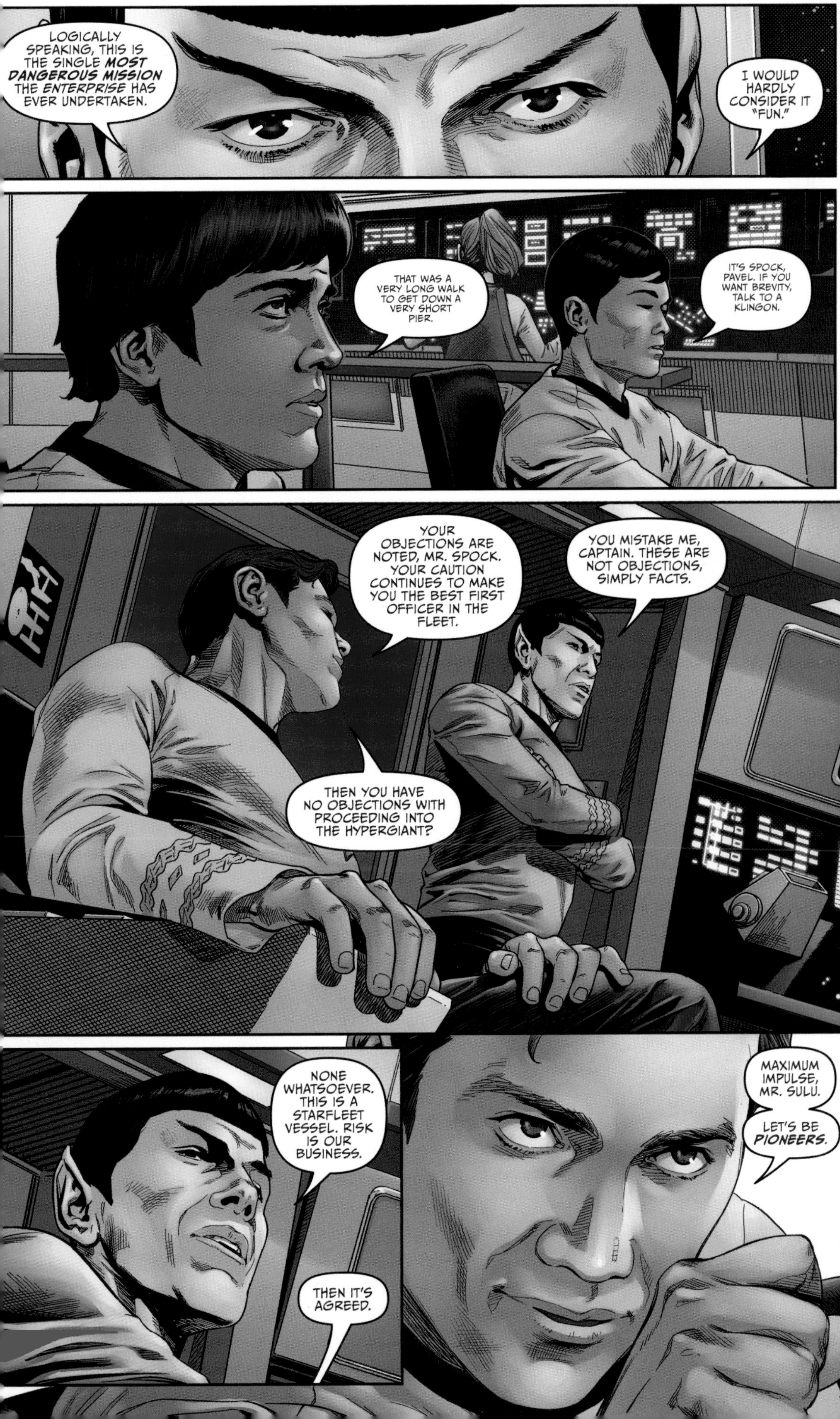
LOGICALLY SPEAKING, THIS IS THE SINGLE **MOST DANGEROUS MISSION** THE *ENTERPRISE* HAS EVER UNDERTAKEN.
I WOULD HARDLY CONSIDER IT "FUN."
THAT WAS A VERY LONG WALK TO GET DOWN A VERY SHORT PIER.
IT'S SPOCK, PAVEL. IF YOU WANT BREVITY, TALK TO A KLINGON.
YOUR OBJECTIONS ARE NOTED, MR. SPOCK. YOUR CAUTION CONTINUES TO MAKE YOU THE BEST FIRST OFFICER IN THE FLEET.
YOU MISTAKE ME, CAPTAIN. THESE ARE NOT OBJECTIONS, SIMPLY FACTS.
THEN YOU HAVE NO OBJECTIONS WITH PROCEEDING INTO THE HYPERGIANT?
NONE WHATSOEVER. THIS IS A STARFLEET VESSEL. RISK IS OUR BUSINESS.
THEN IT'S AGREED.
MAXIMUM IMPULSE, MR. SULU.
LET'S BE **PIONEERS**.

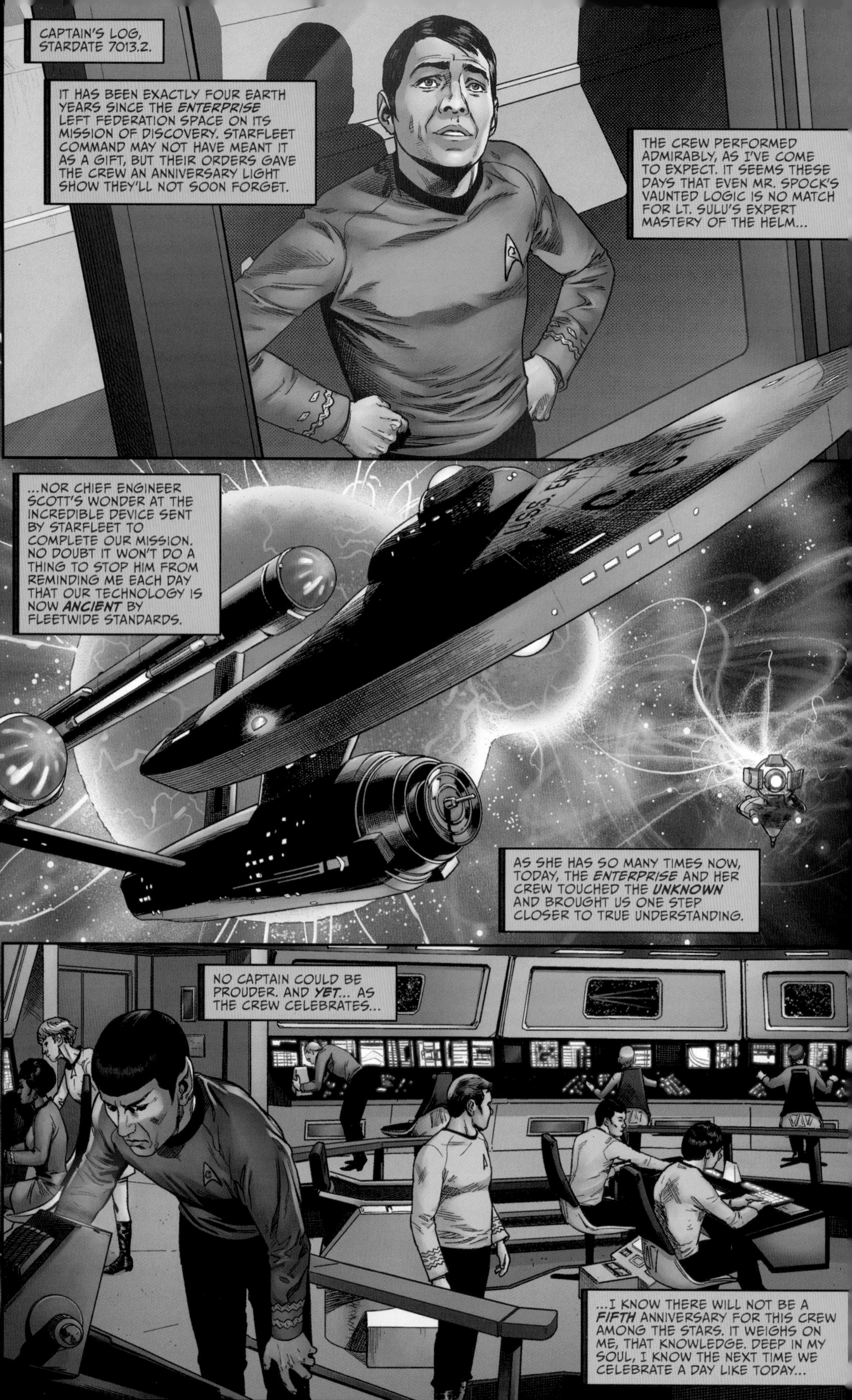
CAPTAIN'S LOG, STARDATE 7013.2.
IT HAS BEEN EXACTLY FOUR EARTH YEARS SINCE THE *ENTERPRISE* LEFT FEDERATION SPACE ON ITS MISSION OF DISCOVERY. STARFLEET COMMAND MAY NOT HAVE MEANT IT AS A GIFT, BUT THEIR ORDERS GAVE THE CREW AN ANNIVERSARY LIGHT SHOW THEY'LL NOT SOON FORGET.
THE CREW PERFORMED ADMIRABLY, AS I'VE COME TO EXPECT. IT SEEMS THESE DAYS THAT EVEN MR. SPOCK'S VAUNTED LOGIC IS NO MATCH FOR LT. SULU'S EXPERT MASTERY OF THE HELM...
...NOR CHIEF ENGINEER SCOTT'S WONDER AT THE INCREDIBLE DEVICE SENT BY STARFLEET TO COMPLETE OUR MISSION. NO DOUBT IT WON'T DO A THING TO STOP HIM FROM REMINDING ME EACH DAY THAT OUR TECHNOLOGY IS NOW ***ANCIENT*** BY FLEETWIDE STANDARDS.
AS SHE HAS SO MANY TIMES NOW, TODAY, THE *ENTERPRISE* AND HER CREW TOUCHED THE ***UNKNOWN*** AND BROUGHT US ONE STEP CLOSER TO TRUE UNDERSTANDING.
NO CAPTAIN COULD BE PROUDER. AND ***YET***... AS THE CREW CELEBRATES...
...I KNOW THERE WILL NOT BE A ***FIFTH*** ANNIVERSARY FOR THIS CREW AMONG THE STARS. IT WEIGHS ON ME, THAT KNOWLEDGE. DEEP IN MY SOUL, I KNOW THE NEXT TIME WE CELEBRATE A DAY LIKE TODAY...

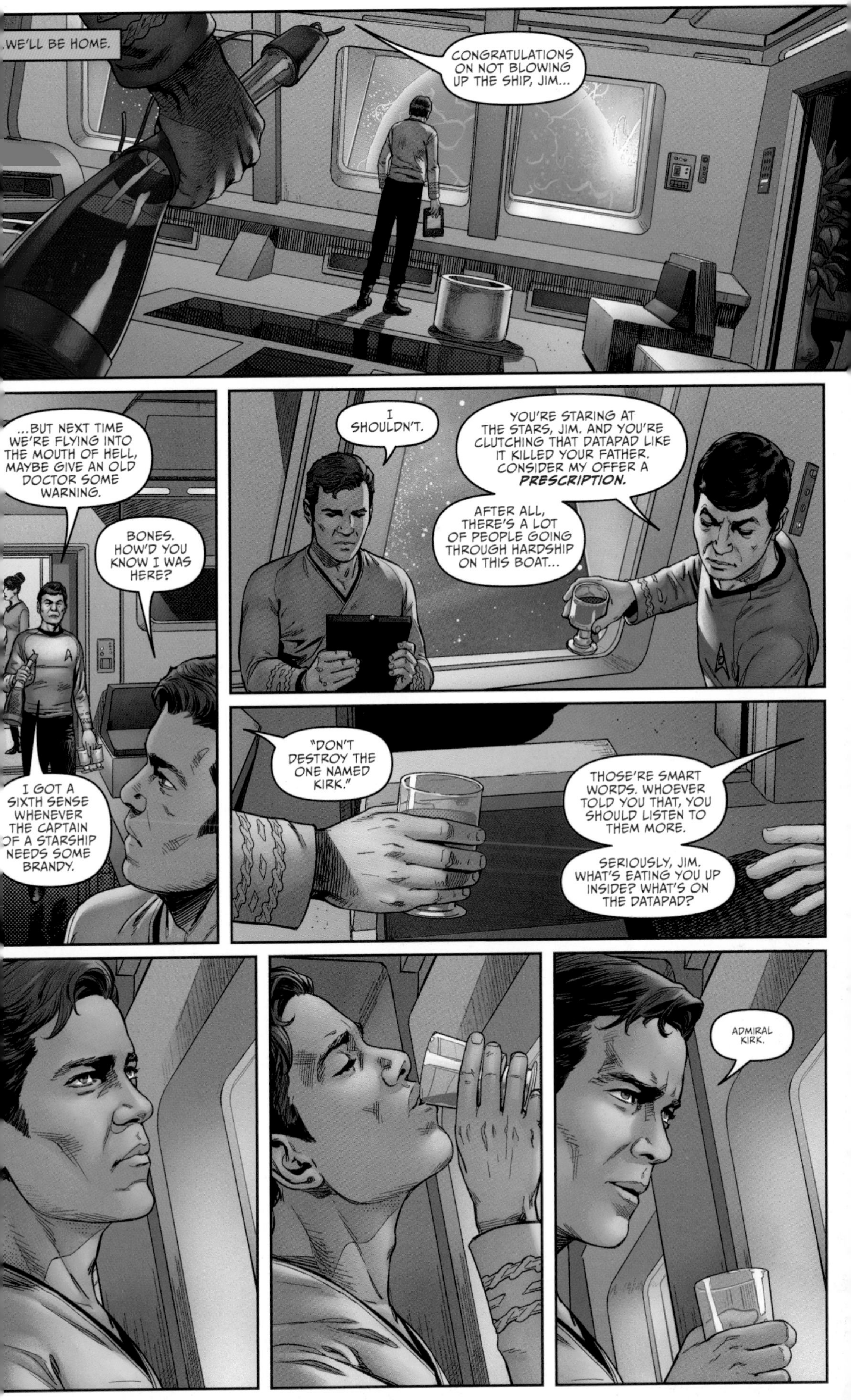
...WE'LL BE HOME.
CONGRATULATIONS ON NOT BLOWING UP THE SHIP, JIM...
...BUT NEXT TIME WE'RE FLYING INTO THE MOUTH OF HELL, MAYBE GIVE AN OLD DOCTOR SOME WARNING.
BONES. HOW'D YOU KNOW I WAS HERE?
I GOT A SIXTH SENSE WHENEVER THE CAPTAIN OF A STARSHIP NEEDS SOME BRANDY.
I SHOULDN'T.
YOU'RE STARING AT THE STARS, JIM. AND YOU'RE CLUTCHING THAT DATAPAD LIKE IT KILLED YOUR FATHER. CONSIDER MY OFFER A PRESCRIPTION.
AFTER ALL, THERE'S A LOT OF PEOPLE GOING THROUGH HARDSHIP ON THIS BOAT...
"DON'T DESTROY THE ONE NAMED KIRK."
THOSE'RE SMART WORDS. WHOEVER TOLD YOU THAT, YOU SHOULD LISTEN TO THEM MORE.
SERIOUSLY, JIM. WHAT'S EATING YOU UP INSIDE? WHAT'S ON THE DATAPAD?
ADMIRAL KIRK.

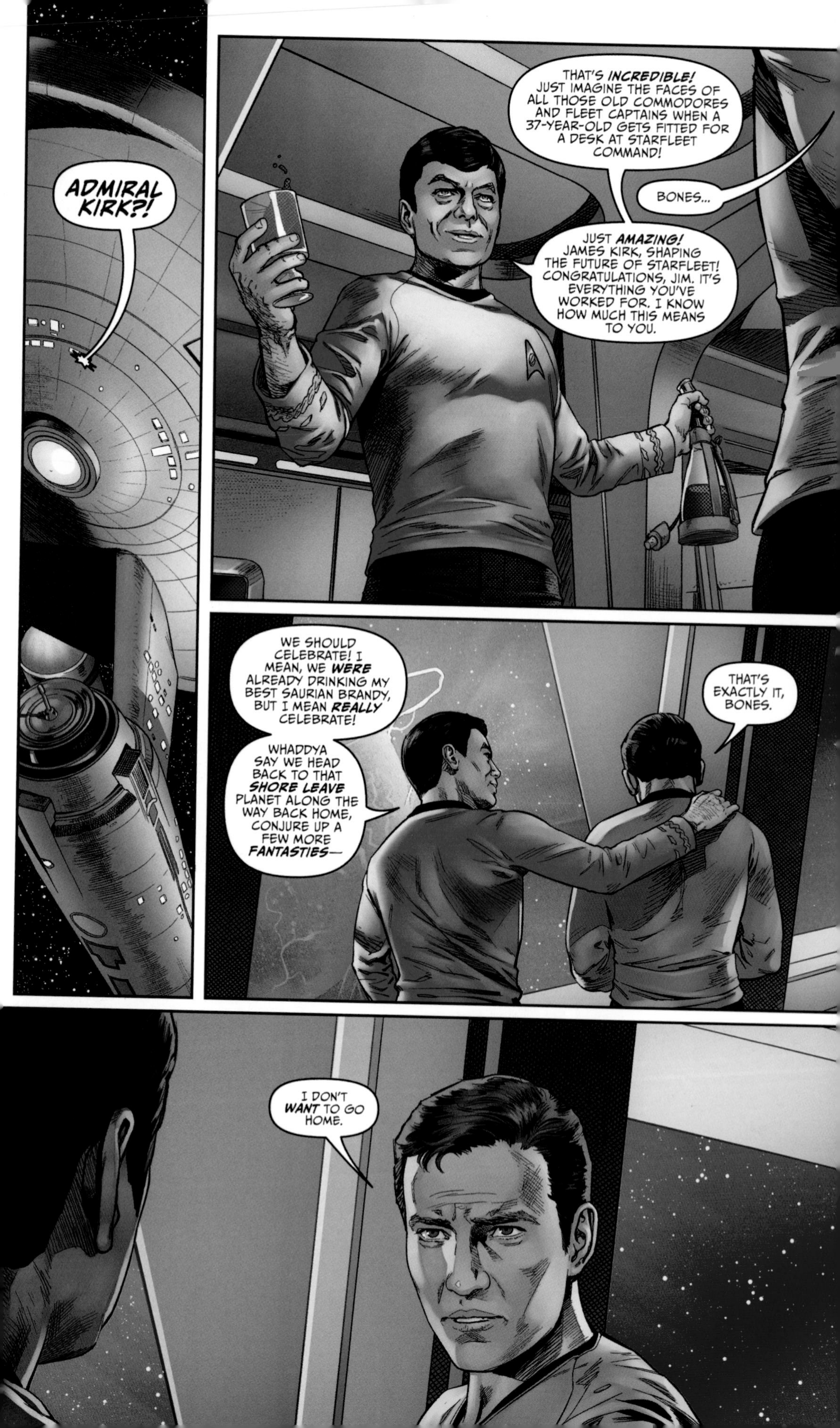
ADMIRAL KIRK?!
THAT'S INCREDIBLE! JUST IMAGINE THE FACES OF ALL THOSE OLD COMMODORES AND FLEET CAPTAINS WHEN A 37-YEAR-OLD GETS FITTED FOR A DESK AT STARFLEET COMMAND!
BONES...
JUST AMAZING! JAMES KIRK, SHAPING THE FUTURE OF STARFLEET! CONGRATULATIONS, JIM. IT'S EVERYTHING YOU'VE WORKED FOR. I KNOW HOW MUCH THIS MEANS TO YOU.
WE SHOULD CELEBRATE! I MEAN, WE WERE ALREADY DRINKING MY BEST SAURIAN BRANDY, BUT I MEAN REALLY CELEBRATE!
WHADDYA SAY WE HEAD BACK TO THAT SHORE LEAVE PLANET ALONG THE WAY BACK HOME, CONJURE UP A FEW MORE FANTASTIES—
THAT'S EXACTLY IT, BONES.
I DON'T WANT TO GO HOME.

I'M NOT SURE... HOW TO EXPLAIN.

SEE, MY DAD WAS A GREAT STUDENT OF THE CLASSICS.

WE HAD A WHOLE LIBRARY OF THEM ON THE FARM IN IOWA—OLD BOOKS, NOT DATAPADS. LIKE THAT LAWYER ON STARBASE 11, JUST **STACKS** OF THEM IN THE OLD BARN. I STILL REMEMBER LOOKING UP AT THE TITLES.

GILGAMESH. SINUHE. JOURNEY TO THE WEST. THE ODYSSEY.

BUT INSTEAD OF LETTING ME READ THEM, MY DAD WOULD RECITE THEM TO ME. HE TOLD ME AND SAM THAT'S HOW IT WAS **MEANT TO BE DONE.**

THAT THE ANCIENTS HAD TO KEEP IT ALL IN THEIR HEAD, SO THEY COULD READ IT WITH TOTAL CONFIDENCE.

IT SEEMED LIKE MAGIC TO ME. HOW COULD ONE MAN REMEMBER ALL THOSE WORDS? SPOCK, SURE, BUT A MAN OF ANCIENT MESOPOTAMIA? MEMORIZING **HUNDREDS** OF PAGES THAT HE COULDN'T EVEN **WRITE DOWN?**

BUT WHEN SOMETHING LOOKS IMPOSSIBLE, THERE'S ALWAYS A TRICK.

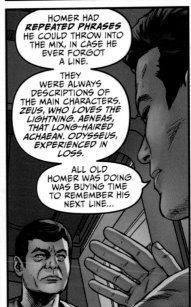

HOMER HAD **REPEATED PHRASES** HE COULD THROW INTO THE MIX, IN CASE HE EVER FORGOT A LINE.

THEY WERE ALWAYS DESCRIPTIONS OF THE MAIN CHARACTERS. ZEUS, WHO LOVES THE LIGHTNING. AENEAS, THAT LONG-HAIRED ACHAEAN. ODYSSEUS, EXPERIENCED IN LOSS.

ALL OLD HOMER WAS DOING WAS BUYING TIME TO REMEMBER HIS NEXT LINE...

...BUT THOSE DESCRIPTIONS LASTED THOUSANDS OF YEARS.

ONE MAN SAID IT ENOUGH AND THAT'S WHAT THOSE PEOPLE BECAME TO HISTORY.

THERE'S NOT A DAY THAT GOES BY THAT I DON'T SAY IT.

"CAPTAIN JAMES T. KIRK OF THE **U.S.S. ENTERPRISE.**"

I JUST DON'T KNOW WHO I AM IF I'M **NOT.**

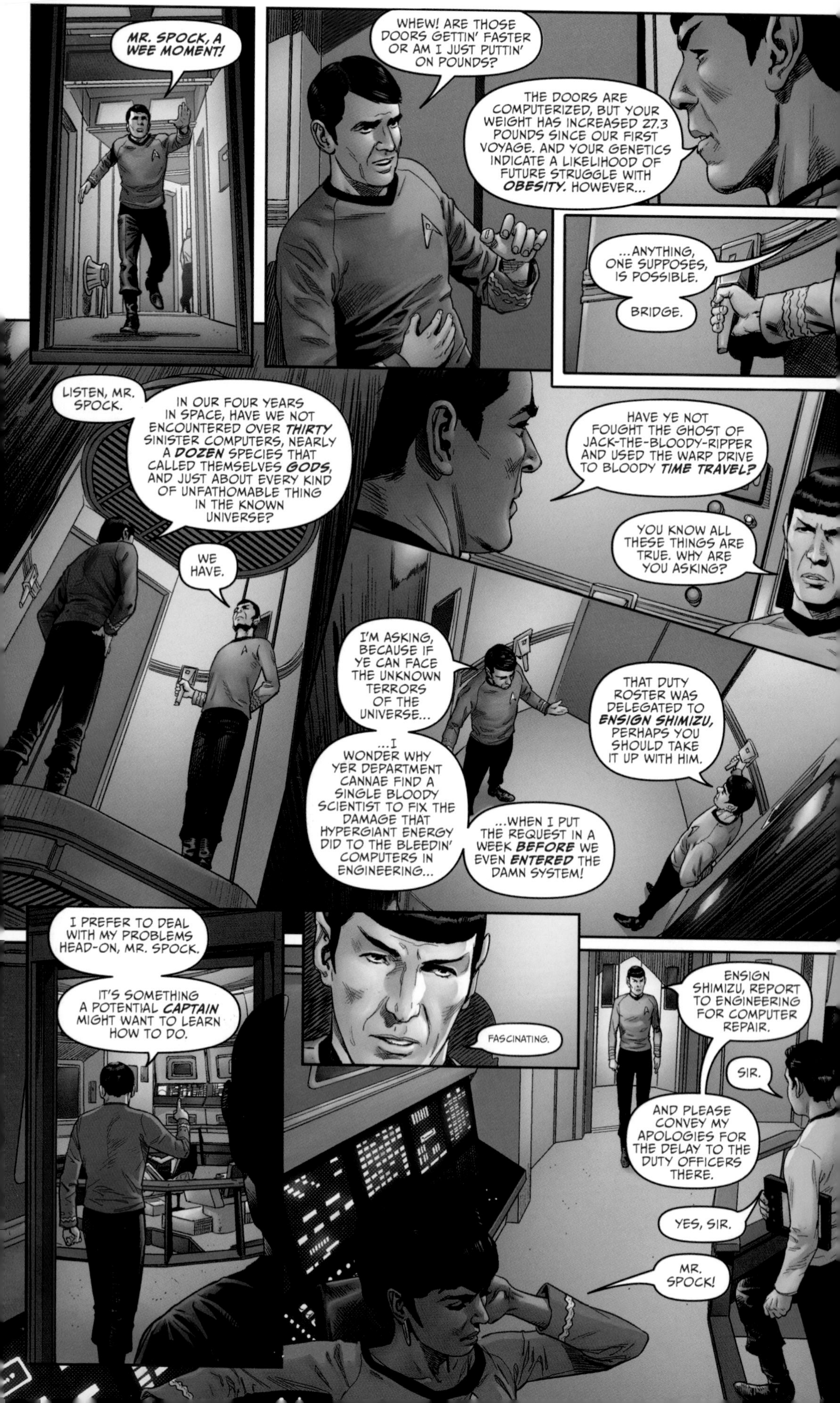
MR. SPOCK, A WEE MOMENT!
WHEW! ARE THOSE DOORS GETTIN' FASTER OR AM I JUST PUTTIN' ON POUNDS?
THE DOORS ARE COMPUTERIZED, BUT YOUR WEIGHT HAS INCREASED 27.3 POUNDS SINCE OUR FIRST VOYAGE. AND YOUR GENETICS INDICATE A LIKELIHOOD OF FUTURE STRUGGLE WITH OBESITY. HOWEVER...
...ANYTHING, ONE SUPPOSES, IS POSSIBLE.
BRIDGE.
LISTEN, MR. SPOCK.
IN OUR FOUR YEARS IN SPACE, HAVE WE NOT ENCOUNTERED OVER THIRTY SINISTER COMPUTERS, NEARLY A DOZEN SPECIES THAT CALLED THEMSELVES GODS, AND JUST ABOUT EVERY KIND OF UNFATHOMABLE THING IN THE KNOWN UNIVERSE?
WE HAVE.
HAVE YE NOT FOUGHT THE GHOST OF JACK-THE-BLOODY-RIPPER AND USED THE WARP DRIVE TO BLOODY TIME TRAVEL?
YOU KNOW ALL THESE THINGS ARE TRUE. WHY ARE YOU ASKING?
I'M ASKING, BECAUSE IF YE CAN FACE THE UNKNOWN TERRORS OF THE UNIVERSE...
...I WONDER WHY YER DEPARTMENT CANNAE FIND A SINGLE BLOODY SCIENTIST TO FIX THE DAMAGE THAT HYPERGIANT ENERGY DID TO THE BLEEDIN' COMPUTERS IN ENGINEERING...
...WHEN I PUT THE REQUEST IN A WEEK BEFORE WE EVEN ENTERED THE DAMN SYSTEM!
THAT DUTY ROSTER WAS DELEGATED TO ENSIGN SHIMIZU, PERHAPS YOU SHOULD TAKE IT UP WITH HIM.
I PREFER TO DEAL WITH MY PROBLEMS HEAD-ON, MR. SPOCK.
IT'S SOMETHING A POTENTIAL CAPTAIN MIGHT WANT TO LEARN HOW TO DO.
FASCINATING.
ENSIGN SHIMIZU, REPORT TO ENGINEERING FOR COMPUTER REPAIR.
SIR.
AND PLEASE CONVEY MY APOLOGIES FOR THE DELAY TO THE DUTY OFFICERS THERE.
YES, SIR.
MR. SPOCK!

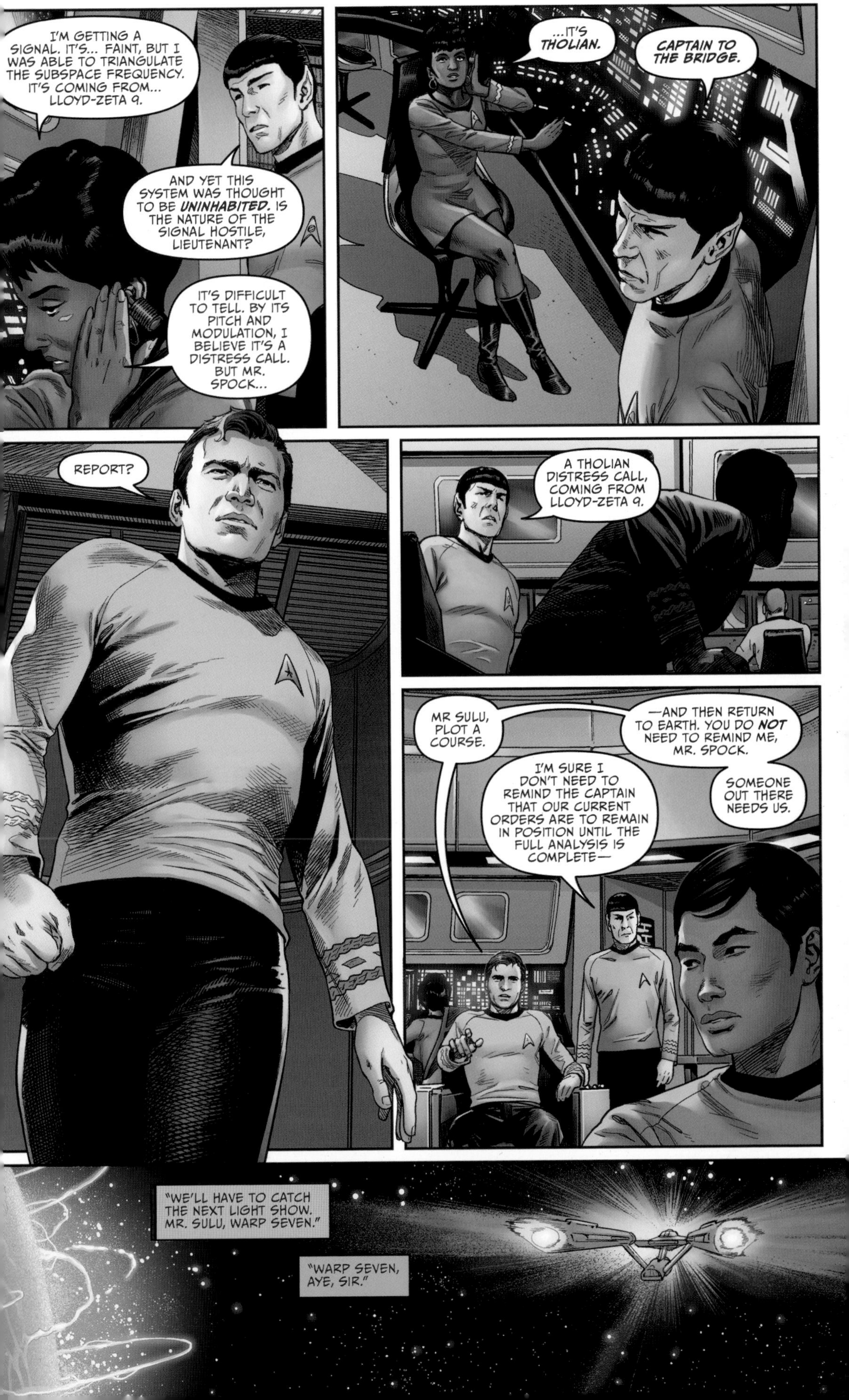
I'M GETTING A SIGNAL. IT'S... FAINT, BUT I WAS ABLE TO TRIANGULATE THE SUBSPACE FREQUENCY. IT'S COMING FROM... LLOYD-ZETA 9.
AND YET THIS SYSTEM WAS THOUGHT TO BE UNINHABITED. IS THE NATURE OF THE SIGNAL HOSTILE, LIEUTENANT?
IT'S DIFFICULT TO TELL. BY ITS PITCH AND MODULATION, I BELIEVE IT'S A DISTRESS CALL. BUT MR. SPOCK...
...IT'S THOLIAN.
CAPTAIN TO THE BRIDGE.
REPORT?
A THOLIAN DISTRESS CALL, COMING FROM LLOYD-ZETA 9.
I'M SURE I DON'T NEED TO REMIND THE CAPTAIN THAT OUR CURRENT ORDERS ARE TO REMAIN IN POSITION UNTIL THE FULL ANALYSIS IS COMPLETE—
—AND THEN RETURN TO EARTH. YOU DO NOT NEED TO REMIND ME, MR. SPOCK.
SOMEONE OUT THERE NEEDS US.
MR SULU, PLOT A COURSE.
"WE'LL HAVE TO CATCH THE NEXT LIGHT SHOW. MR. SULU, WARP SEVEN."
"WARP SEVEN, AYE, SIR."

LLOYD-ZETA 9.
LIFESIGNS: ZERO.

...WE'RE TOO LATE.

IN POINT OF FACT, WE WILL ONLY BE "TOO LATE" ONCE OUR CURRENT PLANETARY POSITION IS FACING THE SUN, AT WHICH POINT THE TEMPERATURE OF THIS SETTLEMENT WILL RISE TO OVER **400 KELVINS**.

THEN LET'S NOT WASTE TIME. FULL SCANS, MR. SPOCK. SECURITY, PHASERS TO STUN. BONES, ARE YOU GETTING ANYTHING?

JIM, THOLIANS ARE MADE OF **LIVING CRYSTAL**. THEY DON'T HAVE HEARTS OR LUNGS. THEY HAVE **FURNACES**!

THERE'S NO TELLING IF THEY'D EVEN REGISTER ON MY EQUIPMENT!

THEY'RE **ALIVE**, BONES. ISN'T THAT YOUR **SPECIALTY**?

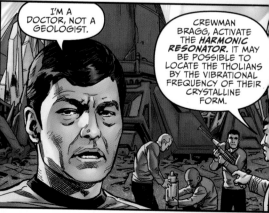

I'M A DOCTOR, NOT A GEOLOGIST.

CREWMAN BRAGG, ACTIVATE THE **HARMONIC RESONATOR**. IT MAY BE POSSIBLE TO LOCATE THE THOLIANS BY THE VIBRATIONAL FREQUENCY OF THEIR CRYSTALLINE FORM.

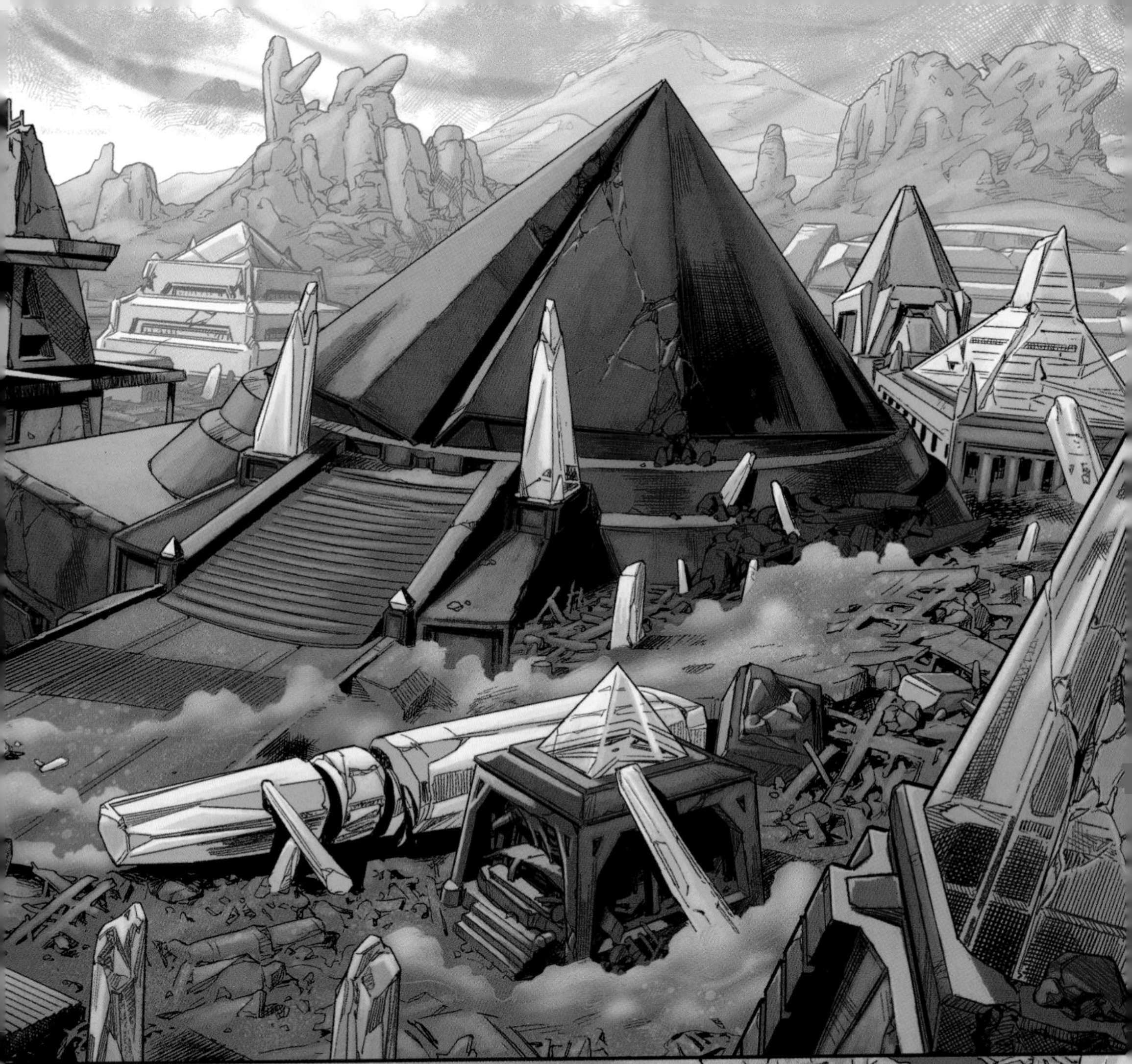

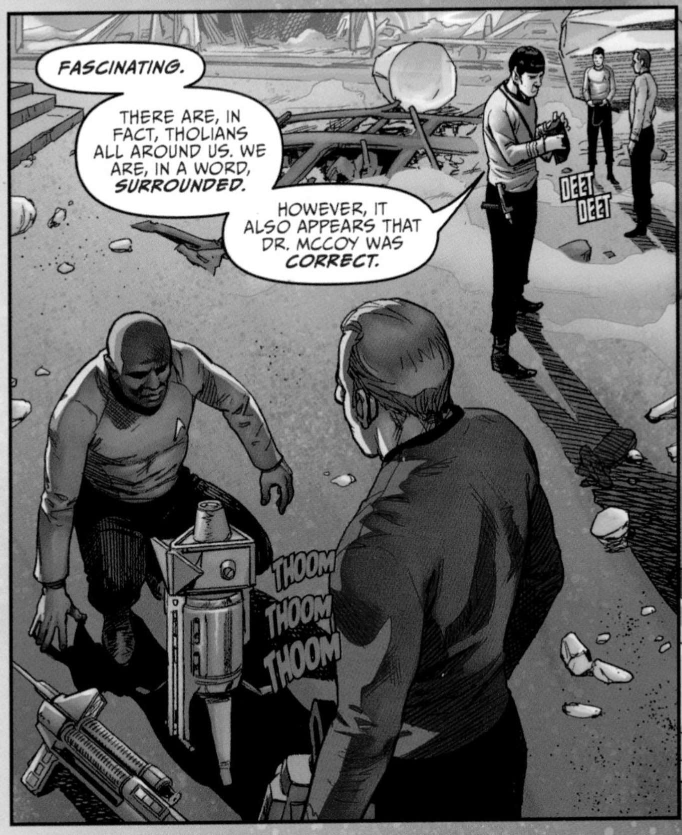
FASCINATING.
THERE ARE, IN FACT, THOLIANS ALL AROUND US. WE ARE, IN A WORD, SURROUNDED.
HOWEVER, IT ALSO APPEARS THAT DR. MCCOY WAS CORRECT.
DEET DEET
THOOM THOOM THOOM

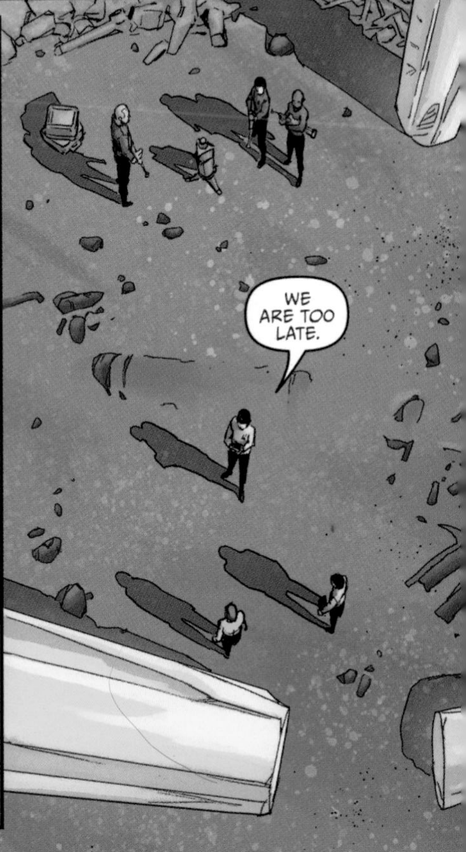
WE ARE TOO LATE.

THERE'S NO PHASER DAMAGE. I'M NOT SEEING ANY... PROJECTILE CASINGS.

THE THOLIANS' UNIQUE BIOLOGY RENDERS THEM VIRTUALLY IMMUNE TO PHASER FIRE. THEIR "SKIN" HAS THE RELATIVE DENSITY OF ANDORIAN DIAMOND.

...DAMMIT.

BUT SOMETHING KILLED THEM. ALL OF THEM.

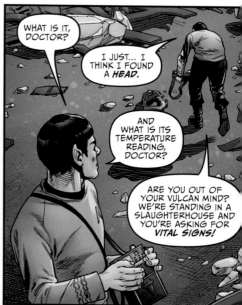

WHAT IS IT, DOCTOR?

I JUST... I THINK I FOUND A HEAD.

AND WHAT IS ITS TEMPERATURE READING, DOCTOR?

ARE YOU OUT OF YOUR VULCAN MIND? WE'RE STANDING IN A SLAUGHTERHOUSE AND YOU'RE ASKING FOR VITAL SIGNS!

BONES. THE TEMPERATURE.

JIM... IT'S ZERO. ABSOLUTE ZERO.

COLD. EXTREME COLD. SPOCK, GIVEN WHAT WE KNOW ABOUT THOLIANS, AN ATTACK UTILIZING THAT KIND OF WEAPON—

—WOULD SUGGEST EXTREME FAMILIARITY WITH THOLIAN BIOLOGY AND DEFENSE CAPABILITIES, CAPTAIN.

BUT THE THOLIANS ARE PRACTICALLY HERMITS! GET CLOSE ENOUGH TO THEIR SPACE AND THEY PUT YOU IN ONE OF THEIR DAMNED WEBS! WHO WOULD EVEN BEGIN TO KNOW HOW TO DO THIS?

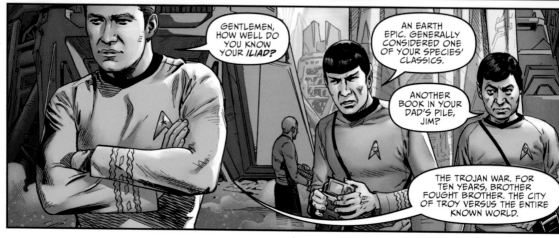

GENTLEMEN, HOW WELL DO YOU KNOW YOUR ILIAD?

AN EARTH EPIC. GENERALLY CONSIDERED ONE OF YOUR SPECIES' CLASSICS.

ANOTHER BOOK IN YOUR DAD'S PILE, JIM?

THE TROJAN WAR. FOR TEN YEARS, BROTHER FOUGHT BROTHER. THE CITY OF TROY VERSUS THE ENTIRE KNOWN WORLD.

BUT THEY WERE *ALL GREEK.*

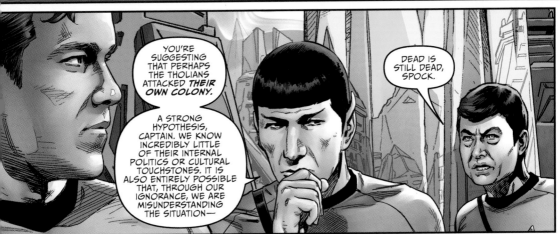

YOU'RE SUGGESTING THAT PERHAPS THE THOLIANS ATTACKED *THEIR OWN COLONY.*

A STRONG HYPOTHESIS, CAPTAIN. WE KNOW INCREDIBLY LITTLE OF THEIR INTERNAL POLITICS OR CULTURAL TOUCHSTONES. IT IS ALSO ENTIRELY POSSIBLE THAT, THROUGH OUR IGNORANCE, WE ARE MISUNDERSTANDING THE SITUATION—

DEAD IS STILL DEAD, SPOCK.

HEY, *STOP!* DON'T *COME* ANY—

AYEEE!

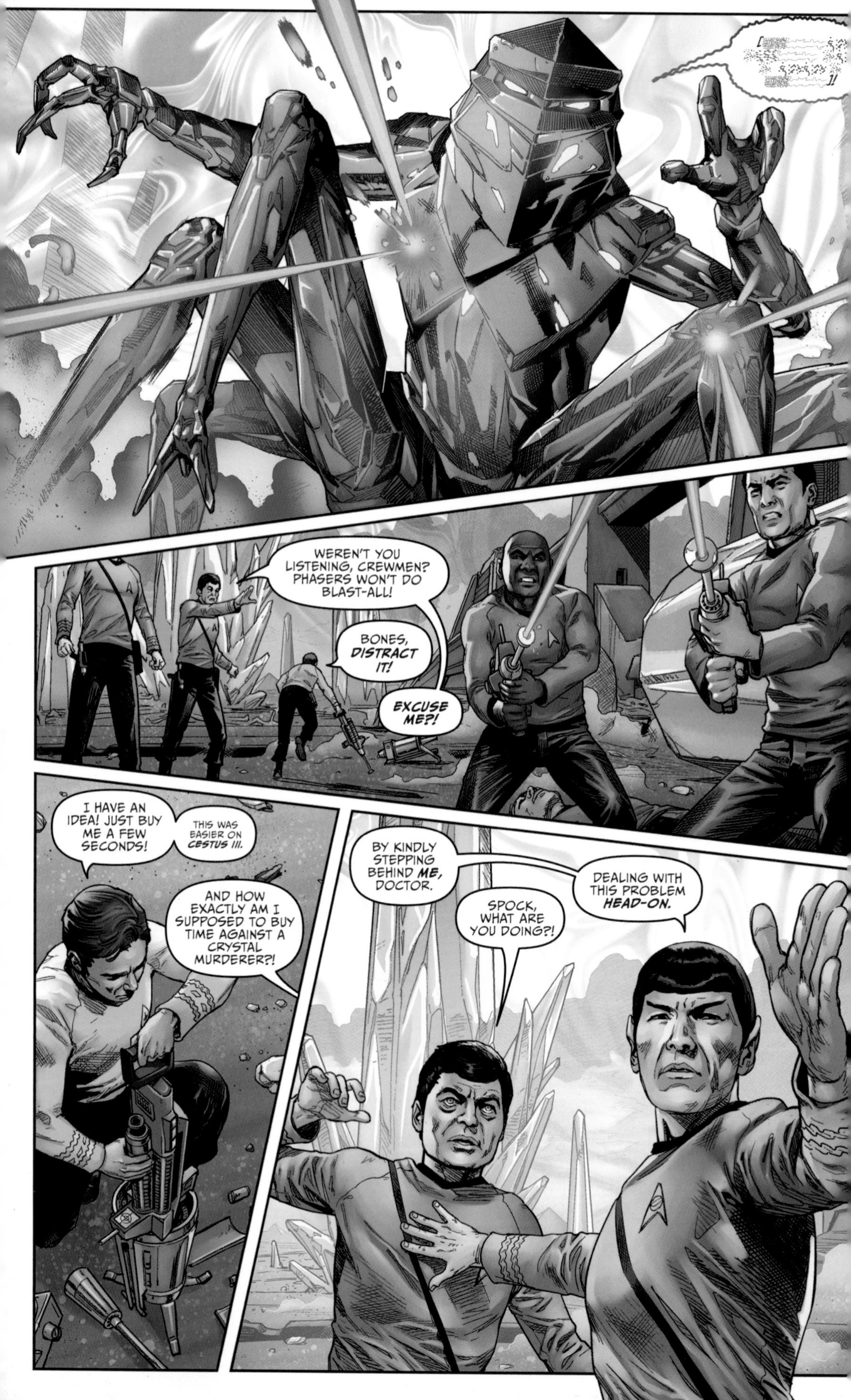
WEREN'T YOU LISTENING, CREWMEN? PHASERS WON'T DO BLAST-ALL!
BONES, DISTRACT IT!
EXCUSE ME?!
I HAVE AN IDEA! JUST BUY ME A FEW SECONDS!
THIS WAS EASIER ON CESTUS III.
AND HOW EXACTLY AM I SUPPOSED TO BUY TIME AGAINST A CRYSTAL MURDERER?!
SPOCK, WHAT ARE YOU DOING?!
DEALING WITH THIS PROBLEM HEAD-ON.
BY KINDLY STEPPING BEHIND ME, DOCTOR.

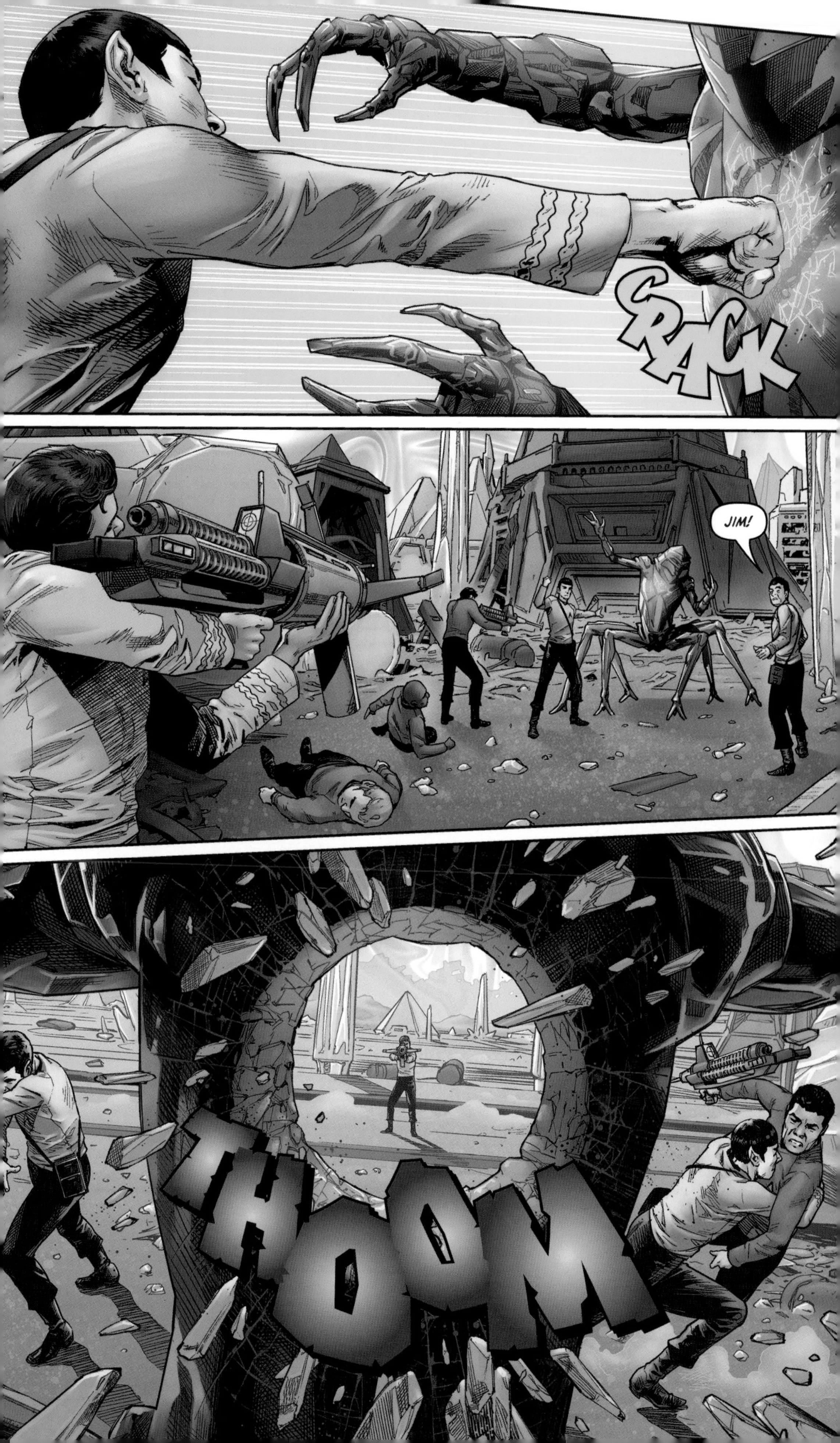
CRACK
JIM!
THOOM

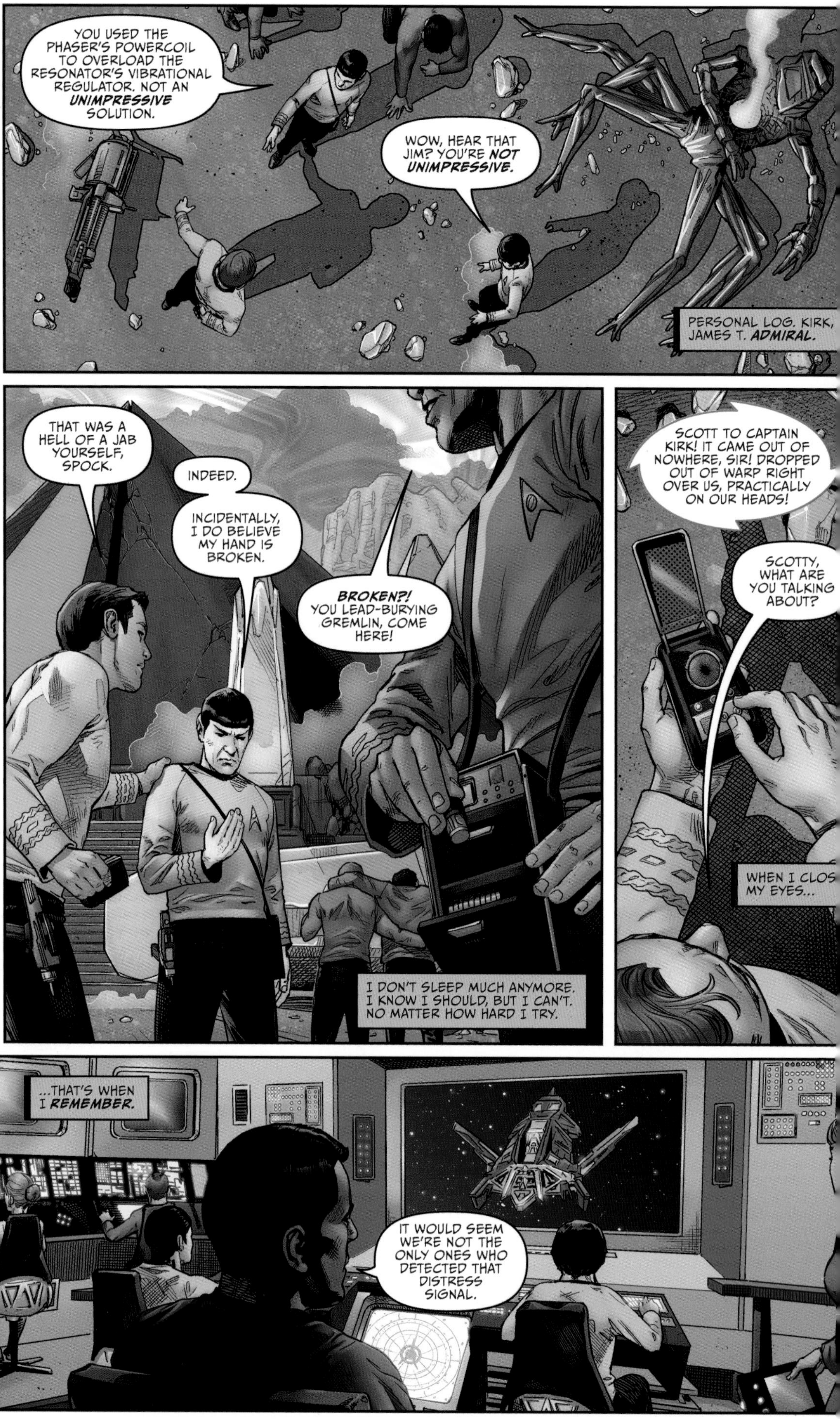
YOU USED THE PHASER'S POWERCOIL TO OVERLOAD THE RESONATOR'S VIBRATIONAL REGULATOR. NOT AN UNIMPRESSIVE SOLUTION.
WOW, HEAR THAT JIM? YOU'RE NOT UNIMPRESSIVE.
PERSONAL LOG. KIRK, JAMES T. ADMIRAL.
THAT WAS A HELL OF A JAB YOURSELF, SPOCK.
INDEED.
INCIDENTALLY, I DO BELIEVE MY HAND IS BROKEN.
BROKEN?! YOU LEAD-BURYING GREMLIN, COME HERE!
I DON'T SLEEP MUCH ANYMORE. I KNOW I SHOULD, BUT I CAN'T. NO MATTER HOW HARD I TRY.
SCOTT TO CAPTAIN KIRK! IT CAME OUT OF NOWHERE, SIR! DROPPED OUT OF WARP RIGHT OVER US, PRACTICALLY ON OUR HEADS!
SCOTTY, WHAT ARE YOU TALKING ABOUT?
WHEN I CLOS MY EYES...
...THAT'S WHEN I REMEMBER.
IT WOULD SEEM WE'RE NOT THE ONLY ONES WHO DETECTED THAT DISTRESS SIGNAL.

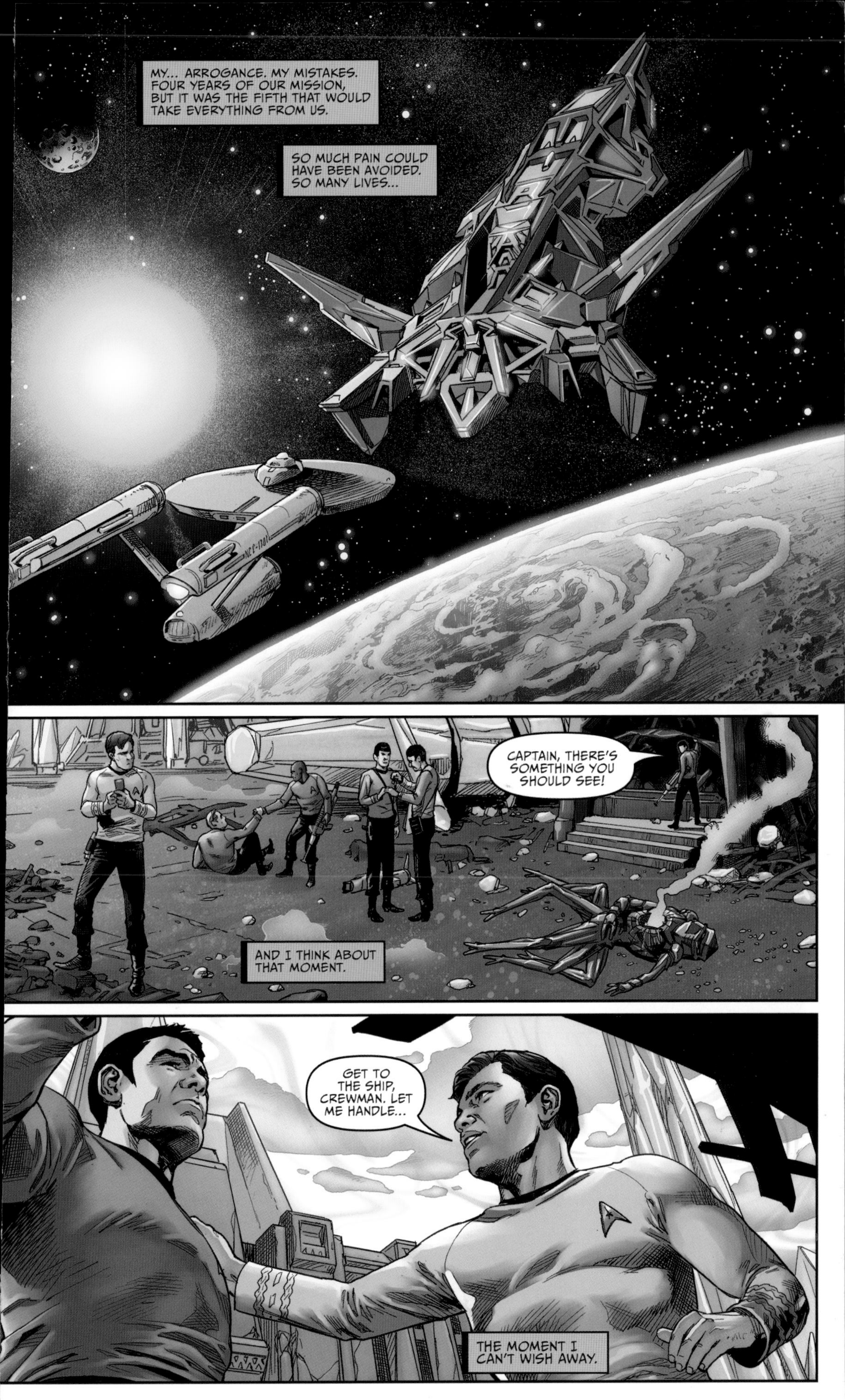
MY... ARROGANCE. MY MISTAKES. FOUR YEARS OF OUR MISSION, BUT IT WAS THE FIFTH THAT WOULD TAKE EVERYTHING FROM US.
SO MUCH PAIN COULD HAVE BEEN AVOIDED. SO MANY LIVES...
CAPTAIN, THERE'S SOMETHING YOU SHOULD SEE!
AND I THINK ABOUT THAT MOMENT.
GET TO THE SHIP, CREWMAN. LET ME HANDLE...
THE MOMENT I CAN'T WISH AWAY.

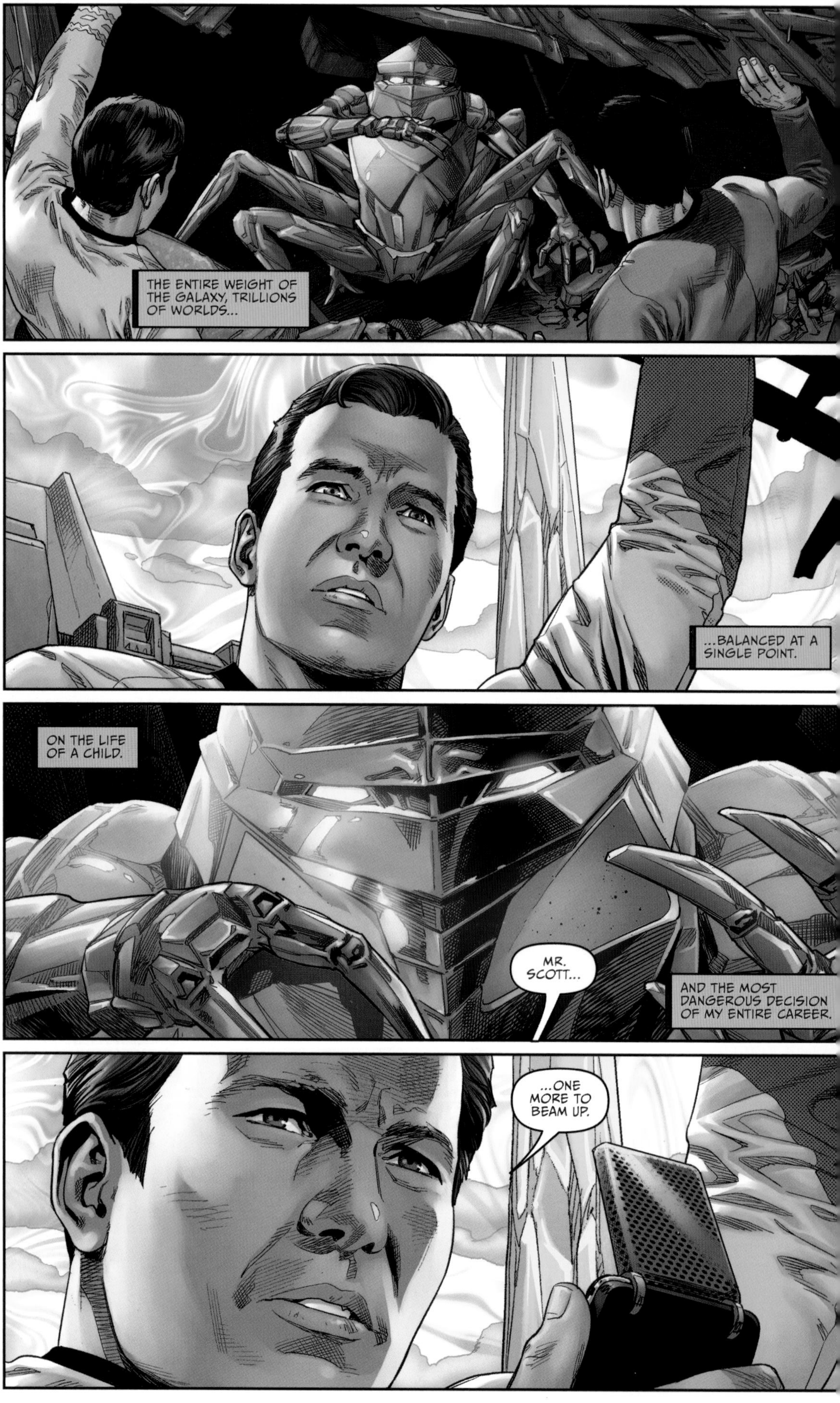
THE ENTIRE WEIGHT OF THE GALAXY, TRILLIONS OF WORLDS...
...BALANCED AT A SINGLE POINT.
ON THE LIFE OF A CHILD.
MR. SCOTT...
AND THE MOST DANGEROUS DECISION OF MY ENTIRE CAREER.
...ONE MORE TO BEAM UP.

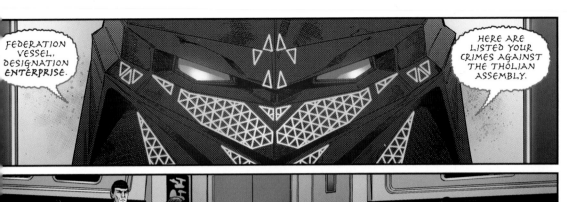

FEDERATION VESSEL, DESIGNATION ENTERPRISE.

HERE ARE LISTED YOUR CRIMES AGAINST THE THOLIAN ASSEMBLY.

YOU HAVE VIOLATED OUR ANCESTRAL TERRITORY WITHOUT OUR CONSENT.

YOU HAVE ALTERED THIS SYSTEM'S SOLAR BODY WITHOUT OUR CONSENT.

YOU HAVE MEDDLED IN AN INTERNAL MATTER ON THE COLONY YOU DESIGNATE AS LLOYD-ZETA 9 WITHOUT OUR CONSENT.

THE FORCEFIELD IS HOLDING, DOCTOR!

I ONLY HOPE I GOT THE THOLIAN ATMOSPHERE HALFWAY RIGHT...

WORST OF ALL, YOU HAVE MURDERED ONE OF OUR OWN...

...AND KIDNAPPED ANOTHER.

RETURN THE SURVIVOR TO US. WIPE YOUR SENSOR DATA. ONLY THEN WILL WE CONSIDER ALLOWING YOUR VESSEL TO LEAVE.

CAPTAIN, WE SHOULD COMPLY. THIS COURSE OF ACTION IS EXTREMELY LIKELY TO RESULT IN, AT MINIMUM, A DIPLOMATIC INCIDENT—

NOT UNTIL I KNOW WHAT KILLED THOSE PEOPLE ON THE SURFACE, MR. SPOCK.

THIS IS CAPTAIN JAMES T. KIRK OF THE STARSHIP ENTERPRISE. WE ARE NOT RESPONSIBLE FOR THE DEVASTATION BELOW.

WE HAVE TAKEN THE SURVIVING CHILD INTO OUR CUSTODY ONLY TO ASSURE THEIR SAFETY WHILE WE CONDUCT OUR INVESTIGATION.

IT IS OUR BELIEF THAT A THOLIAN SPLINTER GROUP OR TERRORIST ORGANIZATION ATTACKED YOUR COLONY AND—

KEPTIN!

THE THOLIANS ARE POWERING SOME KIND OF WEAPON!

VERY WELL. IF THREATS ARE NOT SUFFICIENT TO ENSURE YOU COMPLY, WE WILL INSTEAD SPEAK IN A WAY YOU PRIMITIVE PEOPLE CAN UNDERSTAND...

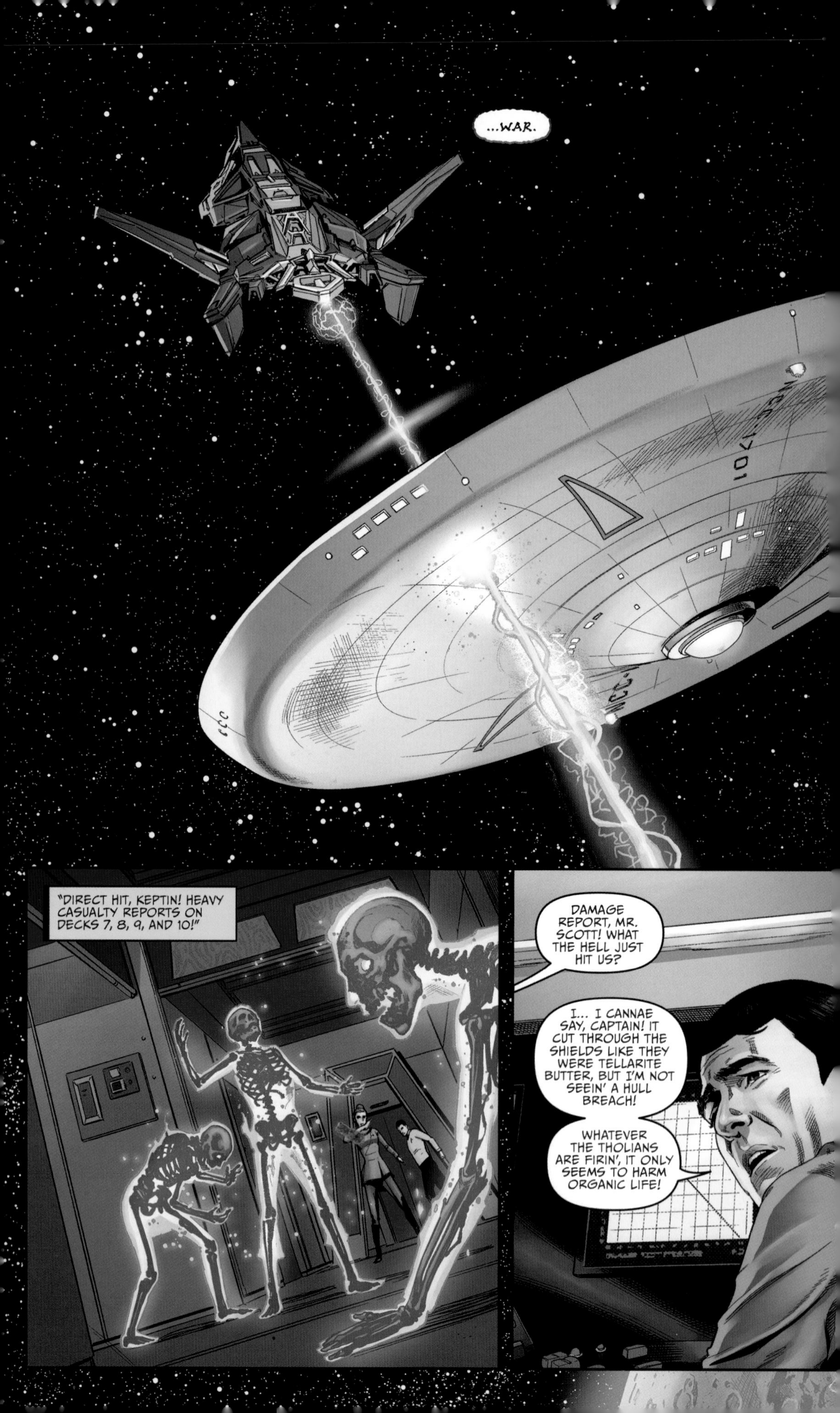
...WAR.
"DIRECT HIT, KEPTIN! HEAVY CASUALTY REPORTS ON DECKS 7, 8, 9, AND 10!"
DAMAGE REPORT, MR. SCOTT! WHAT THE HELL JUST HIT US?
I... I CANNAE SAY, CAPTAIN! IT CUT THROUGH THE SHIELDS LIKE THEY WERE TELLARITE BUTTER, BUT I'M NOT SEEIN' A HULL BREACH!
WHATEVER THE THOLIANS ARE FIRIN', IT ONLY SEEMS TO HARM ORGANIC LIFE!

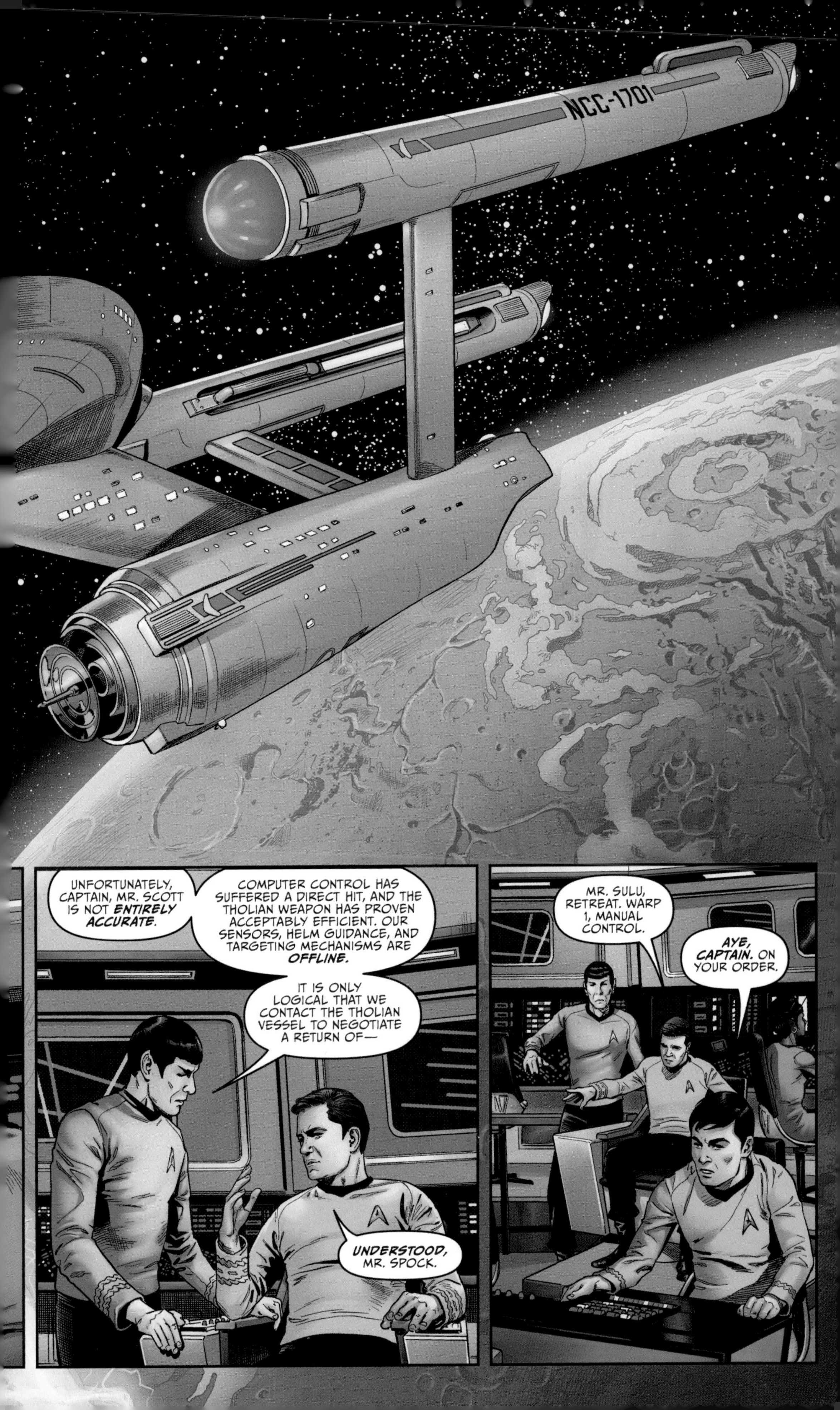

NCC-1701
UNFORTUNATELY, CAPTAIN, MR. SCOTT IS NOT ENTIRELY ACCURATE.
COMPUTER CONTROL HAS SUFFERED A DIRECT HIT, AND THE THOLIAN WEAPON HAS PROVEN ACCEPTABLY EFFICIENT. OUR SENSORS, HELM GUIDANCE, AND TARGETING MECHANISMS ARE OFFLINE.
IT IS ONLY LOGICAL THAT WE CONTACT THE THOLIAN VESSEL TO NEGOTIATE A RETURN OF—
UNDERSTOOD, MR. SPOCK.
MR. SULU, RETREAT. WARP 1, MANUAL CONTROL.
AYE, CAPTAIN. ON YOUR ORDER.

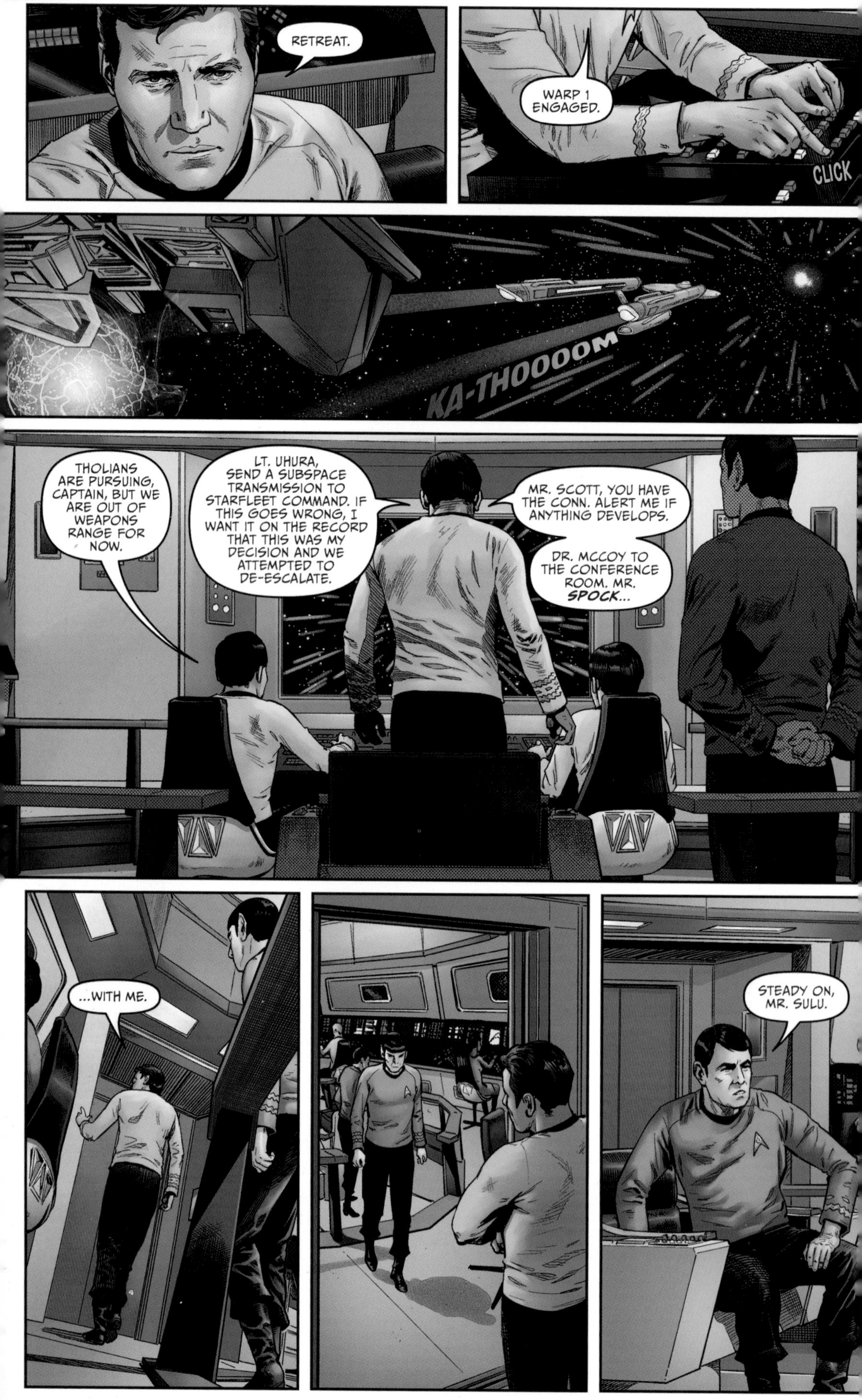
RETREAT.
WARP 1 ENGAGED.
CLICK
KA-THOOOOM
THOLIANS ARE PURSUING, CAPTAIN, BUT WE ARE OUT OF WEAPONS RANGE FOR NOW.
LT. UHURA, SEND A SUBSPACE TRANSMISSION TO STARFLEET COMMAND. IF THIS GOES WRONG, I WANT IT ON THE RECORD THAT THIS WAS MY DECISION AND WE ATTEMPTED TO DE-ESCALATE.
MR. SCOTT, YOU HAVE THE CONN. ALERT ME IF ANYTHING DEVELOPS.
DR. MCCOY TO THE CONFERENCE ROOM. MR. SPOCK...
...WITH ME.
STEADY ON, MR. SULU.

GENTLEMEN. AS YOU'RE WELL AWARE, THE SITUATION IS DIRE.

WE HAVE, AT MOST, AN HOUR TO STRATEGIZE A WAY TO DEFEAT THE THOLIANS.

A PENNY FOR YOUR THOUGHTS.

CAPTAIN, IN THE SPIRIT OF HONESTY, I BELIEVE YOU ARE ACTING EMOTIONALLY.

THE ABDUCTION OF THE THOLIAN CHILD, WHILE WELL-INTENTIONED, HAS ALREADY RESULTED IN THE DEATHS OF *FIVE* MEMBERS OF THE *ENTERPRISE* CREW BY APPARENT DISINTEGRATION.

THE THOLIANS DO NOT NEED TO BE *DEFEATED*, CAPTAIN. THEY NEED TO BE PLACATED, AFTER WHICH THE *ENTERPRISE* MUST WITHDRAW.

I CAN'T BELIEVE I'M SAYING THIS, JIM, BUT I AGREE WITH *SPOCK.*

I'M BARELY KEEPING THAT CRYSTAL SPIDER ALIVE.

I DON'T KNOW THE FIRST THING ABOUT THOLIAN BIOLOGY, AND EVEN IF I *DID*, I HAVE NO IDEA HOW TO ASK MY PATIENT THEIR NAME, LET ALONE WHETHER THEY'RE COMFORTABLE BREATHING OUR AIR.

HELL, I DON'T EVEN KNOW IF THOLIANS *BREATHE!* IT'S A HELL OF A RISK YOU'RE TAKING ON A HUNCH.

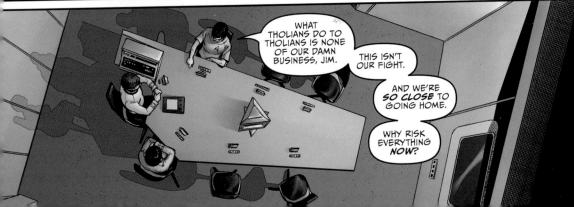

WHAT THOLIANS DO TO THOLIANS IS NONE OF OUR DAMN BUSINESS, JIM.

THIS ISN'T OUR FIGHT.

AND WE'RE *SO CLOSE* TO GOING HOME.

WHY RISK EVERYTHING *NOW?*

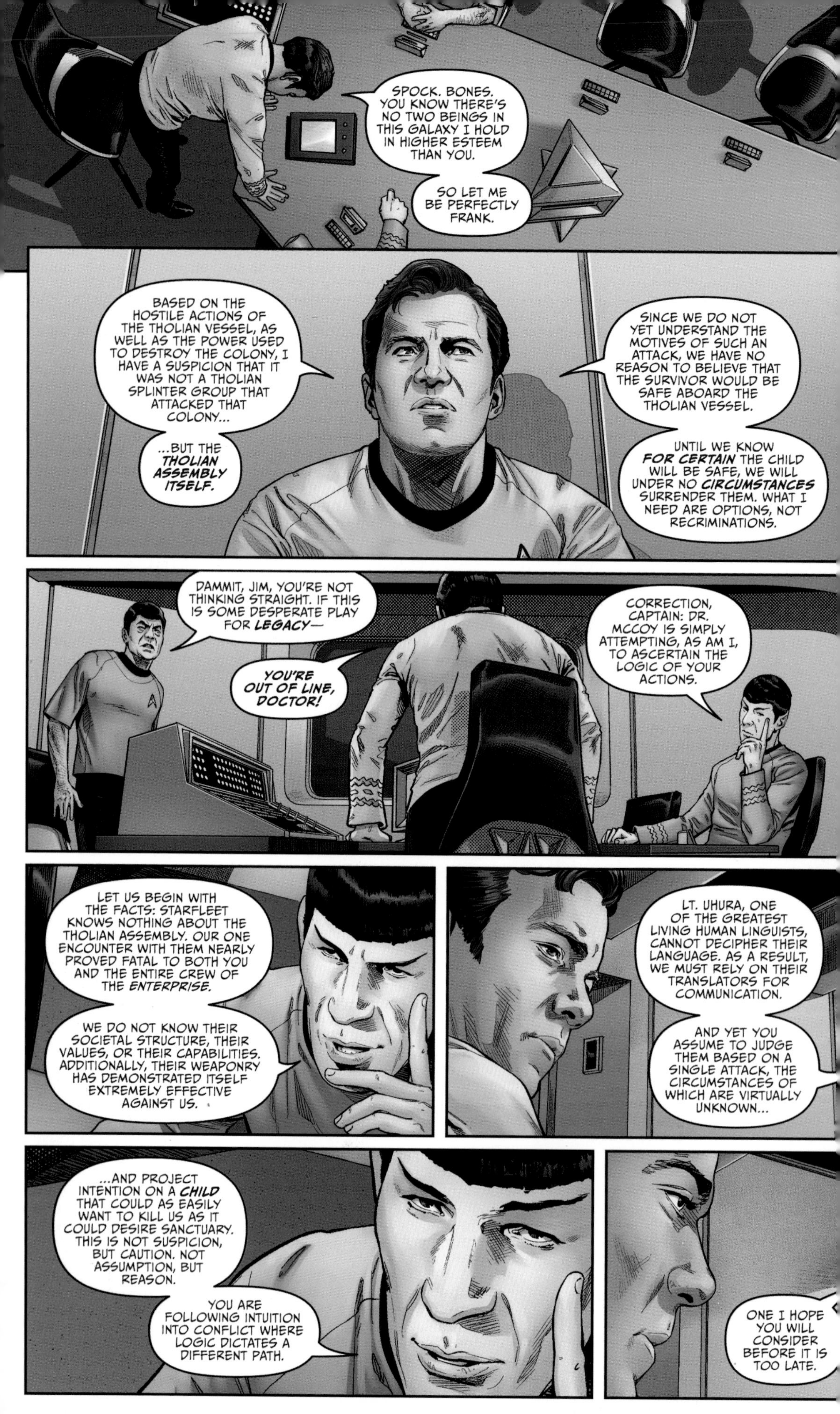
SPOCK. BONES. YOU KNOW THERE'S NO TWO BEINGS IN THIS GALAXY I HOLD IN HIGHER ESTEEM THAN YOU.
SO LET ME BE PERFECTLY FRANK.
BASED ON THE HOSTILE ACTIONS OF THE THOLIAN VESSEL, AS WELL AS THE POWER USED TO DESTROY THE COLONY, I HAVE A SUSPICION THAT IT WAS NOT A THOLIAN SPLINTER GROUP THAT ATTACKED THAT COLONY...
...BUT THE THOLIAN ASSEMBLY ITSELF.
SINCE WE DO NOT YET UNDERSTAND THE MOTIVES OF SUCH AN ATTACK, WE HAVE NO REASON TO BELIEVE THAT THE SURVIVOR WOULD BE SAFE ABOARD THE THOLIAN VESSEL.
UNTIL WE KNOW FOR CERTAIN THE CHILD WILL BE SAFE, WE WILL UNDER NO CIRCUMSTANCES SURRENDER THEM. WHAT I NEED ARE OPTIONS, NOT RECRIMINATIONS.
DAMMIT, JIM, YOU'RE NOT THINKING STRAIGHT. IF THIS IS SOME DESPERATE PLAY FOR LEGACY—
YOU'RE OUT OF LINE, DOCTOR!
CORRECTION, CAPTAIN: DR. MCCOY IS SIMPLY ATTEMPTING, AS AM I, TO ASCERTAIN THE LOGIC OF YOUR ACTIONS.
LET US BEGIN WITH THE FACTS: STARFLEET KNOWS NOTHING ABOUT THE THOLIAN ASSEMBLY. OUR ONE ENCOUNTER WITH THEM NEARLY PROVED FATAL TO BOTH YOU AND THE ENTIRE CREW OF THE ENTERPRISE.
WE DO NOT KNOW THEIR SOCIETAL STRUCTURE, THEIR VALUES, OR THEIR CAPABILITIES. ADDITIONALLY, THEIR WEAPONRY HAS DEMONSTRATED ITSELF EXTREMELY EFFECTIVE AGAINST US.
LT. UHURA, ONE OF THE GREATEST LIVING HUMAN LINGUISTS, CANNOT DECIPHER THEIR LANGUAGE. AS A RESULT, WE MUST RELY ON THEIR TRANSLATORS FOR COMMUNICATION.
AND YET YOU ASSUME TO JUDGE THEM BASED ON A SINGLE ATTACK, THE CIRCUMSTANCES OF WHICH ARE VIRTUALLY UNKNOWN...
...AND PROJECT INTENTION ON A CHILD THAT COULD AS EASILY WANT TO KILL US AS IT COULD DESIRE SANCTUARY. THIS IS NOT SUSPICION, BUT CAUTION. NOT ASSUMPTION, BUT REASON.
YOU ARE FOLLOWING INTUITION INTO CONFLICT WHERE LOGIC DICTATES A DIFFERENT PATH.
ONE I HOPE YOU WILL CONSIDER BEFORE IT IS TOO LATE.

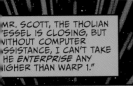

MR. SCOTT, THE THOLIAN VESSEL IS CLOSING, BUT WITHOUT COMPUTER ASSISTANCE, I CAN'T TAKE THE *ENTERPRISE* ANY HIGHER THAN WARP 1."

"SO YER TELLIN' ME OUR OPTIONS ARE KEEP RUNNIN' AND GET SHOT OUT OF THE SKY, OR STOP AND FACE THE MUSIC..."

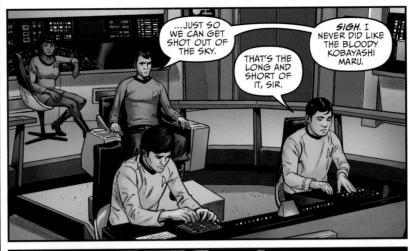

...JUST SO WE CAN GET SHOT OUT OF THE SKY.

THAT'S THE LONG AND SHORT OF IT, SIR.

SIGH. I NEVER DID LIKE THE BLOODY KOBAYASHI MARU.

YOU AND CAPTAIN KIRK HAVE THAT IN COMMON, MR. SCOTT.

WHICH IS WHY HE *HACKED* IT.

WHAT ARE YOU SUGGESTIN', LIEUTENANT? I CAN'T VERY WELL HACK A THOLIAN COMPUTER FROM THE *ENTERPRISE*, NEVERMIND AT *WARP!*

I'M NOT SUGGESTING WE HACK THE *SHIP*, SIR.

I'M SUGGESTING WE HACK THE *SCENARIO.*

SURE, WE DON'T KNOW HOW TO DEFEND AGAINST THE THOLIAN WEAPON OR HOW TO EFFECTIVELY ESCAPE. AND *SURE*, THE COMPUTER'S OFFLINE. BUT MR. SCOTT, YOU'RE SITTING IN A ROOM WITH SEVERAL OF THE *FINEST MINDS* IN STARFLEET.

WHY RELY ON A COMPUTER WHEN YOU COULD PUT *US* TO USE?

ANYONE EVER TELL YOU YOU'RE A BLOODY GENIUS, LT. UHURA?

THEN LET ME BE THE FIRST TO RECTIFY THAT.

NOT SINCE THE ACADEMY, MR. SCOTT.

LT. UHURA IS A BLOODY GENIUS AND FOR THE NEXT THIRTY MINUTES, WE'RE DOIN' *EXACTLY* WHAT SHE SAYS.

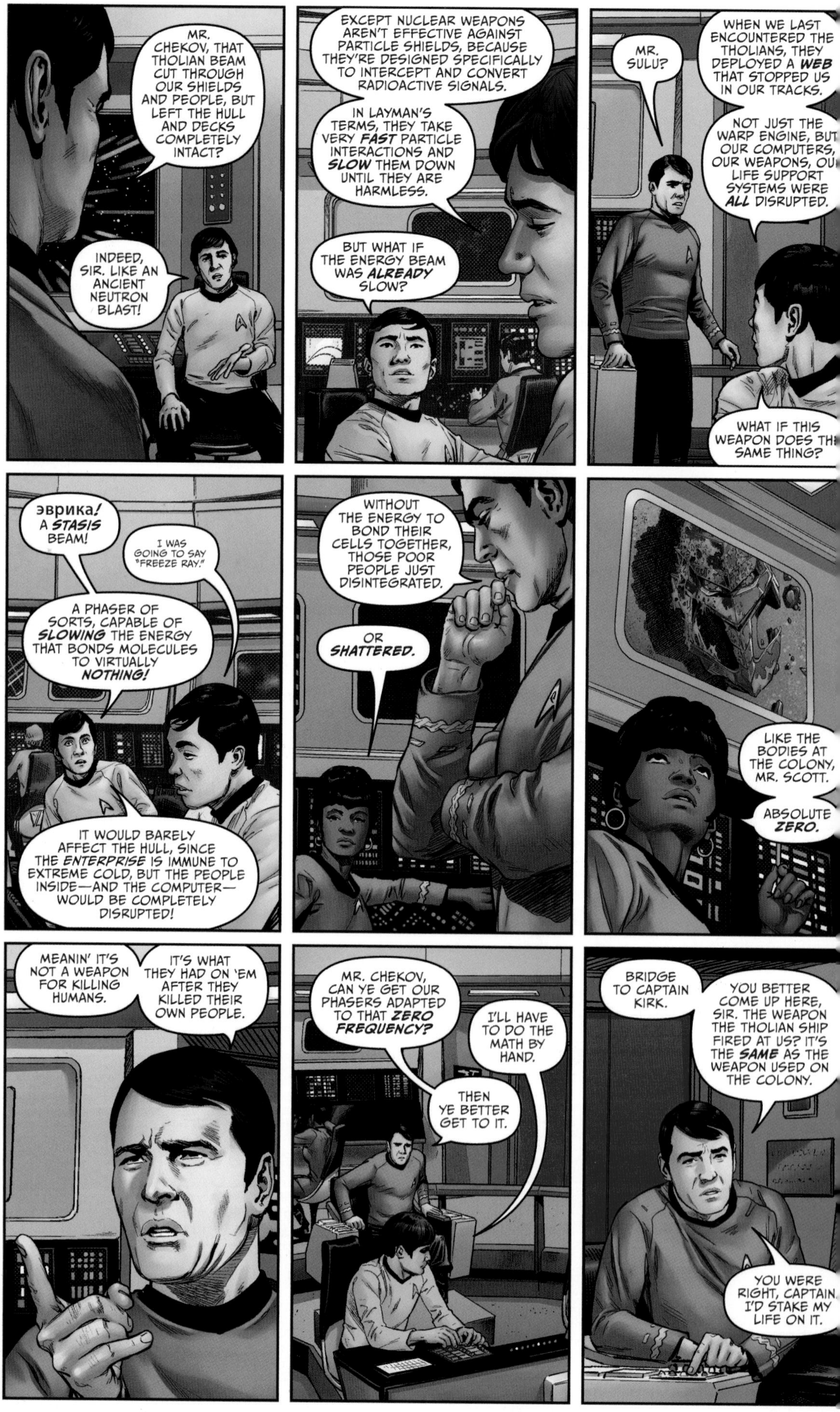

MR. CHEKOV, THAT THOLIAN BEAM CUT THROUGH OUR SHIELDS AND PEOPLE, BUT LEFT THE HULL AND DECKS COMPLETELY INTACT?
INDEED, SIR. LIKE AN ANCIENT NEUTRON BLAST!
EXCEPT NUCLEAR WEAPONS AREN'T EFFECTIVE AGAINST PARTICLE SHIELDS, BECAUSE THEY'RE DESIGNED SPECIFICALLY TO INTERCEPT AND CONVERT RADIOACTIVE SIGNALS.
IN LAYMAN'S TERMS, THEY TAKE VERY FAST PARTICLE INTERACTIONS AND SLOW THEM DOWN UNTIL THEY ARE HARMLESS.
BUT WHAT IF THE ENERGY BEAM WAS ALREADY SLOW?
MR. SULU?
WHEN WE LAST ENCOUNTERED THE THOLIANS, THEY DEPLOYED A WEB THAT STOPPED US IN OUR TRACKS.
NOT JUST THE WARP ENGINE, BUT OUR COMPUTERS, OUR WEAPONS, OUR LIFE SUPPORT SYSTEMS WERE ALL DISRUPTED.
WHAT IF THIS WEAPON DOES THE SAME THING?
эврика! A STASIS BEAM!
I WAS GOING TO SAY "FREEZE RAY."
A PHASER OF SORTS, CAPABLE OF SLOWING THE ENERGY THAT BONDS MOLECULES TO VIRTUALLY NOTHING!
IT WOULD BARELY AFFECT THE HULL, SINCE THE ENTERPRISE IS IMMUNE TO EXTREME COLD, BUT THE PEOPLE INSIDE—AND THE COMPUTER—WOULD BE COMPLETELY DISRUPTED!
WITHOUT THE ENERGY TO BOND THEIR CELLS TOGETHER, THOSE POOR PEOPLE JUST DISINTEGRATED.
OR SHATTERED.
LIKE THE BODIES AT THE COLONY, MR. SCOTT.
ABSOLUTE ZERO.
MEANIN' IT'S NOT A WEAPON FOR KILLING HUMANS.
IT'S WHAT THEY HAD ON 'EM AFTER THEY KILLED THEIR OWN PEOPLE.
MR. CHEKOV, CAN YE GET OUR PHASERS ADAPTED TO THAT ZERO FREQUENCY?
I'LL HAVE TO DO THE MATH BY HAND.
THEN YE BETTER GET TO IT.
BRIDGE TO CAPTAIN KIRK.
YOU BETTER COME UP HERE, SIR. THE WEAPON THE THOLIAN SHIP FIRED AT US? IT'S THE SAME AS THE WEAPON USED ON THE COLONY.
YOU WERE RIGHT, CAPTAIN. I'D STAKE MY LIFE ON IT.

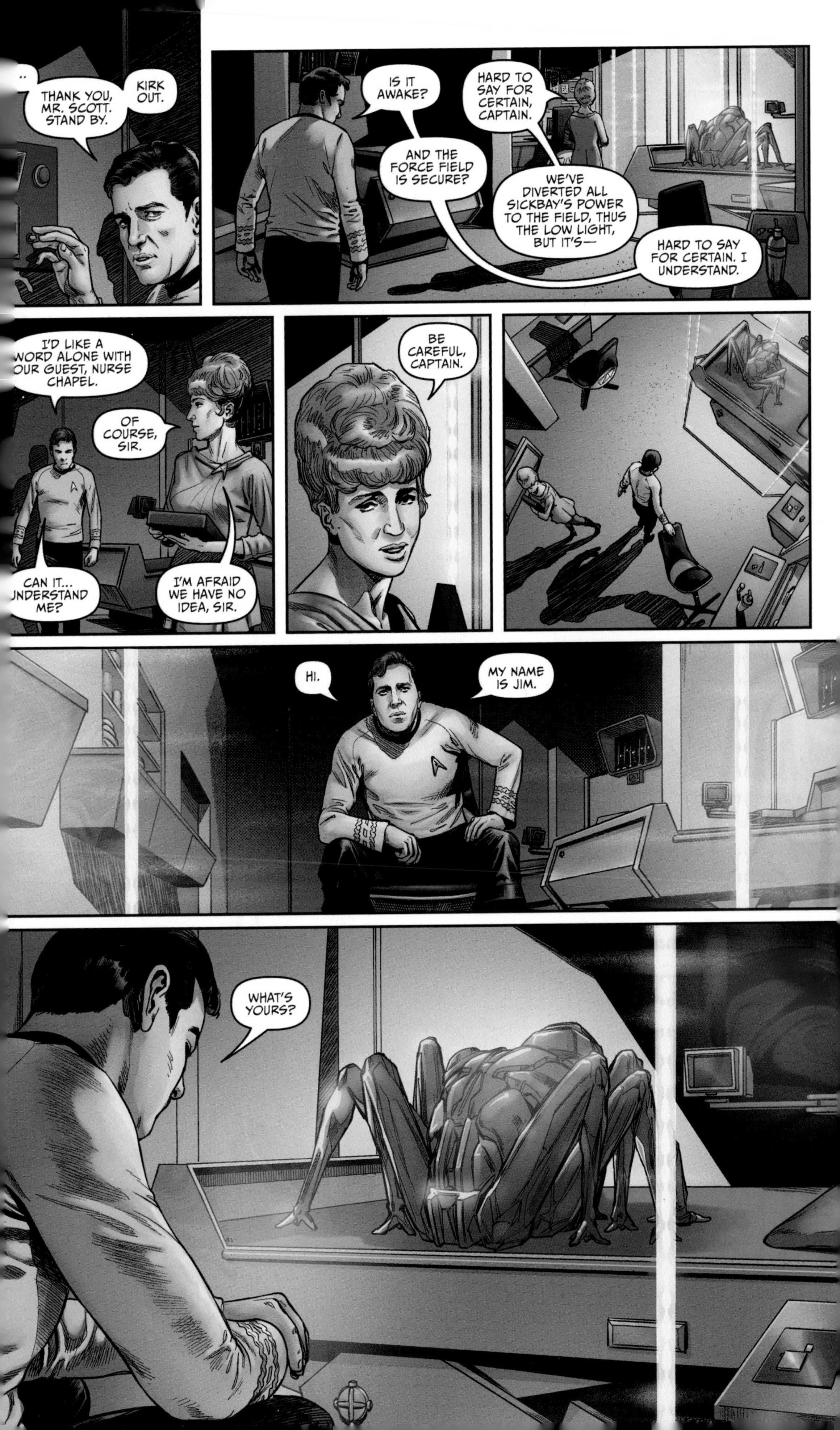
..
THANK YOU, MR. SCOTT. STAND BY.
KIRK OUT.
IS IT AWAKE?
HARD TO SAY FOR CERTAIN, CAPTAIN.
AND THE FORCE FIELD IS SECURE?
WE'VE DIVERTED ALL SICKBAY'S POWER TO THE FIELD, THUS THE LOW LIGHT, BUT IT'S—
HARD TO SAY FOR CERTAIN. I UNDERSTAND.
I'D LIKE A WORD ALONE WITH OUR GUEST, NURSE CHAPEL.
OF COURSE, SIR.
CAN IT... UNDERSTAND ME?
I'M AFRAID WE HAVE NO IDEA, SIR.
BE CAREFUL, CAPTAIN.
HI.
MY NAME IS JIM.
WHAT'S YOURS?

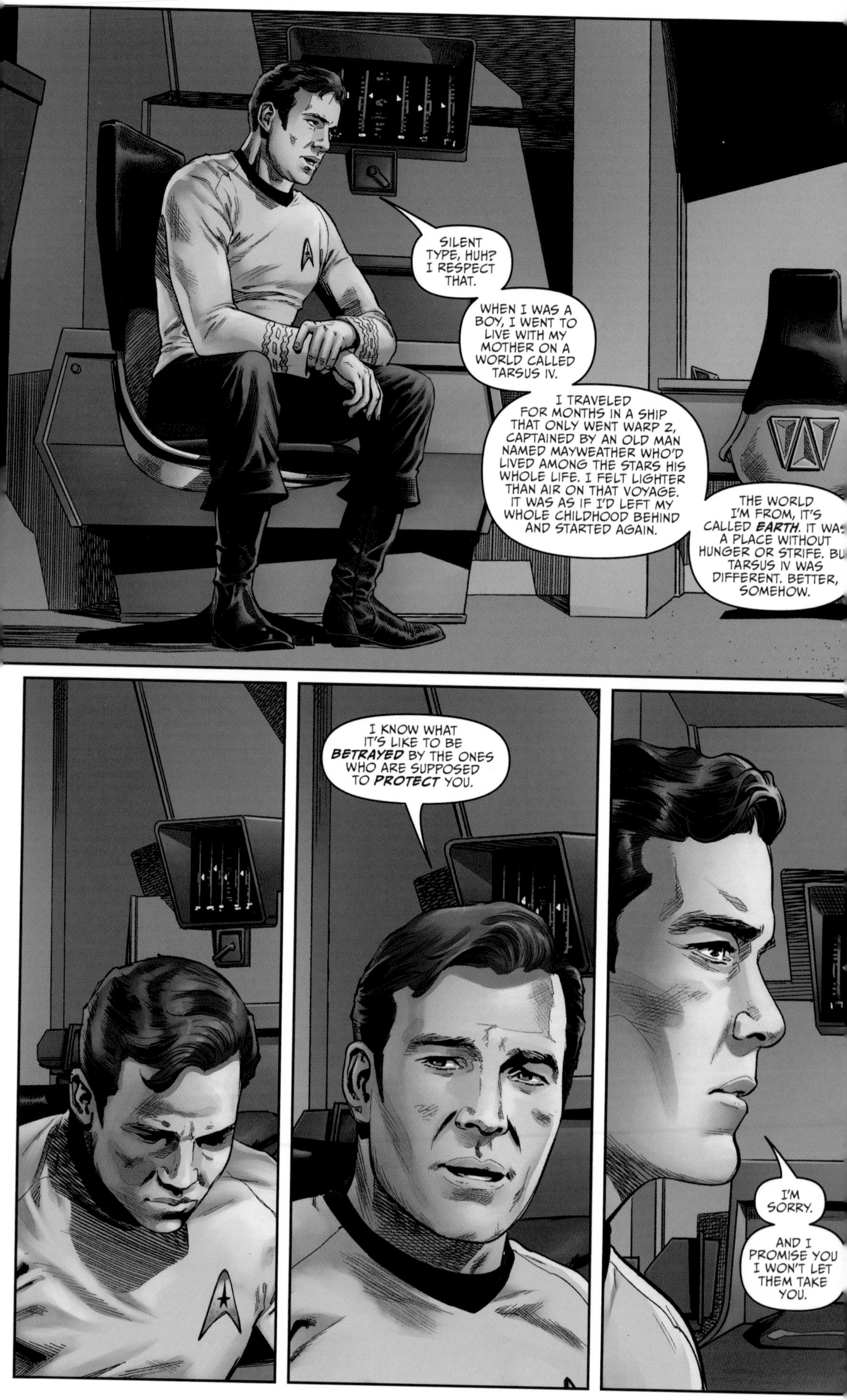
SILENT TYPE, HUH? I RESPECT THAT.
WHEN I WAS A BOY, I WENT TO LIVE WITH MY MOTHER ON A WORLD CALLED TARSUS IV.
I TRAVELED FOR MONTHS IN A SHIP THAT ONLY WENT WARP 2, CAPTAINED BY AN OLD MAN NAMED MAYWEATHER WHO'D LIVED AMONG THE STARS HIS WHOLE LIFE. I FELT LIGHTER THAN AIR ON THAT VOYAGE. IT WAS AS IF I'D LEFT MY WHOLE CHILDHOOD BEHIND AND STARTED AGAIN.
THE WORLD I'M FROM, IT'S CALLED **EARTH**. IT WAS A PLACE WITHOUT HUNGER OR STRIFE. BU TARSUS IV WAS DIFFERENT. BETTER, SOMEHOW.
I KNOW WHAT IT'S LIKE TO BE **BETRAYED** BY THE ONES WHO ARE SUPPOSED TO **PROTECT** YOU.
I'M SORRY.
AND I PROMISE YOU I WON'T LET THEM TAKE YOU.

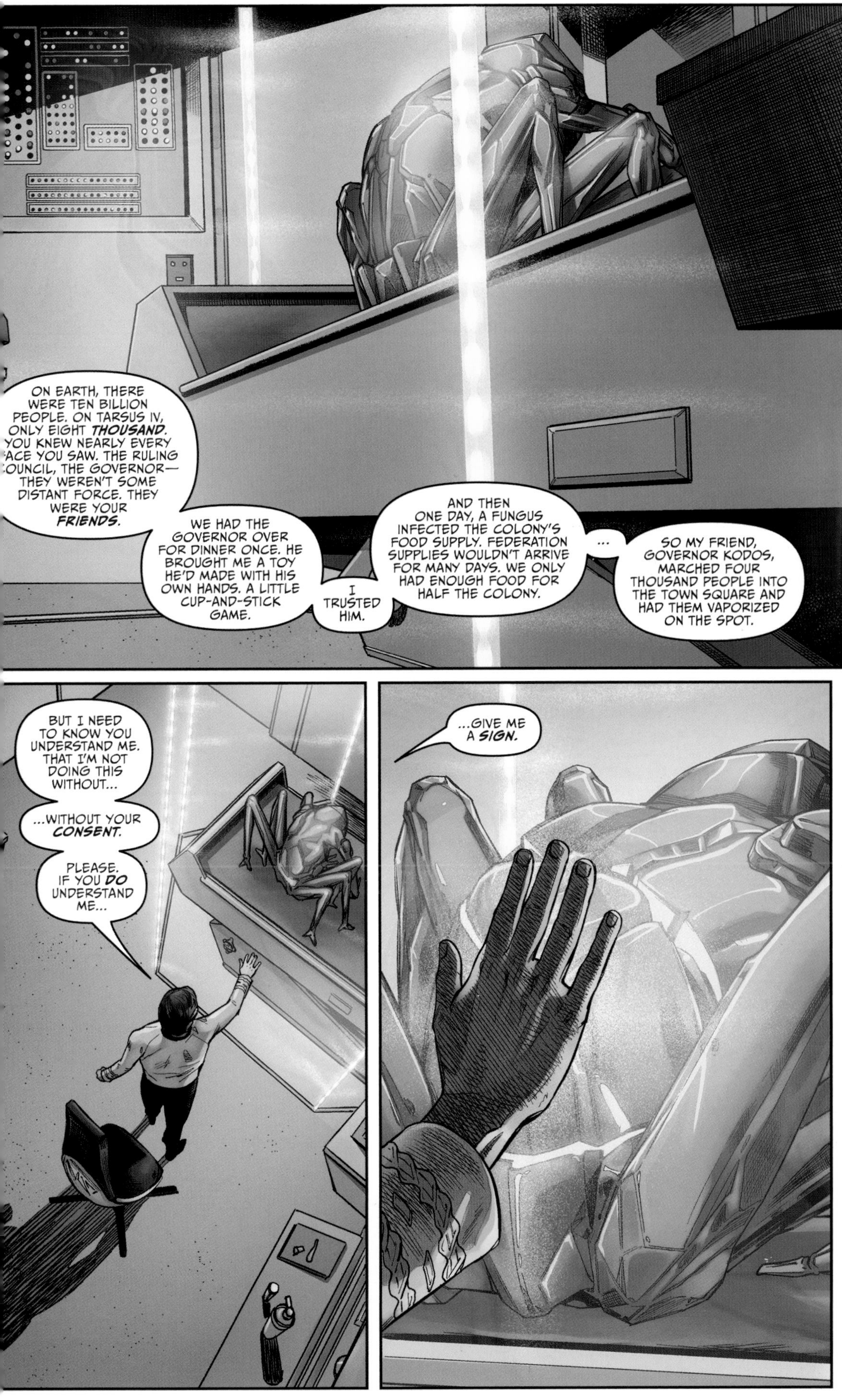
ON EARTH, THERE WERE TEN BILLION PEOPLE. ON TARSUS IV, ONLY EIGHT THOUSAND. YOU KNEW NEARLY EVERY FACE YOU SAW. THE RULING COUNCIL, THE GOVERNOR— THEY WEREN'T SOME DISTANT FORCE. THEY WERE YOUR FRIENDS.
WE HAD THE GOVERNOR OVER FOR DINNER ONCE. HE BROUGHT ME A TOY HE'D MADE WITH HIS OWN HANDS. A LITTLE CUP-AND-STICK GAME.
I TRUSTED HIM.
AND THEN ONE DAY, A FUNGUS INFECTED THE COLONY'S FOOD SUPPLY. FEDERATION SUPPLIES WOULDN'T ARRIVE FOR MANY DAYS. WE ONLY HAD ENOUGH FOOD FOR HALF THE COLONY.
...
SO MY FRIEND, GOVERNOR KODOS, MARCHED FOUR THOUSAND PEOPLE INTO THE TOWN SQUARE AND HAD THEM VAPORIZED ON THE SPOT.
BUT I NEED TO KNOW YOU UNDERSTAND ME. THAT I'M NOT DOING THIS WITHOUT...
...WITHOUT YOUR CONSENT.
PLEASE. IF YOU DO UNDERSTAND ME...
...GIVE ME A SIGN.

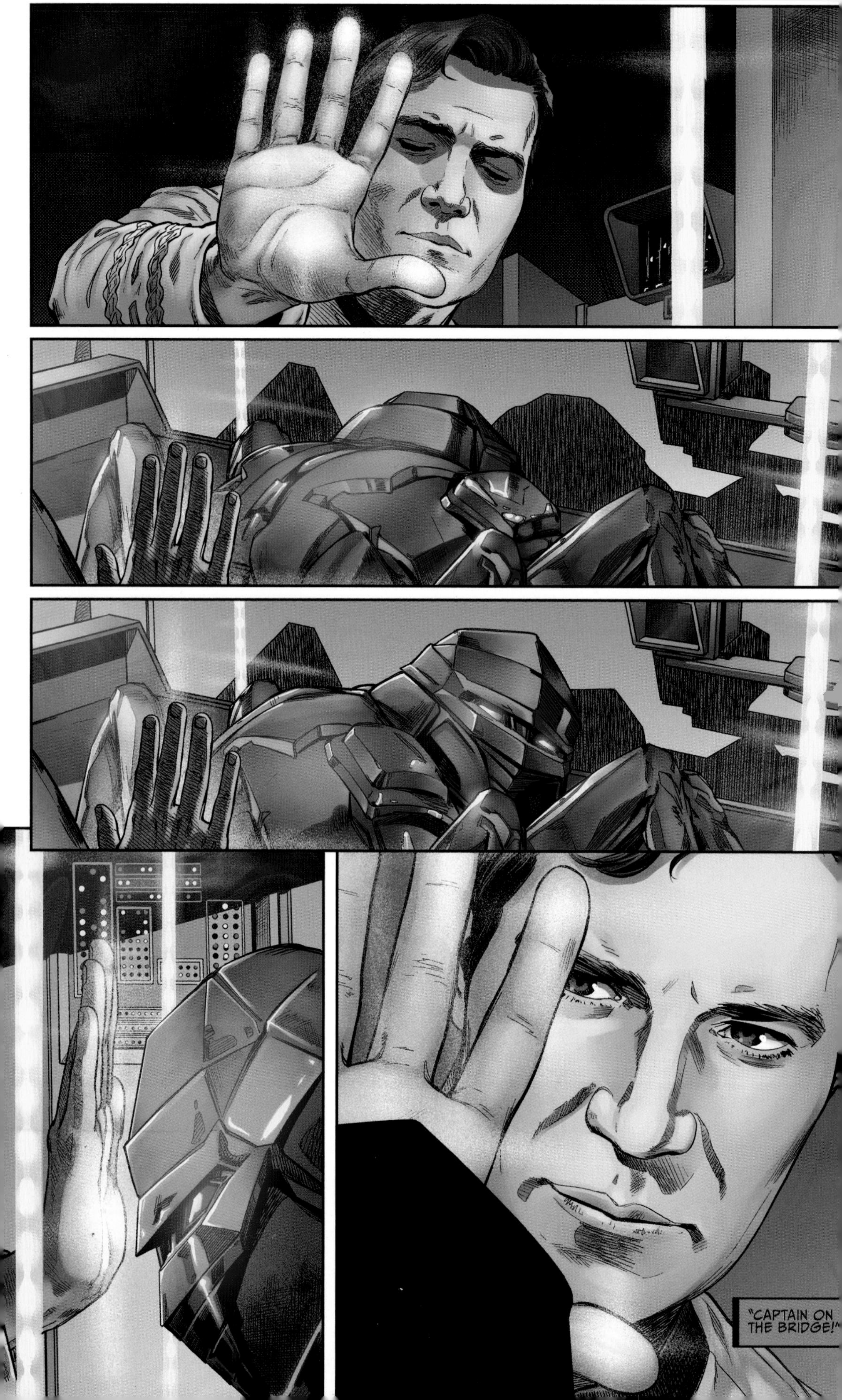
"CAPTAIN ON THE BRIDGE!"

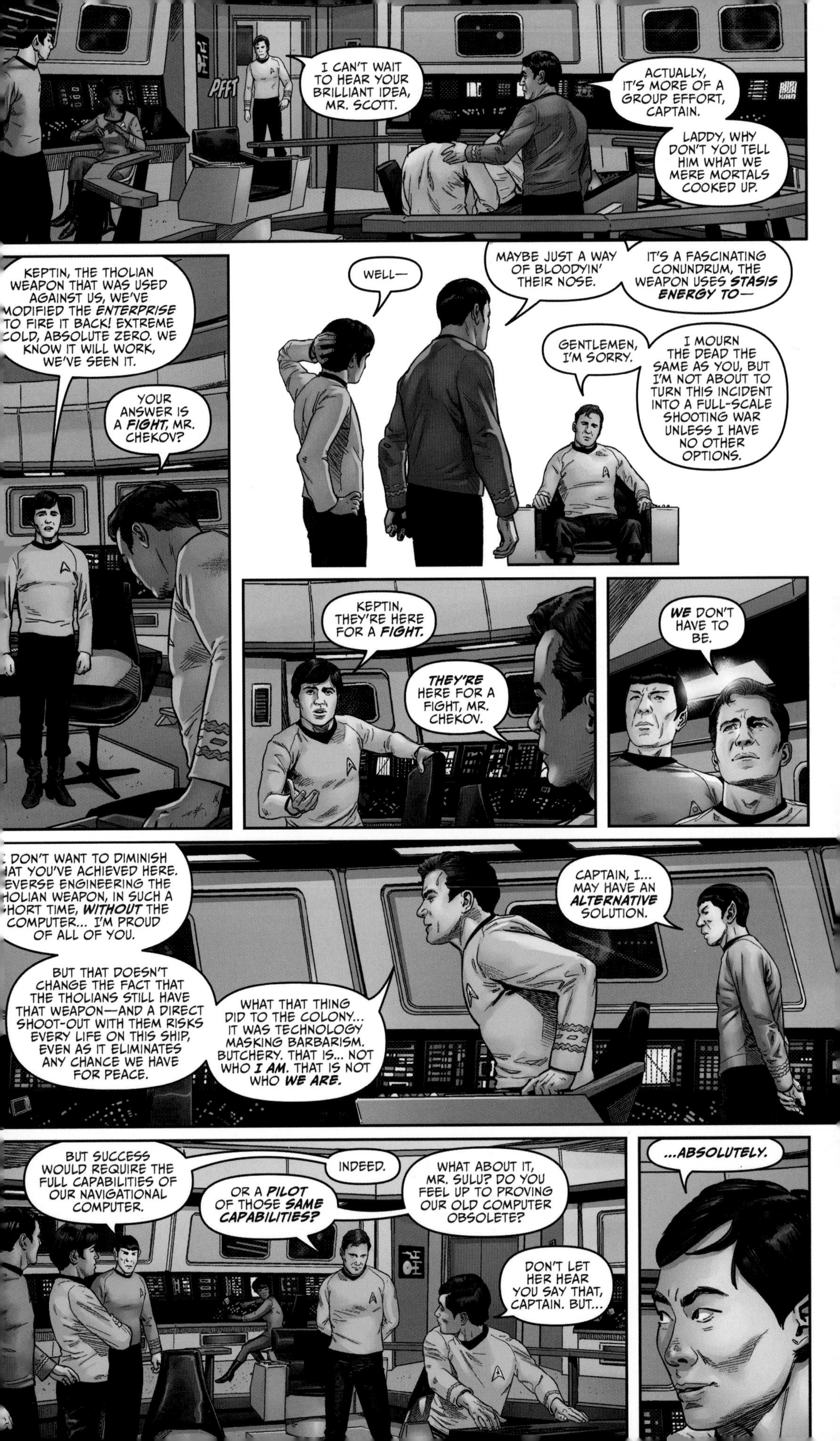
PFFT
I CAN'T WAIT TO HEAR YOUR BRILLIANT IDEA, MR. SCOTT.
ACTUALLY, IT'S MORE OF A GROUP EFFORT, CAPTAIN.
LADDY, WHY DON'T YOU TELL HIM WHAT WE MERE MORTALS COOKED UP.
WELL—
MAYBE JUST A WAY OF BLOODYIN' THEIR NOSE.
IT'S A FASCINATING CONUNDRUM, THE WEAPON USES *STASIS ENERGY* TO—
GENTLEMEN, I'M SORRY.
I MOURN THE DEAD THE SAME AS YOU, BUT I'M NOT ABOUT TO TURN THIS INCIDENT INTO A FULL-SCALE SHOOTING WAR UNLESS I HAVE NO OTHER OPTIONS.
KEPTIN, THE THOLIAN WEAPON THAT WAS USED AGAINST US, WE'VE MODIFIED THE *ENTERPRISE* TO FIRE IT BACK! EXTREME COLD, ABSOLUTE ZERO. WE KNOW IT WILL WORK, WE'VE SEEN IT.
YOUR ANSWER IS A *FIGHT*, MR. CHEKOV?
KEPTIN, THEY'RE HERE FOR A *FIGHT.*
THEY'RE HERE FOR A FIGHT, MR. CHEKOV.
WE DON'T HAVE TO BE.
DON'T WANT TO DIMINISH HAT YOU'VE ACHIEVED HERE. EVERSE ENGINEERING THE HOLIAN WEAPON, IN SUCH A HORT TIME, *WITHOUT* THE COMPUTER... I'M PROUD OF ALL OF YOU.
BUT THAT DOESN'T CHANGE THE FACT THAT THE THOLIANS STILL HAVE THAT WEAPON—AND A DIRECT SHOOT-OUT WITH THEM RISKS EVERY LIFE ON THIS SHIP, EVEN AS IT ELIMINATES ANY CHANCE WE HAVE FOR PEACE.
WHAT THAT THING DID TO THE COLONY... IT WAS TECHNOLOGY MASKING BARBARISM. BUTCHERY. THAT IS... NOT WHO *I AM*. THAT IS NOT WHO *WE ARE.*
CAPTAIN, I... MAY HAVE AN *ALTERNATIVE* SOLUTION.
BUT SUCCESS WOULD REQUIRE THE FULL CAPABILITIES OF OUR NAVIGATIONAL COMPUTER.
INDEED.
OR A *PILOT* OF THOSE *SAME CAPABILITIES?*
WHAT ABOUT IT, MR. SULU? DO YOU FEEL UP TO PROVING OUR OLD COMPUTER OBSOLETE?
DON'T LET HER HEAR YOU SAY THAT, CAPTAIN. BUT...
...ABSOLUTELY.

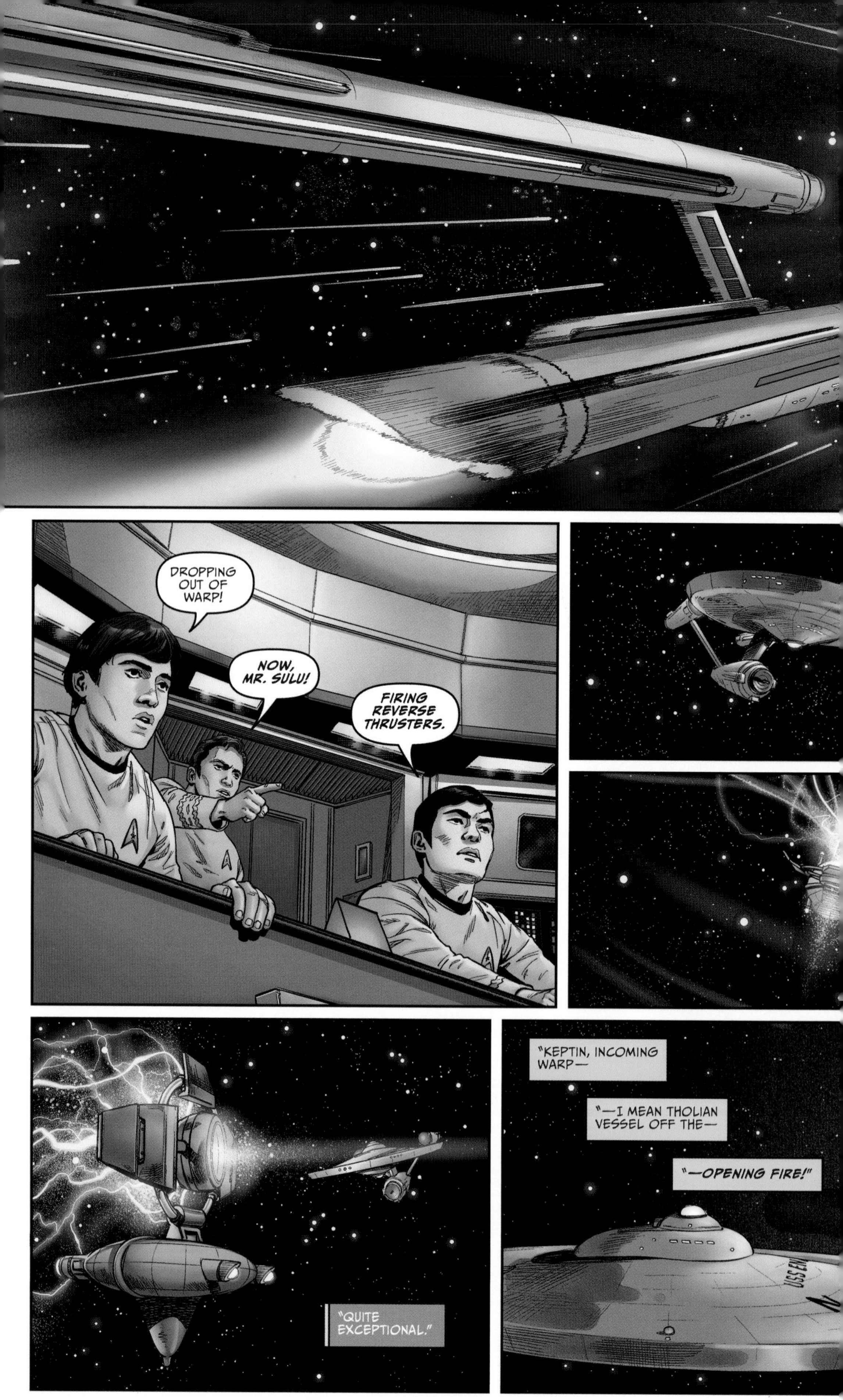
DROPPING OUT OF WARP!
NOW, MR. SULU!
FIRING REVERSE THRUSTERS.
"QUITE EXCEPTIONAL."
"KEPTIN, INCOMING WARP—
"—I MEAN THOLIAN VESSEL OFF THE—
"—OPENING FIRE!"

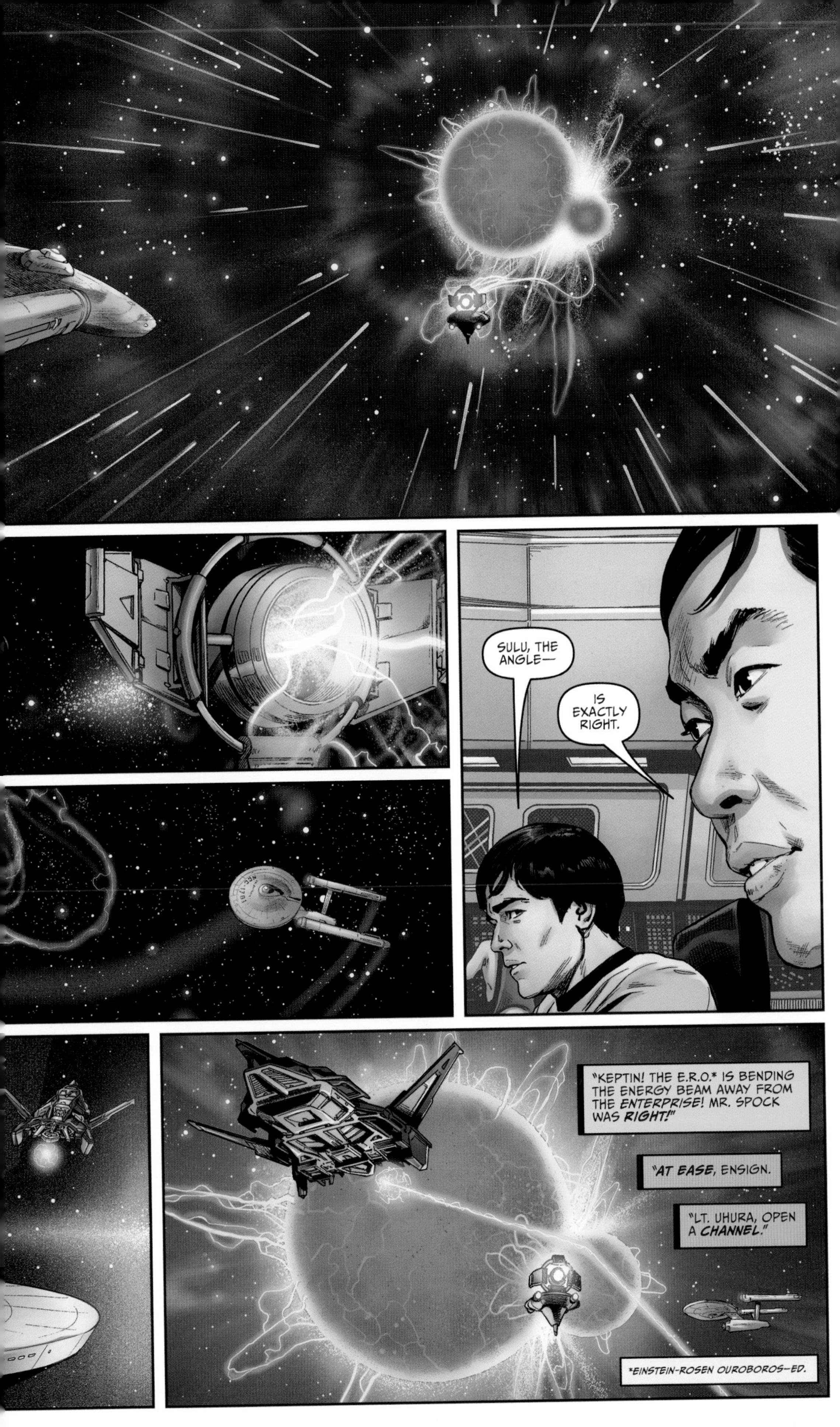

SULU, THE ANGLE—
IS EXACTLY RIGHT.
"KEPTIN! THE E.R.O.* IS BENDING THE ENERGY BEAM AWAY FROM THE *ENTERPRISE*! MR. SPOCK WAS ***RIGHT!***"
"***AT EASE***, ENSIGN.
"LT. UHURA, OPEN A ***CHANNEL***."
*EINSTEIN-ROSEN OUROBOROS—ED.

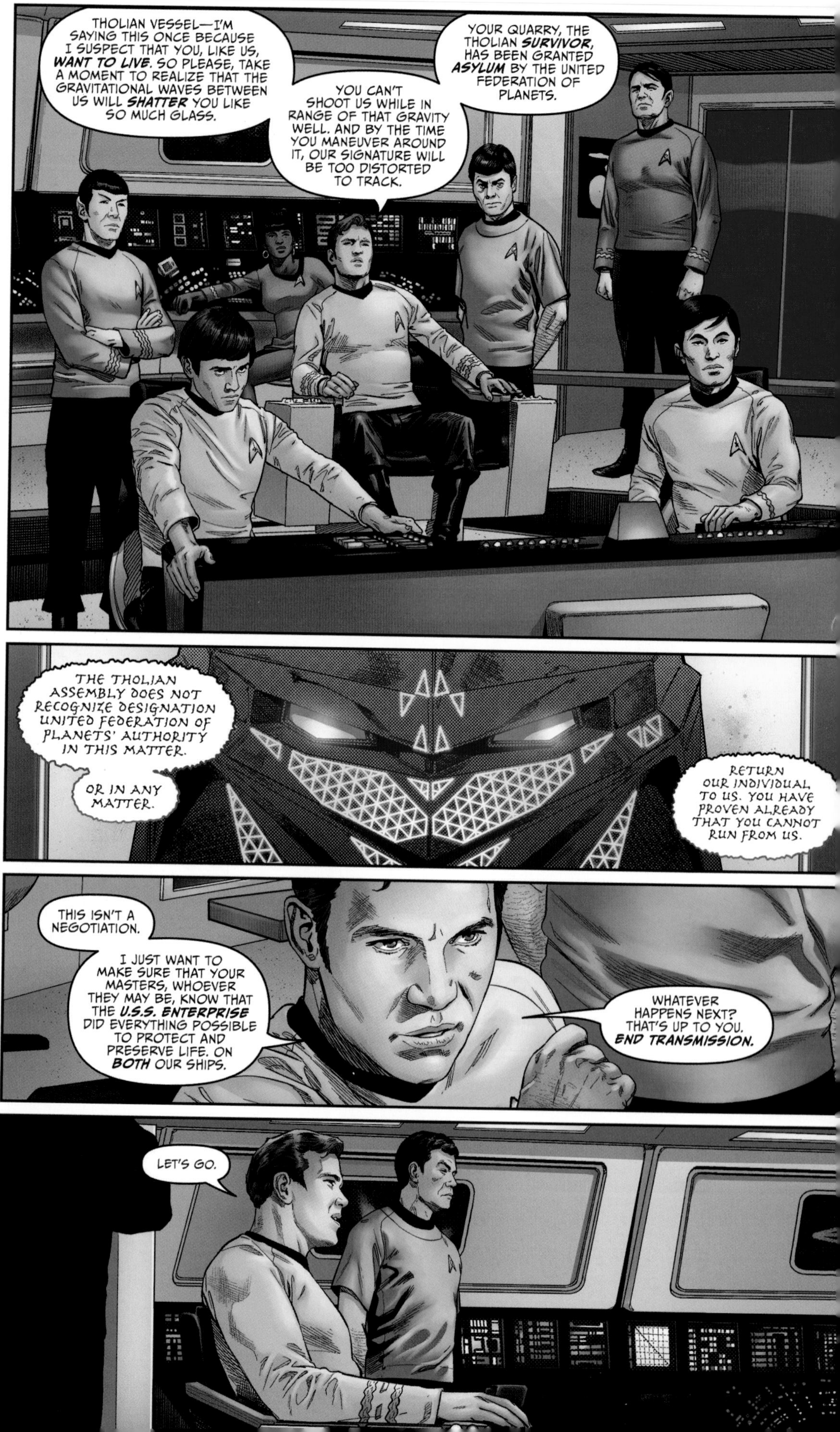
THOLIAN VESSEL—I'M SAYING THIS ONCE BECAUSE I SUSPECT THAT YOU, LIKE US, WANT TO LIVE. SO PLEASE, TAKE A MOMENT TO REALIZE THAT THE GRAVITATIONAL WAVES BETWEEN US WILL SHATTER YOU LIKE SO MUCH GLASS.
YOU CAN'T SHOOT US WHILE IN RANGE OF THAT GRAVITY WELL. AND BY THE TIME YOU MANEUVER AROUND IT, OUR SIGNATURE WILL BE TOO DISTORTED TO TRACK.
YOUR QUARRY, THE THOLIAN SURVIVOR, HAS BEEN GRANTED ASYLUM BY THE UNITED FEDERATION OF PLANETS.
THE THOLIAN ASSEMBLY DOES NOT RECOGNIZE DESIGNATION UNITED FEDERATION OF PLANETS' AUTHORITY IN THIS MATTER.
OR IN ANY MATTER.
RETURN OUR INDIVIDUAL TO US. YOU HAVE PROVEN ALREADY THAT YOU CANNOT RUN FROM US.
THIS ISN'T A NEGOTIATION.
I JUST WANT TO MAKE SURE THAT YOUR MASTERS, WHOEVER THEY MAY BE, KNOW THAT THE U.S.S. ENTERPRISE DID EVERYTHING POSSIBLE TO PROTECT AND PRESERVE LIFE. ON BOTH OUR SHIPS.
WHATEVER HAPPENS NEXT? THAT'S UP TO YOU. END TRANSMISSION.
LET'S GO.

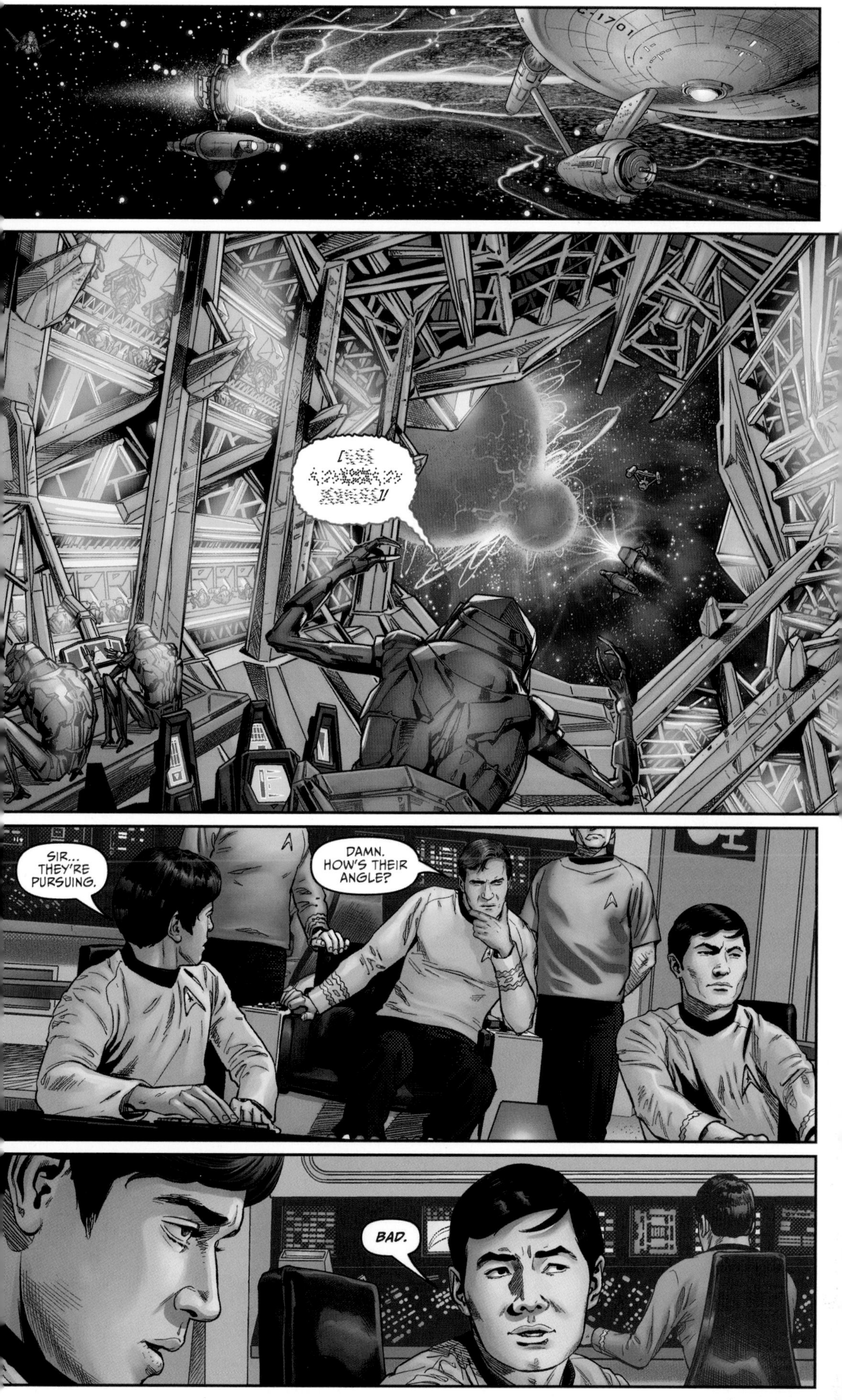
SIR... THEY'RE PURSUING.
DAMN. HOW'S THEIR ANGLE?
BAD.

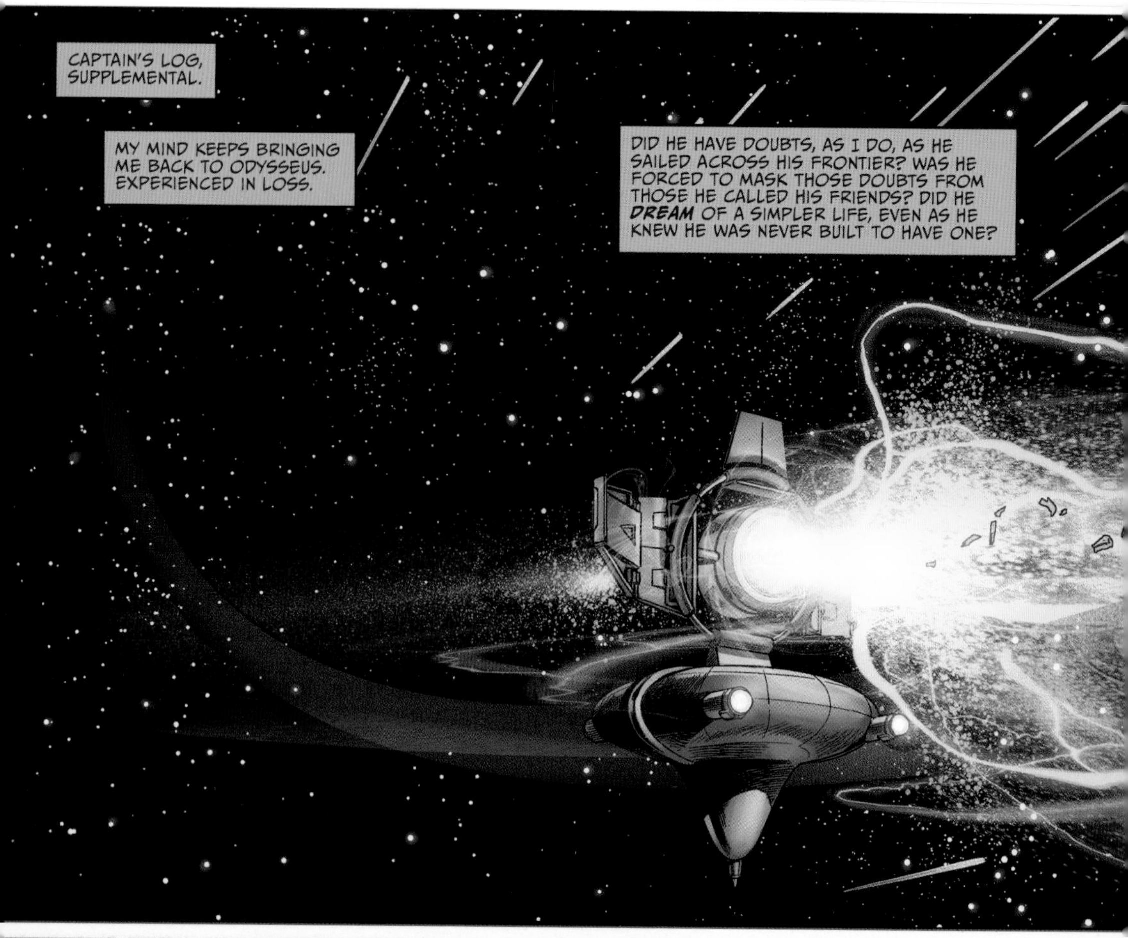
CAPTAIN'S LOG, SUPPLEMENTAL.
MY MIND KEEPS BRINGING ME BACK TO ODYSSEUS. EXPERIENCED IN LOSS.
DID HE HAVE DOUBTS, AS I DO, AS HE SAILED ACROSS HIS FRONTIER? WAS HE FORCED TO MASK THOSE DOUBTS FROM THOSE HE CALLED HIS FRIENDS? DID HE DREAM OF A SIMPLER LIFE, EVEN AS HE KNEW HE WAS NEVER BUILT TO HAVE ONE?

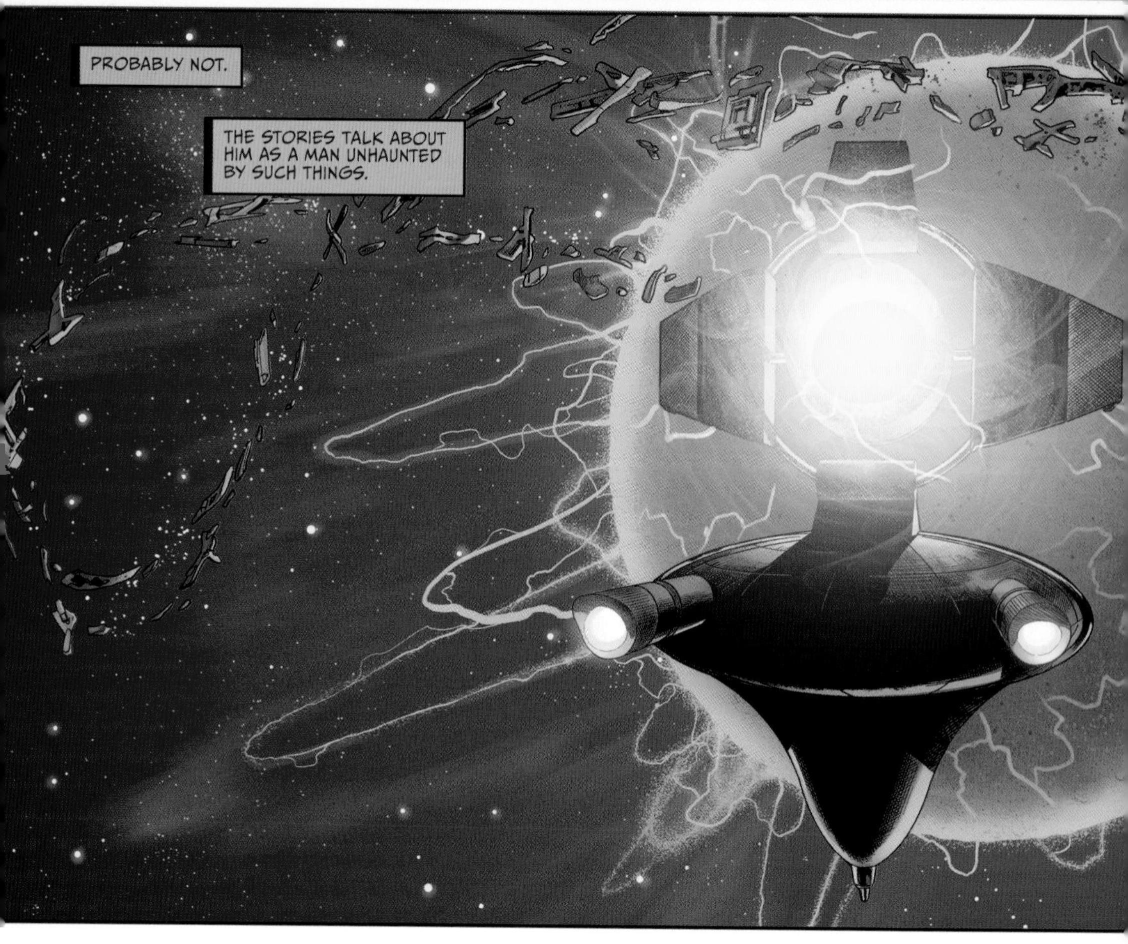
PROBABLY NOT.
THE STORIES TALK ABOUT HIM AS A MAN UNHAUNTED BY SUCH THINGS.

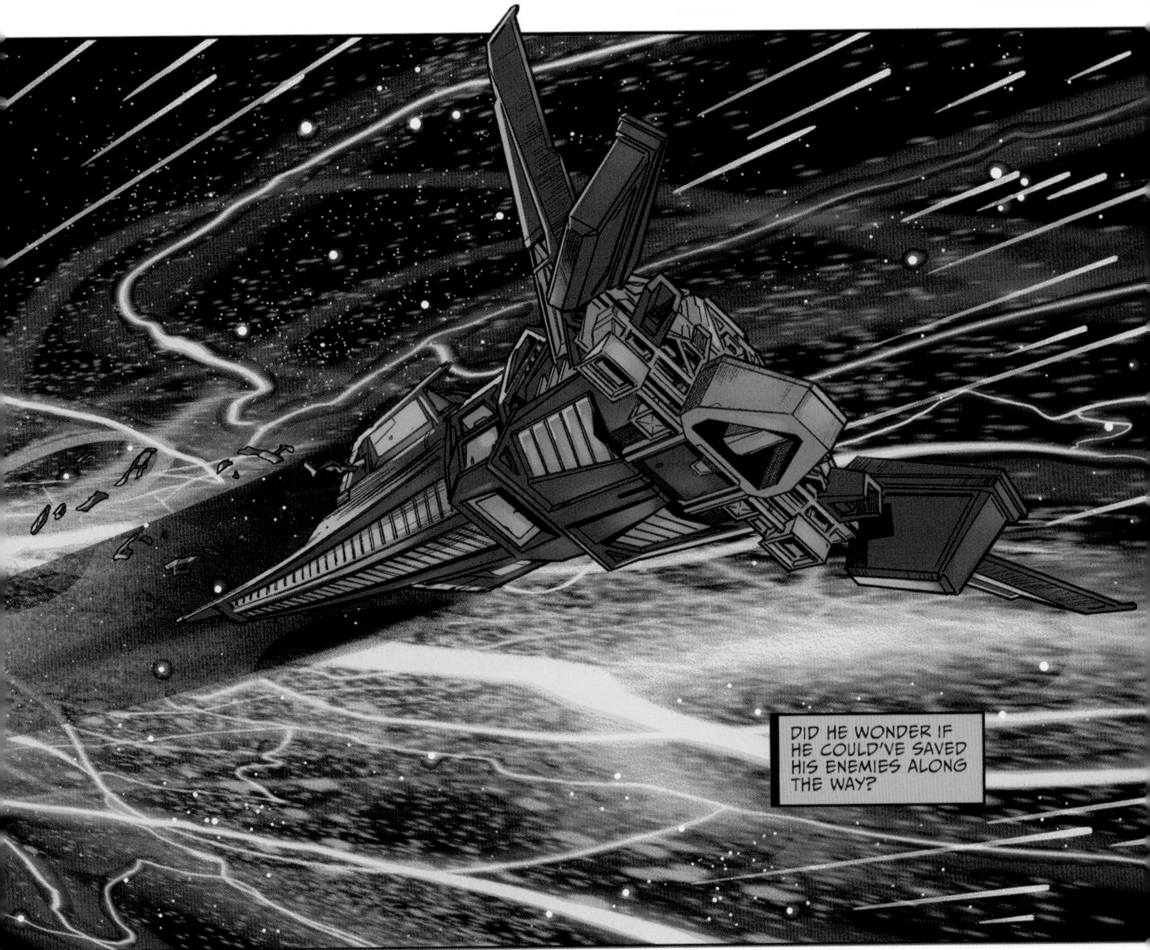
DID HE WONDER IF HE COULD'VE SAVED HIS ENEMIES ALONG THE WAY?

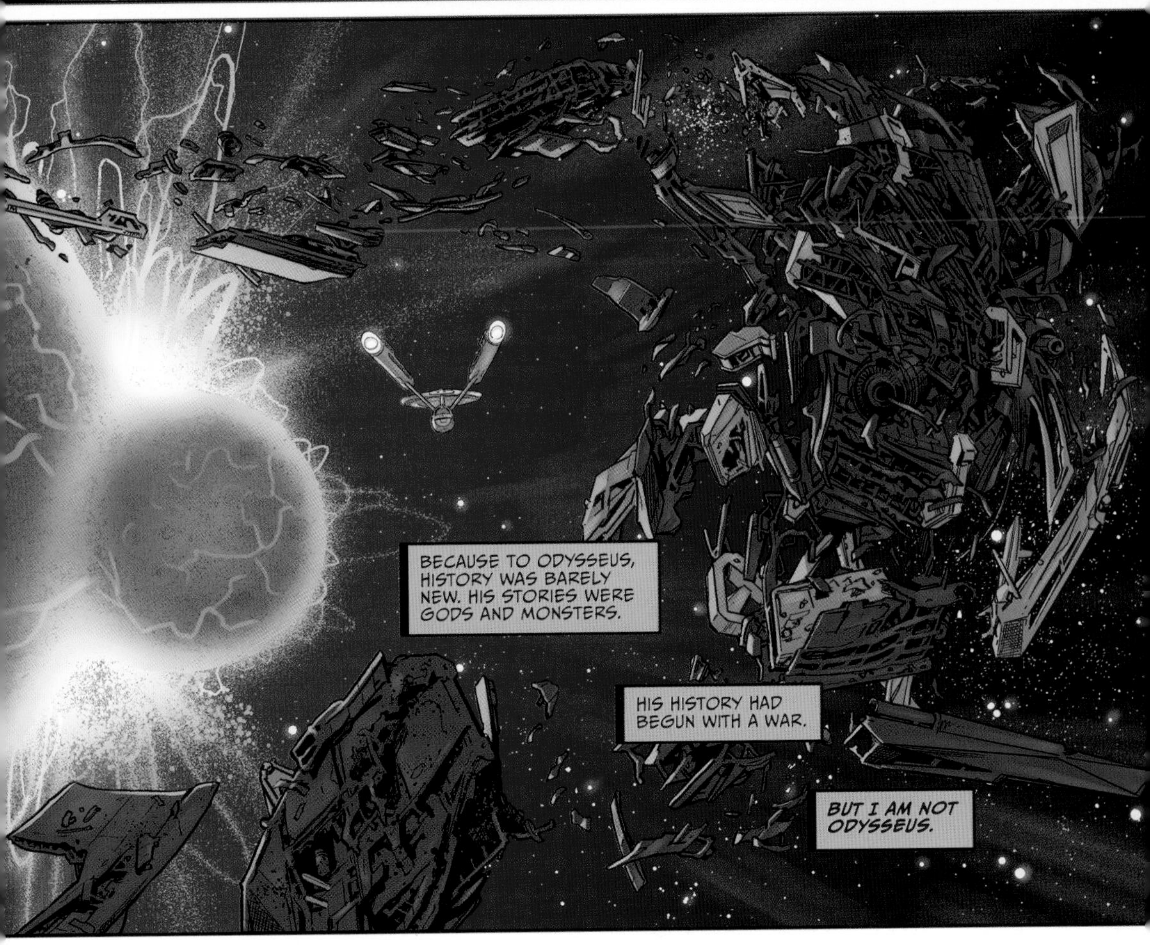
BECAUSE TO ODYSSEUS, HISTORY WAS BARELY NEW. HIS STORIES WERE GODS AND MONSTERS.
HIS HISTORY HAD BEGUN WITH A WAR.
BUT I AM NOT ODYSSEUS.

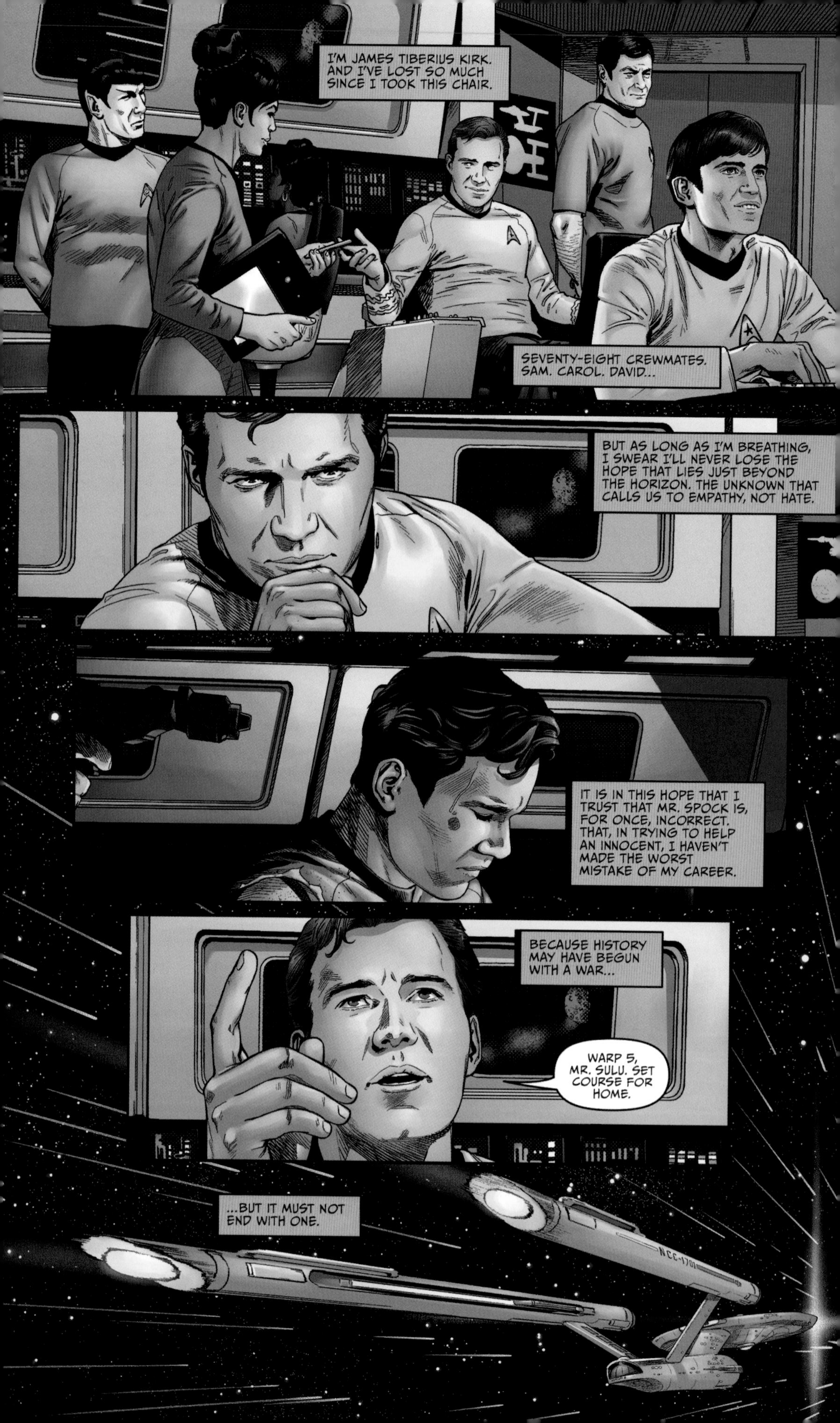

I'M JAMES TIBERIUS KIRK. AND I'VE LOST SO MUCH SINCE I TOOK THIS CHAIR.
SEVENTY-EIGHT CREWMATES. SAM. CAROL. DAVID...
BUT AS LONG AS I'M BREATHING, I SWEAR I'LL NEVER LOSE THE HOPE THAT LIES JUST BEYOND THE HORIZON. THE UNKNOWN THAT CALLS US TO EMPATHY, NOT HATE.
IT IS IN THIS HOPE THAT I TRUST THAT MR. SPOCK IS, FOR ONCE, INCORRECT. THAT, IN TRYING TO HELP AN INNOCENT, I HAVEN'T MADE THE WORST MISTAKE OF MY CAREER.
BECAUSE HISTORY MAY HAVE BEGUN WITH A WAR...
WARP 5, MR. SULU. SET COURSE FOR HOME.
...BUT IT MUST NOT END WITH ONE.
NCC-1701

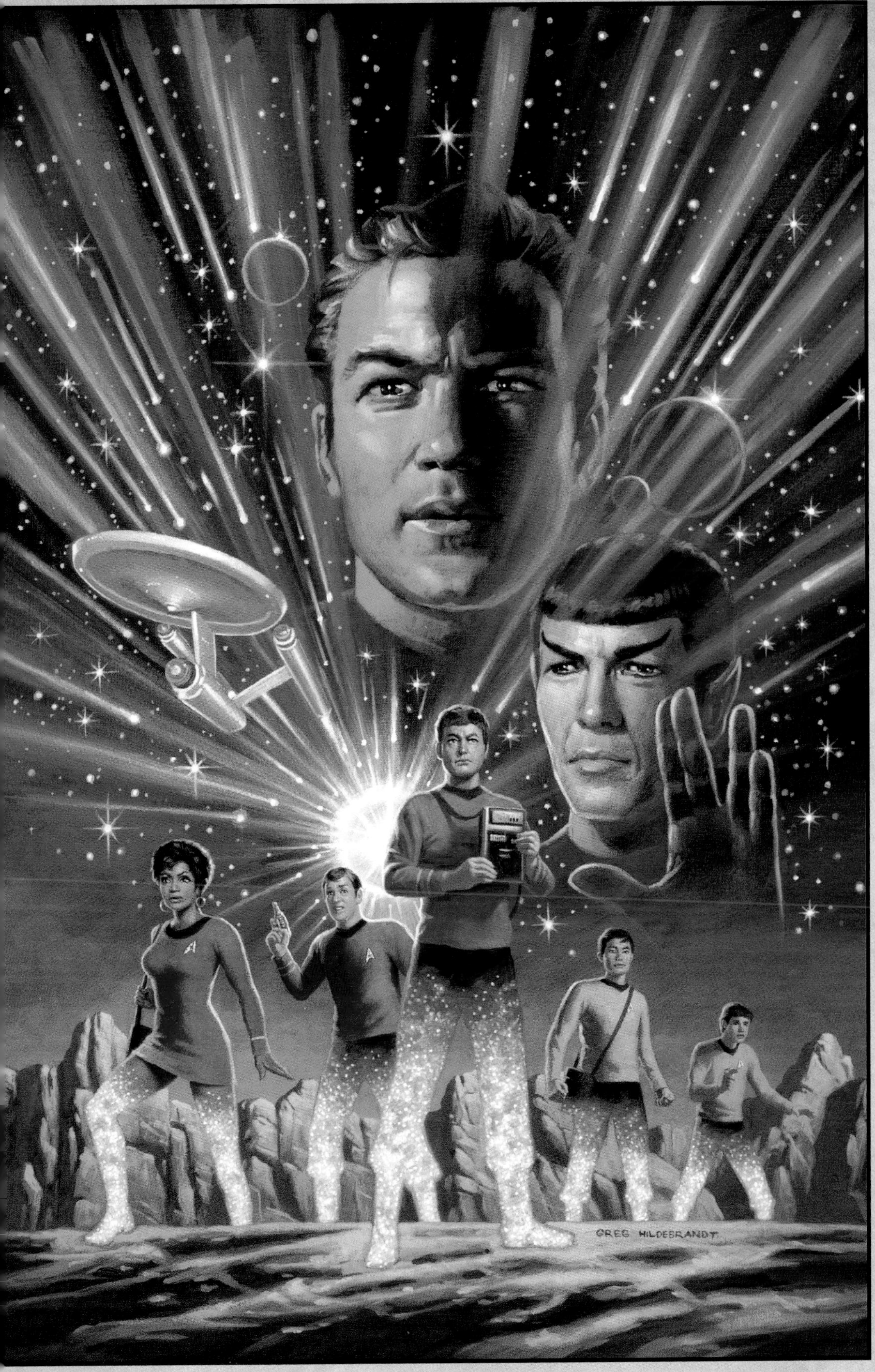
GREG HILDEBRANDT

ART BY GREG HILDEBRANDT

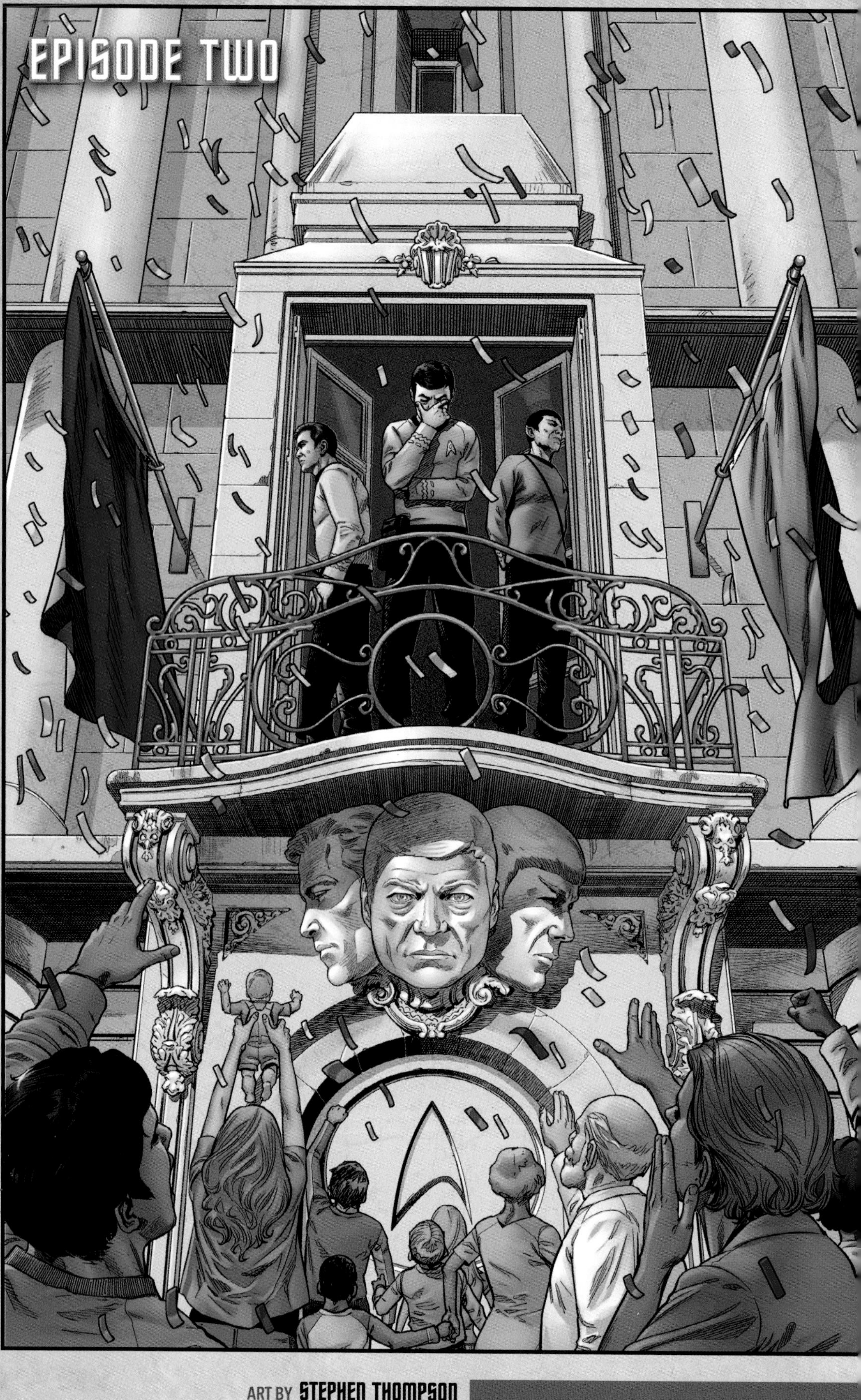
EPISODE TWO

ART BY STEPHEN THOMPSON

COLORS BY CHARLIE KIRCHOFF

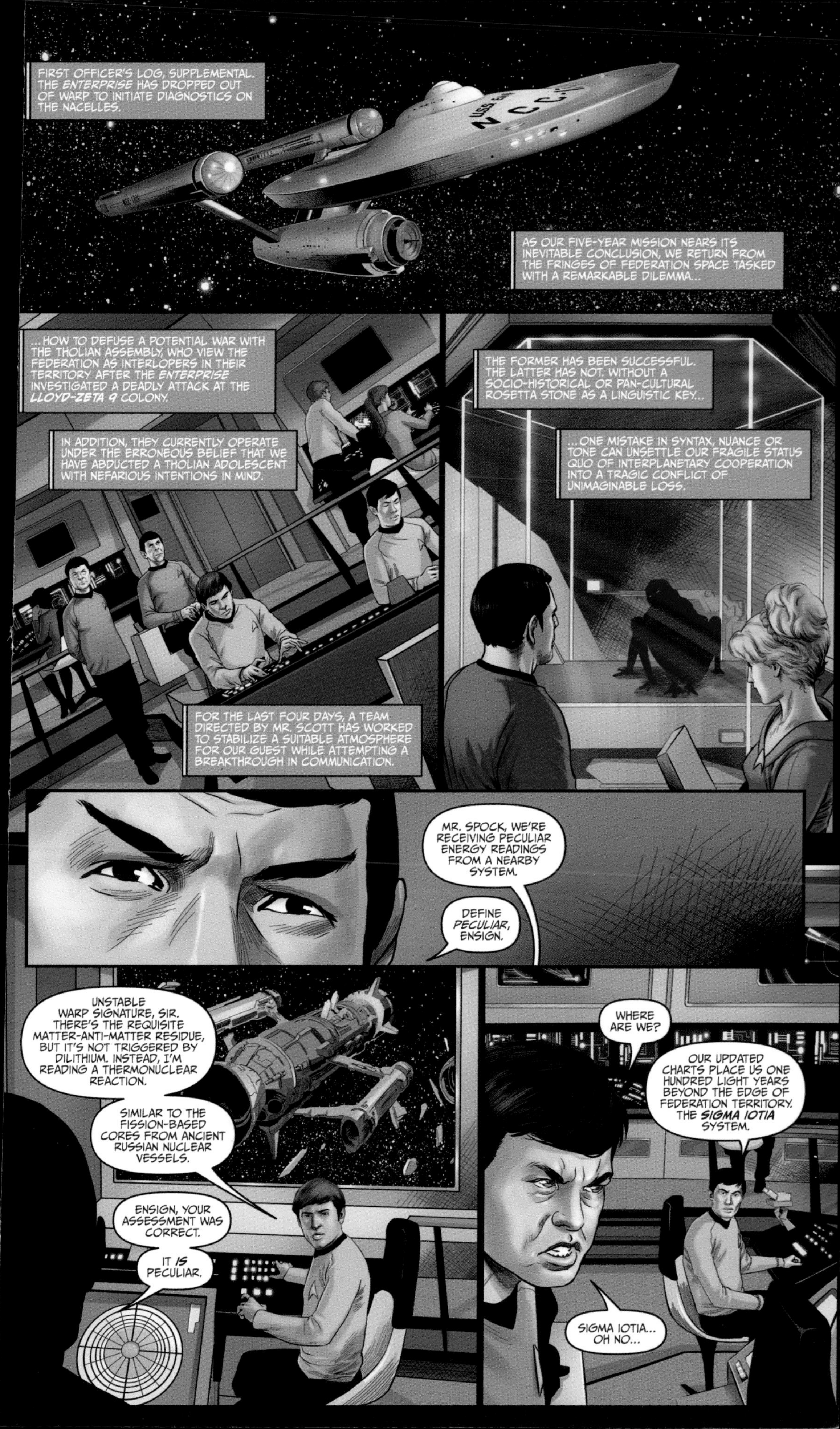
FIRST OFFICER'S LOG, SUPPLEMENTAL. THE ENTERPRISE HAS DROPPED OUT OF WARP TO INITIATE DIAGNOSTICS ON THE NACELLES.
AS OUR FIVE-YEAR MISSION NEARS ITS INEVITABLE CONCLUSION, WE RETURN FROM THE FRINGES OF FEDERATION SPACE TASKED WITH A REMARKABLE DILEMMA...
...HOW TO DEFUSE A POTENTIAL WAR WITH THE THOLIAN ASSEMBLY, WHO VIEW THE FEDERATION AS INTERLOPERS IN THEIR TERRITORY AFTER THE ENTERPRISE INVESTIGATED A DEADLY ATTACK AT THE LLOYD-ZETA 9 COLONY.
IN ADDITION, THEY CURRENTLY OPERATE UNDER THE ERRONEOUS BELIEF THAT WE HAVE ABDUCTED A THOLIAN ADOLESCENT WITH NEFARIOUS INTENTIONS IN MIND.
FOR THE LAST FOUR DAYS, A TEAM DIRECTED BY MR. SCOTT HAS WORKED TO STABILIZE A SUITABLE ATMOSPHERE FOR OUR GUEST WHILE ATTEMPTING A BREAKTHROUGH IN COMMUNICATION.
THE FORMER HAS BEEN SUCCESSFUL. THE LATTER HAS NOT. WITHOUT A SOCIO-HISTORICAL OR PAN-CULTURAL ROSETTA STONE AS A LINGUISTIC KEY...
...ONE MISTAKE IN SYNTAX, NUANCE OR TONE CAN UNSETTLE OUR FRAGILE STATUS QUO OF INTERPLANETARY COOPERATION INTO A TRAGIC CONFLICT OF UNIMAGINABLE LOSS.
MR. SPOCK, WE'RE RECEIVING PECULIAR ENERGY READINGS FROM A NEARBY SYSTEM.
DEFINE PECULIAR, ENSIGN.
UNSTABLE WARP SIGNATURE, SIR. THERE'S THE REQUISITE MATTER-ANTI-MATTER RESIDUE, BUT IT'S NOT TRIGGERED BY DILITHIUM. INSTEAD, I'M READING A THERMONUCLEAR REACTION.
SIMILAR TO THE FISSION-BASED CORES FROM ANCIENT RUSSIAN NUCLEAR VESSELS.
ENSIGN, YOUR ASSESSMENT WAS CORRECT.
IT IS PECULIAR.
WHERE ARE WE?
OUR UPDATED CHARTS PLACE US ONE HUNDRED LIGHT YEARS BEYOND THE EDGE OF FEDERATION TERRITORY. THE SIGMA IOTIA SYSTEM.
SIGMA IOTIA... OH NO...

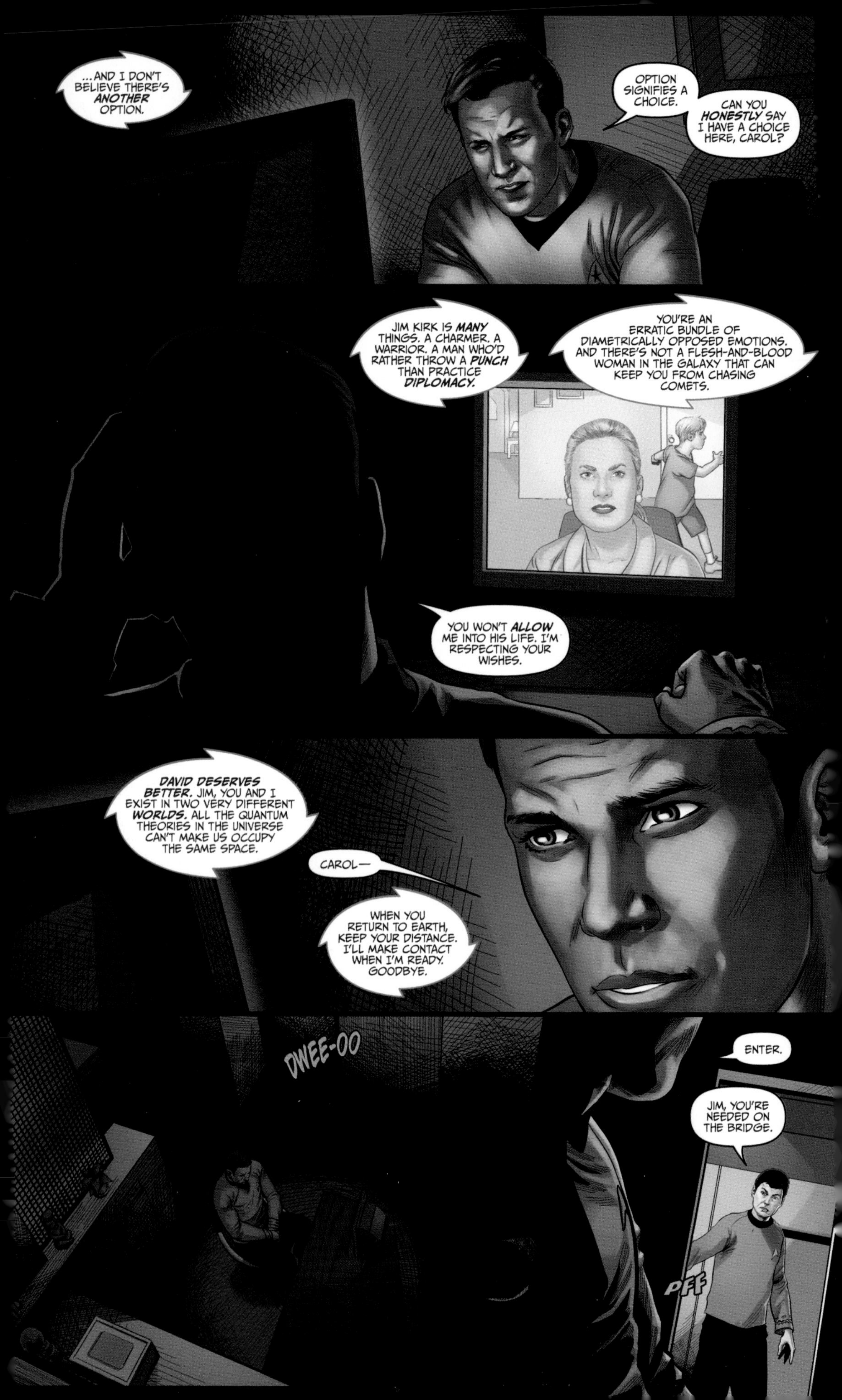
...AND I DON'T BELIEVE THERE'S ANOTHER OPTION.
OPTION SIGNIFIES A CHOICE.
CAN YOU HONESTLY SAY I HAVE A CHOICE HERE, CAROL?
JIM KIRK IS MANY THINGS. A CHARMER. A WARRIOR. A MAN WHO'D RATHER THROW A PUNCH THAN PRACTICE DIPLOMACY.
YOU'RE AN ERRATIC BUNDLE OF DIAMETRICALLY OPPOSED EMOTIONS. AND THERE'S NOT A FLESH-AND-BLOOD WOMAN IN THE GALAXY THAT CAN KEEP YOU FROM CHASING COMETS.
YOU WON'T ALLOW ME INTO HIS LIFE. I'M RESPECTING YOUR WISHES.
DAVID DESERVES BETTER. JIM, YOU AND I EXIST IN TWO VERY DIFFERENT WORLDS. ALL THE QUANTUM THEORIES IN THE UNIVERSE CAN'T MAKE US OCCUPY THE SAME SPACE.
CAROL—
WHEN YOU RETURN TO EARTH, KEEP YOUR DISTANCE. I'LL MAKE CONTACT WHEN I'M READY. GOODBYE.
DWEE-OO
ENTER.
JIM, YOU'RE NEEDED ON THE BRIDGE.
PFF

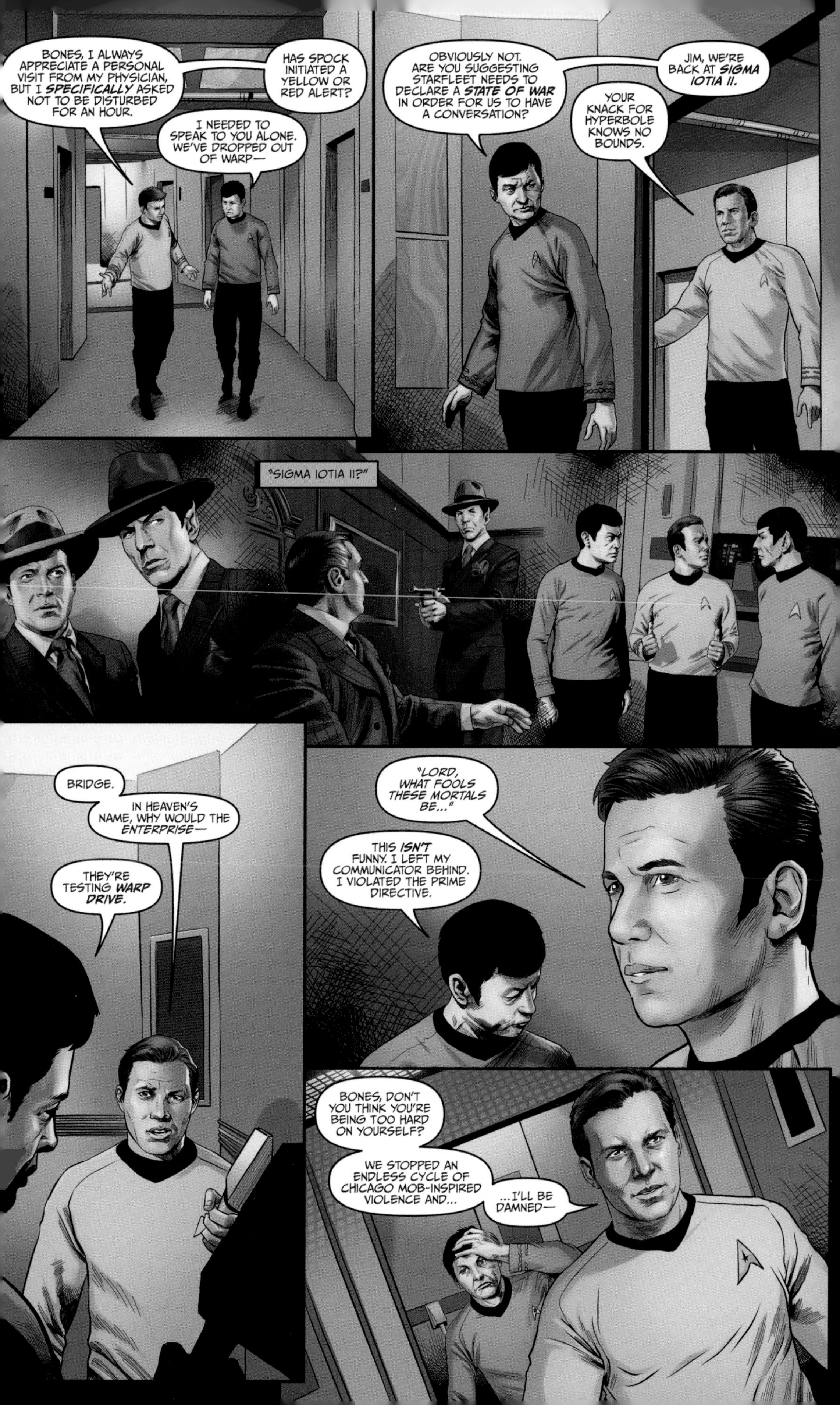
BONES, I ALWAYS APPRECIATE A PERSONAL VISIT FROM MY PHYSICIAN, BUT I *SPECIFICALLY* ASKED NOT TO BE DISTURBED FOR AN HOUR.
HAS SPOCK INITIATED A YELLOW OR RED ALERT?
I NEEDED TO SPEAK TO YOU ALONE. WE'VE DROPPED OUT OF WARP—
OBVIOUSLY NOT. ARE YOU SUGGESTING STARFLEET NEEDS TO DECLARE A *STATE OF WAR* IN ORDER FOR US TO HAVE A CONVERSATION?
JIM, WE'RE BACK AT *SIGMA IOTIA II.*
YOUR KNACK FOR HYPERBOLE KNOWS NO BOUNDS.
"SIGMA IOTIA II?"
BRIDGE.
IN HEAVEN'S NAME, WHY WOULD THE *ENTERPRISE*—
THEY'RE TESTING *WARP DRIVE.*
"LORD, WHAT FOOLS THESE MORTALS BE..."
THIS *ISN'T* FUNNY. I LEFT MY COMMUNICATOR BEHIND. I VIOLATED THE PRIME DIRECTIVE.
BONES, DON'T YOU THINK YOU'RE BEING TOO HARD ON YOURSELF?
WE STOPPED AN ENDLESS CYCLE OF CHICAGO MOB-INSPIRED VIOLENCE AND...
...I'LL BE DAMNED—

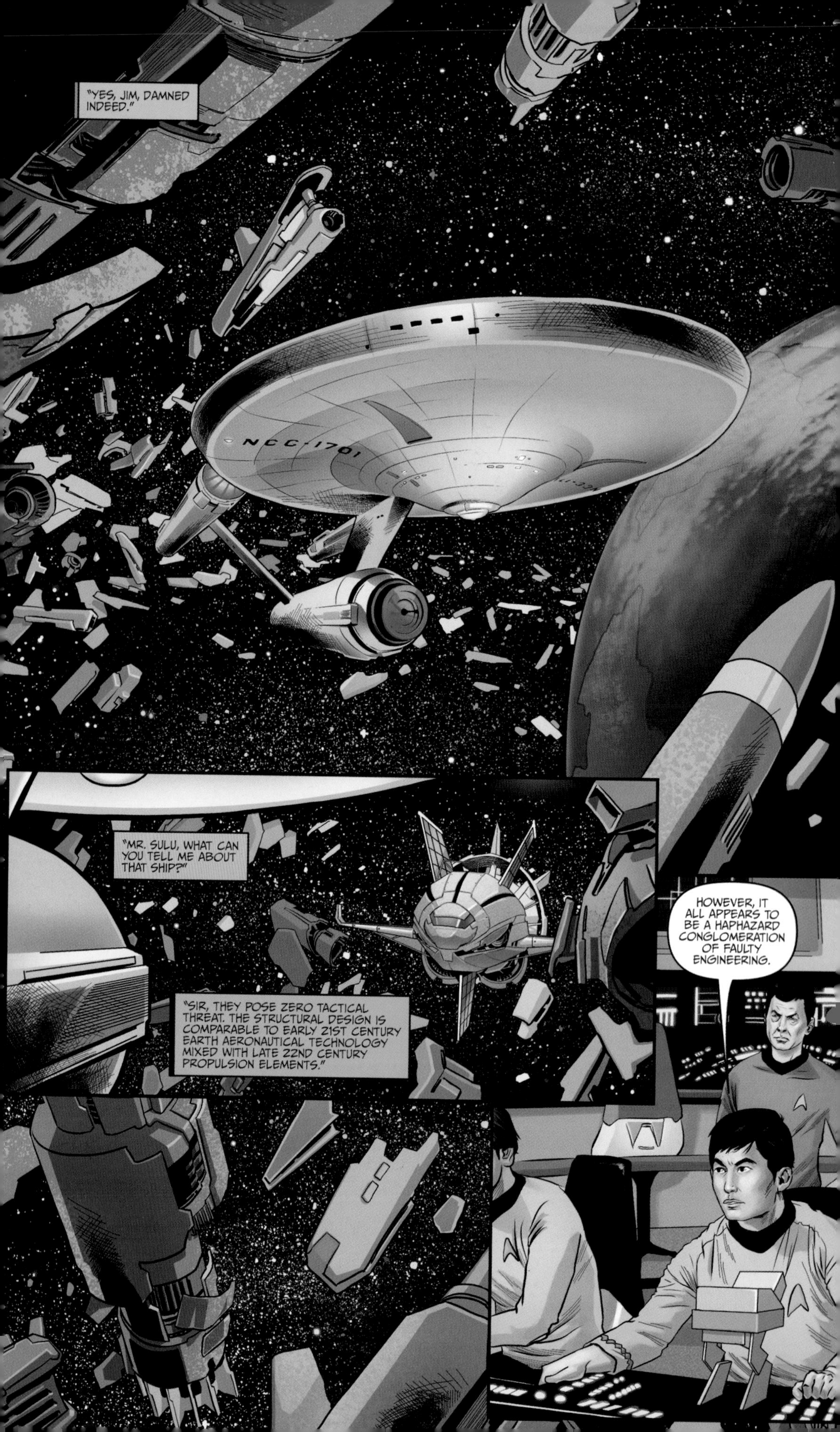
"YES, JIM, DAMNED INDEED."
NCC-1701
"MR. SULU, WHAT CAN YOU TELL ME ABOUT THAT SHIP?"
"SIR, THEY POSE ZERO TACTICAL THREAT. THE STRUCTURAL DESIGN IS COMPARABLE TO EARLY 21ST CENTURY EARTH AERONAUTICAL TECHNOLOGY MIXED WITH LATE 22ND CENTURY PROPULSION ELEMENTS."
HOWEVER, IT ALL APPEARS TO BE A HAPHAZARD CONGLOMERATION OF FAULTY ENGINEERING.

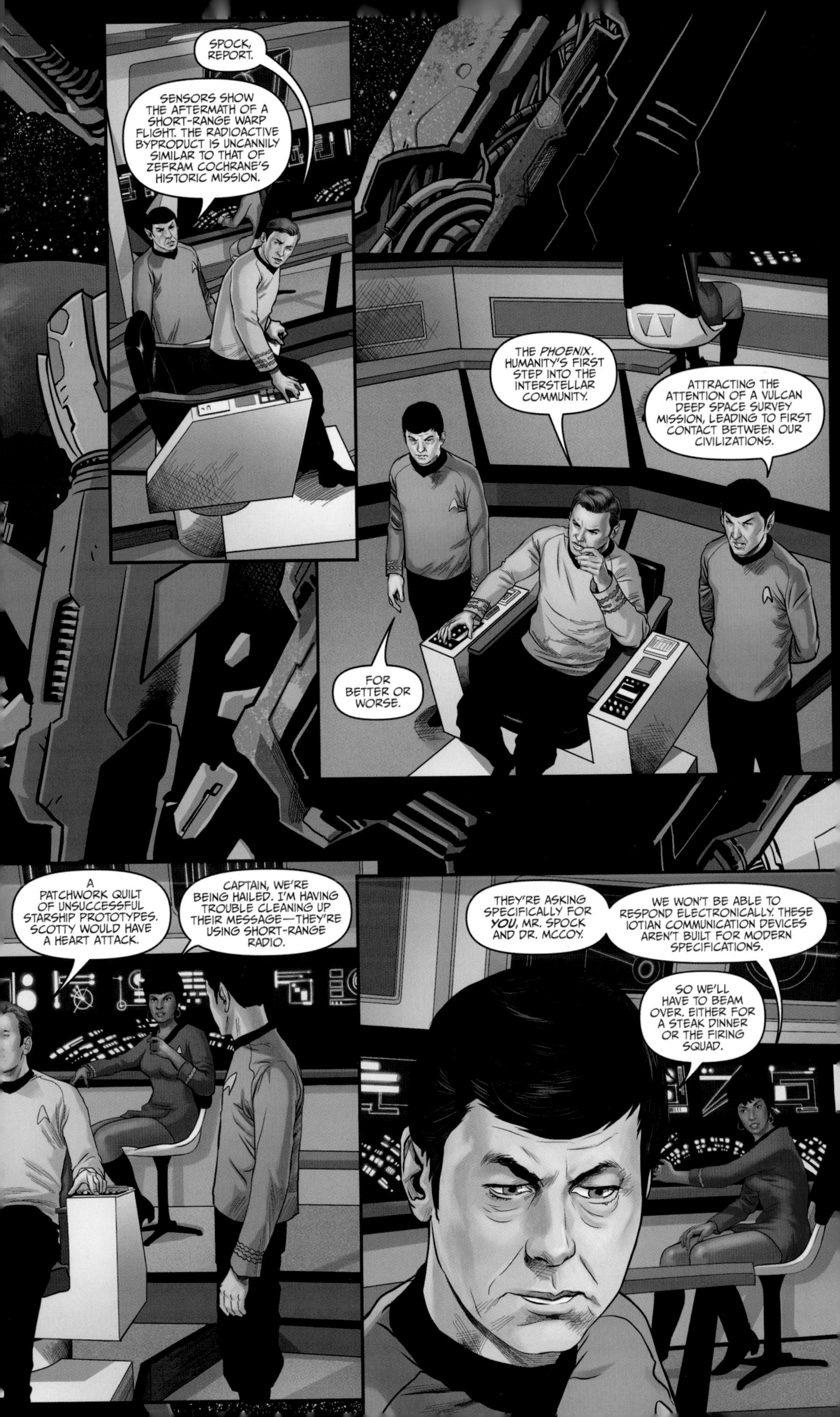
SPOCK, REPORT.
SENSORS SHOW THE AFTERMATH OF A SHORT-RANGE WARP FLIGHT. THE RADIOACTIVE BYPRODUCT IS UNCANNILY SIMILAR TO THAT OF ZEFRAM COCHRANE'S HISTORIC MISSION.
THE *PHOENIX*. HUMANITY'S FIRST STEP INTO THE INTERSTELLAR COMMUNITY.
ATTRACTING THE ATTENTION OF A VULCAN DEEP SPACE SURVEY MISSION, LEADING TO FIRST CONTACT BETWEEN OUR CIVILIZATIONS.
FOR BETTER OR WORSE.
A PATCHWORK QUILT OF UNSUCCESSFUL STARSHIP PROTOTYPES. SCOTTY WOULD HAVE A HEART ATTACK.
CAPTAIN, WE'RE BEING HAILED. I'M HAVING TROUBLE CLEANING UP THEIR MESSAGE—THEY'RE USING SHORT-RANGE RADIO.
THEY'RE ASKING SPECIFICALLY FOR ***YOU***, MR. SPOCK AND DR. MCCOY.
WE WON'T BE ABLE TO RESPOND ELECTRONICALLY. THESE IOTIAN COMMUNICATION DEVICES AREN'T BUILT FOR MODERN SPECIFICATIONS.
SO WE'LL HAVE TO BEAM OVER. EITHER FOR A STEAK DINNER OR THE FIRING SQUAD.

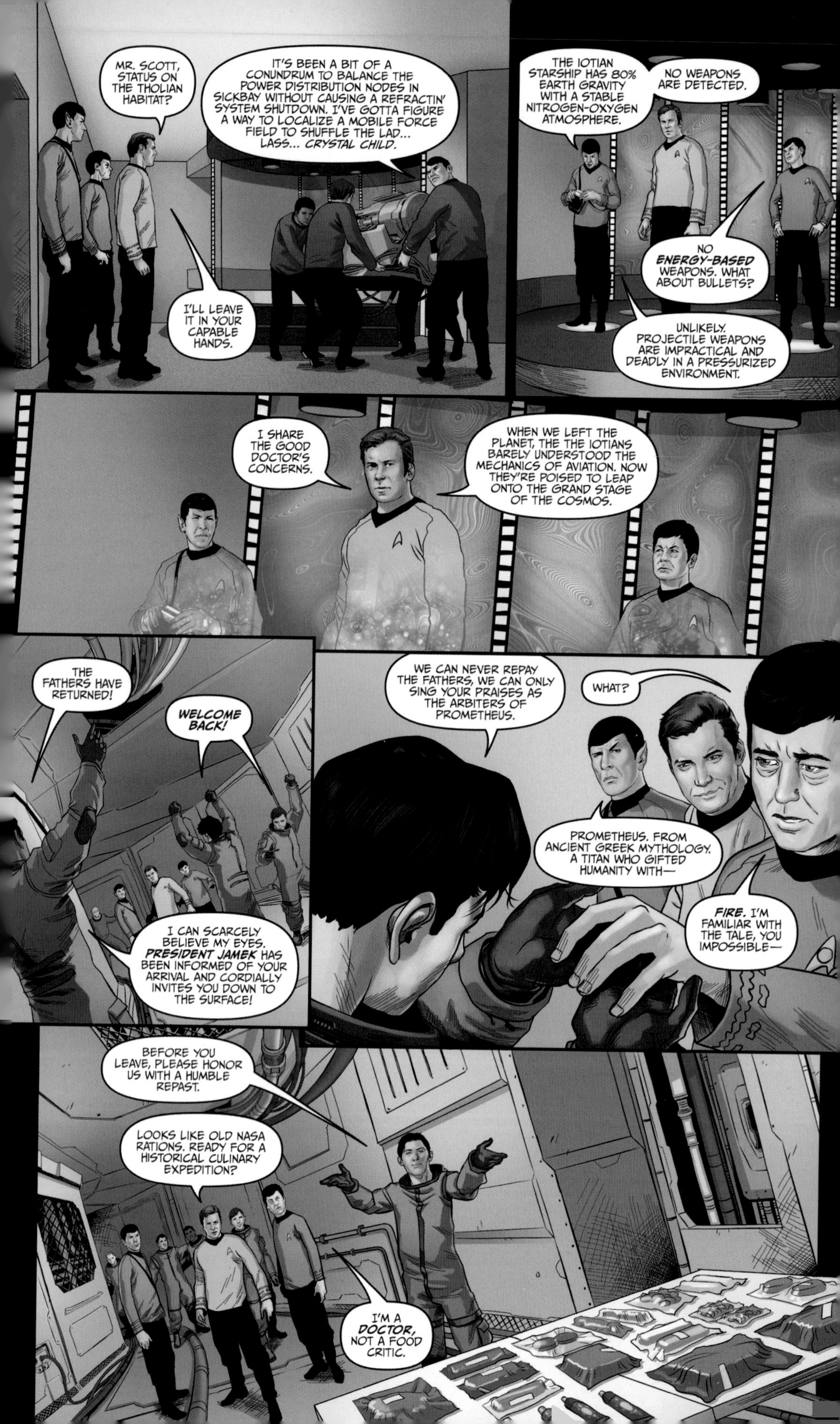
MR. SCOTT, STATUS ON THE THOLIAN HABITAT?
IT'S BEEN A BIT OF A CONUNDRUM TO BALANCE THE POWER DISTRIBUTION NODES IN SICKBAY WITHOUT CAUSING A REFRACTIN' SYSTEM SHUTDOWN. I'VE GOTTA FIGURE A WAY TO LOCALIZE A MOBILE FORCE FIELD TO SHUFFLE THE LAD... LASS... *CRYSTAL CHILD*.
I'LL LEAVE IT IN YOUR CAPABLE HANDS.
THE IOTIAN STARSHIP HAS 80% EARTH GRAVITY WITH A STABLE NITROGEN-OXYGEN ATMOSPHERE.
NO WEAPONS ARE DETECTED.
NO ***ENERGY-BASED*** WEAPONS. WHAT ABOUT BULLETS?
UNLIKELY. PROJECTILE WEAPONS ARE IMPRACTICAL AND DEADLY IN A PRESSURIZED ENVIRONMENT.
I SHARE THE GOOD DOCTOR'S CONCERNS.
WHEN WE LEFT THE PLANET, THE THE IOTIANS BARELY UNDERSTOOD THE MECHANICS OF AVIATION. NOW THEY'RE POISED TO LEAP ONTO THE GRAND STAGE OF THE COSMOS.
THE FATHERS HAVE RETURNED!
WELCOME BACK!
I CAN SCARCELY BELIEVE MY EYES. ***PRESIDENT JAMEK*** HAS BEEN INFORMED OF YOUR ARRIVAL AND CORDIALLY INVITES YOU DOWN TO THE SURFACE!
WE CAN NEVER REPAY THE FATHERS, WE CAN ONLY SING YOUR PRAISES AS THE ARBITERS OF PROMETHEUS.
WHAT?
PROMETHEUS. FROM ANCIENT GREEK MYTHOLOGY. A TITAN WHO GIFTED HUMANITY WITH—
FIRE. I'M FAMILIAR WITH THE TALE, YOU IMPOSSIBLE—
BEFORE YOU LEAVE, PLEASE HONOR US WITH A HUMBLE REPAST.
LOOKS LIKE OLD NASA RATIONS. READY FOR A HISTORICAL CULINARY EXPEDITION?
I'M A ***DOCTOR,*** NOT A FOOD CRITIC.

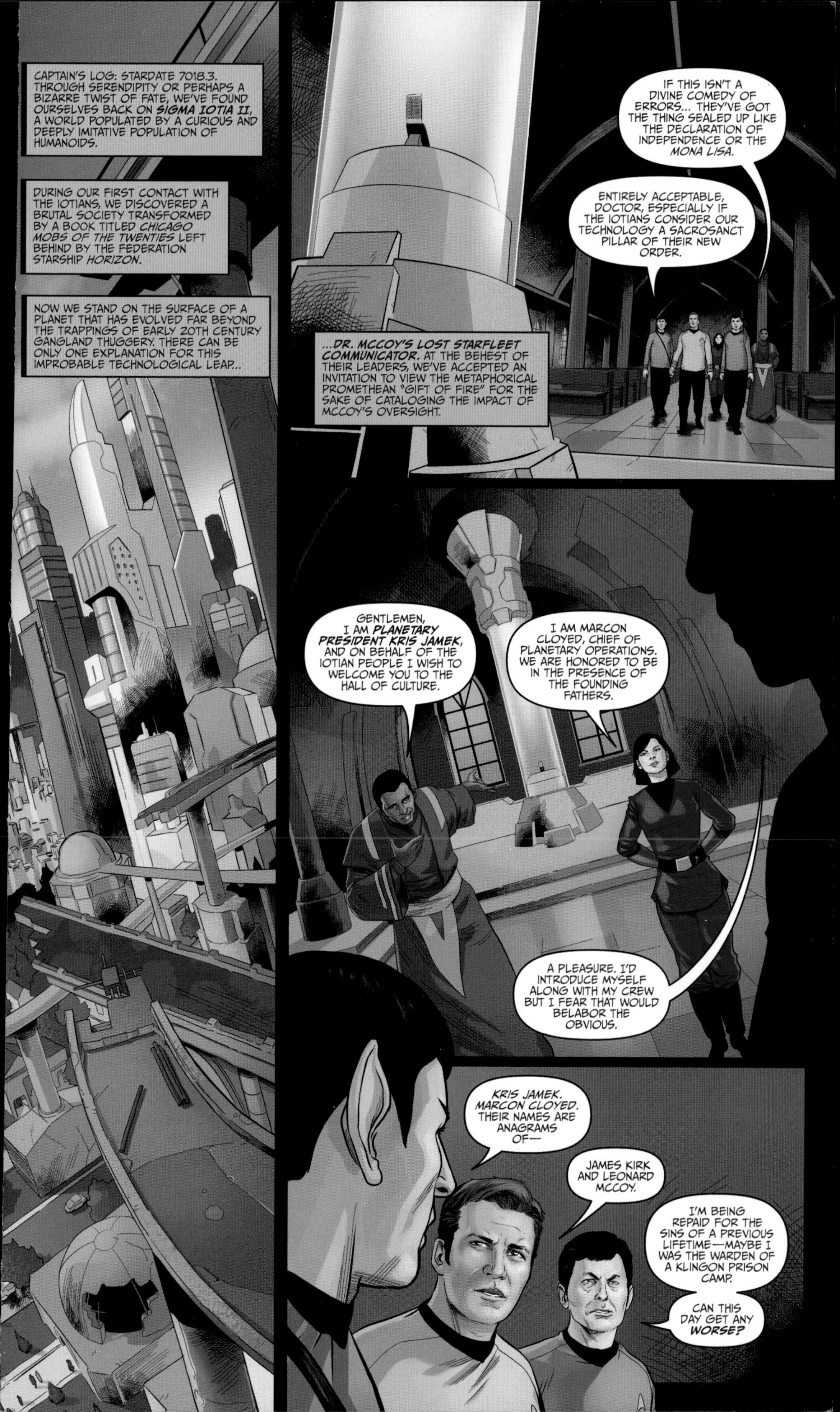
CAPTAIN'S LOG: STARDATE 7018.3. THROUGH SERENDIPITY OR PERHAPS A BIZARRE TWIST OF FATE, WE'VE FOUND OURSELVES BACK ON *SIGMA IOTIA II*, A WORLD POPULATED BY A CURIOUS AND DEEPLY IMITATIVE POPULATION OF HUMANOIDS.
DURING OUR FIRST CONTACT WITH THE IOTIANS, WE DISCOVERED A BRUTAL SOCIETY TRANSFORMED BY A BOOK TITLED *CHICAGO MOBS OF THE TWENTIES* LEFT BEHIND BY THE FEDERATION STARSHIP *HORIZON*.
NOW WE STAND ON THE SURFACE OF A PLANET THAT HAS EVOLVED FAR BEYOND THE TRAPPINGS OF EARLY 20TH CENTURY GANGLAND THUGGERY. THERE CAN BE ONLY ONE EXPLANATION FOR THIS IMPROBABLE TECHNOLOGICAL LEAP...
...***DR. MCCOY'S LOST STARFLEET COMMUNICATOR.*** AT THE BEHEST OF THEIR LEADERS, WE'VE ACCEPTED AN INVITATION TO VIEW THE METAPHORICAL PROMETHEAN "GIFT OF FIRE" FOR THE SAKE OF CATALOGING THE IMPACT OF MCCOY'S OVERSIGHT.
IF THIS ISN'T A DIVINE COMEDY OF ERRORS... THEY'VE GOT THE THING SEALED UP LIKE THE DECLARATION OF INDEPENDENCE OR THE *MONA LISA*.
ENTIRELY ACCEPTABLE, DOCTOR, ESPECIALLY IF THE IOTIANS CONSIDER OUR TECHNOLOGY A SACROSANCT PILLAR OF THEIR NEW ORDER.
GENTLEMEN, I AM ***PLANETARY PRESIDENT KRIS JAMEK***, AND ON BEHALF OF THE IOTIAN PEOPLE I WISH TO WELCOME YOU TO THE HALL OF CULTURE.
I AM MARCON CLOYED, CHIEF OF PLANETARY OPERATIONS. WE ARE HONORED TO BE IN THE PRESENCE OF THE FOUNDING FATHERS.
A PLEASURE. I'D INTRODUCE MYSELF ALONG WITH MY CREW BUT I FEAR THAT WOULD BELABOR THE OBVIOUS.
KRIS JAMEK. MARCON CLOYED. THEIR NAMES ARE ANAGRAMS OF—
JAMES KIRK AND LEONARD MCCOY.
I'M BEING REPAID FOR THE SINS OF A PREVIOUS LIFETIME—MAYBE I WAS THE WARDEN OF A KLINGON PRISON CAMP.
CAN THIS DAY GET ANY ***WORSE?***

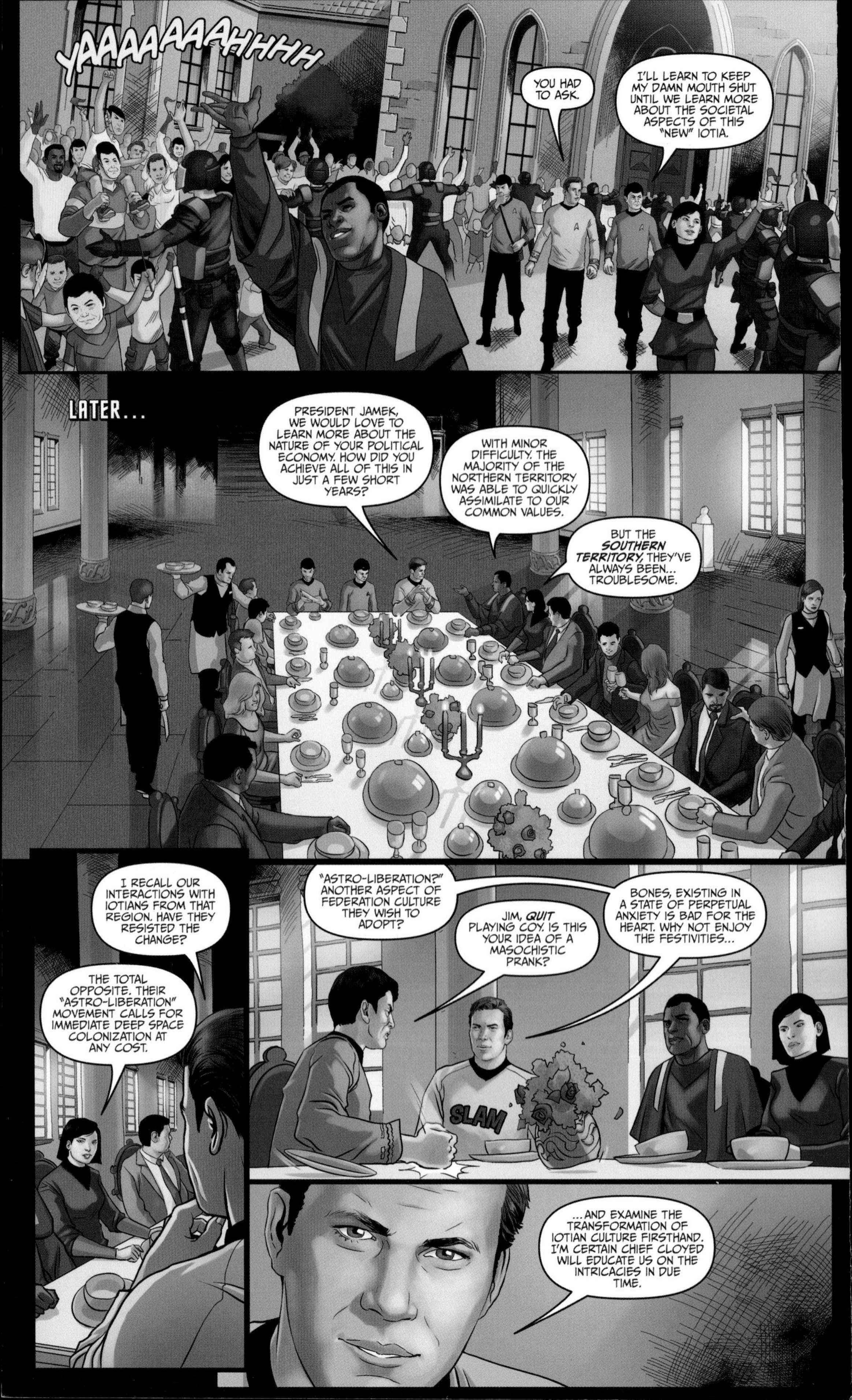
YAAAAAAAHHHH
YOU HAD TO ASK.
I'LL LEARN TO KEEP MY DAMN MOUTH SHUT UNTIL WE LEARN MORE ABOUT THE SOCIETAL ASPECTS OF THIS "NEW" IOTIA.
LATER...
PRESIDENT JAMEK, WE WOULD LOVE TO LEARN MORE ABOUT THE NATURE OF YOUR POLITICAL ECONOMY. HOW DID YOU ACHIEVE ALL OF THIS IN JUST A FEW SHORT YEARS?
WITH MINOR DIFFICULTY. THE MAJORITY OF THE NORTHERN TERRITORY WAS ABLE TO QUICKLY ASSIMILATE TO OUR COMMON VALUES.
BUT THE *SOUTHERN TERRITORY,* THEY'VE ALWAYS BEEN... TROUBLESOME.
I RECALL OUR INTERACTIONS WITH IOTIANS FROM THAT REGION. HAVE THEY RESISTED THE CHANGE?
THE TOTAL OPPOSITE. THEIR "ASTRO-LIBERATION" MOVEMENT CALLS FOR IMMEDIATE DEEP SPACE COLONIZATION AT ANY COST.
"ASTRO-LIBERATION?" ANOTHER ASPECT OF FEDERATION CULTURE THEY WISH TO ADOPT?
JIM, *QUIT* PLAYING COY. IS THIS YOUR IDEA OF A MASOCHISTIC PRANK?
BONES, EXISTING IN A STATE OF PERPETUAL ANXIETY IS BAD FOR THE HEART. WHY NOT ENJOY THE FESTIVITIES...
SLAM
...AND EXAMINE THE TRANSFORMATION OF IOTIAN CULTURE FIRSTHAND. I'M CERTAIN CHIEF CLOYED WILL EDUCATE US ON THE INTRICACIES IN DUE TIME.

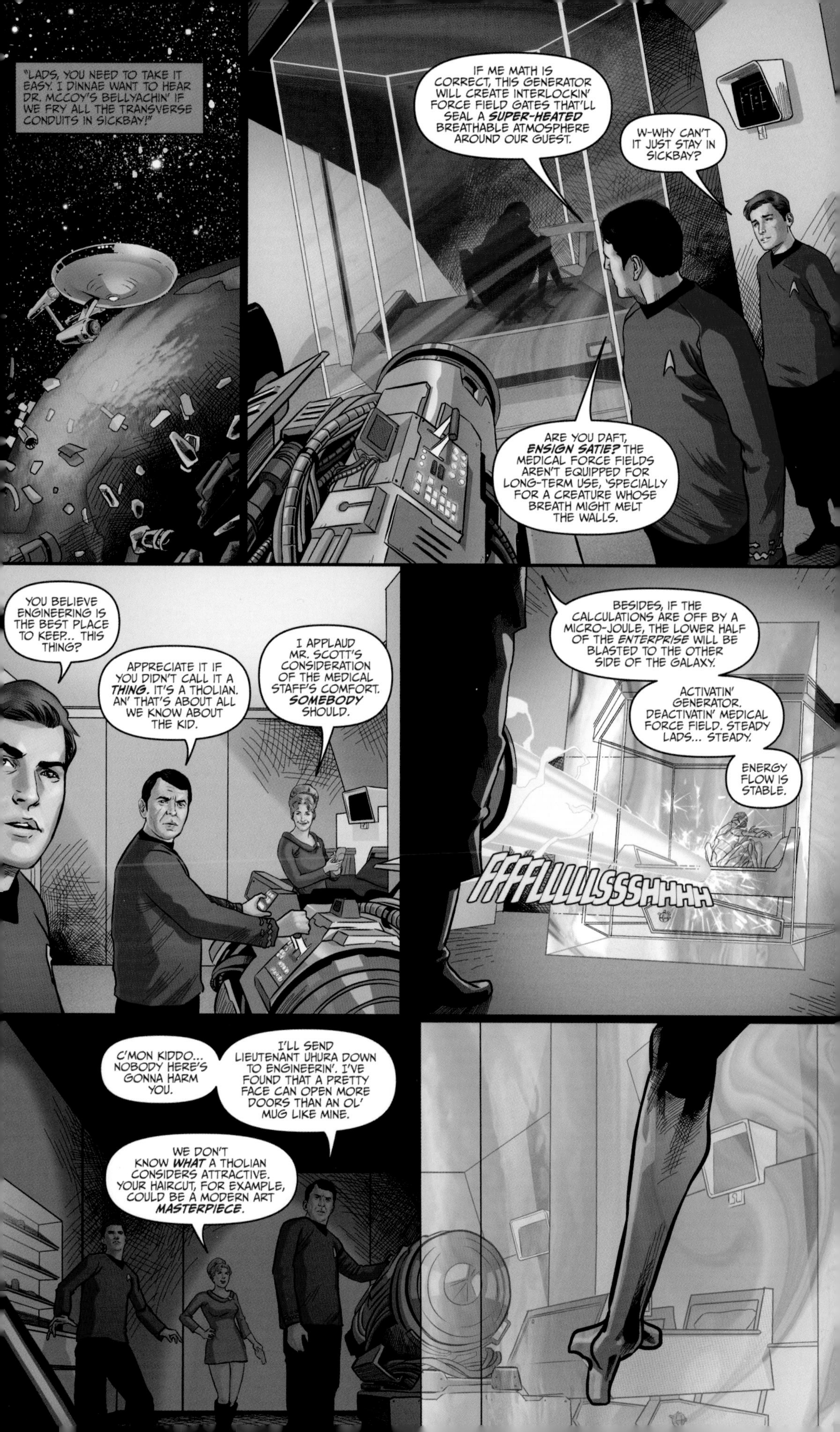
"LADS, YOU NEED TO TAKE IT EASY. I DINNAE WANT TO HEAR DR. MCCOY'S BELLYACHIN' IF WE FRY ALL THE TRANSVERSE CONDUITS IN SICKBAY!"
IF ME MATH IS CORRECT, THIS GENERATOR WILL CREATE INTERLOCKIN' FORCE FIELD GATES THAT'LL SEAL A ***SUPER-HEATED*** BREATHABLE ATMOSPHERE AROUND OUR GUEST.
W-WHY CAN'T IT JUST STAY IN SICKBAY?
ARE YOU DAFT, ***ENSIGN SATIE?*** THE MEDICAL FORCE FIELDS AREN'T EQUIPPED FOR LONG-TERM USE, 'SPECIALLY FOR A CREATURE WHOSE BREATH MIGHT MELT THE WALLS.
YOU BELIEVE ENGINEERING IS THE BEST PLACE TO KEEP... THIS THING?
APPRECIATE IT IF YOU DIDN'T CALL IT A ***THING***. IT'S A THOLIAN. AN' THAT'S ABOUT ALL WE KNOW ABOUT THE KID.
I APPLAUD MR. SCOTT'S CONSIDERATION OF THE MEDICAL STAFF'S COMFORT. ***SOMEBODY*** SHOULD.
BESIDES, IF THE CALCULATIONS ARE OFF BY A MICRO-JOULE, THE LOWER HALF OF THE *ENTERPRISE* WILL BE BLASTED TO THE OTHER SIDE OF THE GALAXY.
ACTIVATIN' GENERATOR. DEACTIVATIN' MEDICAL FORCE FIELD. STEADY LADS... STEADY.
ENERGY FLOW IS STABLE.
FFFFLLLLLLSSSHHHH
C'MON KIDDO... NOBODY HERE'S GONNA HARM YOU.
I'LL SEND LIEUTENANT UHURA DOWN TO ENGINEERIN'. I'VE FOUND THAT A PRETTY FACE CAN OPEN MORE DOORS THAN AN OL' MUG LIKE MINE.
WE DON'T KNOW ***WHAT*** A THOLIAN CONSIDERS ATTRACTIVE. YOUR HAIRCUT, FOR EXAMPLE, COULD BE A MODERN ART ***MASTERPIECE***.

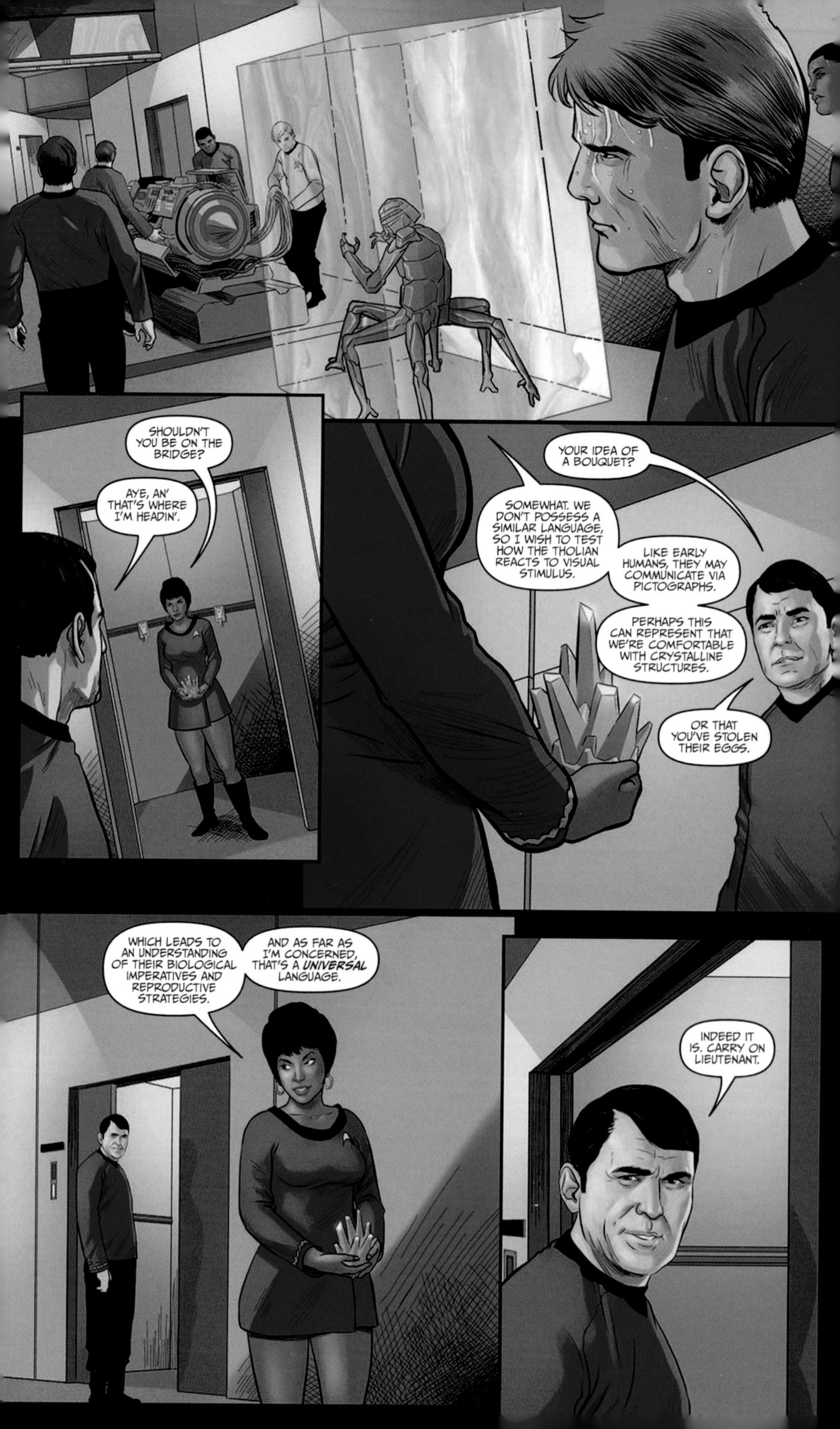
SHOULDN'T YOU BE ON THE BRIDGE?
AYE, AN' THAT'S WHERE I'M HEADIN'.
YOUR IDEA OF A BOUQUET?
SOMEWHAT. WE DON'T POSSESS A SIMILAR LANGUAGE, SO I WISH TO TEST HOW THE THOLIAN REACTS TO VISUAL STIMULUS.
LIKE EARLY HUMANS, THEY MAY COMMUNICATE VIA PICTOGRAPHS.
PERHAPS THIS CAN REPRESENT THAT WE'RE COMFORTABLE WITH CRYSTALLINE STRUCTURES.
OR THAT YOU'VE STOLEN THEIR EGGS.
WHICH LEADS TO AN UNDERSTANDING OF THEIR BIOLOGICAL IMPERATIVES AND REPRODUCTIVE STRATEGIES.
AND AS FAR AS I'M CONCERNED, THAT'S A *UNIVERSAL* LANGUAGE.
INDEED IT IS. CARRY ON LIEUTENANT.

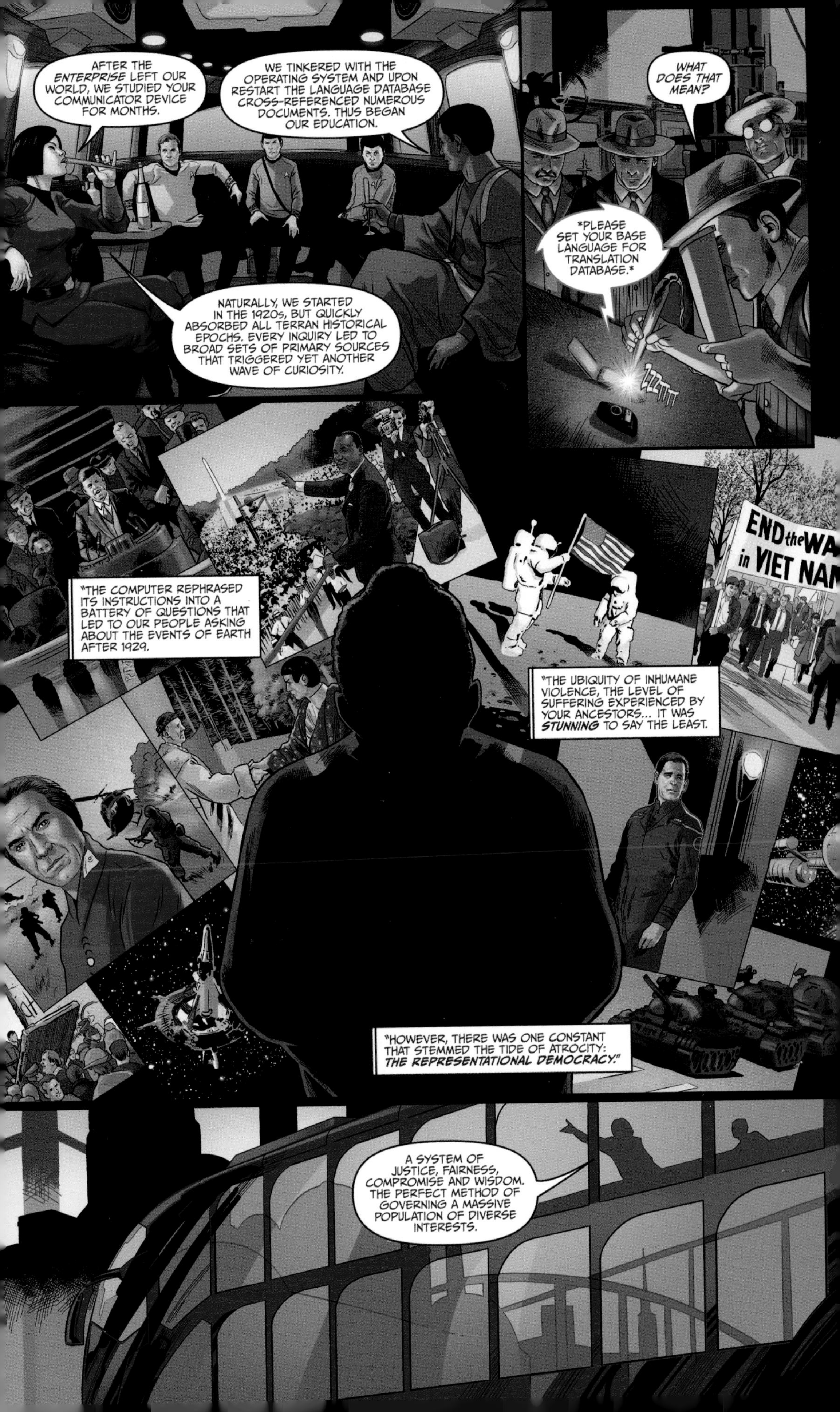
AFTER THE *ENTERPRISE* LEFT OUR WORLD, WE STUDIED YOUR COMMUNICATOR DEVICE FOR MONTHS.
WE TINKERED WITH THE OPERATING SYSTEM AND UPON RESTART THE LANGUAGE DATABASE CROSS-REFERENCED NUMEROUS DOCUMENTS. THUS BEGAN OUR EDUCATION.
NATURALLY, WE STARTED IN THE 1920s, BUT QUICKLY ABSORBED ALL TERRAN HISTORICAL EPOCHS. EVERY INQUIRY LED TO BROAD SETS OF PRIMARY SOURCES THAT TRIGGERED YET ANOTHER WAVE OF CURIOSITY.
WHAT DOES THAT MEAN?
PLEASE SET YOUR BASE LANGUAGE FOR TRANSLATION DATABASE.
ZZZTTTT
END the WA
in VIET NAM
"THE COMPUTER REPHRASED ITS INSTRUCTIONS INTO A BATTERY OF QUESTIONS THAT LED TO OUR PEOPLE ASKING ABOUT THE EVENTS OF EARTH AFTER 1929.
"THE UBIQUITY OF INHUMANE VIOLENCE, THE LEVEL OF SUFFERING EXPERIENCED BY YOUR ANCESTORS... IT WAS ***STUNNING*** TO SAY THE LEAST.
"HOWEVER, THERE WAS ONE CONSTANT THAT STEMMED THE TIDE OF ATROCITY: ***THE REPRESENTATIONAL DEMOCRACY.***"
A SYSTEM OF JUSTICE, FAIRNESS, COMPROMISE AND WISDOM. THE PERFECT METHOD OF GOVERNING A MASSIVE POPULATION OF DIVERSE INTERESTS.

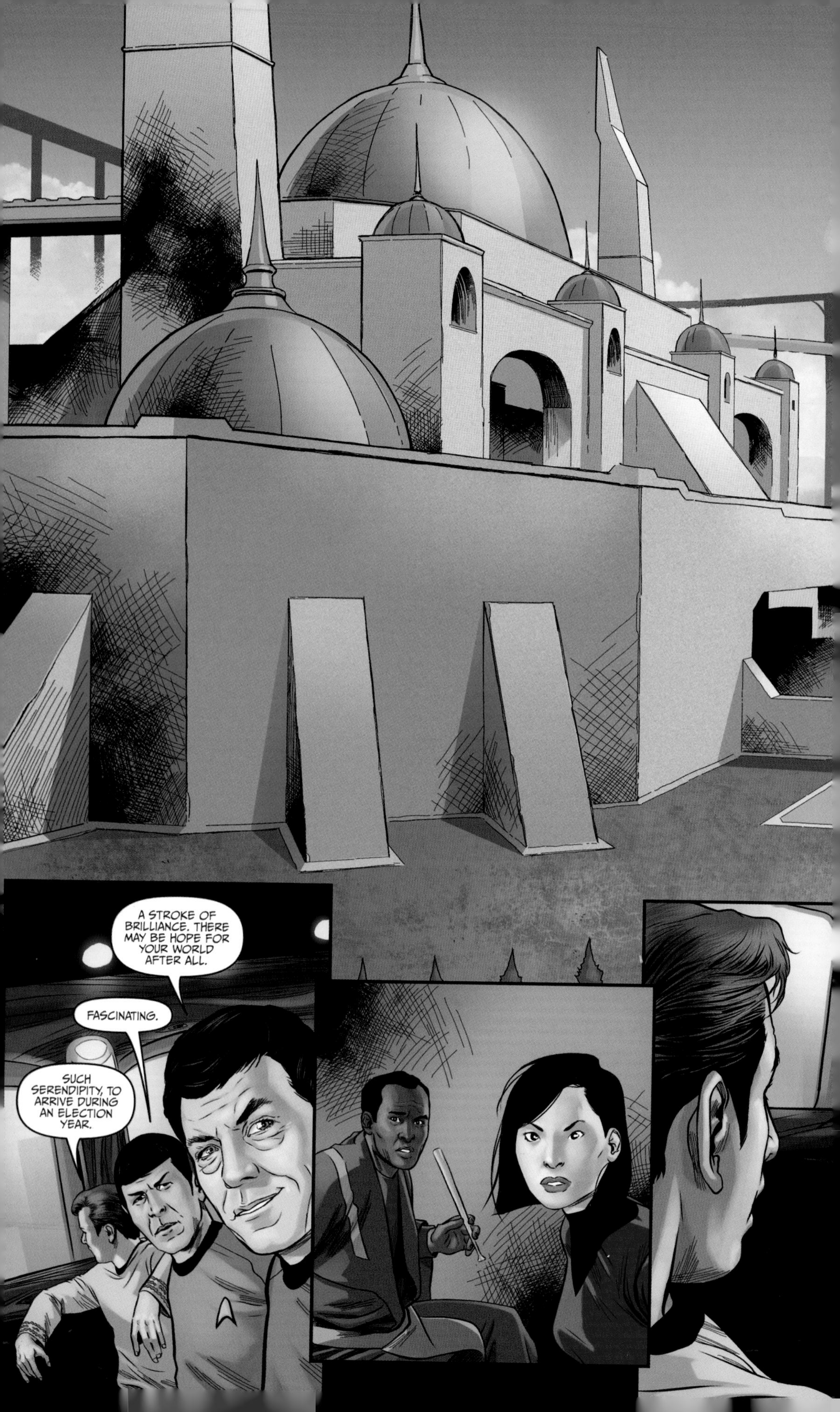
A STROKE OF BRILLIANCE. THERE MAY BE HOPE FOR YOUR WORLD AFTER ALL.
FASCINATING.
SUCH SERENDIPITY, TO ARRIVE DURING AN ELECTION YEAR.

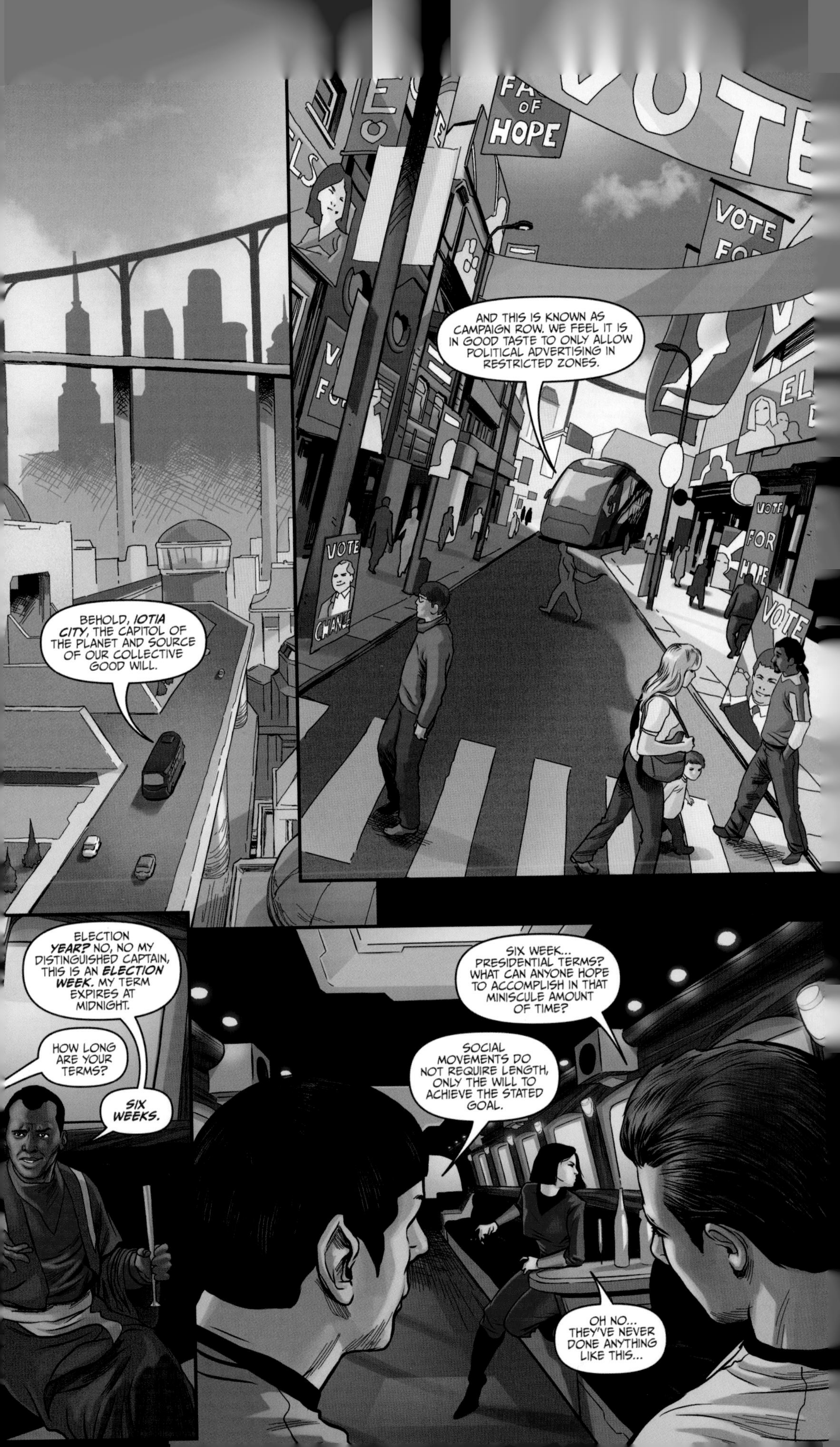

BEHOLD, IOTIA CITY, THE CAPITOL OF THE PLANET AND SOURCE OF OUR COLLECTIVE GOOD WILL.
VOTE
HOPE
AND THIS IS KNOWN AS CAMPAIGN ROW. WE FEEL IT IS IN GOOD TASTE TO ONLY ALLOW POLITICAL ADVERTISING IN RESTRICTED ZONES.
VOTE CHANGE
VOTE FOR HOPE
VOTE
ELECTION YEAR? NO, NO MY DISTINGUISHED CAPTAIN, THIS IS AN ELECTION WEEK. MY TERM EXPIRES AT MIDNIGHT.
HOW LONG ARE YOUR TERMS?
SIX WEEKS.
SIX WEEK... PRESIDENTIAL TERMS? WHAT CAN ANYONE HOPE TO ACCOMPLISH IN THAT MINISCULE AMOUNT OF TIME?
SOCIAL MOVEMENTS DO NOT REQUIRE LENGTH, ONLY THE WILL TO ACHIEVE THE STATED GOAL.
OH NO... THEY'VE NEVER DONE ANYTHING LIKE THIS...

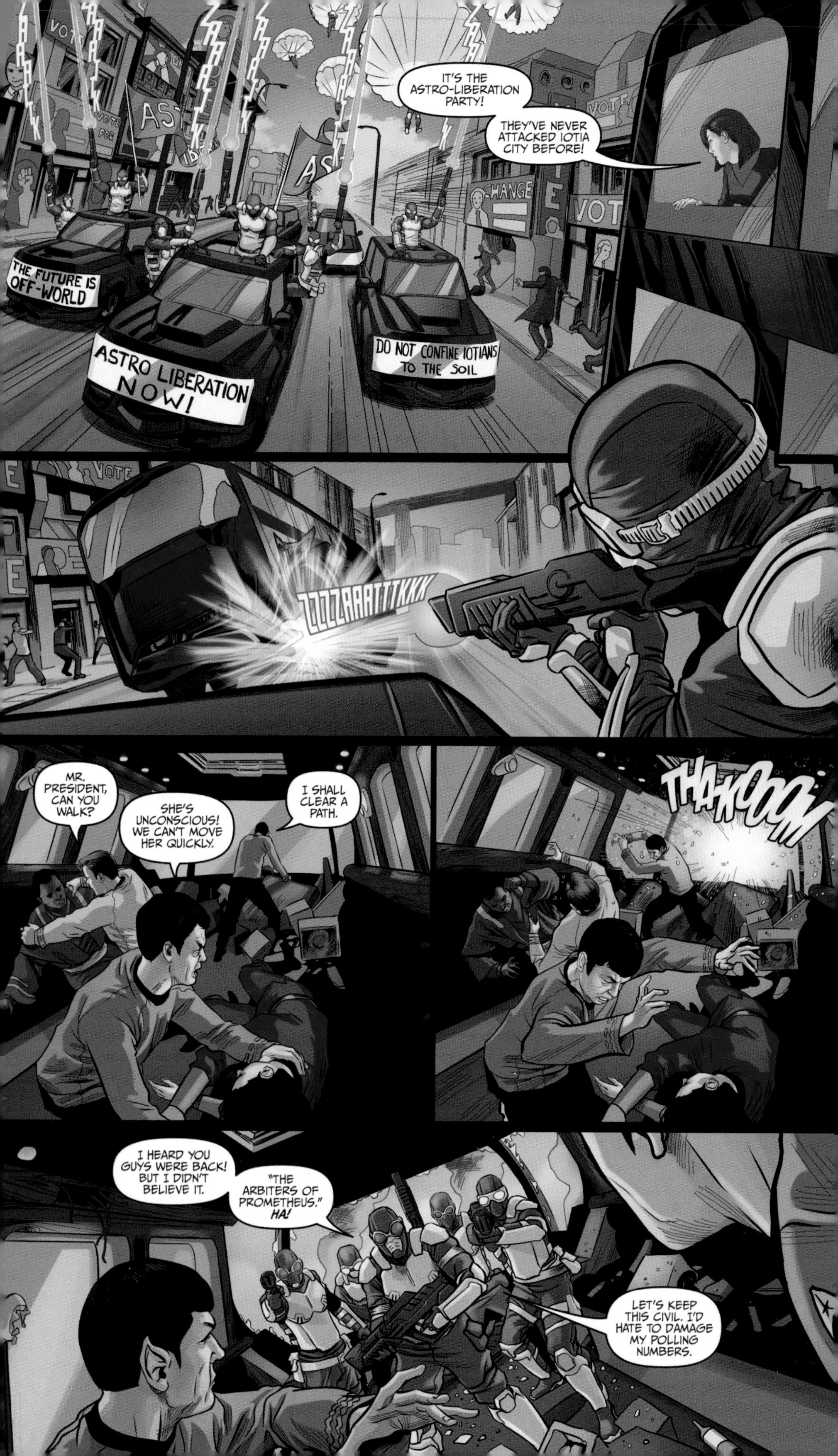

IT'S THE ASTRO-LIBERATION PARTY!
THEY'VE NEVER ATTACKED IOTIA CITY BEFORE!
THE FUTURE IS OFF-WORLD
ASTRO LIBERATION NOW!
DO NOT CONFINE IOTIANS TO THE SOIL
ZZZZAAATTTKKK
MR. PRESIDENT, CAN YOU WALK?
SHE'S UNCONSCIOUS! WE CAN'T MOVE HER QUICKLY.
I SHALL CLEAR A PATH.
THAKOOOM
I HEARD YOU GUYS WERE BACK! BUT I DIDN'T BELIEVE IT.
"THE ARBITERS OF PROMETHEUS." HA!
LET'S KEEP THIS CIVIL. I'D HATE TO DAMAGE MY POLLING NUMBERS.

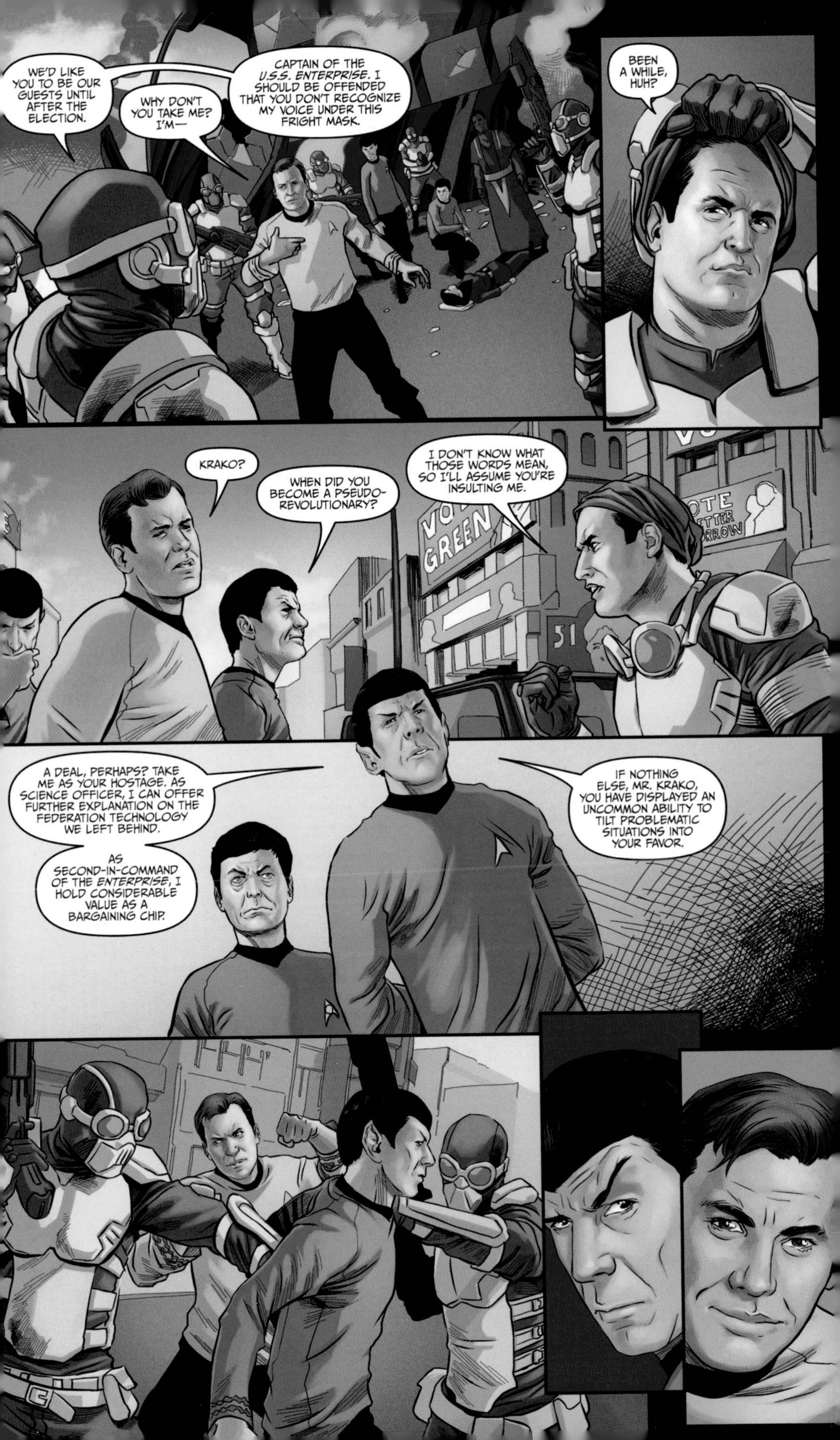
WE'D LIKE YOU TO BE OUR GUESTS UNTIL AFTER THE ELECTION.
WHY DON'T YOU TAKE ME? I'M—
CAPTAIN OF THE *U.S.S. ENTERPRISE*. I SHOULD BE OFFENDED THAT YOU DON'T RECOGNIZE MY VOICE UNDER THIS FRIGHT MASK.
BEEN A WHILE, HUH?
KRAKO?
WHEN DID YOU BECOME A PSEUDO-REVOLUTIONARY?
I DON'T KNOW WHAT THOSE WORDS MEAN, SO I'LL ASSUME YOU'RE INSULTING ME.
VOTE GREEN
51
A DEAL, PERHAPS? TAKE ME AS YOUR HOSTAGE. AS SCIENCE OFFICER, I CAN OFFER FURTHER EXPLANATION ON THE FEDERATION TECHNOLOGY WE LEFT BEHIND.
AS SECOND-IN-COMMAND OF THE *ENTERPRISE*, I HOLD CONSIDERABLE VALUE AS A BARGAINING CHIP.
IF NOTHING ELSE, MR. KRAKO, YOU HAVE DISPLAYED AN UNCOMMON ABILITY TO TILT PROBLEMATIC SITUATIONS INTO YOUR FAVOR.

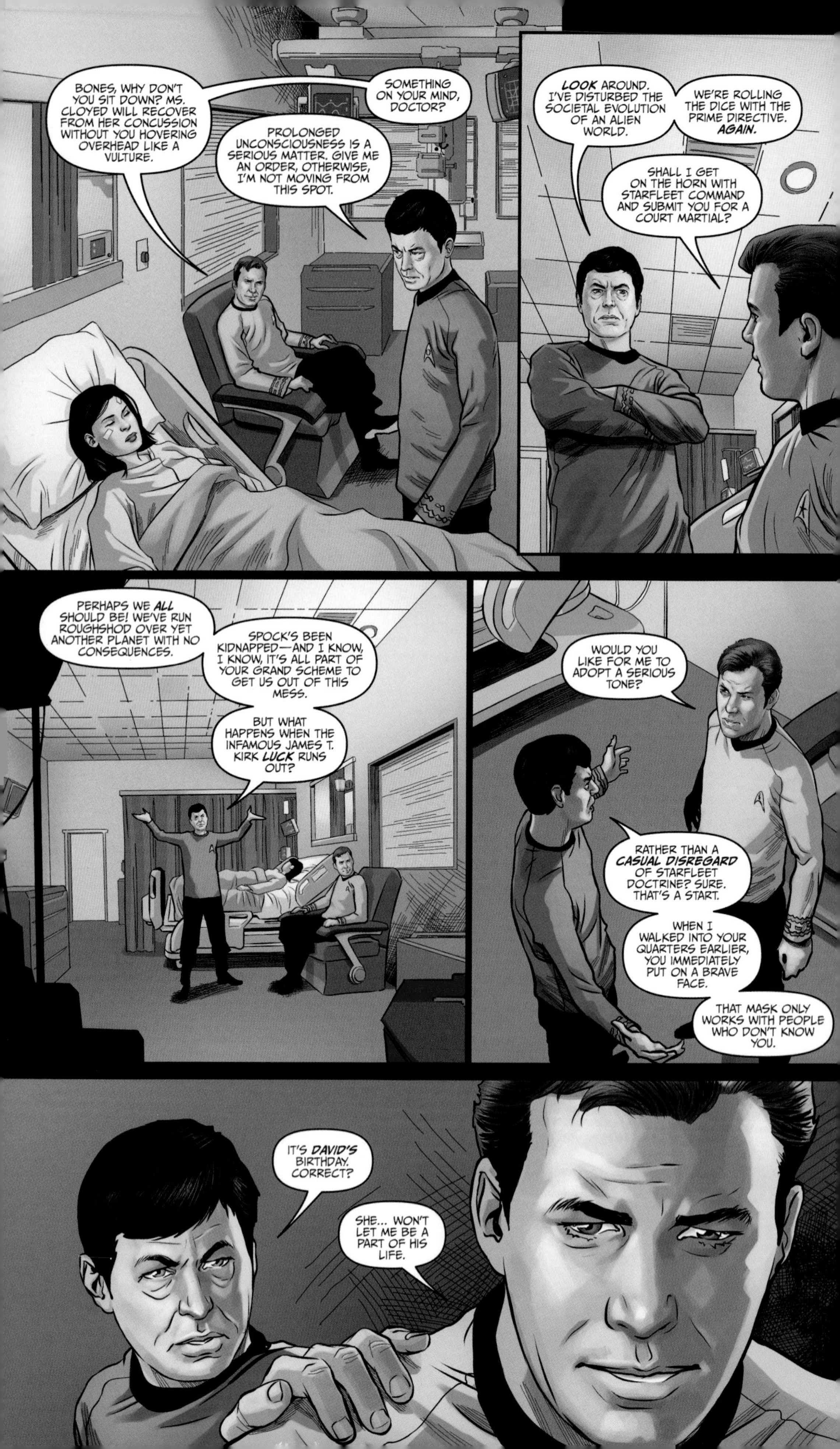
SOMETHING ON YOUR MIND, DOCTOR?
BONES, WHY DON'T YOU SIT DOWN? MS. CLOYED WILL RECOVER FROM HER CONCUSSION WITHOUT YOU HOVERING OVERHEAD LIKE A VULTURE.
PROLONGED UNCONSCIOUSNESS IS A SERIOUS MATTER. GIVE ME AN ORDER, OTHERWISE, I'M NOT MOVING FROM THIS SPOT.
WE'RE ROLLING THE DICE WITH THE PRIME DIRECTIVE. AGAIN.
LOOK AROUND. I'VE DISTURBED THE SOCIETAL EVOLUTION OF AN ALIEN WORLD.
SHALL I GET ON THE HORN WITH STARFLEET COMMAND AND SUBMIT YOU FOR A COURT MARTIAL?
PERHAPS WE ALL SHOULD BE! WE'VE RUN ROUGHSHOD OVER YET ANOTHER PLANET WITH NO CONSEQUENCES.
SPOCK'S BEEN KIDNAPPED—AND I KNOW, I KNOW, IT'S ALL PART OF YOUR GRAND SCHEME TO GET US OUT OF THIS MESS.
BUT WHAT HAPPENS WHEN THE INFAMOUS JAMES T. KIRK LUCK RUNS OUT?
WOULD YOU LIKE FOR ME TO ADOPT A SERIOUS TONE?
RATHER THAN A CASUAL DISREGARD OF STARFLEET DOCTRINE? SURE. THAT'S A START.
WHEN I WALKED INTO YOUR QUARTERS EARLIER, YOU IMMEDIATELY PUT ON A BRAVE FACE.
THAT MASK ONLY WORKS WITH PEOPLE WHO DON'T KNOW YOU.
IT'S DAVID'S BIRTHDAY. CORRECT?
SHE... WON'T LET ME BE A PART OF HIS LIFE.

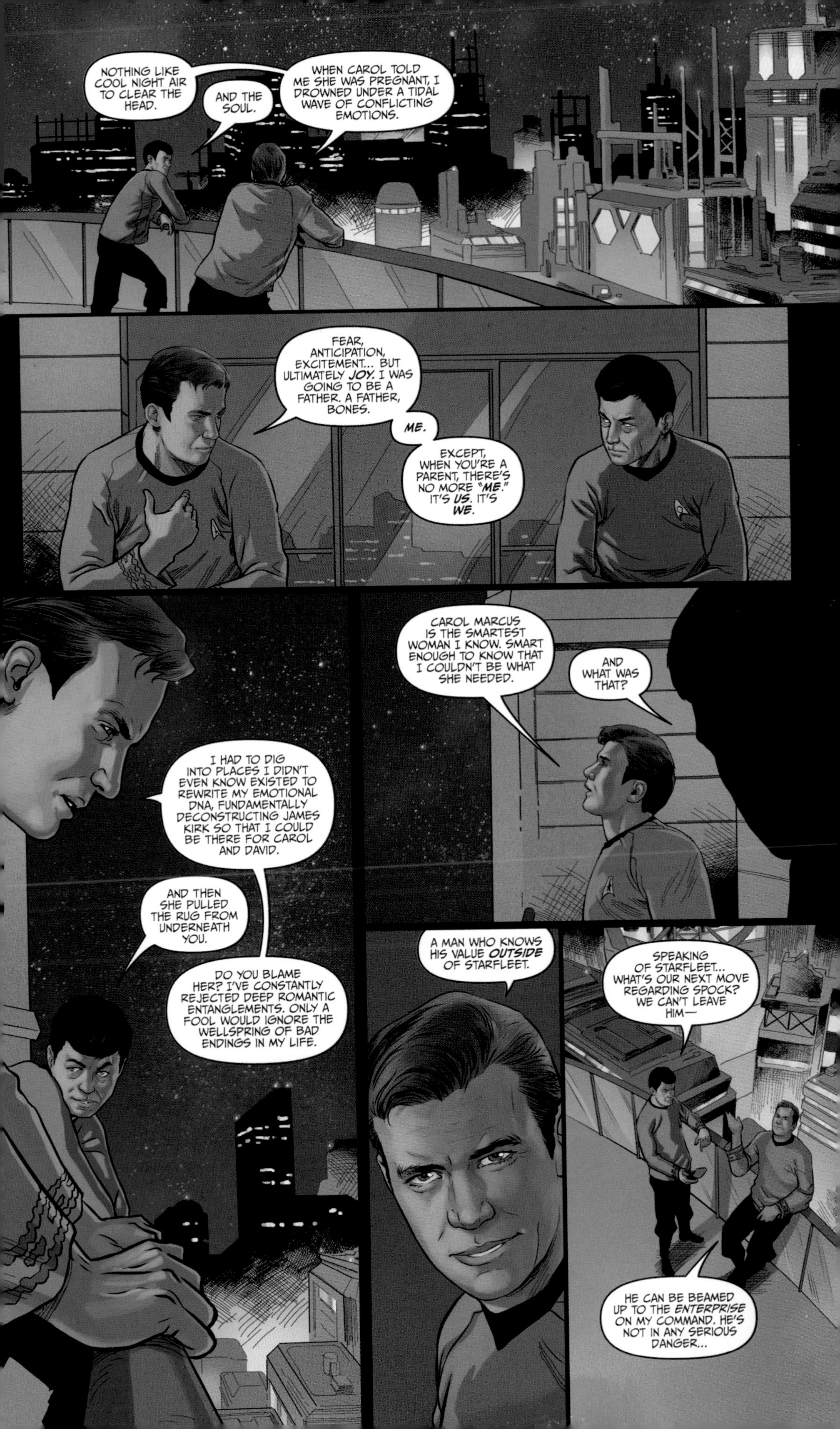
NOTHING LIKE COOL NIGHT AIR TO CLEAR THE HEAD.
AND THE SOUL.
WHEN CAROL TOLD ME SHE WAS PREGNANT, I DROWNED UNDER A TIDAL WAVE OF CONFLICTING EMOTIONS.
FEAR, ANTICIPATION, EXCITEMENT... BUT ULTIMATELY *JOY*. I WAS GOING TO BE A FATHER. A FATHER, BONES.
ME.
EXCEPT, WHEN YOU'RE A PARENT, THERE'S NO MORE "*ME*." IT'S *US*. IT'S *WE*.
I HAD TO DIG INTO PLACES I DIDN'T EVEN KNOW EXISTED TO REWRITE MY EMOTIONAL DNA, FUNDAMENTALLY DECONSTRUCTING JAMES KIRK SO THAT I COULD BE THERE FOR CAROL AND DAVID.
AND THEN SHE PULLED THE RUG FROM UNDERNEATH YOU.
DO YOU BLAME HER? I'VE CONSTANTLY REJECTED DEEP ROMANTIC ENTANGLEMENTS. ONLY A FOOL WOULD IGNORE THE WELLSPRING OF BAD ENDINGS IN MY LIFE.
CAROL MARCUS IS THE SMARTEST WOMAN I KNOW. SMART ENOUGH TO KNOW THAT I COULDN'T BE WHAT SHE NEEDED.
AND WHAT WAS THAT?
A MAN WHO KNOWS HIS VALUE *OUTSIDE* OF STARFLEET.
SPEAKING OF STARFLEET... WHAT'S OUR NEXT MOVE REGARDING SPOCK? WE CAN'T LEAVE HIM—
HE CAN BE BEAMED UP TO THE *ENTERPRISE* ON MY COMMAND. HE'S NOT IN ANY SERIOUS DANGER...

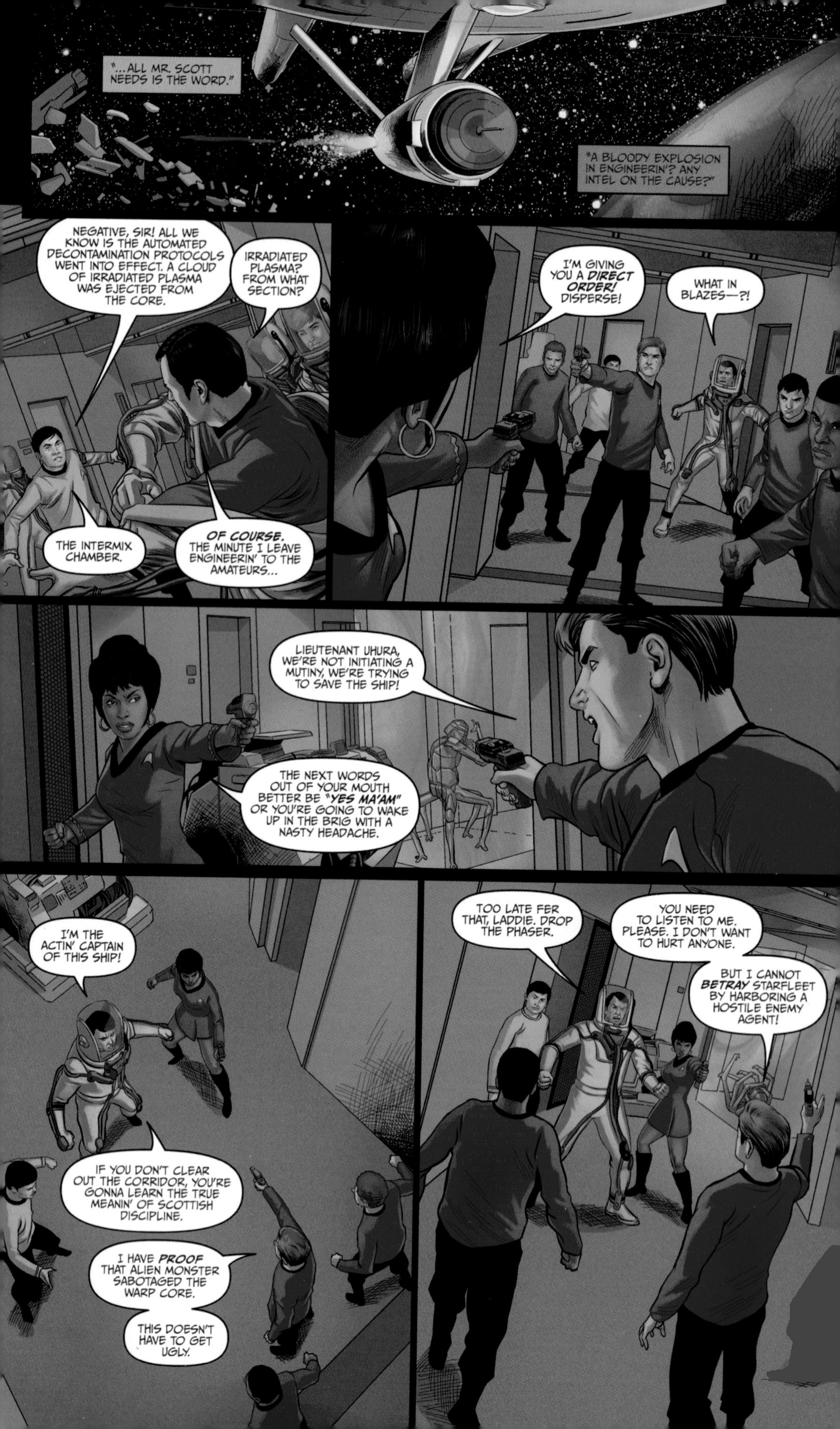
"...ALL MR. SCOTT NEEDS IS THE WORD."
"A BLOODY EXPLOSION IN ENGINEERIN'? ANY INTEL ON THE CAUSE?"
NEGATIVE, SIR! ALL WE KNOW IS THE AUTOMATED DECONTAMINATION PROTOCOLS WENT INTO EFFECT. A CLOUD OF IRRADIATED PLASMA WAS EJECTED FROM THE CORE.
IRRADIATED PLASMA? FROM WHAT SECTION?
THE INTERMIX CHAMBER.
OF COURSE. THE MINUTE I LEAVE ENGINEERIN' TO THE AMATEURS...
I'M GIVING YOU A DIRECT ORDER! DISPERSE!
WHAT IN BLAZES—?!
LIEUTENANT UHURA, WE'RE NOT INITIATING A MUTINY, WE'RE TRYING TO SAVE THE SHIP!
THE NEXT WORDS OUT OF YOUR MOUTH BETTER BE "YES MA'AM" OR YOU'RE GOING TO WAKE UP IN THE BRIG WITH A NASTY HEADACHE.
I'M THE ACTIN' CAPTAIN OF THIS SHIP!
IF YOU DON'T CLEAR OUT THE CORRIDOR, YOU'RE GONNA LEARN THE TRUE MEANIN' OF SCOTTISH DISCIPLINE.
I HAVE PROOF THAT ALIEN MONSTER SABOTAGED THE WARP CORE.
THIS DOESN'T HAVE TO GET UGLY.
TOO LATE FER THAT, LADDIE. DROP THE PHASER.
YOU NEED TO LISTEN TO ME. PLEASE. I DON'T WANT TO HURT ANYONE.
BUT I CANNOT BETRAY STARFLEET BY HARBORING A HOSTILE ENEMY AGENT!

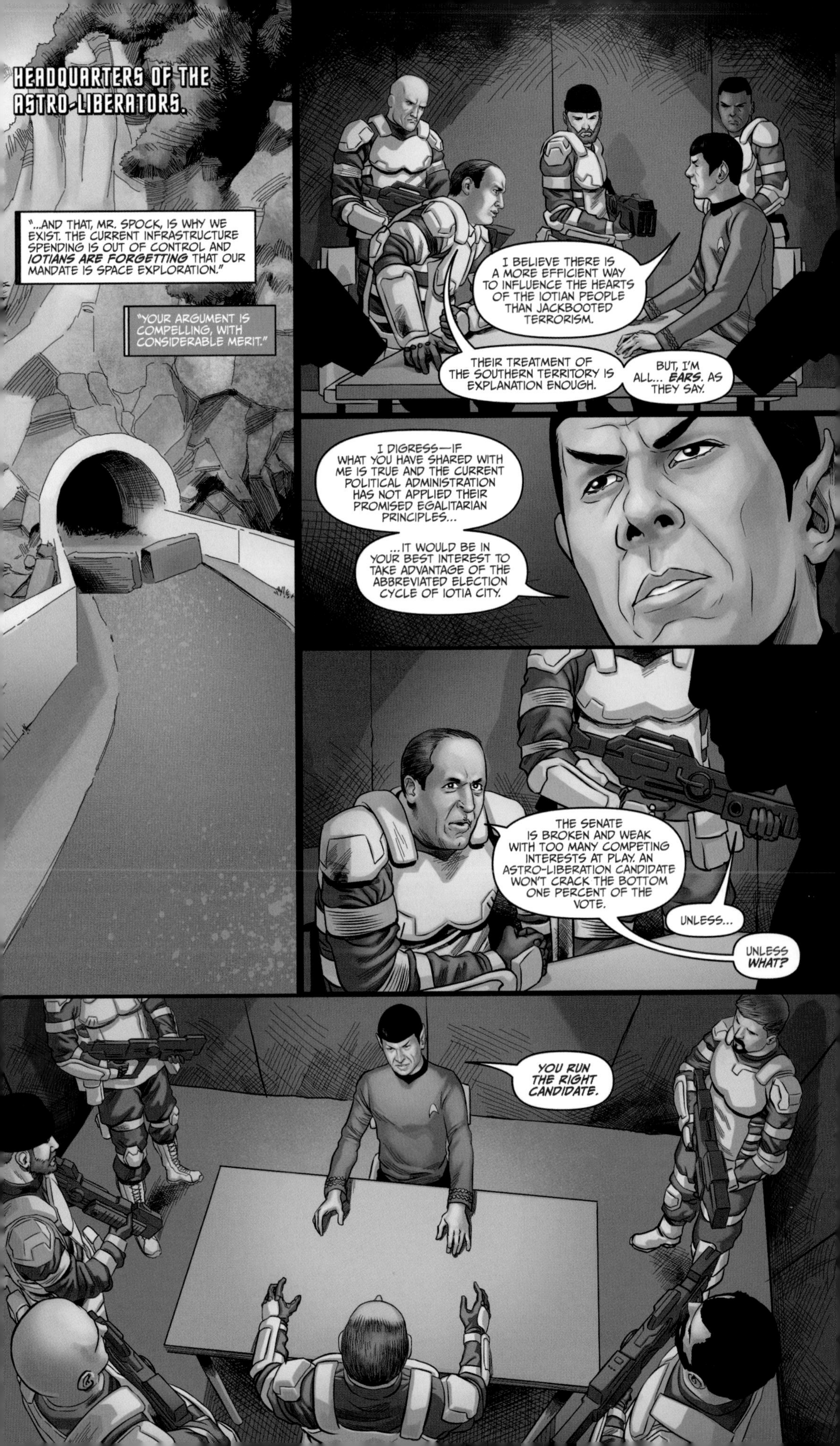
HEADQUARTERS OF THE ASTRO-LIBERATORS.
"...AND THAT, MR. SPOCK, IS WHY WE EXIST. THE CURRENT INFRASTRUCTURE SPENDING IS OUT OF CONTROL AND IOTIANS ARE FORGETTING THAT OUR MANDATE IS SPACE EXPLORATION."
"YOUR ARGUMENT IS COMPELLING, WITH CONSIDERABLE MERIT."
I BELIEVE THERE IS A MORE EFFICIENT WAY TO INFLUENCE THE HEARTS OF THE IOTIAN PEOPLE THAN JACKBOOTED TERRORISM.
THEIR TREATMENT OF THE SOUTHERN TERRITORY IS EXPLANATION ENOUGH.
BUT, I'M ALL... EARS, AS THEY SAY.
I DIGRESS—IF WHAT YOU HAVE SHARED WITH ME IS TRUE AND THE CURRENT POLITICAL ADMINISTRATION HAS NOT APPLIED THEIR PROMISED EGALITARIAN PRINCIPLES...
...IT WOULD BE IN YOUR BEST INTEREST TO TAKE ADVANTAGE OF THE ABBREVIATED ELECTION CYCLE OF IOTIA CITY.
THE SENATE IS BROKEN AND WEAK WITH TOO MANY COMPETING INTERESTS AT PLAY. AN ASTRO-LIBERATION CANDIDATE WON'T CRACK THE BOTTOM ONE PERCENT OF THE VOTE.
UNLESS...
UNLESS WHAT?
YOU RUN THE RIGHT CANDIDATE.

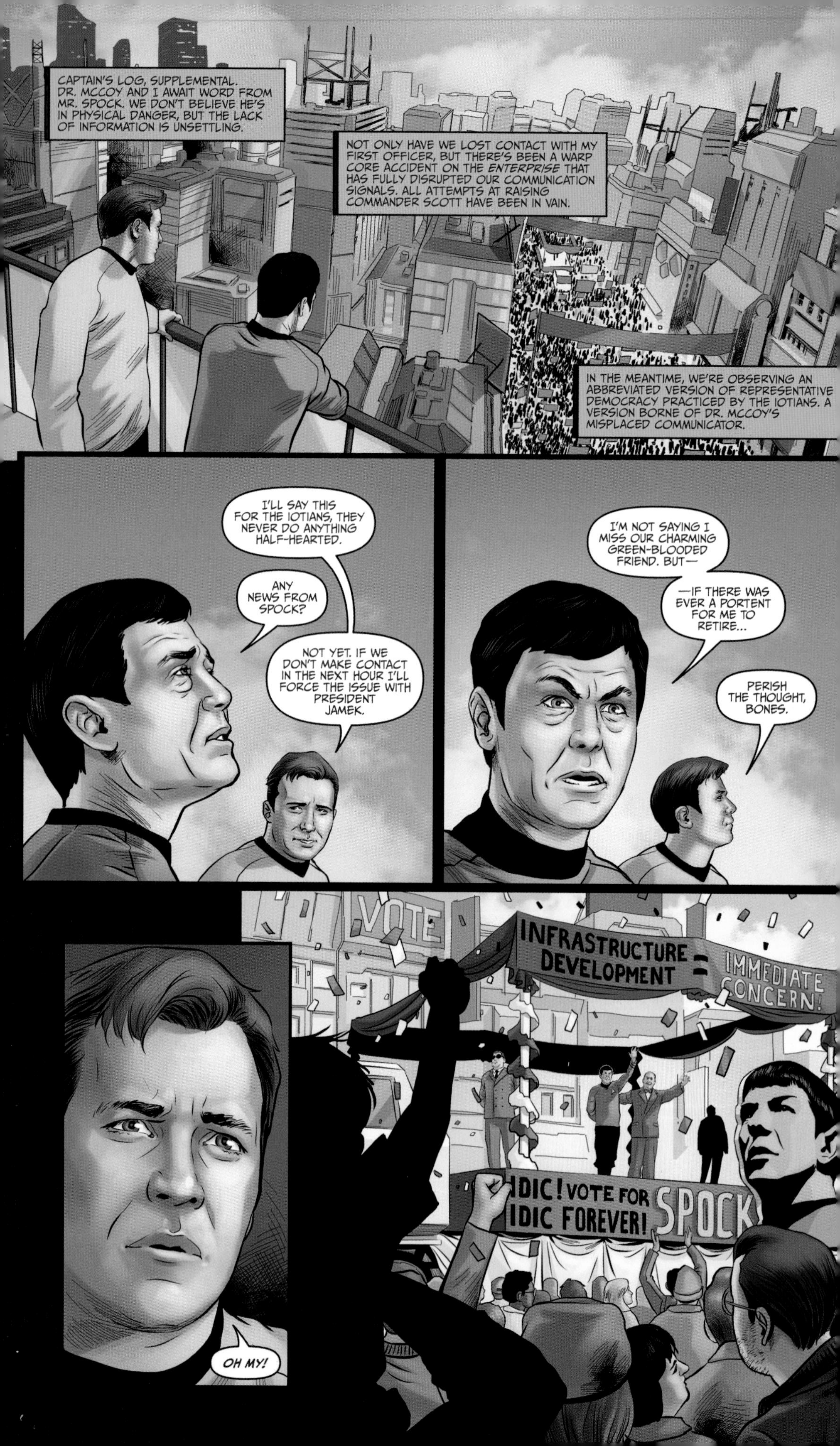
CAPTAIN'S LOG, SUPPLEMENTAL. DR. MCCOY AND I AWAIT WORD FROM MR. SPOCK. WE DON'T BELIEVE HE'S IN PHYSICAL DANGER, BUT THE LACK OF INFORMATION IS UNSETTLING.
NOT ONLY HAVE WE LOST CONTACT WITH MY FIRST OFFICER, BUT THERE'S BEEN A WARP CORE ACCIDENT ON THE *ENTERPRISE* THAT HAS FULLY DISRUPTED OUR COMMUNICATION SIGNALS. ALL ATTEMPTS AT RAISING COMMANDER SCOTT HAVE BEEN IN VAIN.
IN THE MEANTIME, WE'RE OBSERVING AN ABBREVIATED VERSION OF REPRESENTATIVE DEMOCRACY PRACTICED BY THE IOTIANS. A VERSION BORNE OF DR. MCCOY'S MISPLACED COMMUNICATOR.
I'LL SAY THIS FOR THE IOTIANS, THEY NEVER DO ANYTHING HALF-HEARTED.
ANY NEWS FROM SPOCK?
NOT YET. IF WE DON'T MAKE CONTACT IN THE NEXT HOUR I'LL FORCE THE ISSUE WITH PRESIDENT JAMEK.
I'M NOT SAYING I MISS OUR CHARMING GREEN-BLOODED FRIEND. BUT—
—IF THERE WAS EVER A PORTENT FOR ME TO RETIRE...
PERISH THE THOUGHT, BONES.
VOTE
INFRASTRUCTURE DEVELOPMENT = IMMEDIATE CONCERN!
IDIC! VOTE FOR IDIC FOREVER! SPOCK
OH MY!

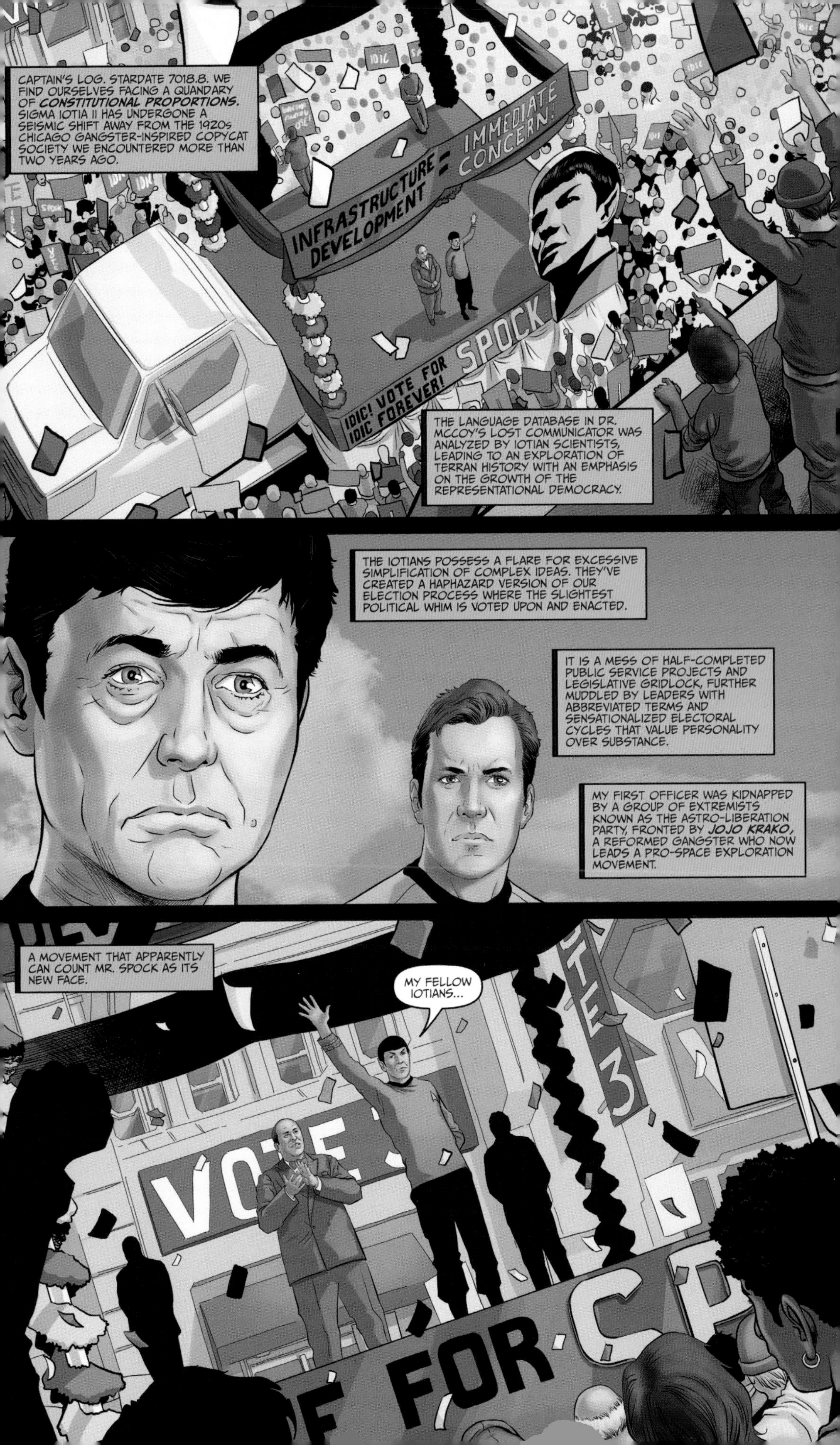
CAPTAIN'S LOG. STARDATE 7018.8. WE FIND OURSELVES FACING A QUANDARY OF ***CONSTITUTIONAL PROPORTIONS.*** SIGMA IOTIA II HAS UNDERGONE A SEISMIC SHIFT AWAY FROM THE 1920s CHICAGO GANGSTER-INSPIRED COPYCAT SOCIETY WE ENCOUNTERED MORE THAN TWO YEARS AGO.
INFRASTRUCTURE DEVELOPMENT = IMMEDIATE CONCERN!
IDIC! VOTE FOR SPOCK
IDIC FOREVER!
THE LANGUAGE DATABASE IN DR. MCCOY'S LOST COMMUNICATOR WAS ANALYZED BY IOTIAN SCIENTISTS, LEADING TO AN EXPLORATION OF TERRAN HISTORY WITH AN EMPHASIS ON THE GROWTH OF THE REPRESENTATIONAL DEMOCRACY.
THE IOTIANS POSSESS A FLARE FOR EXCESSIVE SIMPLIFICATION OF COMPLEX IDEAS. THEY'VE CREATED A HAPHAZARD VERSION OF OUR ELECTION PROCESS WHERE THE SLIGHTEST POLITICAL WHIM IS VOTED UPON AND ENACTED.
IT IS A MESS OF HALF-COMPLETED PUBLIC SERVICE PROJECTS AND LEGISLATIVE GRIDLOCK, FURTHER MUDDLED BY LEADERS WITH ABBREVIATED TERMS AND SENSATIONALIZED ELECTORAL CYCLES THAT VALUE PERSONALITY OVER SUBSTANCE.
MY FIRST OFFICER WAS KIDNAPPED BY A GROUP OF EXTREMISTS KNOWN AS THE ASTRO-LIBERATION PARTY, FRONTED BY ***JOJO KRAKO,*** A REFORMED GANGSTER WHO NOW LEADS A PRO-SPACE EXPLORATION MOVEMENT.
A MOVEMENT THAT APPARENTLY CAN COUNT MR. SPOCK AS ITS NEW FACE.
MY FELLOW IOTIANS...
VOTE
FOR

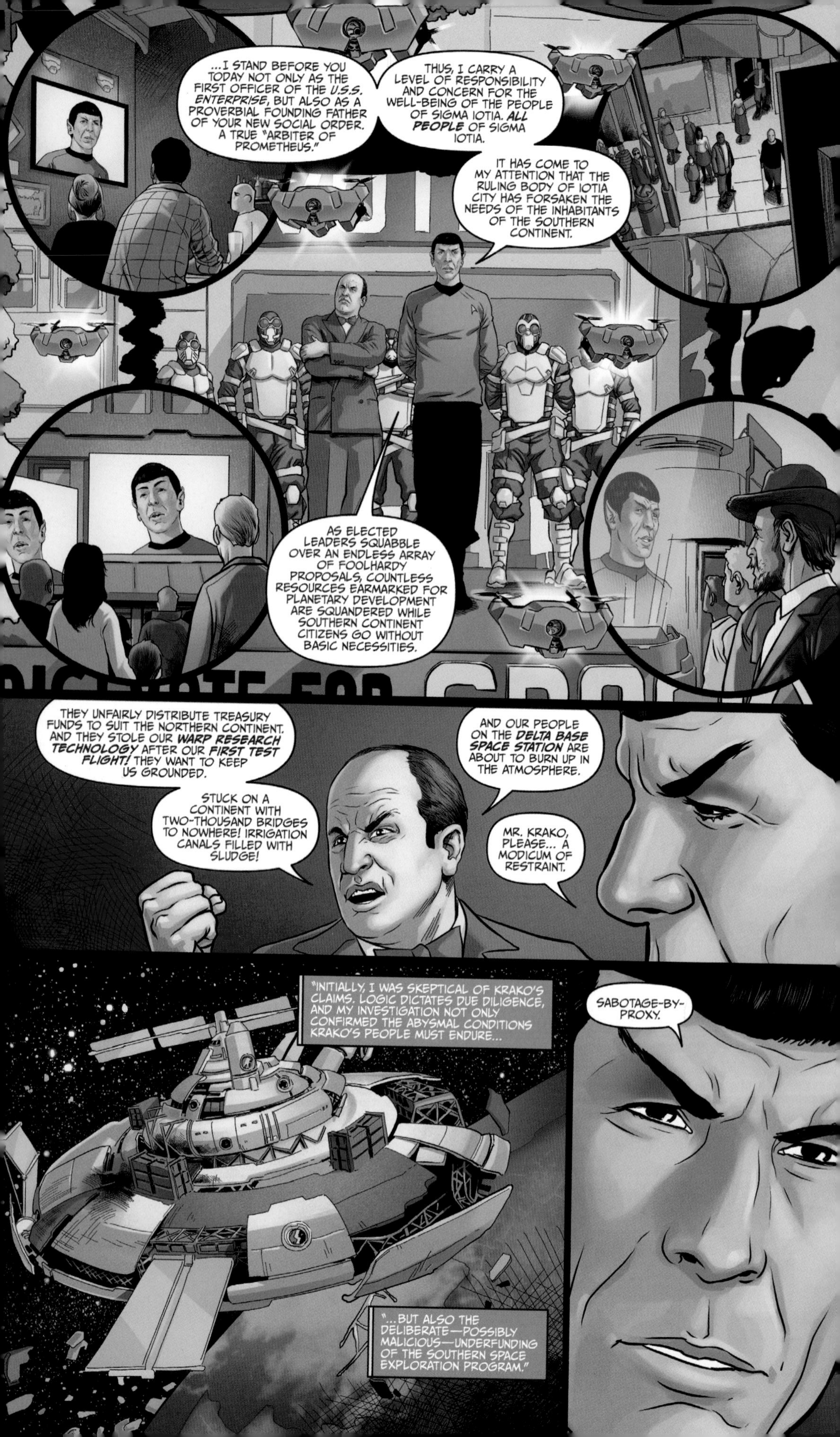
...I STAND BEFORE YOU TODAY NOT ONLY AS THE FIRST OFFICER OF THE *U.S.S. ENTERPRISE*, BUT ALSO AS A PROVERBIAL FOUNDING FATHER OF YOUR NEW SOCIAL ORDER. A TRUE "ARBITER OF PROMETHEUS."
THUS, I CARRY A LEVEL OF RESPONSIBILITY AND CONCERN FOR THE WELL-BEING OF THE PEOPLE OF SIGMA IOTIA. ***ALL PEOPLE*** OF SIGMA IOTIA.
IT HAS COME TO MY ATTENTION THAT THE RULING BODY OF IOTIA CITY HAS FORSAKEN THE NEEDS OF THE INHABITANTS OF THE SOUTHERN CONTINENT.
AS ELECTED LEADERS SQUABBLE OVER AN ENDLESS ARRAY OF FOOLHARDY PROPOSALS, COUNTLESS RESOURCES EARMARKED FOR PLANETARY DEVELOPMENT ARE SQUANDERED WHILE SOUTHERN CONTINENT CITIZENS GO WITHOUT BASIC NECESSITIES.
THEY UNFAIRLY DISTRIBUTE TREASURY FUNDS TO SUIT THE NORTHERN CONTINENT. AND THEY STOLE OUR ***WARP RESEARCH TECHNOLOGY*** AFTER OUR ***FIRST TEST FLIGHT!*** THEY WANT TO KEEP US GROUNDED.
STUCK ON A CONTINENT WITH TWO-THOUSAND BRIDGES TO NOWHERE! IRRIGATION CANALS FILLED WITH SLUDGE!
AND OUR PEOPLE ON THE ***DELTA BASE SPACE STATION*** ARE ABOUT TO BURN UP IN THE ATMOSPHERE.
MR. KRAKO, PLEASE... A MODICUM OF RESTRAINT.
"INITIALLY, I WAS SKEPTICAL OF KRAKO'S CLAIMS. LOGIC DICTATES DUE DILIGENCE, AND MY INVESTIGATION NOT ONLY CONFIRMED THE ABYSMAL CONDITIONS KRAKO'S PEOPLE MUST ENDURE...
SABOTAGE-BY-PROXY.
"...BUT ALSO THE DELIBERATE—POSSIBLY MALICIOUS—UNDERFUNDING OF THE SOUTHERN SPACE EXPLORATION PROGRAM."

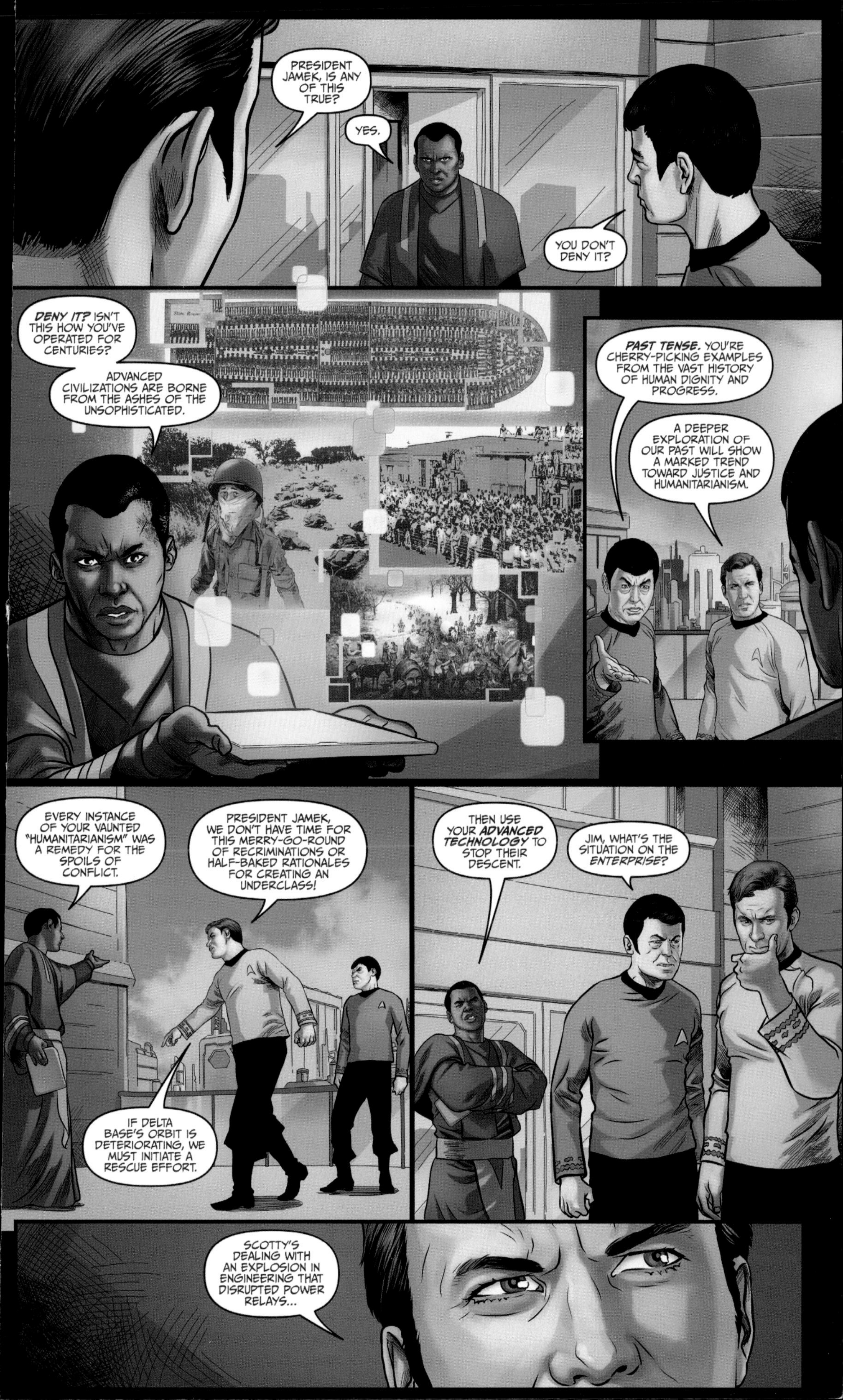
PRESIDENT JAMEK, IS ANY OF THIS TRUE?
YES.
YOU DON'T DENY IT?
DENY IT? ISN'T THIS HOW YOU'VE OPERATED FOR CENTURIES?
ADVANCED CIVILIZATIONS ARE BORNE FROM THE ASHES OF THE UNSOPHISTICATED.
PAST TENSE. YOU'RE CHERRY-PICKING EXAMPLES FROM THE VAST HISTORY OF HUMAN DIGNITY AND PROGRESS.
A DEEPER EXPLORATION OF OUR PAST WILL SHOW A MARKED TREND TOWARD JUSTICE AND HUMANITARIANISM.
EVERY INSTANCE OF YOUR VAUNTED "HUMANITARIANISM" WAS A REMEDY FOR THE SPOILS OF CONFLICT.
PRESIDENT JAMEK, WE DON'T HAVE TIME FOR THIS MERRY-GO-ROUND OF RECRIMINATIONS OR HALF-BAKED RATIONALES FOR CREATING AN UNDERCLASS!
IF DELTA BASE'S ORBIT IS DETERIORATING, WE MUST INITIATE A RESCUE EFFORT.
THEN USE YOUR ADVANCED TECHNOLOGY TO STOP THEIR DESCENT.
JIM, WHAT'S THE SITUATION ON THE ENTERPRISE?
SCOTTY'S DEALING WITH AN EXPLOSION IN ENGINEERING THAT DISRUPTED POWER RELAYS...

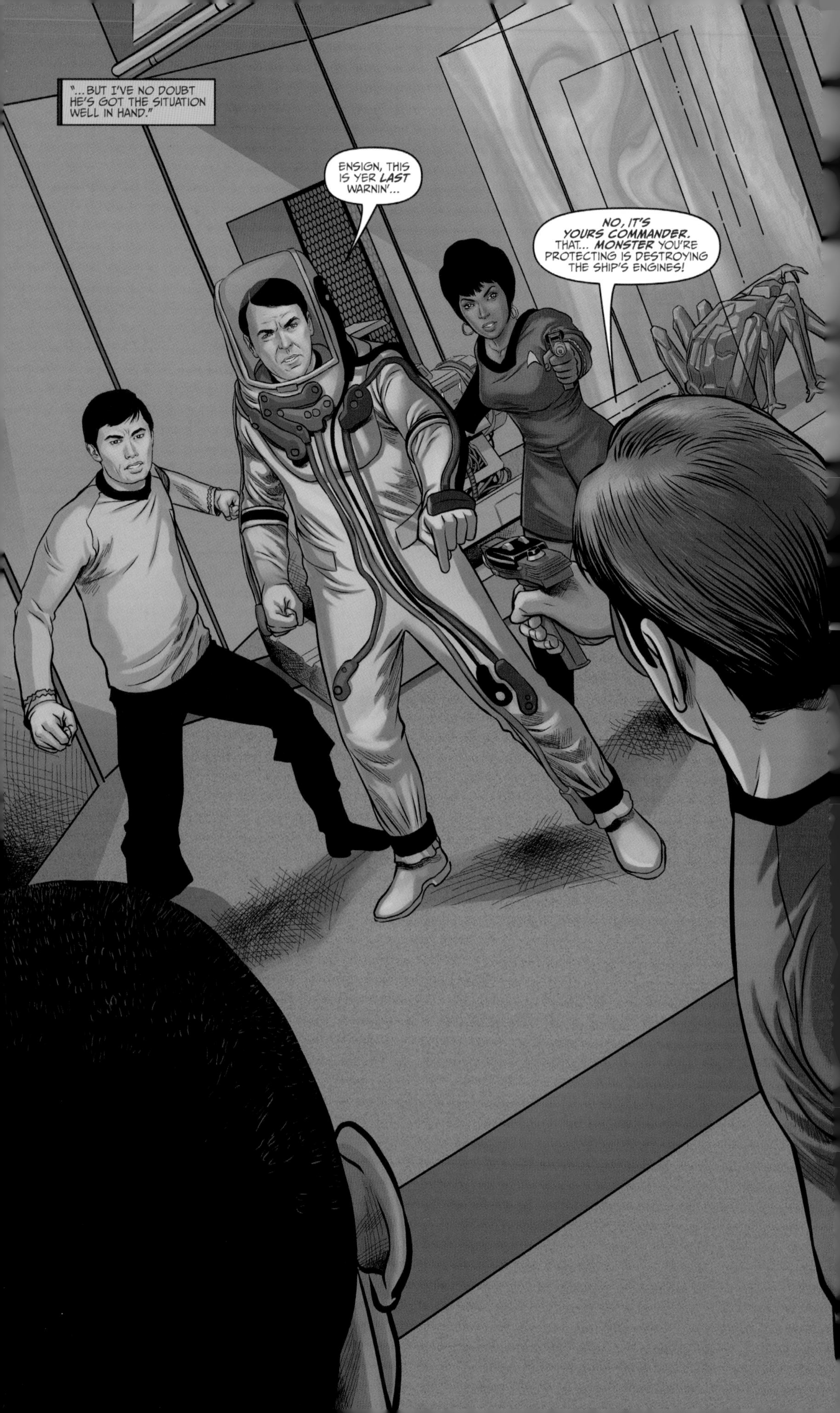
"...BUT I'VE NO DOUBT HE'S GOT THE SITUATION WELL IN HAND."
ENSIGN, THIS IS YER LAST WARNIN'...
NO, IT'S YOURS COMMANDER. THAT... MONSTER YOU'RE PROTECTING IS DESTROYING THE SHIP'S ENGINES!

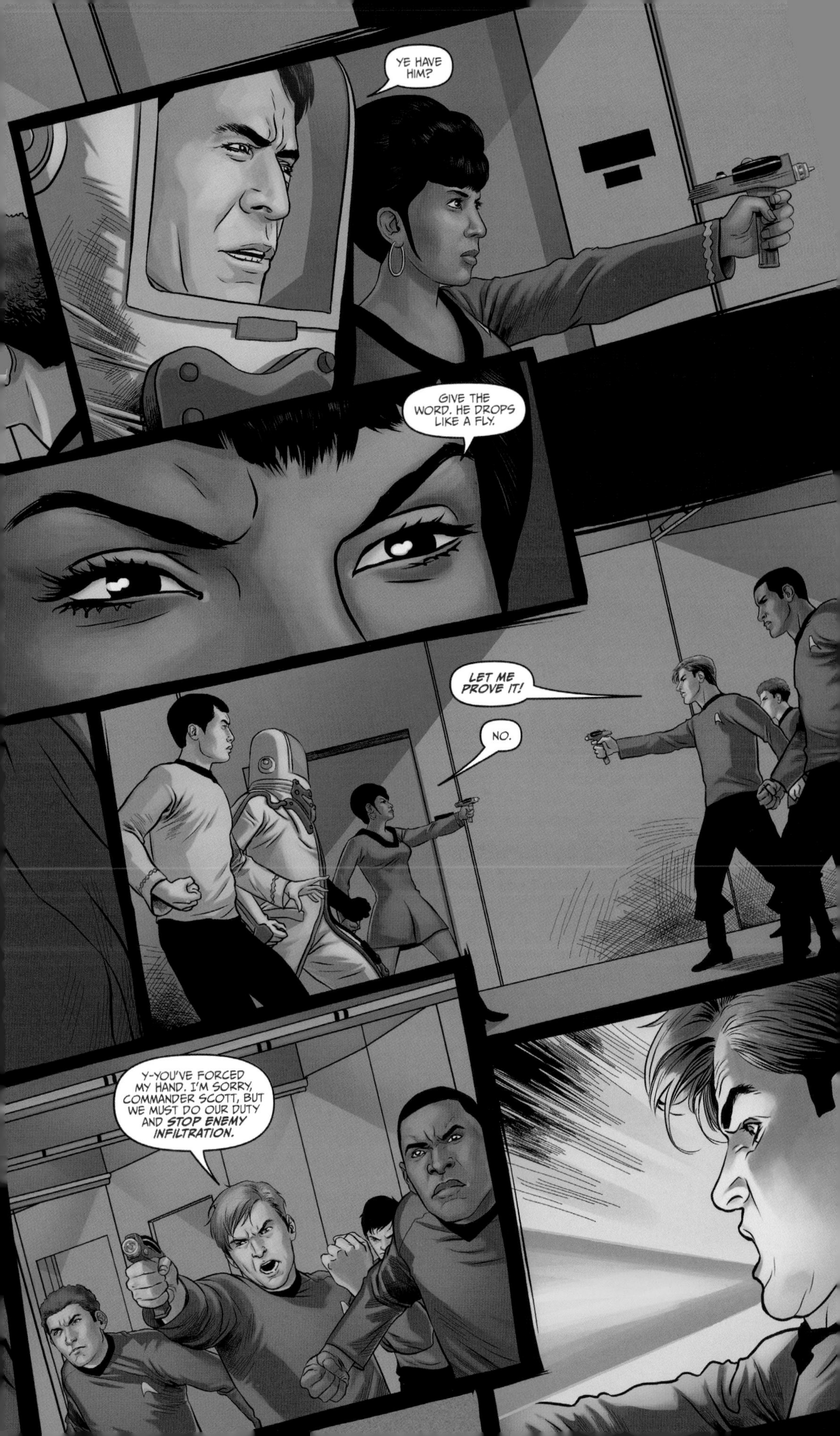
YE HAVE HIM?
GIVE THE WORD. HE DROPS LIKE A FLY.
LET ME PROVE IT!
NO.
Y-YOU'VE FORCED MY HAND. I'M SORRY, COMMANDER SCOTT, BUT WE MUST DO OUR DUTY AND STOP ENEMY INFILTRATION.

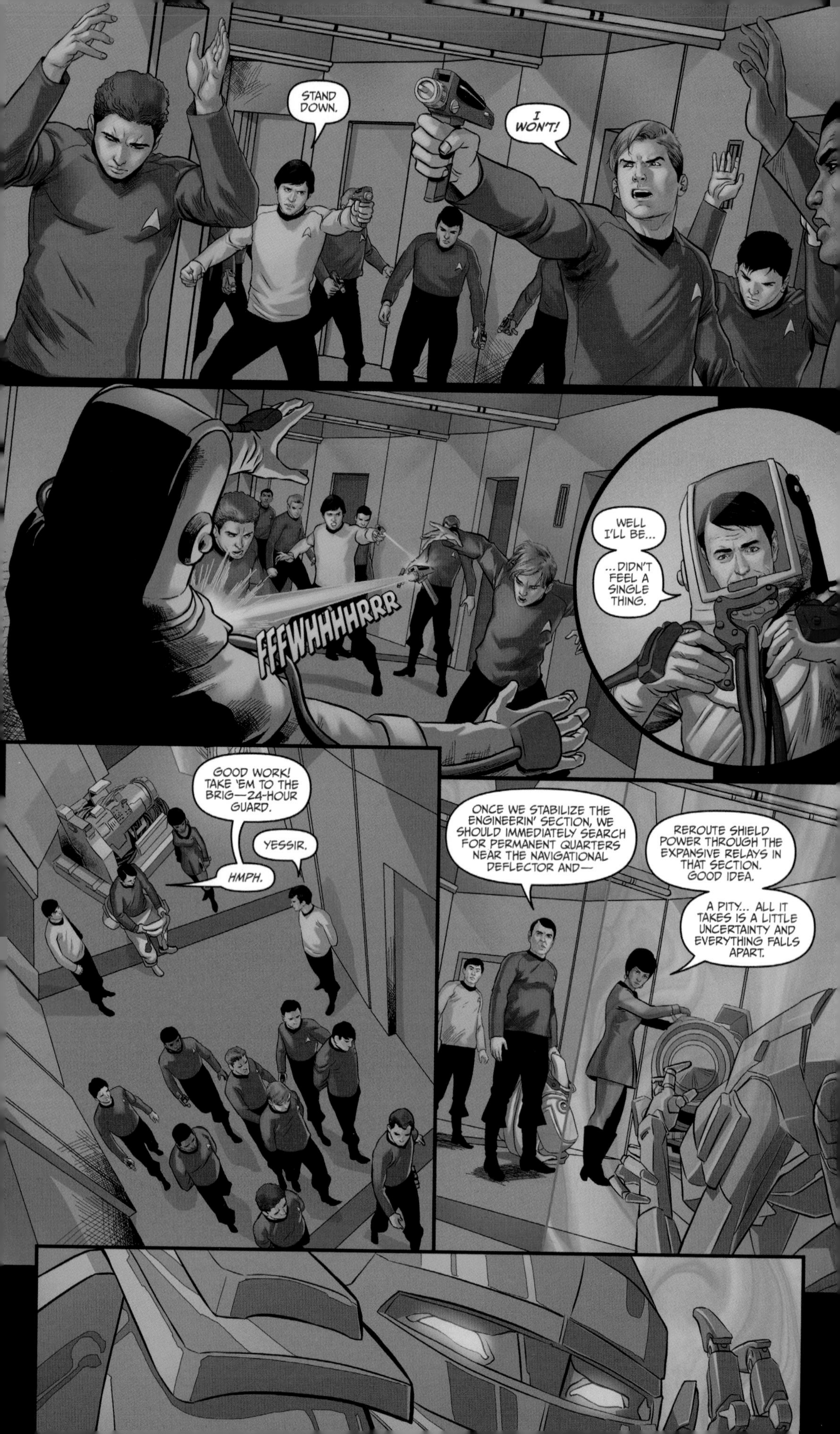
STAND DOWN.
I WON'T!
FFFWHHHHRRR
WELL I'LL BE...
...DIDN'T FEEL A SINGLE THING.
GOOD WORK! TAKE 'EM TO THE BRIG—24-HOUR GUARD.
YESSIR.
HMPH.
ONCE WE STABILIZE THE ENGINEERIN' SECTION, WE SHOULD IMMEDIATELY SEARCH FOR PERMANENT QUARTERS NEAR THE NAVIGATIONAL DEFLECTOR AND—
REROUTE SHIELD POWER THROUGH THE EXPANSIVE RELAYS IN THAT SECTION. GOOD IDEA.
A PITY... ALL IT TAKES IS A LITTLE UNCERTAINTY AND EVERYTHING FALLS APART.

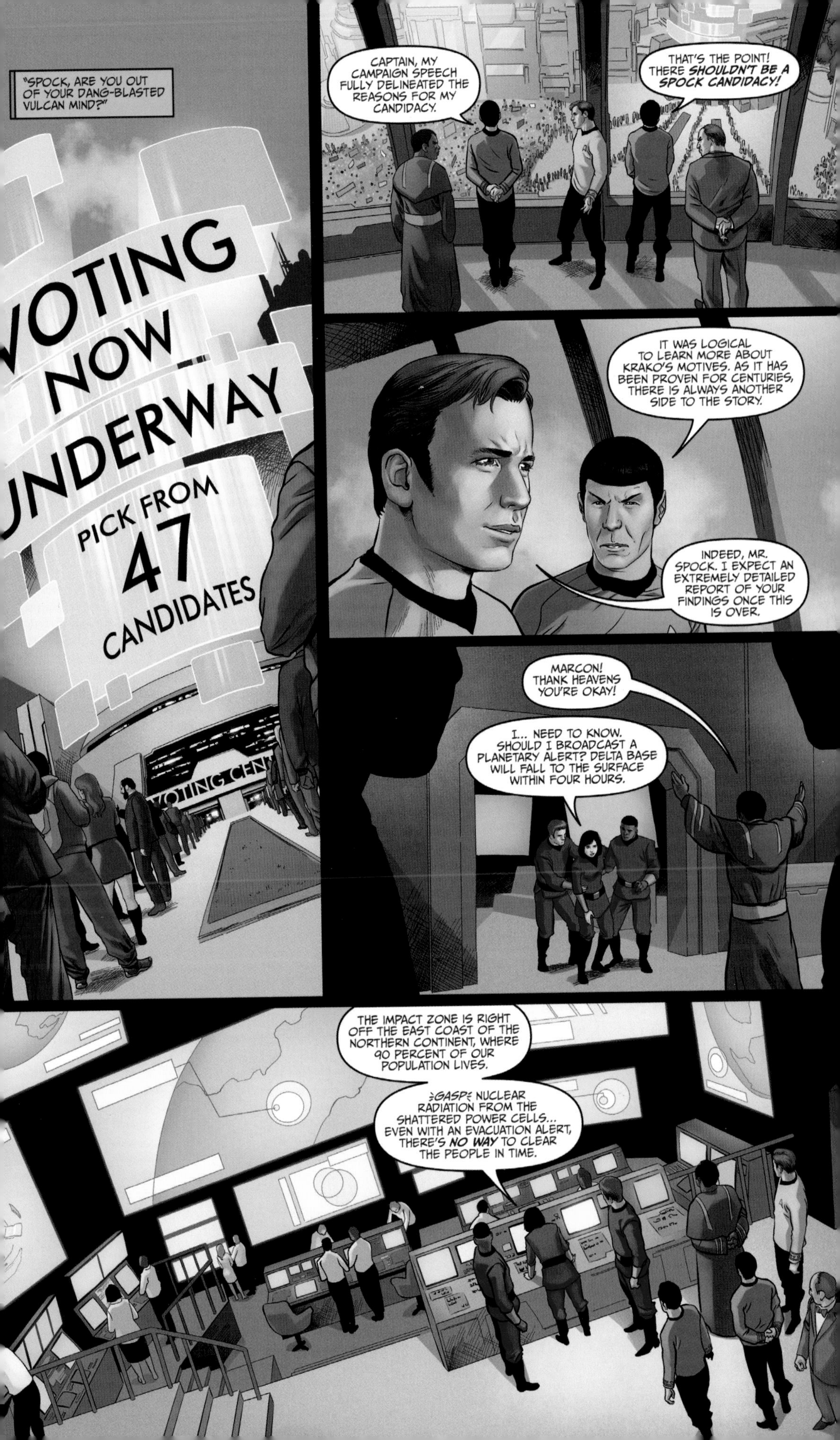
"SPOCK, ARE YOU OUT OF YOUR DANG-BLASTED VULCAN MIND?"
VOTING NOW UNDERWAY
PICK FROM 47 CANDIDATES
VOTING CEN
CAPTAIN, MY CAMPAIGN SPEECH FULLY DELINEATED THE REASONS FOR MY CANDIDACY.
THAT'S THE POINT! THERE SHOULDN'T BE A SPOCK CANDIDACY!
IT WAS LOGICAL TO LEARN MORE ABOUT KRAKO'S MOTIVES. AS IT HAS BEEN PROVEN FOR CENTURIES, THERE IS ALWAYS ANOTHER SIDE TO THE STORY.
INDEED, MR. SPOCK. I EXPECT AN EXTREMELY DETAILED REPORT OF YOUR FINDINGS ONCE THIS IS OVER.
MARCON! THANK HEAVENS YOU'RE OKAY!
I... NEED TO KNOW. SHOULD I BROADCAST A PLANETARY ALERT? DELTA BASE WILL FALL TO THE SURFACE WITHIN FOUR HOURS.
THE IMPACT ZONE IS RIGHT OFF THE EAST COAST OF THE NORTHERN CONTINENT, WHERE 90 PERCENT OF OUR POPULATION LIVES.
GASP NUCLEAR RADIATION FROM THE SHATTERED POWER CELLS... EVEN WITH AN EVACUATION ALERT, THERE'S NO WAY TO CLEAR THE PEOPLE IN TIME.

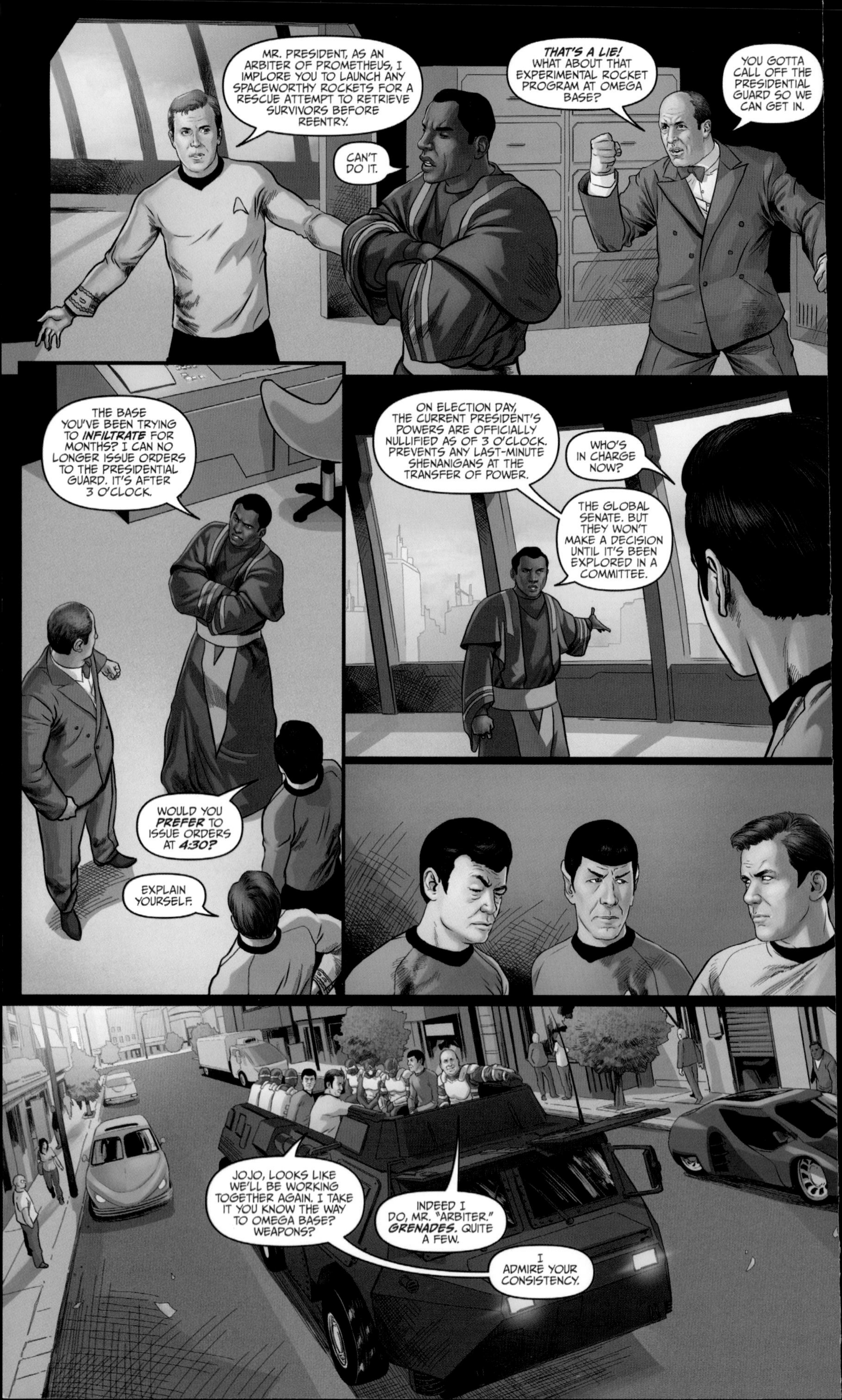
MR. PRESIDENT, AS AN ARBITER OF PROMETHEUS, I IMPLORE YOU TO LAUNCH ANY SPACEWORTHY ROCKETS FOR A RESCUE ATTEMPT TO RETRIEVE SURVIVORS BEFORE REENTRY.
CAN'T DO IT.
THAT'S A LIE! WHAT ABOUT THAT EXPERIMENTAL ROCKET PROGRAM AT OMEGA BASE?
YOU GOTTA CALL OFF THE PRESIDENTIAL GUARD SO WE CAN GET IN.
THE BASE YOU'VE BEEN TRYING TO INFILTRATE FOR MONTHS? I CAN NO LONGER ISSUE ORDERS TO THE PRESIDENTIAL GUARD. IT'S AFTER 3 O'CLOCK.
WOULD YOU PREFER TO ISSUE ORDERS AT 4:30?
EXPLAIN YOURSELF.
ON ELECTION DAY, THE CURRENT PRESIDENT'S POWERS ARE OFFICIALLY NULLIFIED AS OF 3 O'CLOCK. PREVENTS ANY LAST-MINUTE SHENANIGANS AT THE TRANSFER OF POWER.
WHO'S IN CHARGE NOW?
THE GLOBAL SENATE. BUT THEY WON'T MAKE A DECISION UNTIL IT'S BEEN EXPLORED IN A COMMITTEE.
JOJO, LOOKS LIKE WE'LL BE WORKING TOGETHER AGAIN. I TAKE IT YOU KNOW THE WAY TO OMEGA BASE? WEAPONS?
INDEED I DO, MR. "ARBITER." GRENADES. QUITE A FEW.
I ADMIRE YOUR CONSISTENCY.

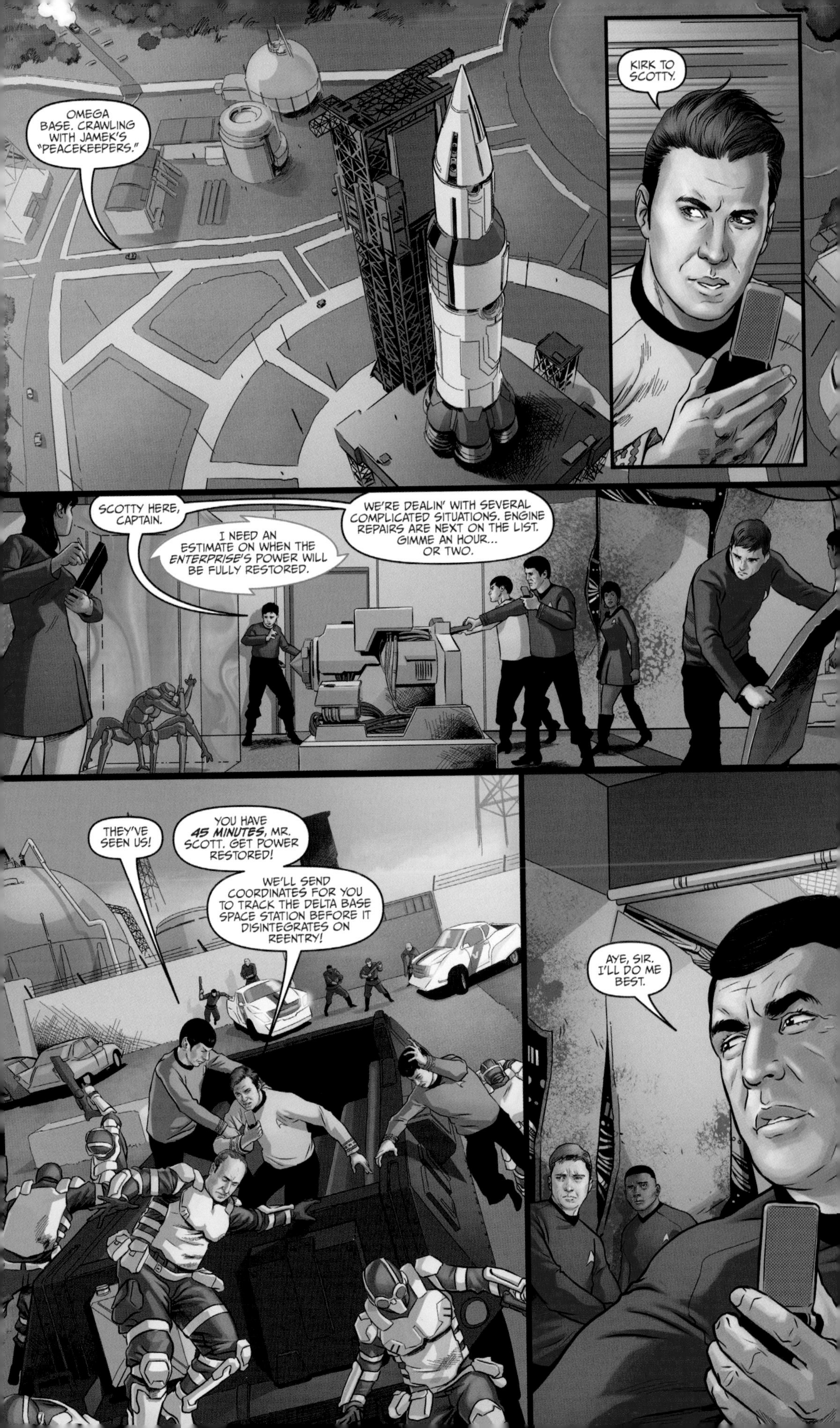

OMEGA BASE. CRAWLING WITH JAMEK'S "PEACEKEEPERS."
KIRK TO SCOTTY.
SCOTTY HERE, CAPTAIN.
I NEED AN ESTIMATE ON WHEN THE *ENTERPRISE'S* POWER WILL BE FULLY RESTORED.
WE'RE DEALIN' WITH SEVERAL COMPLICATED SITUATIONS. ENGINE REPAIRS ARE NEXT ON THE LIST. GIMME AN HOUR... OR TWO.
THEY'VE SEEN US!
YOU HAVE ***45 MINUTES***, MR. SCOTT. GET POWER RESTORED!
WE'LL SEND COORDINATES FOR YOU TO TRACK THE DELTA BASE SPACE STATION BEFORE IT DISINTEGRATES ON REENTRY!
AYE, SIR. I'LL DO ME BEST.

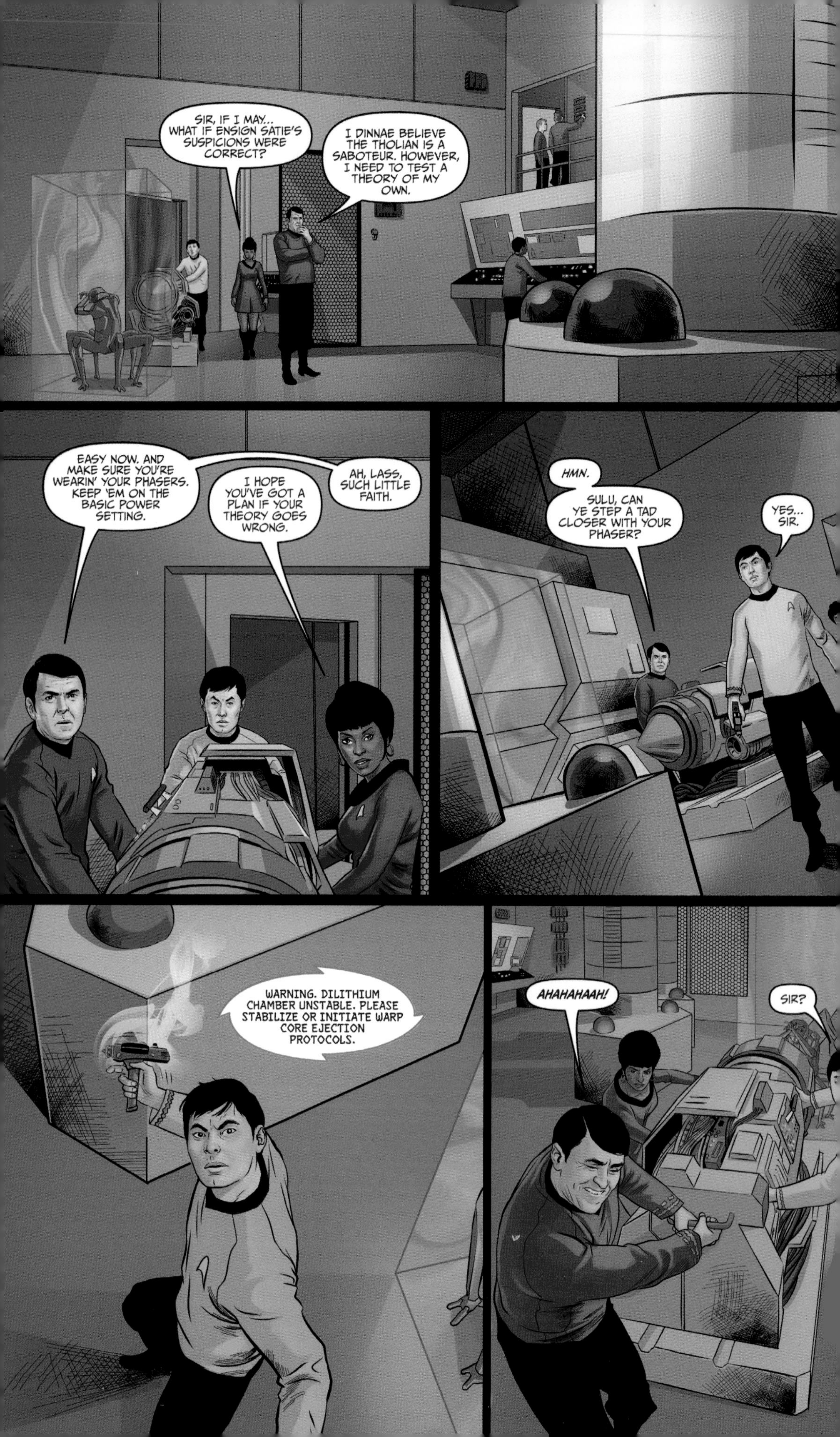
SIR, IF I MAY... WHAT IF ENSIGN SATIE'S SUSPICIONS WERE CORRECT?
I DINNAE BELIEVE THE THOLIAN IS A SABOTEUR. HOWEVER, I NEED TO TEST A THEORY OF MY OWN.
EASY NOW. AND MAKE SURE YOU'RE WEARIN' YOUR PHASERS. KEEP 'EM ON THE BASIC POWER SETTING.
I HOPE YOU'VE GOT A PLAN IF YOUR THEORY GOES WRONG.
AH, LASS, SUCH LITTLE FAITH.
HMN.
SULU, CAN YE STEP A TAD CLOSER WITH YOUR PHASER?
YES... SIR.
WARNING. DILITHIUM CHAMBER UNSTABLE. PLEASE STABILIZE OR INITIATE WARP CORE EJECTION PROTOCOLS.
AHAHAHAAAH!
SIR?

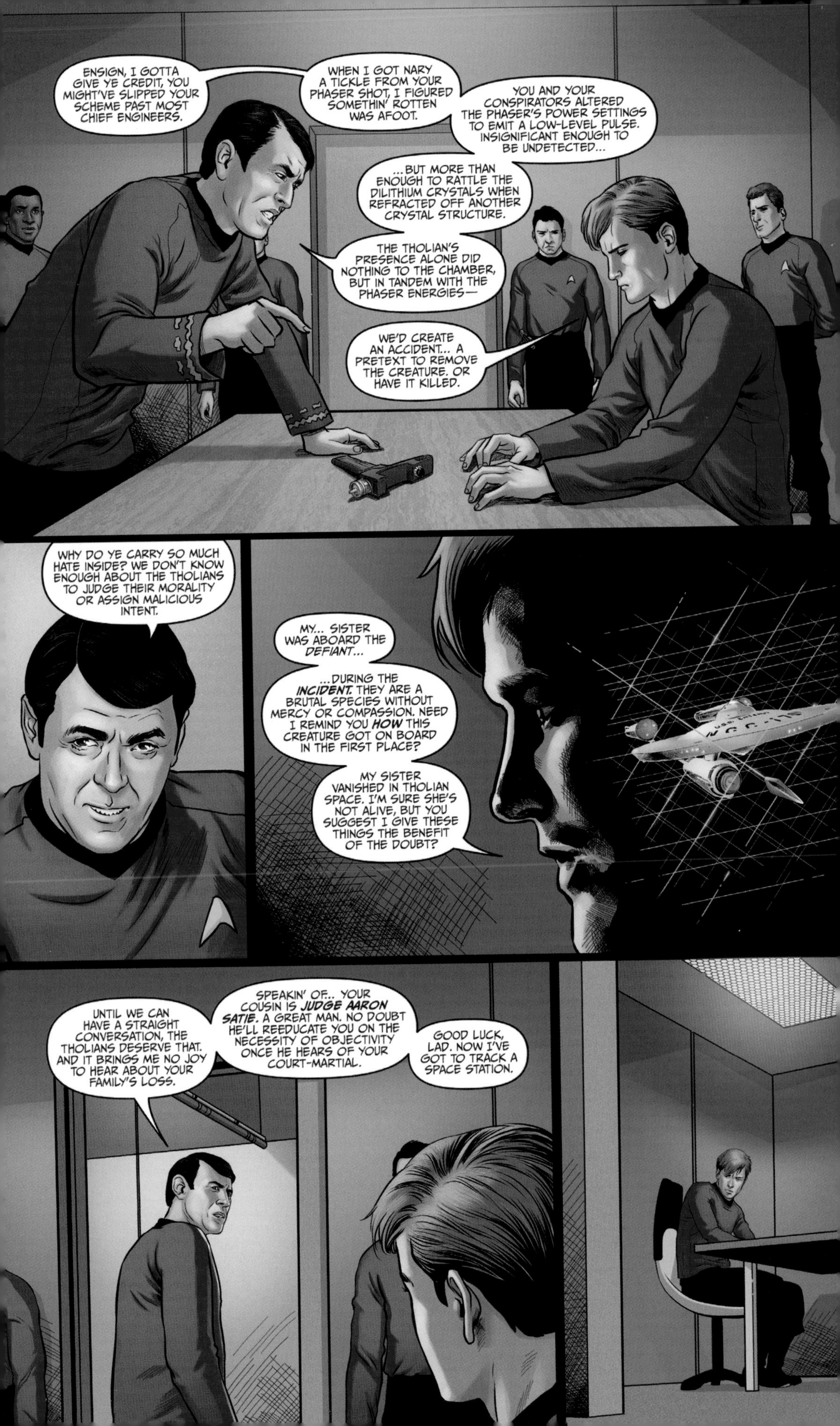
ENSIGN, I GOTTA GIVE YE CREDIT, YOU MIGHT'VE SLIPPED YOUR SCHEME PAST MOST CHIEF ENGINEERS.
WHEN I GOT NARY A TICKLE FROM YOUR PHASER SHOT, I FIGURED SOMETHIN' ROTTEN WAS AFOOT.
YOU AND YOUR CONSPIRATORS ALTERED THE PHASER'S POWER SETTINGS TO EMIT A LOW-LEVEL PULSE. INSIGNIFICANT ENOUGH TO BE UNDETECTED...
...BUT MORE THAN ENOUGH TO RATTLE THE DILITHIUM CRYSTALS WHEN REFRACTED OFF ANOTHER CRYSTAL STRUCTURE.
THE THOLIAN'S PRESENCE ALONE DID NOTHING TO THE CHAMBER, BUT IN TANDEM WITH THE PHASER ENERGIES—
WE'D CREATE AN ACCIDENT... A PRETEXT TO REMOVE THE CREATURE. OR HAVE IT KILLED.
WHY DO YE CARRY SO MUCH HATE INSIDE? WE DON'T KNOW ENOUGH ABOUT THE THOLIANS TO JUDGE THEIR MORALITY OR ASSIGN MALICIOUS INTENT.
MY... SISTER WAS ABOARD THE *DEFIANT*...
...DURING THE ***INCIDENT.*** THEY ARE A BRUTAL SPECIES WITHOUT MERCY OR COMPASSION. NEED I REMIND YOU ***HOW*** THIS CREATURE GOT ON BOARD IN THE FIRST PLACE?
MY SISTER VANISHED IN THOLIAN SPACE. I'M SURE SHE'S NOT ALIVE, BUT YOU SUGGEST I GIVE THESE THINGS THE BENEFIT OF THE DOUBT?
UNTIL WE CAN HAVE A STRAIGHT CONVERSATION, THE THOLIANS DESERVE THAT. AND IT BRINGS ME NO JOY TO HEAR ABOUT YOUR FAMILY'S LOSS.
SPEAKIN' OF.. YOUR COUSIN IS ***JUDGE AARON SATIE.*** A GREAT MAN. NO DOUBT HE'LL REEDUCATE YOU ON THE NECESSITY OF OBJECTIVITY ONCE HE HEARS OF YOUR COURT-MARTIAL.
GOOD LUCK, LAD. NOW I'VE GOT TO TRACK A SPACE STATION.

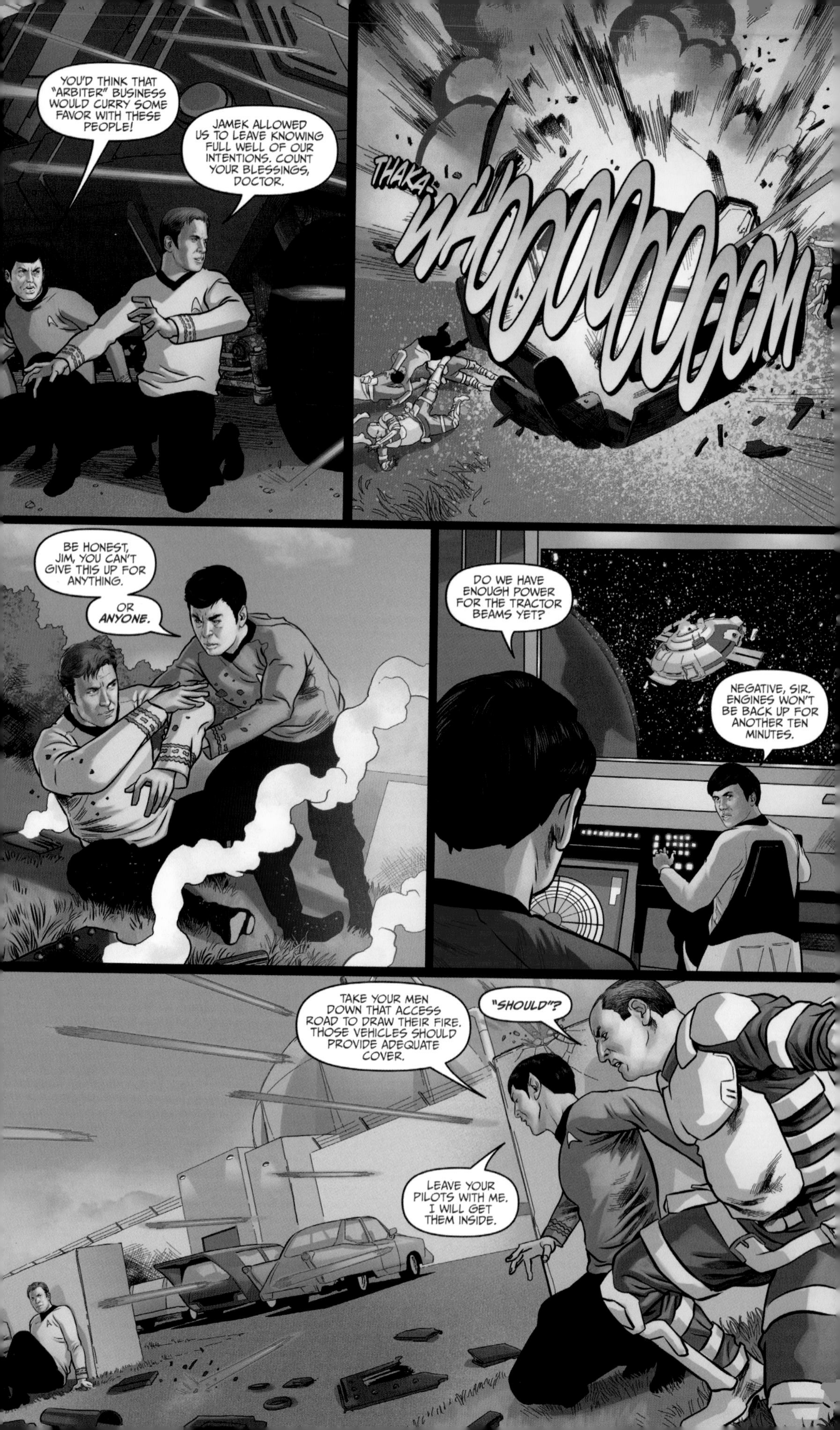
YOU'D THINK THAT "ARBITER" BUSINESS WOULD CURRY SOME FAVOR WITH THESE PEOPLE!
JAMEK ALLOWED US TO LEAVE KNOWING FULL WELL OF OUR INTENTIONS. COUNT YOUR BLESSINGS, DOCTOR.
THAKA-WHOOOOOOOM
BE HONEST, JIM, YOU CAN'T GIVE THIS UP FOR ANYTHING.
OR *ANYONE.*
DO WE HAVE ENOUGH POWER FOR THE TRACTOR BEAMS YET?
NEGATIVE, SIR. ENGINES WON'T BE BACK UP FOR ANOTHER TEN MINUTES.
TAKE YOUR MEN DOWN THAT ACCESS ROAD TO DRAW THEIR FIRE. THOSE VEHICLES SHOULD PROVIDE ADEQUATE COVER.
"SHOULD"?
LEAVE YOUR PILOTS WITH ME. I WILL GET THEM INSIDE.

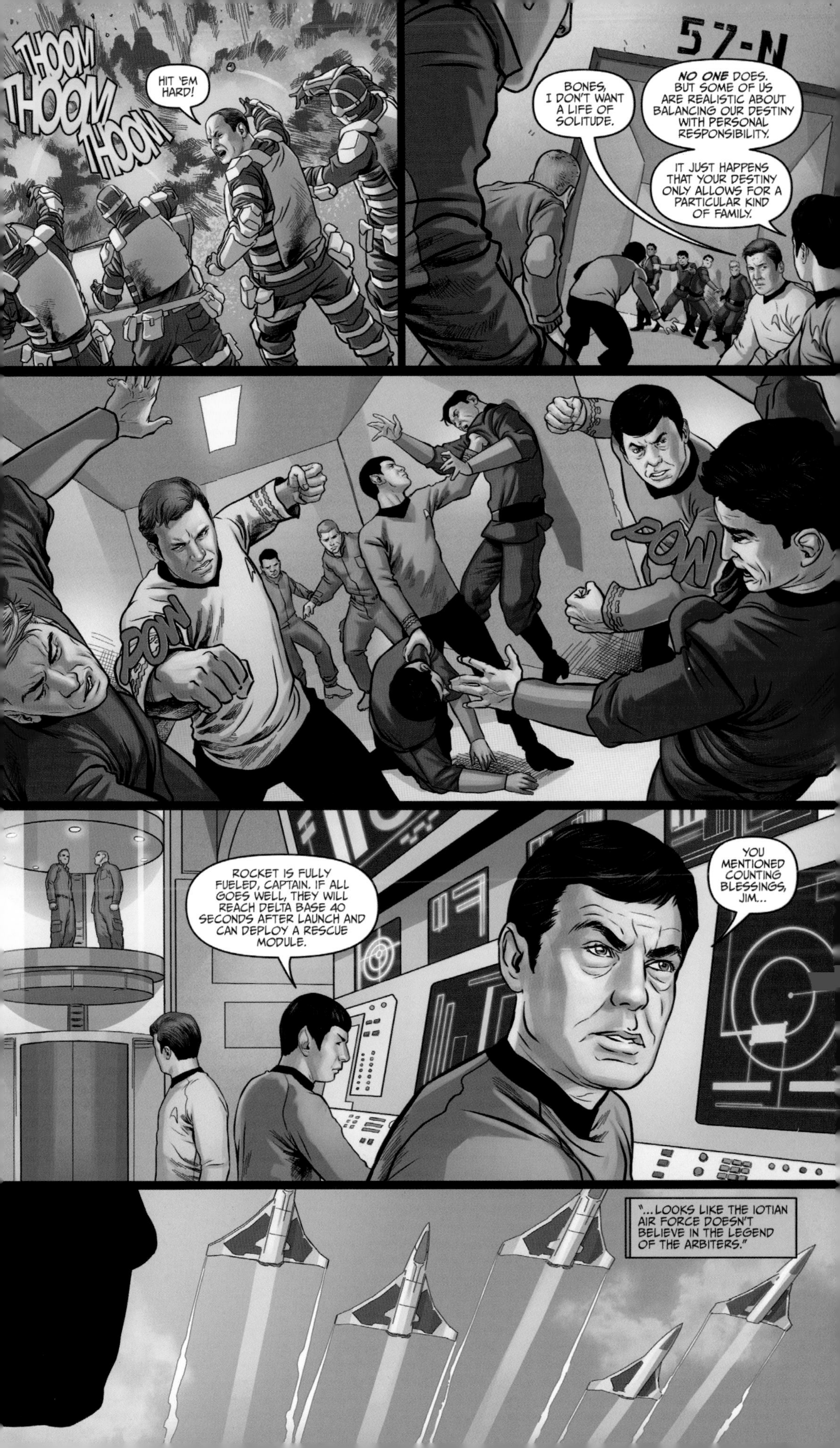
THOOM THOOM THOOM
HIT 'EM HARD!
57-N
BONES, I DON'T WANT A LIFE OF SOLITUDE.
NO ONE DOES. BUT SOME OF US ARE REALISTIC ABOUT BALANCING OUR DESTINY WITH PERSONAL RESPONSIBILITY.
IT JUST HAPPENS THAT YOUR DESTINY ONLY ALLOWS FOR A PARTICULAR KIND OF FAMILY.
POW
POW
ROCKET IS FULLY FUELED, CAPTAIN. IF ALL GOES WELL, THEY WILL REACH DELTA BASE 40 SECONDS AFTER LAUNCH AND CAN DEPLOY A RESCUE MODULE.
YOU MENTIONED COUNTING BLESSINGS, JIM...
"...LOOKS LIKE THE IOTIAN AIR FORCE DOESN'T BELIEVE IN THE LEGEND OF THE ARBITERS."

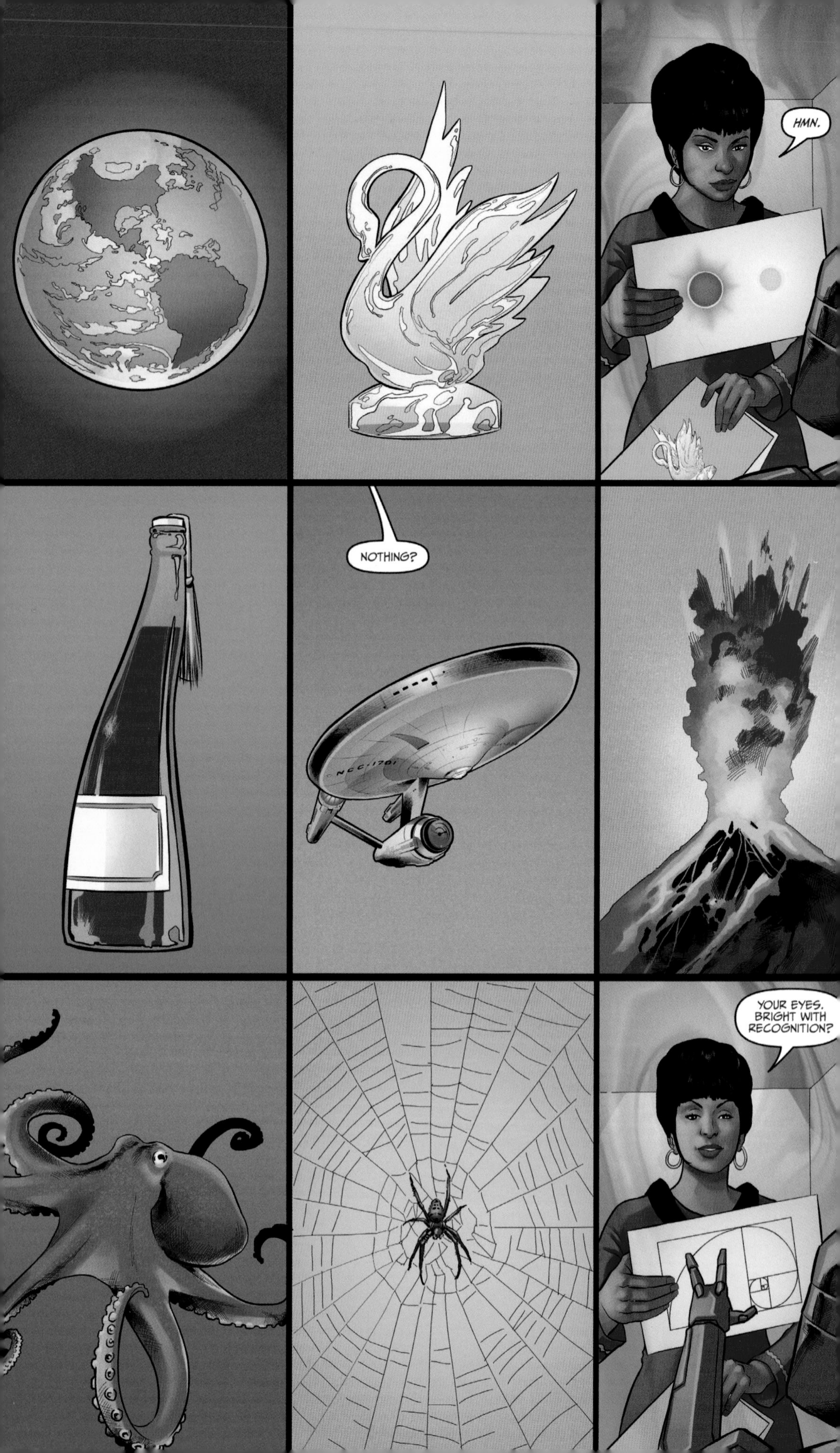
HMN.
NOTHING?
YOUR EYES. BRIGHT WITH RECOGNITION?

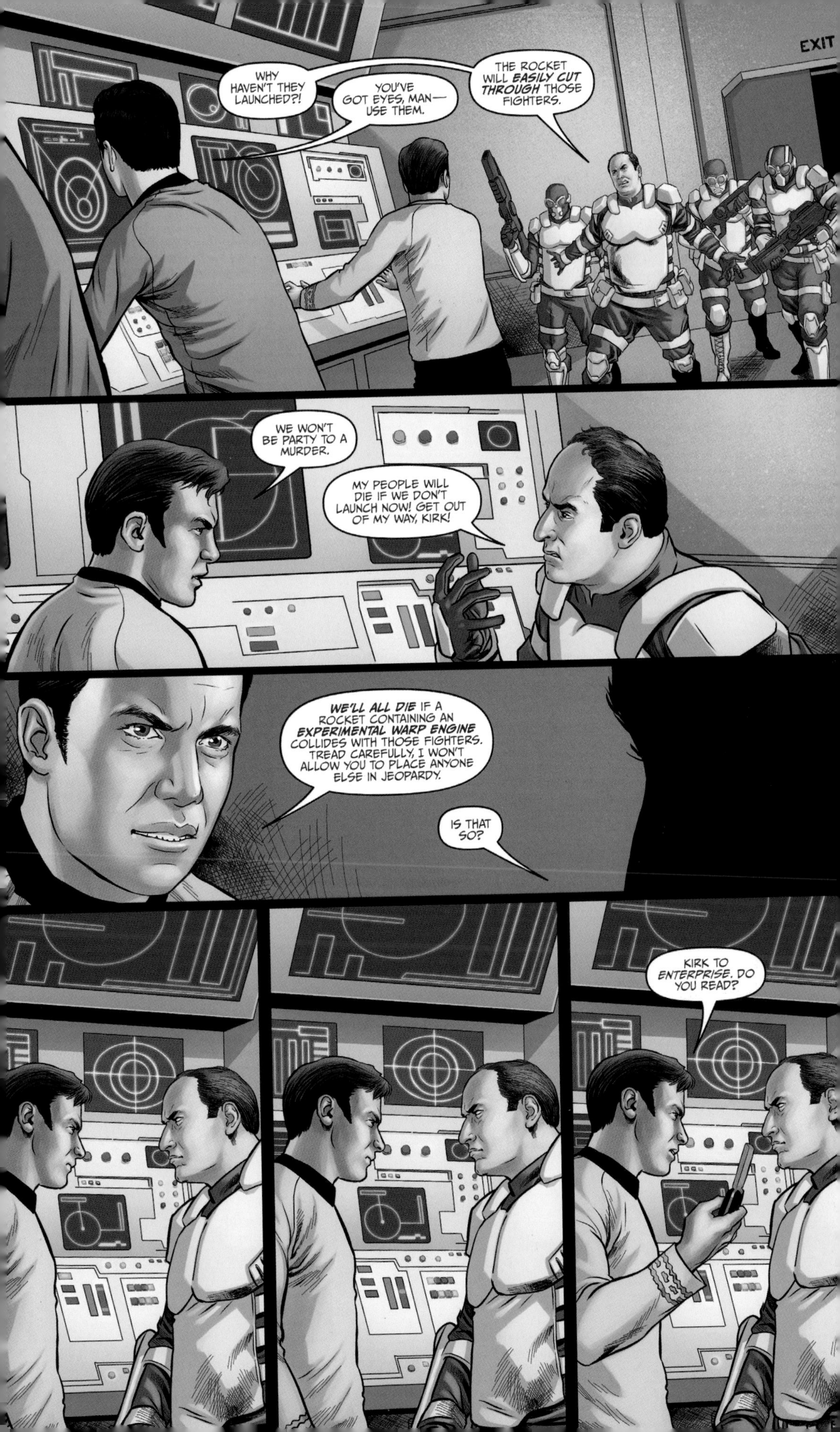
EXIT
WHY HAVEN'T THEY LAUNCHED?!
YOU'VE GOT EYES, MAN— USE THEM.
THE ROCKET WILL **EASILY CUT THROUGH** THOSE FIGHTERS.
WE WON'T BE PARTY TO A MURDER.
MY PEOPLE WILL DIE IF WE DON'T LAUNCH NOW! GET OUT OF MY WAY, KIRK!
WE'LL ALL DIE IF A ROCKET CONTAINING AN **EXPERIMENTAL WARP ENGINE** COLLIDES WITH THOSE FIGHTERS. TREAD CAREFULLY, I WON'T ALLOW YOU TO PLACE ANYONE ELSE IN JEOPARDY.
IS THAT SO?
KIRK TO *ENTERPRISE*. DO YOU READ?

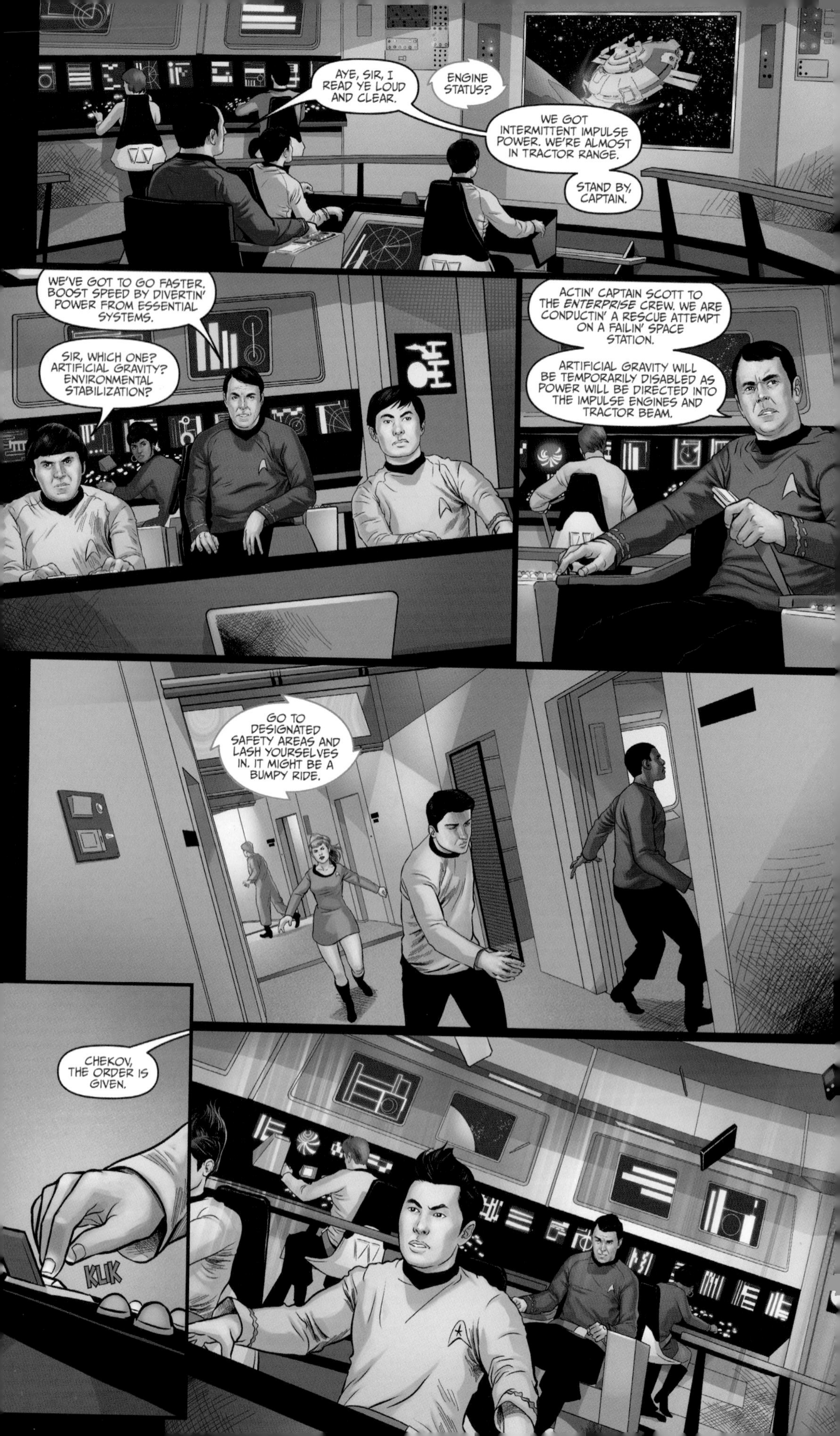
AYE, SIR, I READ YE LOUD AND CLEAR.
ENGINE STATUS?
WE GOT INTERMITTENT IMPULSE POWER. WE'RE ALMOST IN TRACTOR RANGE.
STAND BY, CAPTAIN.
WE'VE GOT TO GO FASTER. BOOST SPEED BY DIVERTIN' POWER FROM ESSENTIAL SYSTEMS.
SIR, WHICH ONE? ARTIFICIAL GRAVITY? ENVIRONMENTAL STABILIZATION?
ACTIN' CAPTAIN SCOTT TO THE *ENTERPRISE* CREW. WE ARE CONDUCTIN' A RESCUE ATTEMPT ON A FAILIN' SPACE STATION.
ARTIFICIAL GRAVITY WILL BE TEMPORARILY DISABLED AS POWER WILL BE DIRECTED INTO THE IMPULSE ENGINES AND TRACTOR BEAM.
GO TO DESIGNATED SAFETY AREAS AND LASH YOURSELVES IN. IT MIGHT BE A BUMPY RIDE.
CHEKOV, THE ORDER IS GIVEN.
KLIK

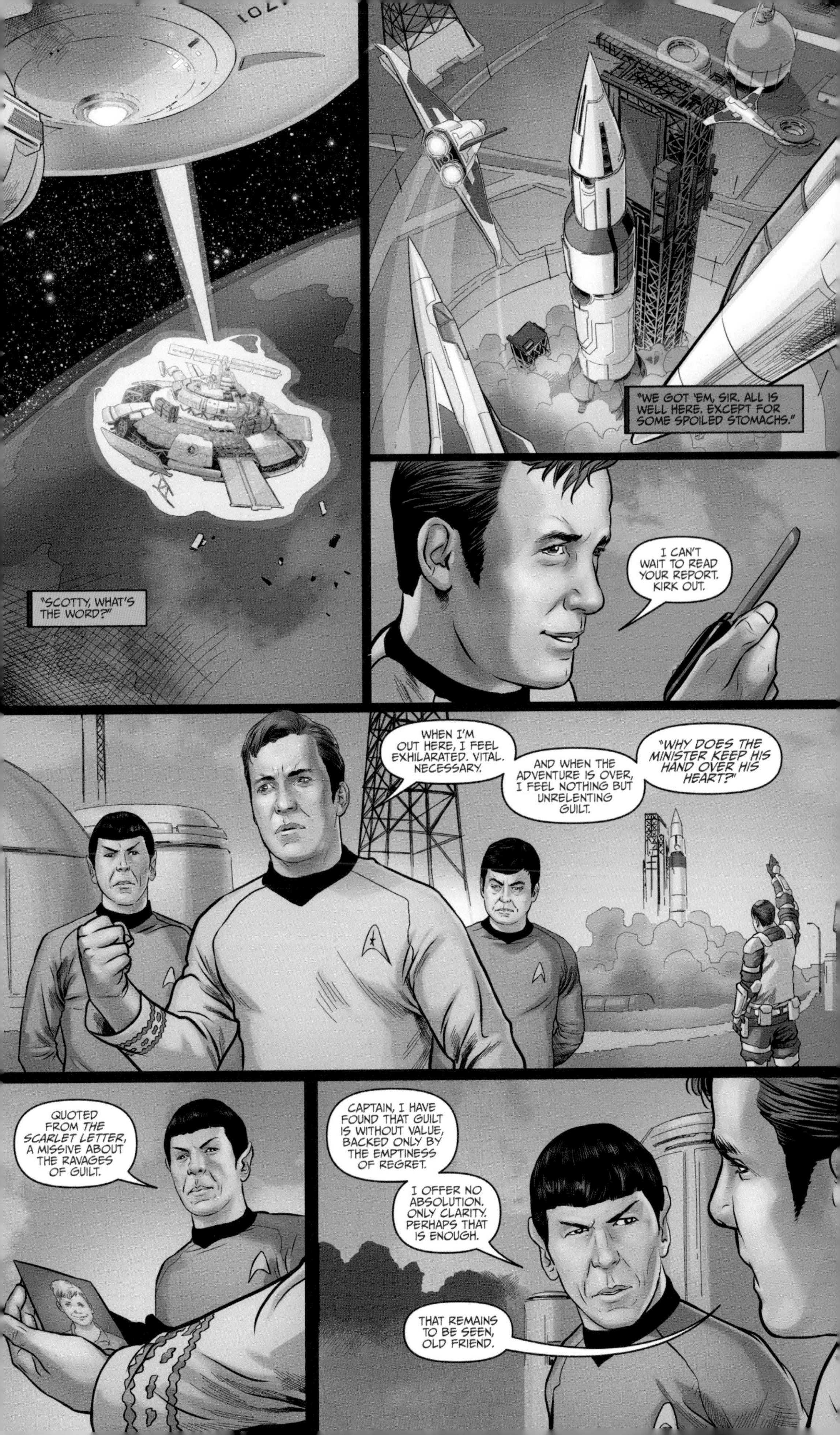
"SCOTTY, WHAT'S THE WORD?"
"WE GOT 'EM, SIR. ALL IS WELL HERE. EXCEPT FOR SOME SPOILED STOMACHS."
I CAN'T WAIT TO READ YOUR REPORT. KIRK OUT.
WHEN I'M OUT HERE, I FEEL EXHILARATED. VITAL. NECESSARY.
AND WHEN THE ADVENTURE IS OVER, I FEEL NOTHING BUT UNRELENTING GUILT.
"WHY DOES THE MINISTER KEEP HIS HAND OVER HIS HEART?"
QUOTED FROM *THE SCARLET LETTER*, A MISSIVE ABOUT THE RAVAGES OF GUILT.
CAPTAIN, I HAVE FOUND THAT GUILT IS WITHOUT VALUE, BACKED ONLY BY THE EMPTINESS OF REGRET.
I OFFER NO ABSOLUTION. ONLY CLARITY. PERHAPS THAT IS ENOUGH.
THAT REMAINS TO BE SEEN, OLD FRIEND.

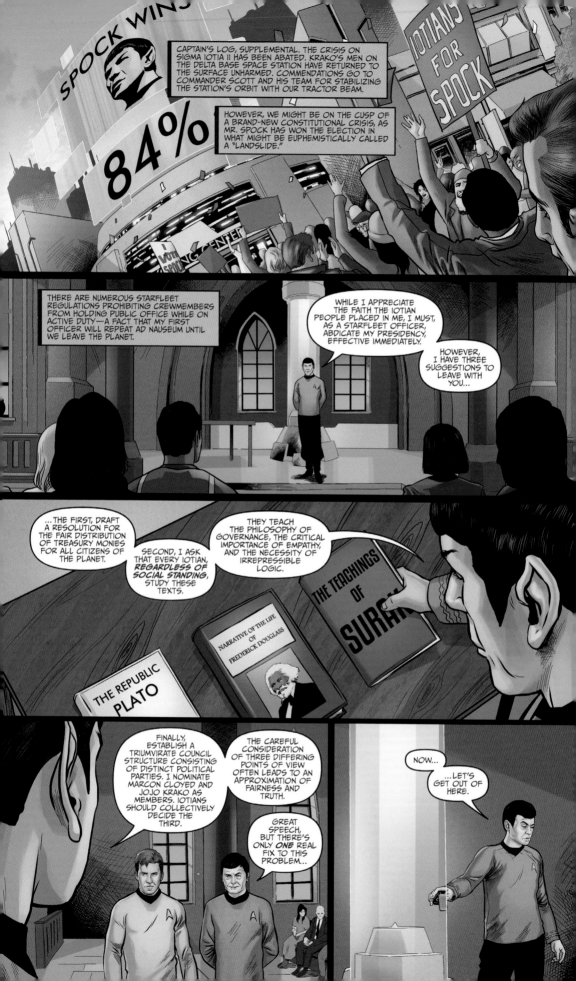

SPOCK WINS

84%

IOTIANS FOR SPOCK

CAPTAIN'S LOG, SUPPLEMENTAL. THE CRISIS ON SIGMA IOTIA II HAS BEEN ABATED. KRAKO'S MEN ON THE DELTA BASE SPACE STATION HAVE RETURNED TO THE SURFACE UNHARMED. COMMENDATIONS GO TO COMMANDER SCOTT AND HIS TEAM FOR STABILIZING THE STATION'S ORBIT WITH OUR TRACTOR BEAM.

HOWEVER, WE MIGHT BE ON THE CUSP OF A BRAND-NEW CONSTITUTIONAL CRISIS, AS MR. SPOCK HAS WON THE ELECTION IN WHAT MIGHT BE EUPHEMISTICALLY CALLED A "LANDSLIDE."

THERE ARE NUMEROUS STARFLEET REGULATIONS PROHIBITING CREWMEMBERS FROM HOLDING PUBLIC OFFICE WHILE ON ACTIVE DUTY—A FACT THAT MY FIRST OFFICER WILL REPEAT AD NAUSEUM UNTIL WE LEAVE THE PLANET.

WHILE I APPRECIATE THE FAITH THE IOTIAN PEOPLE PLACED IN ME, I MUST, AS A STARFLEET OFFICER, ABDICATE MY PRESIDENCY, EFFECTIVE IMMEDIATELY.

HOWEVER, I HAVE THREE SUGGESTIONS TO LEAVE WITH YOU...

...THE FIRST, DRAFT A RESOLUTION FOR THE FAIR DISTRIBUTION OF TREASURY MONIES FOR ALL CITIZENS OF THE PLANET.

SECOND, I ASK THAT EVERY IOTIAN, *REGARDLESS OF SOCIAL STANDING*, STUDY THESE TEXTS.

THEY TEACH THE PHILOSOPHY OF GOVERNANCE, THE CRITICAL IMPORTANCE OF EMPATHY, AND THE NECESSITY OF IRREPRESSIBLE LOGIC.

THE TEACHINGS OF SURAK

NARRATIVE OF THE LIFE OF FREDERICK DOUGLASS

THE REPUBLIC PLATO

FINALLY, ESTABLISH A TRIUMVIRATE COUNCIL STRUCTURE CONSISTING OF DISTINCT POLITICAL PARTIES. I NOMINATE MARCON CLOYED AND JOJO KRAKO AS MEMBERS. IOTIANS SHOULD COLLECTIVELY DECIDE THE THIRD.

THE CAREFUL CONSIDERATION OF THREE DIFFERING POINTS OF VIEW OFTEN LEADS TO AN APPROXIMATION OF FAIRNESS AND TRUTH.

GREAT SPEECH, BUT THERE'S ONLY *ONE* REAL FIX TO THIS PROBLEM...

NOW...

...LET'S GET OUT OF HERE.

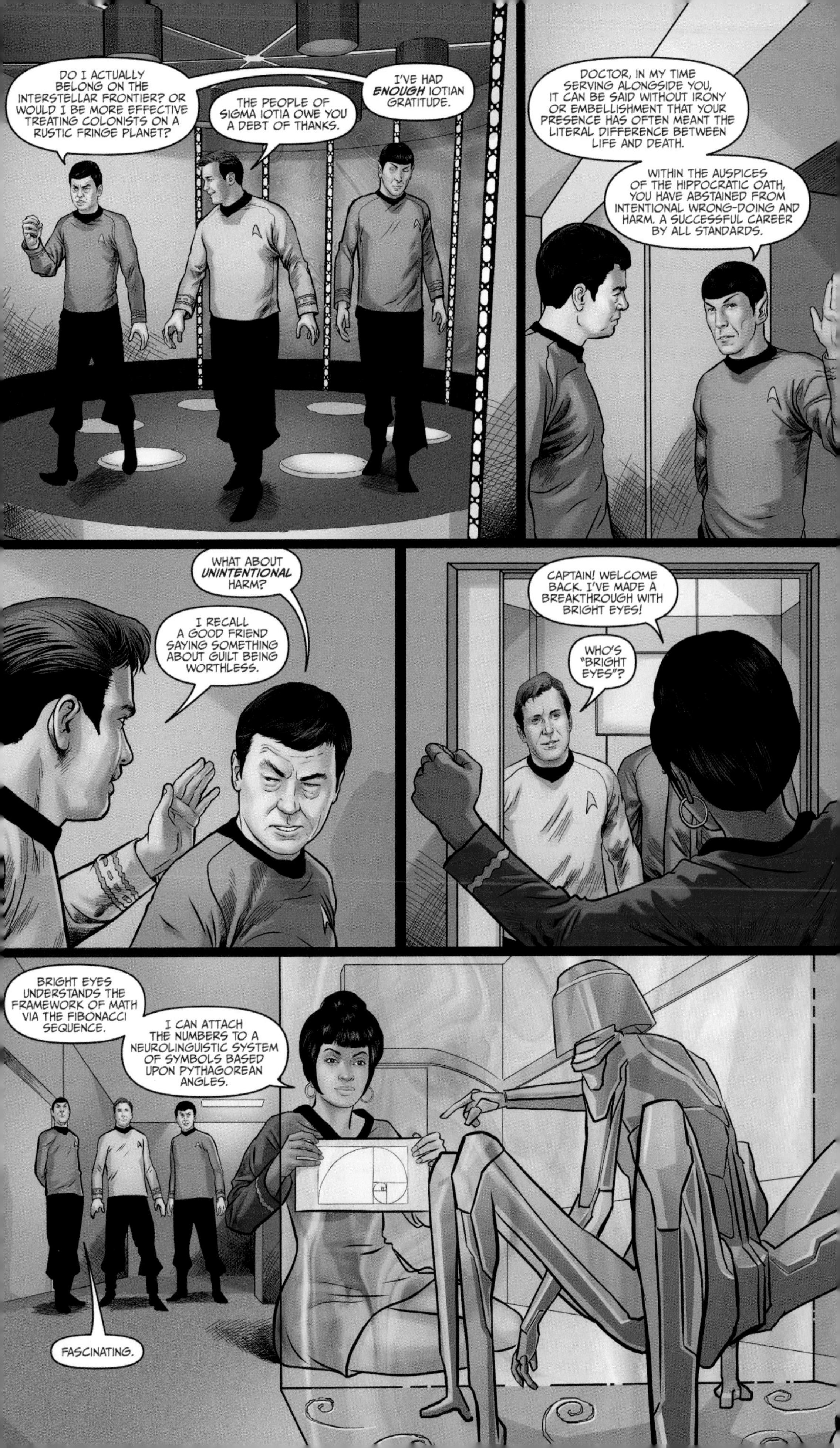
DO I ACTUALLY BELONG ON THE INTERSTELLAR FRONTIER? OR WOULD I BE MORE EFFECTIVE TREATING COLONISTS ON A RUSTIC FRINGE PLANET?
THE PEOPLE OF SIGMA IOTIA OWE YOU A DEBT OF THANKS.
I'VE HAD *ENOUGH* IOTIAN GRATITUDE.
DOCTOR, IN MY TIME SERVING ALONGSIDE YOU, IT CAN BE SAID WITHOUT IRONY OR EMBELLISHMENT THAT YOUR PRESENCE HAS OFTEN MEANT THE LITERAL DIFFERENCE BETWEEN LIFE AND DEATH.
WITHIN THE AUSPICES OF THE HIPPOCRATIC OATH, YOU HAVE ABSTAINED FROM INTENTIONAL WRONG-DOING AND HARM. A SUCCESSFUL CAREER BY ALL STANDARDS.
WHAT ABOUT *UNINTENTIONAL* HARM?
I RECALL A GOOD FRIEND SAYING SOMETHING ABOUT GUILT BEING WORTHLESS.
CAPTAIN! WELCOME BACK. I'VE MADE A BREAKTHROUGH WITH BRIGHT EYES!
WHO'S "BRIGHT EYES"?
BRIGHT EYES UNDERSTANDS THE FRAMEWORK OF MATH VIA THE FIBONACCI SEQUENCE.
I CAN ATTACH THE NUMBERS TO A NEUROLINGUISTIC SYSTEM OF SYMBOLS BASED UPON PYTHAGOREAN ANGLES.
FASCINATING.

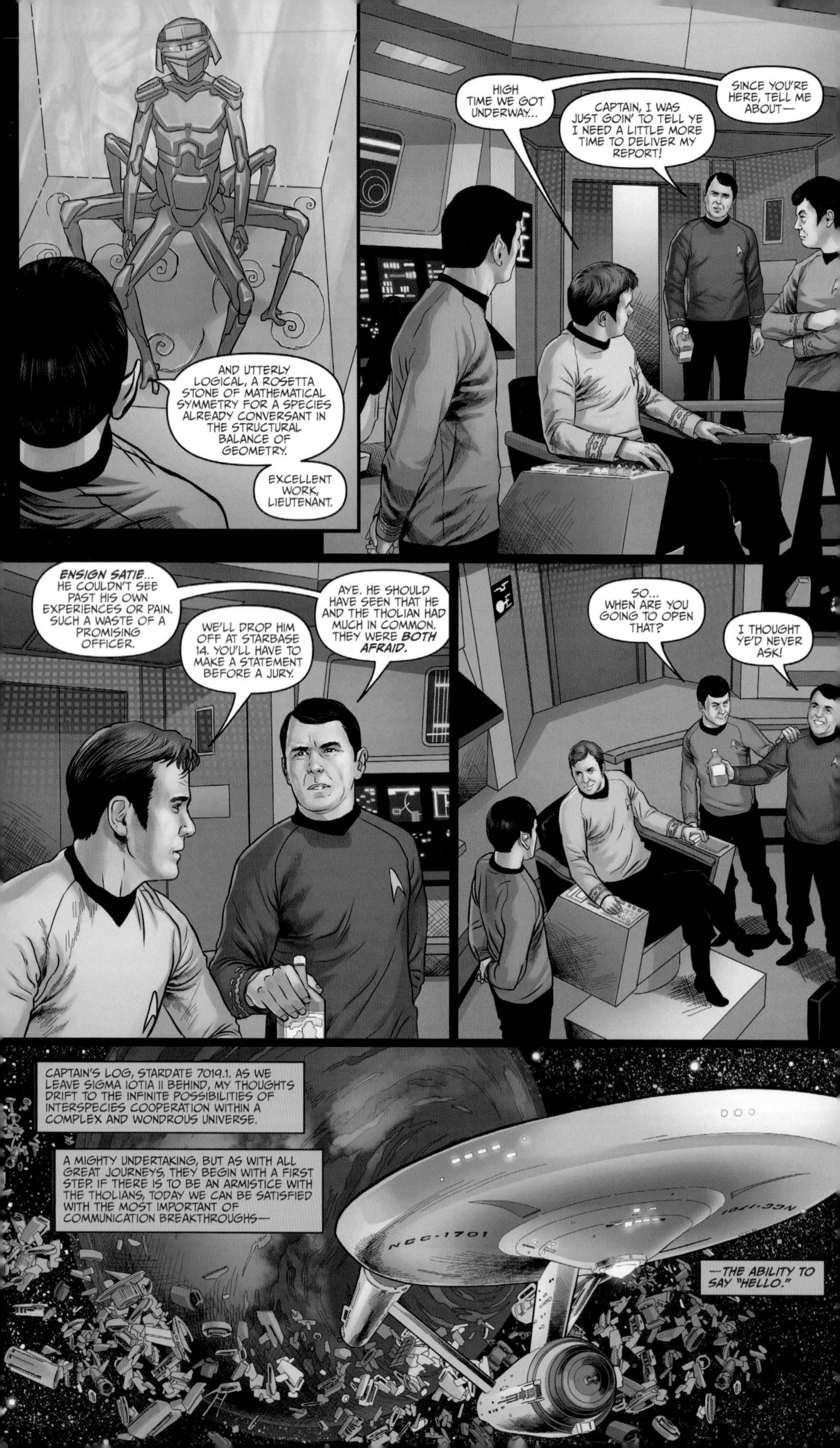
AND UTTERLY LOGICAL, A ROSETTA STONE OF MATHEMATICAL SYMMETRY FOR A SPECIES ALREADY CONVERSANT IN THE STRUCTURAL BALANCE OF GEOMETRY.
EXCELLENT WORK, LIEUTENANT.
HIGH TIME WE GOT UNDERWAY...
SINCE YOU'RE HERE, TELL ME ABOUT—
CAPTAIN, I WAS JUST GOIN' TO TELL YE I NEED A LITTLE MORE TIME TO DELIVER MY REPORT!
ENSIGN SATIE... HE COULDN'T SEE PAST HIS OWN EXPERIENCES OR PAIN. SUCH A WASTE OF A PROMISING OFFICER.
AYE. HE SHOULD HAVE SEEN THAT HE AND THE THOLIAN HAD MUCH IN COMMON. THEY WERE BOTH AFRAID.
WE'LL DROP HIM OFF AT STARBASE 14. YOU'LL HAVE TO MAKE A STATEMENT BEFORE A JURY.
SO... WHEN ARE YOU GOING TO OPEN THAT?
I THOUGHT YE'D NEVER ASK!
CAPTAIN'S LOG, STARDATE 7019.1. AS WE LEAVE SIGMA IOTIA II BEHIND, MY THOUGHTS DRIFT TO THE INFINITE POSSIBILITIES OF INTERSPECIES COOPERATION WITHIN A COMPLEX AND WONDROUS UNIVERSE.
A MIGHTY UNDERTAKING, BUT AS WITH ALL GREAT JOURNEYS, THEY BEGIN WITH A FIRST STEP. IF THERE IS TO BE AN ARMISTICE WITH THE THOLIANS, TODAY WE CAN BE SATISFIED WITH THE MOST IMPORTANT OF COMMUNICATION BREAKTHROUGHS—
NCC-1701
—THE ABILITY TO SAY "HELLO."

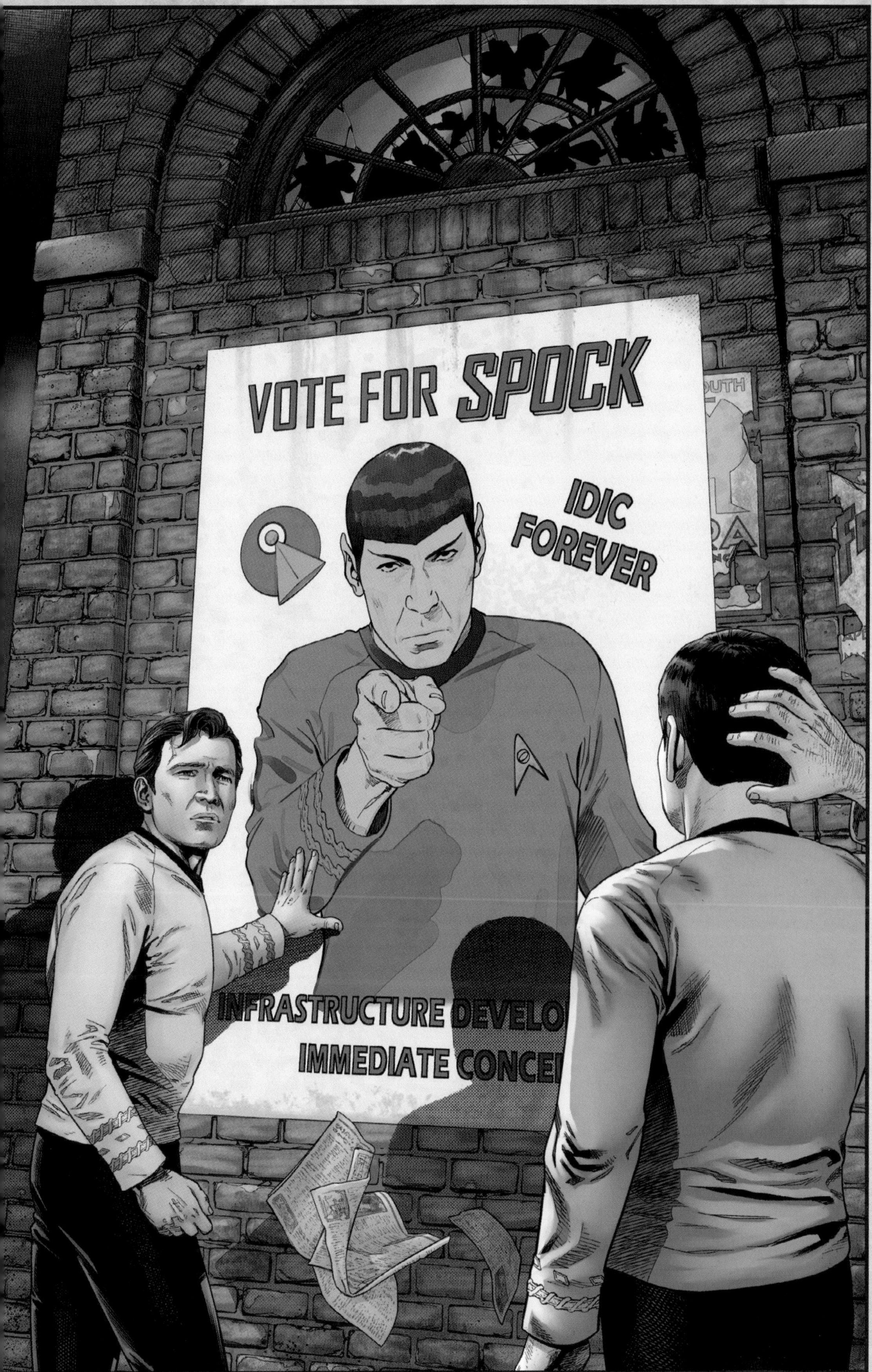
VOTE FOR SPOCK
IDIC FOREVER
INFRASTRUCTURE DEVELO
IMMEDIATE CONCE

ART BY **STEPHEN THOMPSON**

COLORS BY **CHARLIE KIRCHOFF**

EPISODE THREE

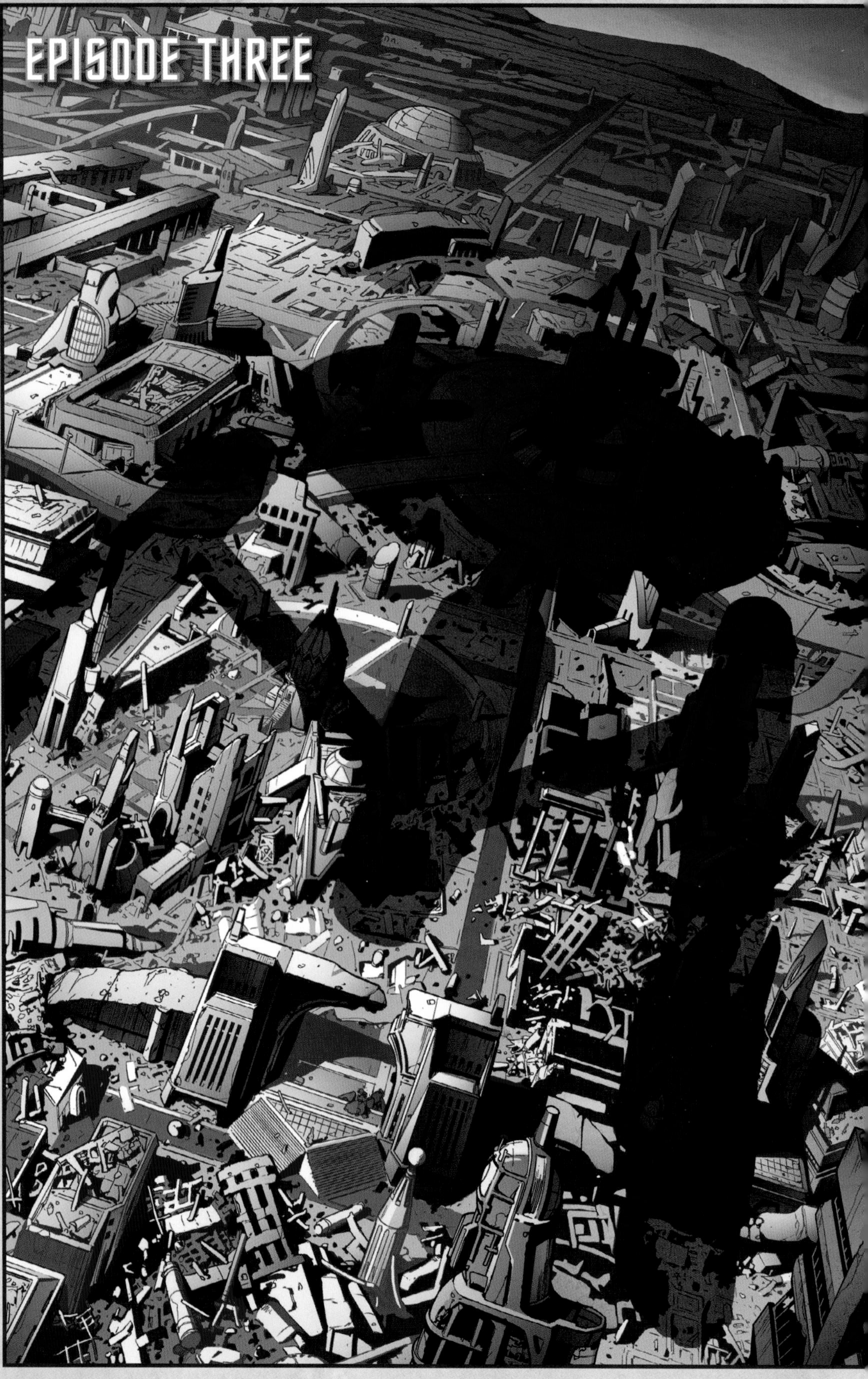

ART BY STEPHEN THOMPSON

COLORS BY DAVID GARCIA CRUZ

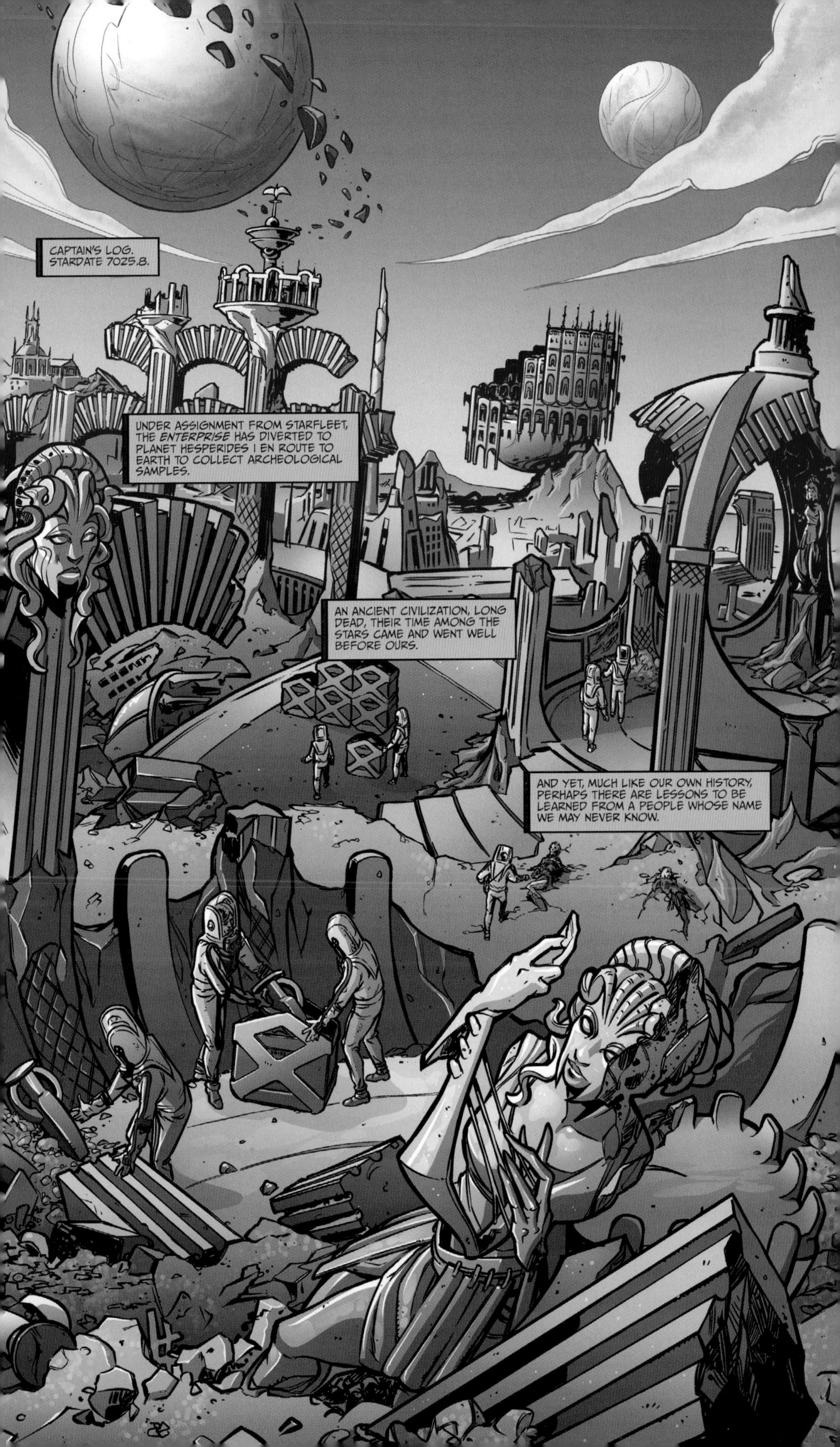
CAPTAIN'S LOG. STARDATE 7025.8.
UNDER ASSIGNMENT FROM STARFLEET, THE *ENTERPRISE* HAS DIVERTED TO PLANET HESPERIDES I EN ROUTE TO EARTH TO COLLECT ARCHEOLOGICAL SAMPLES.
AN ANCIENT CIVILIZATION, LONG DEAD, THEIR TIME AMONG THE STARS CAME AND WENT WELL BEFORE OURS.
AND YET, MUCH LIKE OUR OWN HISTORY, PERHAPS THERE ARE LESSONS TO BE LEARNED FROM A PEOPLE WHOSE NAME WE MAY NEVER KNOW.

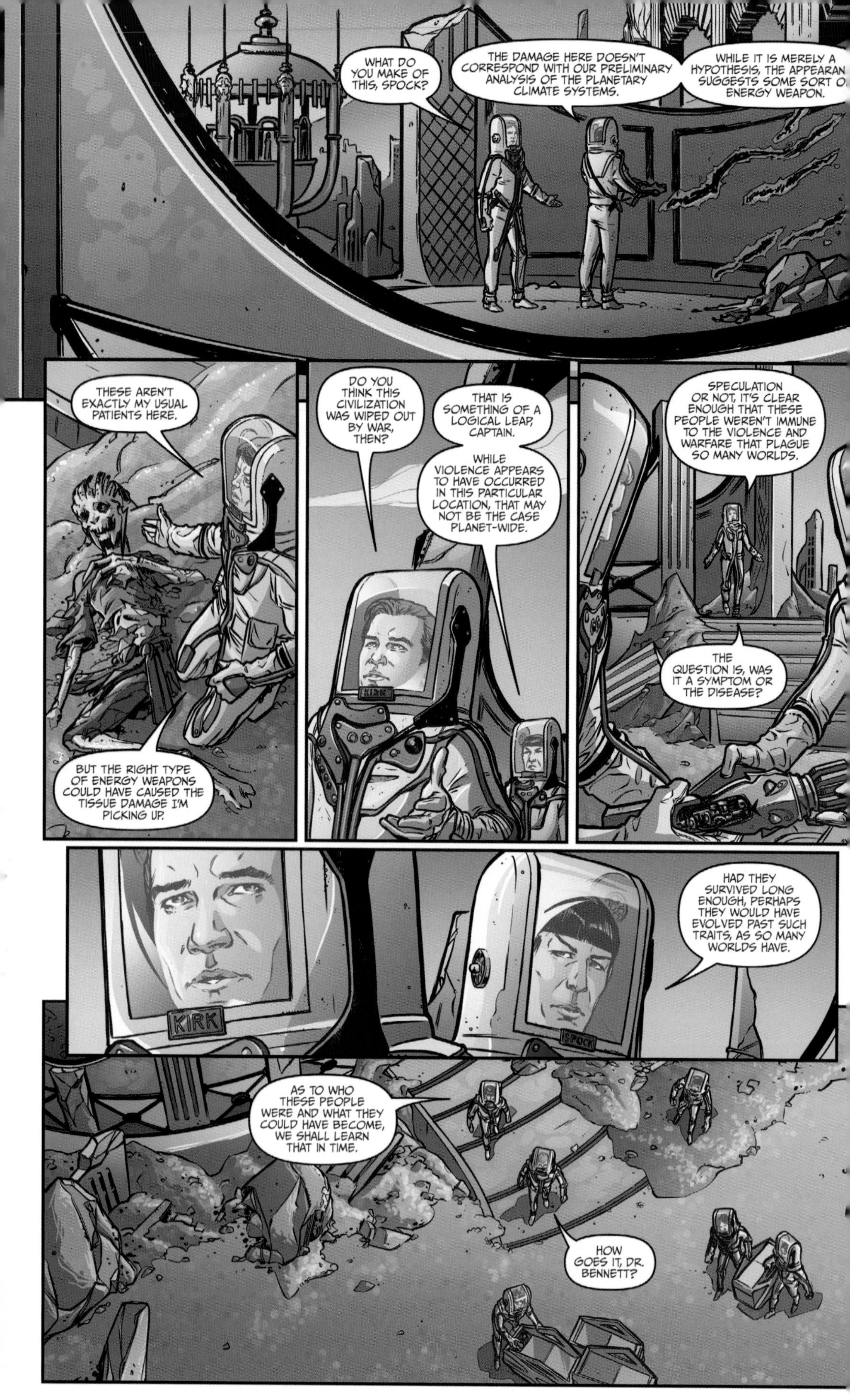
WHAT DO YOU MAKE OF THIS, SPOCK?
THE DAMAGE HERE DOESN'T CORRESPOND WITH OUR PRELIMINARY ANALYSIS OF THE PLANETARY CLIMATE SYSTEMS.
WHILE IT IS MERELY A HYPOTHESIS, THE APPEARAN SUGGESTS SOME SORT O ENERGY WEAPON.
THESE AREN'T EXACTLY MY USUAL PATIENTS HERE.
BUT THE RIGHT TYPE OF ENERGY WEAPONS COULD HAVE CAUSED THE TISSUE DAMAGE I'M PICKING UP.
DO YOU THINK THIS CIVILIZATION WAS WIPED OUT BY WAR, THEN?
THAT IS SOMETHING OF A LOGICAL LEAP, CAPTAIN.
WHILE VIOLENCE APPEARS TO HAVE OCCURRED IN THIS PARTICULAR LOCATION, THAT MAY NOT BE THE CASE PLANET-WIDE.
KIRK
SPECULATION OR NOT, IT'S CLEAR ENOUGH THAT THESE PEOPLE WEREN'T IMMUNE TO THE VIOLENCE AND WARFARE THAT PLAGUE SO MANY WORLDS.
THE QUESTION IS, WAS IT A SYMPTOM OR THE DISEASE?
HAD THEY SURVIVED LONG ENOUGH, PERHAPS THEY WOULD HAVE EVOLVED PAST SUCH TRAITS, AS SO MANY WORLDS HAVE.
KIRK
SPOCK
AS TO WHO THESE PEOPLE WERE AND WHAT THEY COULD HAVE BECOME, WE SHALL LEARN THAT IN TIME.
HOW GOES IT, DR. BENNETT?

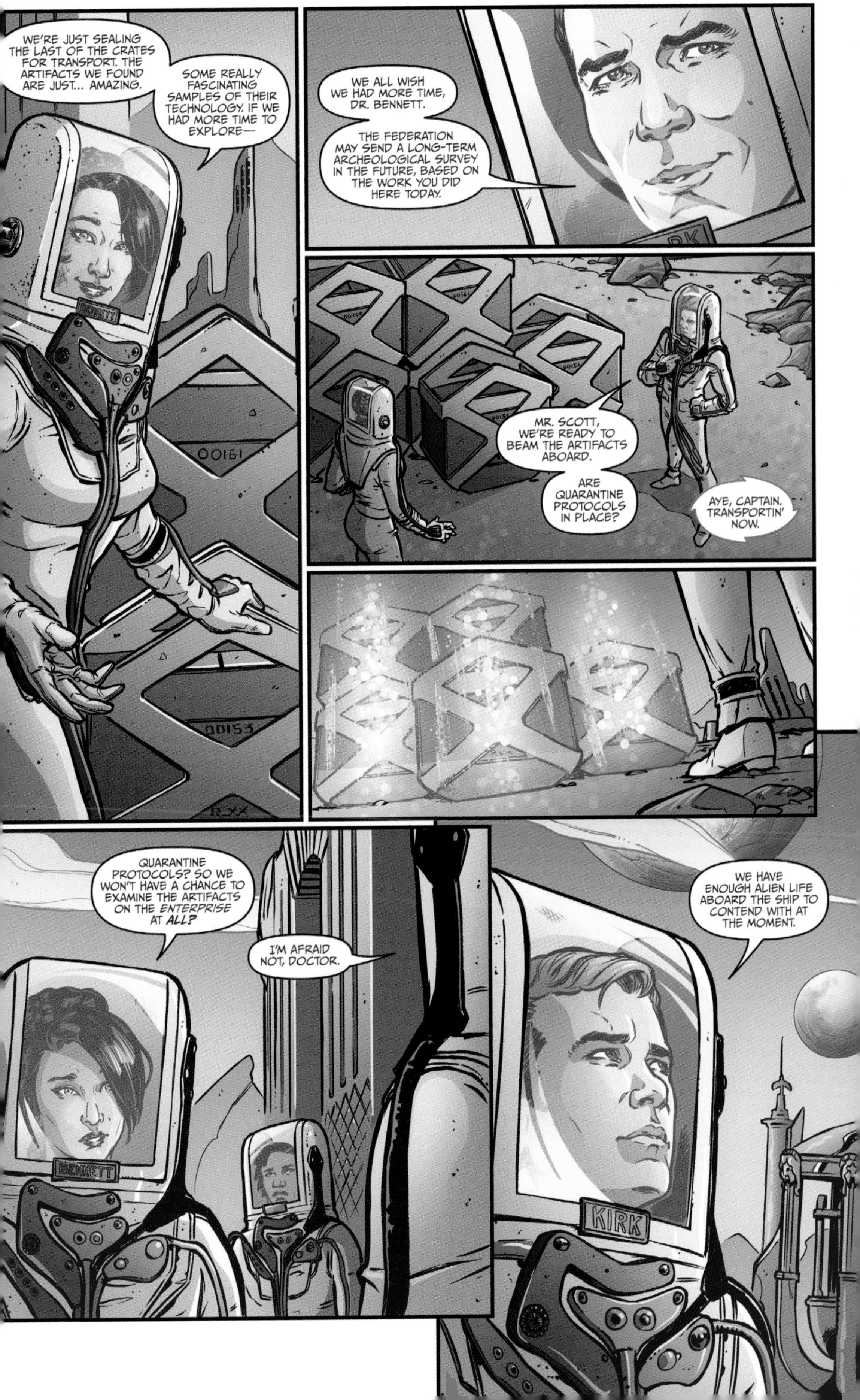
WE'RE JUST SEALING THE LAST OF THE CRATES FOR TRANSPORT. THE ARTIFACTS WE FOUND ARE JUST... AMAZING.
SOME REALLY FASCINATING SAMPLES OF THEIR TECHNOLOGY. IF WE HAD MORE TIME TO EXPLORE—
BENNETT
00161
00153
WE ALL WISH WE HAD MORE TIME, DR. BENNETT.
THE FEDERATION MAY SEND A LONG-TERM ARCHEOLOGICAL SURVEY IN THE FUTURE, BASED ON THE WORK YOU DID HERE TODAY.
MR. SCOTT, WE'RE READY TO BEAM THE ARTIFACTS ABOARD.
ARE QUARANTINE PROTOCOLS IN PLACE?
AYE, CAPTAIN. TRANSPORTIN' NOW.
QUARANTINE PROTOCOLS? SO WE WON'T HAVE A CHANCE TO EXAMINE THE ARTIFACTS ON THE *ENTERPRISE* AT ***ALL?***
I'M AFRAID NOT, DOCTOR.
WE HAVE ENOUGH ALIEN LIFE ABOARD THE SHIP TO CONTEND WITH AT THE MOMENT.
BENNETT
KIRK

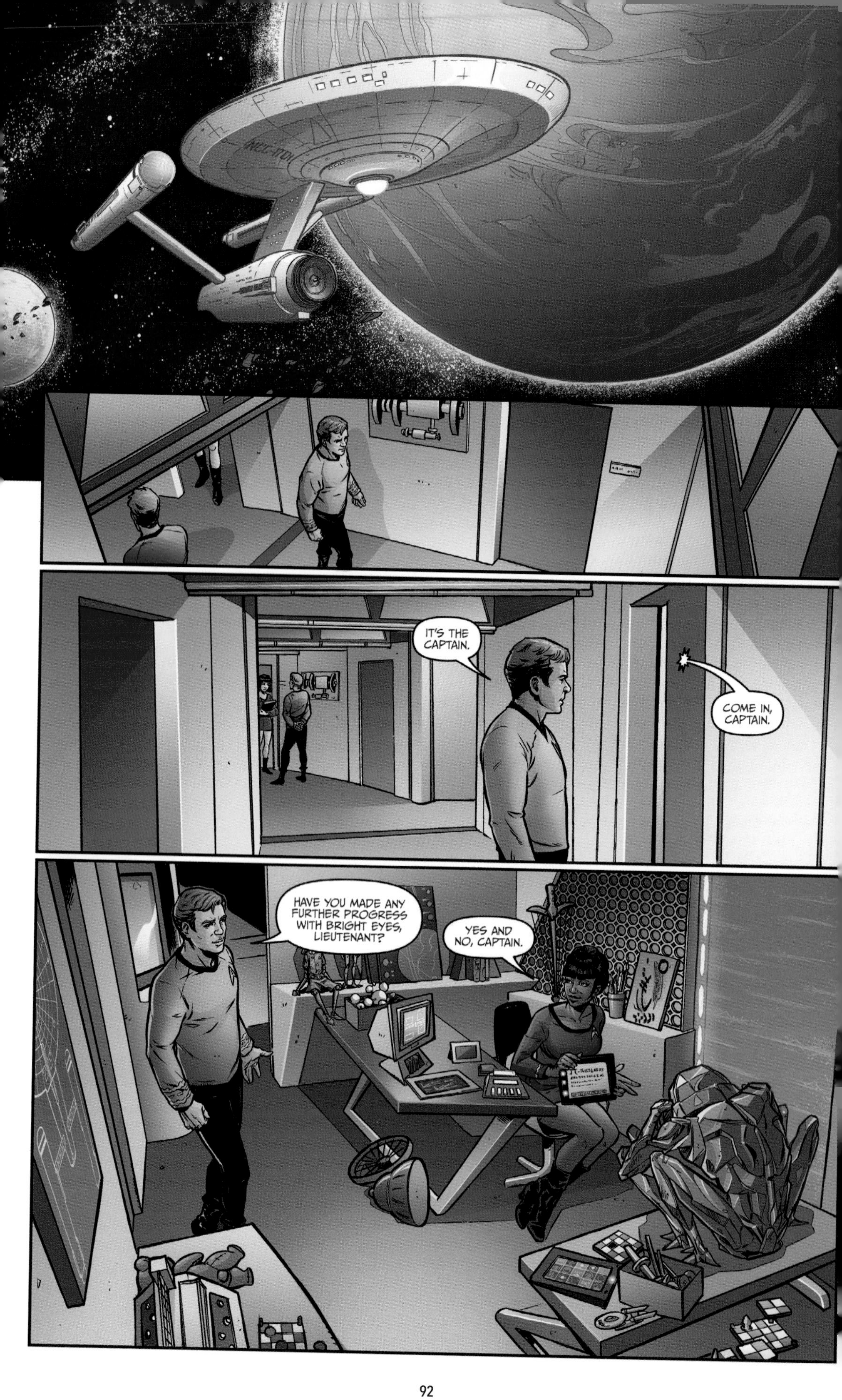
IT'S THE CAPTAIN.
COME IN, CAPTAIN.
HAVE YOU MADE ANY FURTHER PROGRESS WITH BRIGHT EYES, LIEUTENANT?
YES AND NO, CAPTAIN.

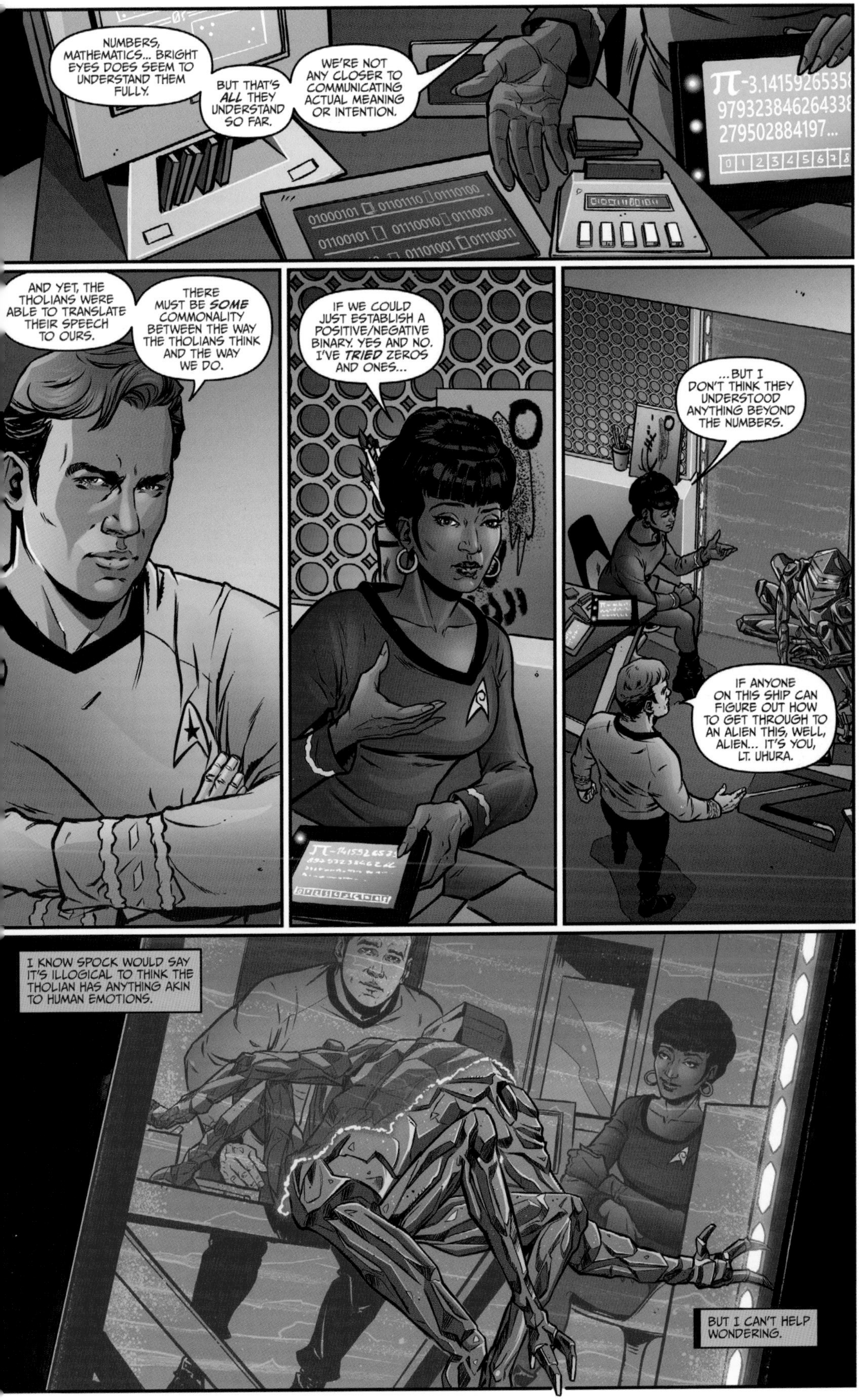
NUMBERS, MATHEMATICS... BRIGHT EYES DOES SEEM TO UNDERSTAND THEM FULLY.
BUT THAT'S ALL THEY UNDERSTAND SO FAR.
WE'RE NOT ANY CLOSER TO COMMUNICATING ACTUAL MEANING OR INTENTION.
π-3.14159265358 97932384626433 279502884197...
AND YET, THE THOLIANS WERE ABLE TO TRANSLATE THEIR SPEECH TO OURS.
THERE MUST BE SOME COMMONALITY BETWEEN THE WAY THE THOLIANS THINK AND THE WAY WE DO.
IF WE COULD JUST ESTABLISH A POSITIVE/NEGATIVE BINARY. YES AND NO. I'VE TRIED ZEROS AND ONES...
...BUT I DON'T THINK THEY UNDERSTOOD ANYTHING BEYOND THE NUMBERS.
IF ANYONE ON THIS SHIP CAN FIGURE OUT HOW TO GET THROUGH TO AN ALIEN THIS, WELL, ALIEN... IT'S YOU, LT. UHURA.
I KNOW SPOCK WOULD SAY IT'S ILLOGICAL TO THINK THE THOLIAN HAS ANYTHING AKIN TO HUMAN EMOTIONS.
BUT I CAN'T HELP WONDERING.

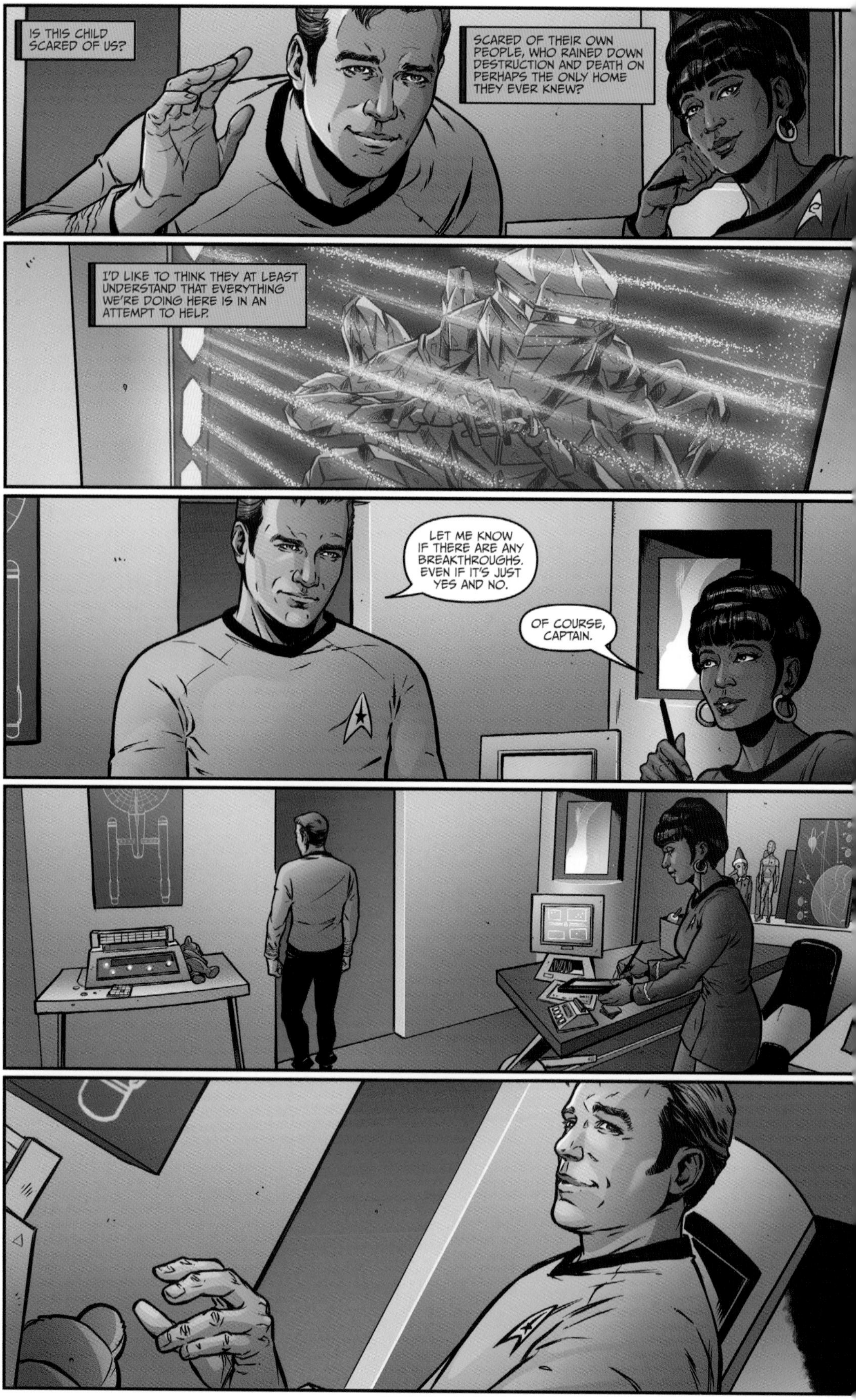
IS THIS CHILD SCARED OF US?
SCARED OF THEIR OWN PEOPLE, WHO RAINED DOWN DESTRUCTION AND DEATH ON PERHAPS THE ONLY HOME THEY EVER KNEW?
I'D LIKE TO THINK THEY AT LEAST UNDERSTAND THAT EVERYTHING WE'RE DOING HERE IS IN AN ATTEMPT TO HELP.
LET ME KNOW IF THERE ARE ANY BREAKTHROUGHS. EVEN IF IT'S JUST YES AND NO.
OF COURSE, CAPTAIN.

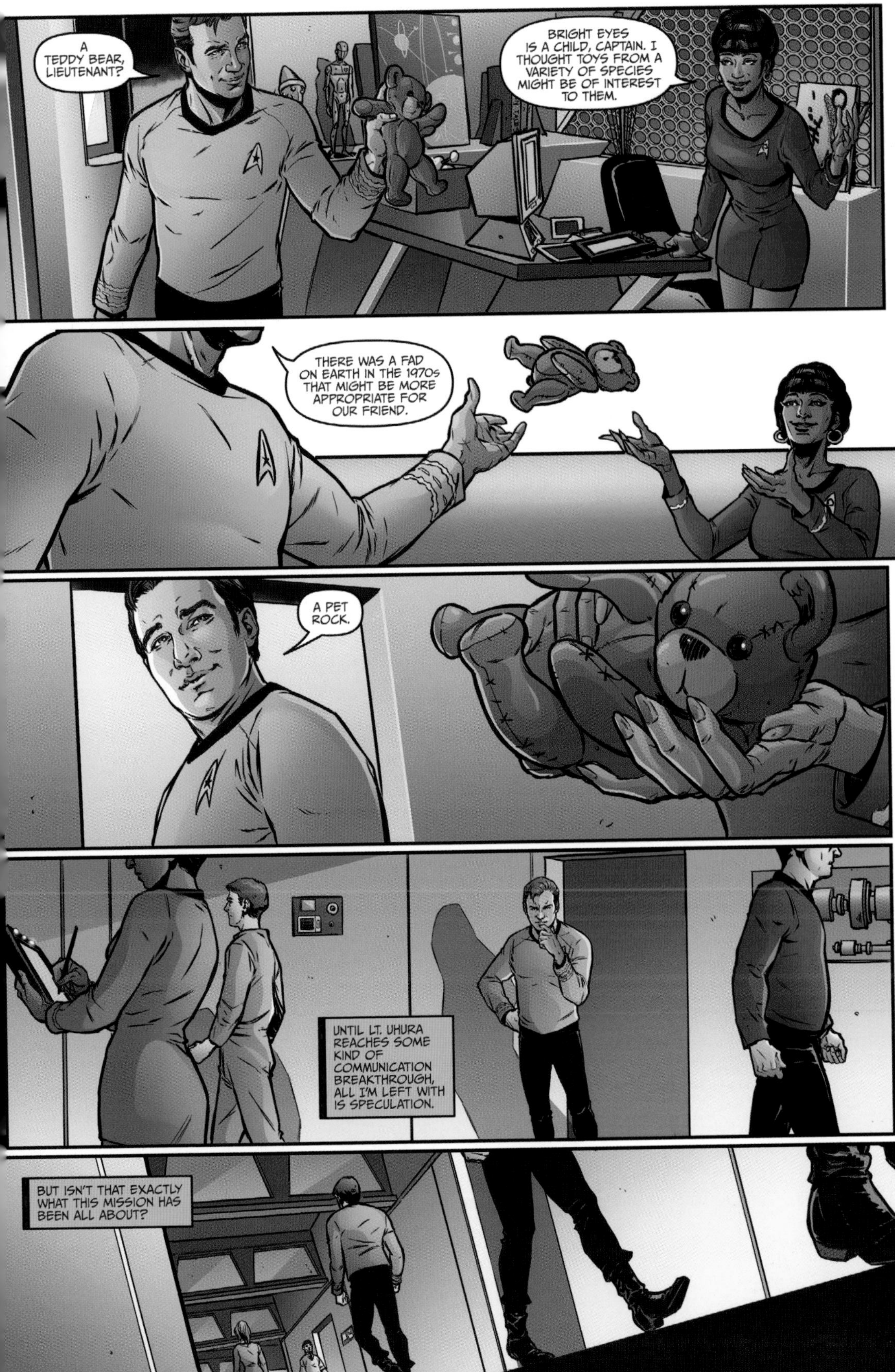
A TEDDY BEAR, LIEUTENANT?
BRIGHT EYES IS A CHILD, CAPTAIN. I THOUGHT TOYS FROM A VARIETY OF SPECIES MIGHT BE OF INTEREST TO THEM.
THERE WAS A FAD ON EARTH IN THE 1970s THAT MIGHT BE MORE APPROPRIATE FOR OUR FRIEND.
A PET ROCK.
UNTIL LT. UHURA REACHES SOME KIND OF COMMUNICATION BREAKTHROUGH, ALL I'M LEFT WITH IS SPECULATION.
BUT ISN'T THAT EXACTLY WHAT THIS MISSION HAS BEEN ALL ABOUT?

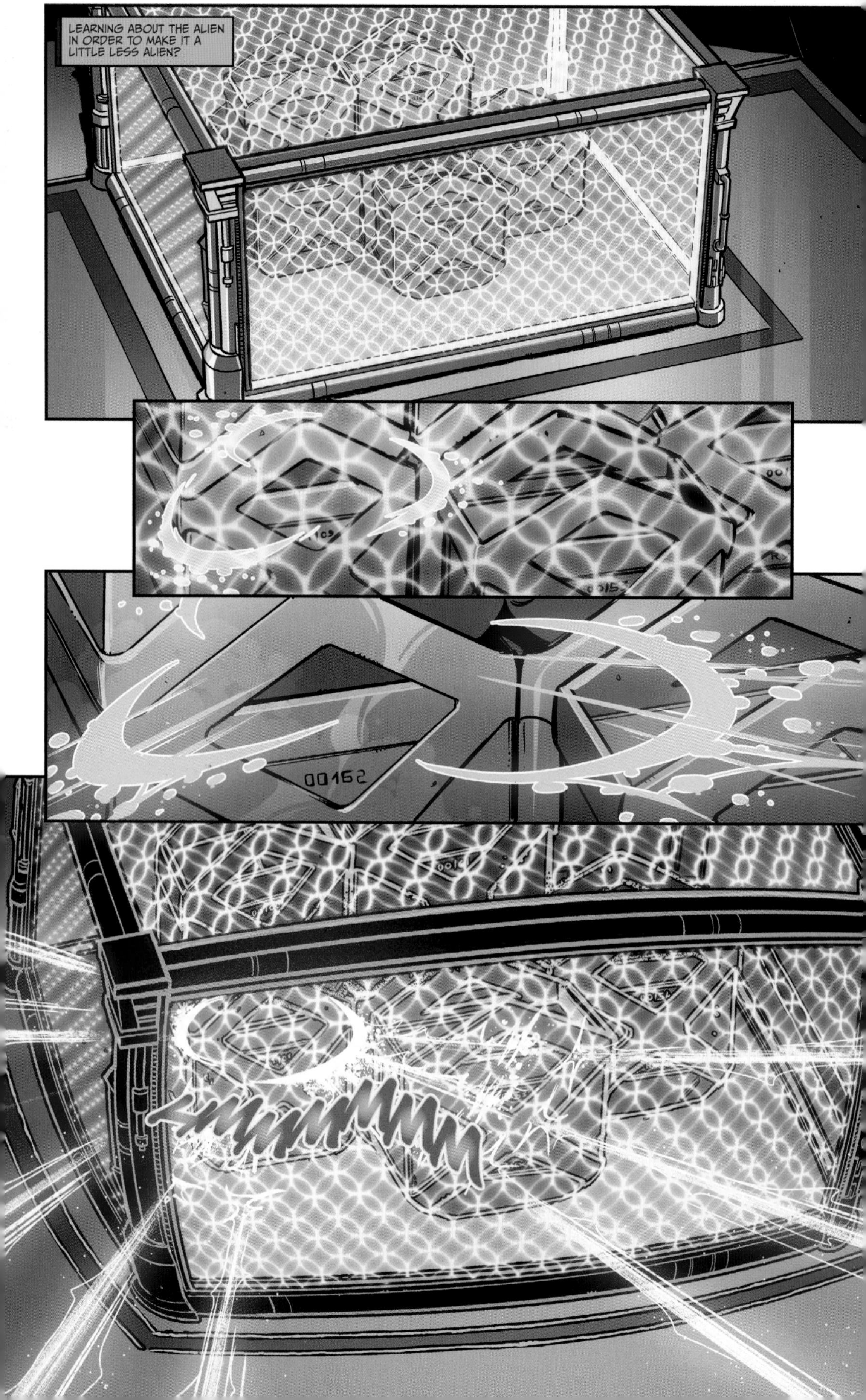
LEARNING ABOUT THE ALIEN IN ORDER TO MAKE IT A LITTLE LESS ALIEN?
00162

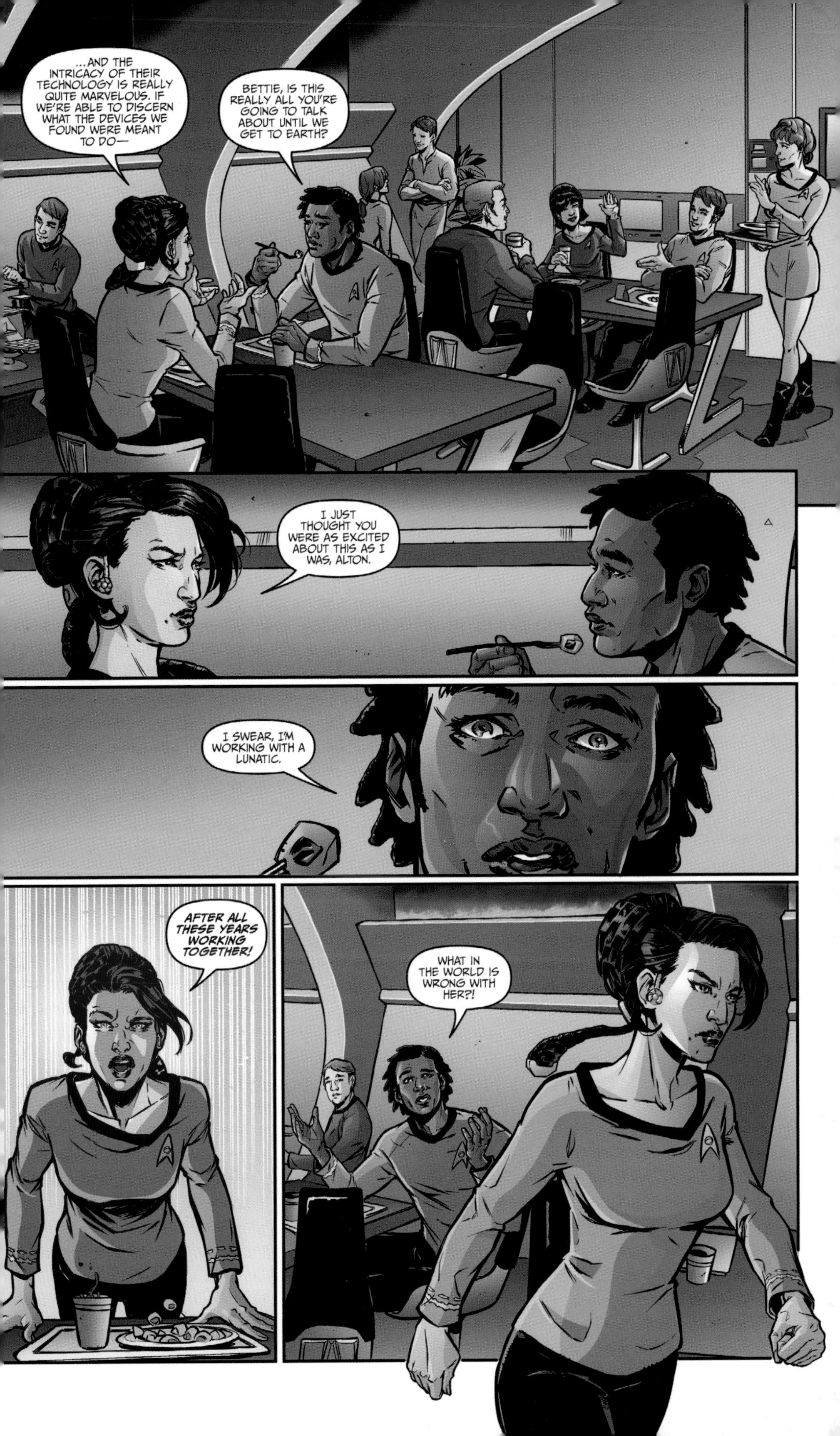
...AND THE INTRICACY OF THEIR TECHNOLOGY IS REALLY QUITE MARVELOUS. IF WE'RE ABLE TO DISCERN WHAT THE DEVICES WE FOUND WERE MEANT TO DO—
BETTIE, IS THIS REALLY ALL YOU'RE GOING TO TALK ABOUT UNTIL WE GET TO EARTH?
I JUST THOUGHT YOU WERE AS EXCITED ABOUT THIS AS I WAS, ALTON.
I SWEAR, I'M WORKING WITH A LUNATIC.
AFTER ALL THESE YEARS WORKING TOGETHER!
WHAT IN THE WORLD IS WRONG WITH HER?!

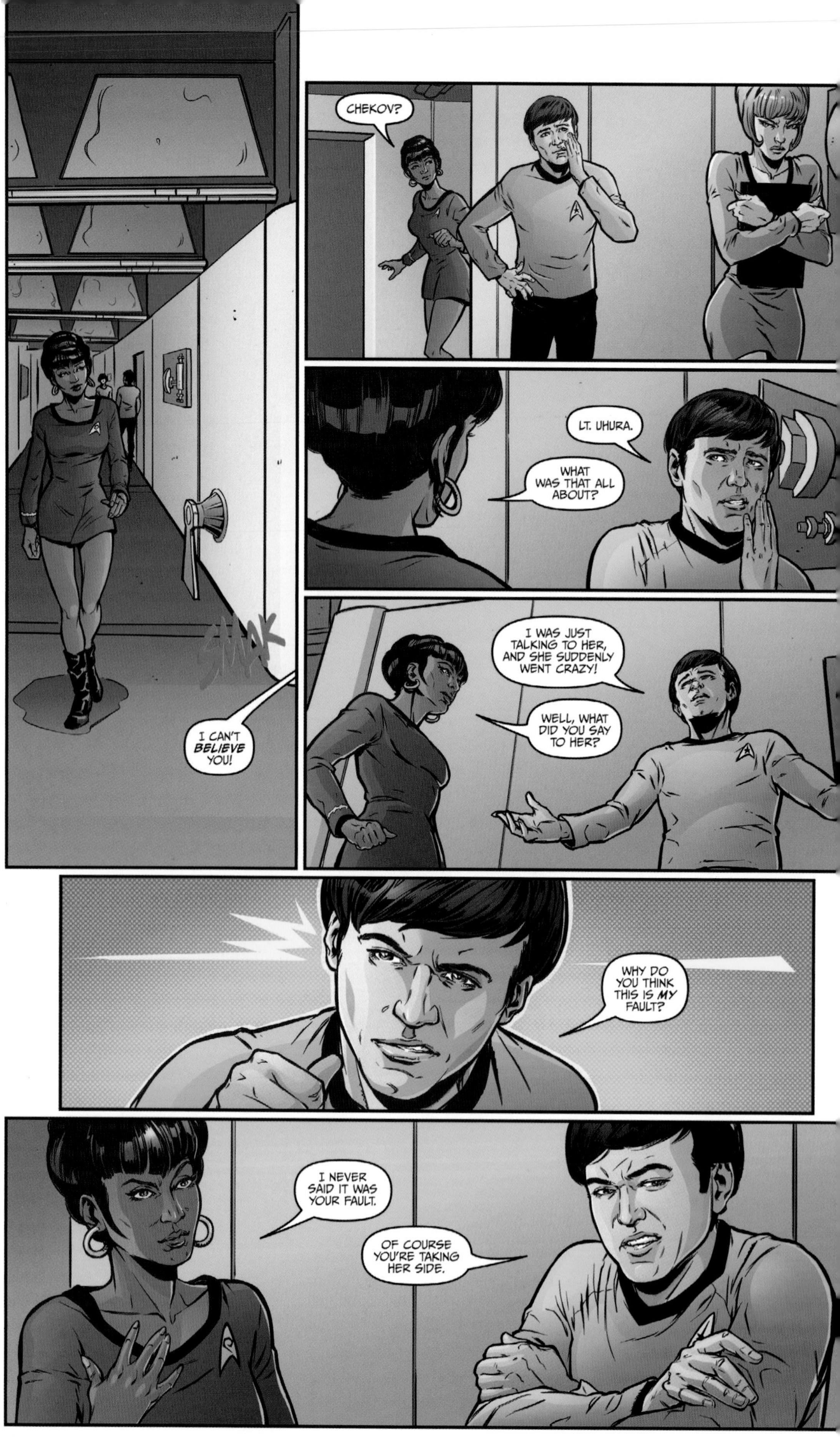
SMAK
I CAN'T BELIEVE YOU!
CHEKOV?
LT. UHURA.
WHAT WAS THAT ALL ABOUT?
I WAS JUST TALKING TO HER, AND SHE SUDDENLY WENT CRAZY!
WELL, WHAT DID YOU SAY TO HER?
WHY DO YOU THINK THIS IS MY FAULT?
I NEVER SAID IT WAS YOUR FAULT.
OF COURSE YOU'RE TAKING HER SIDE.

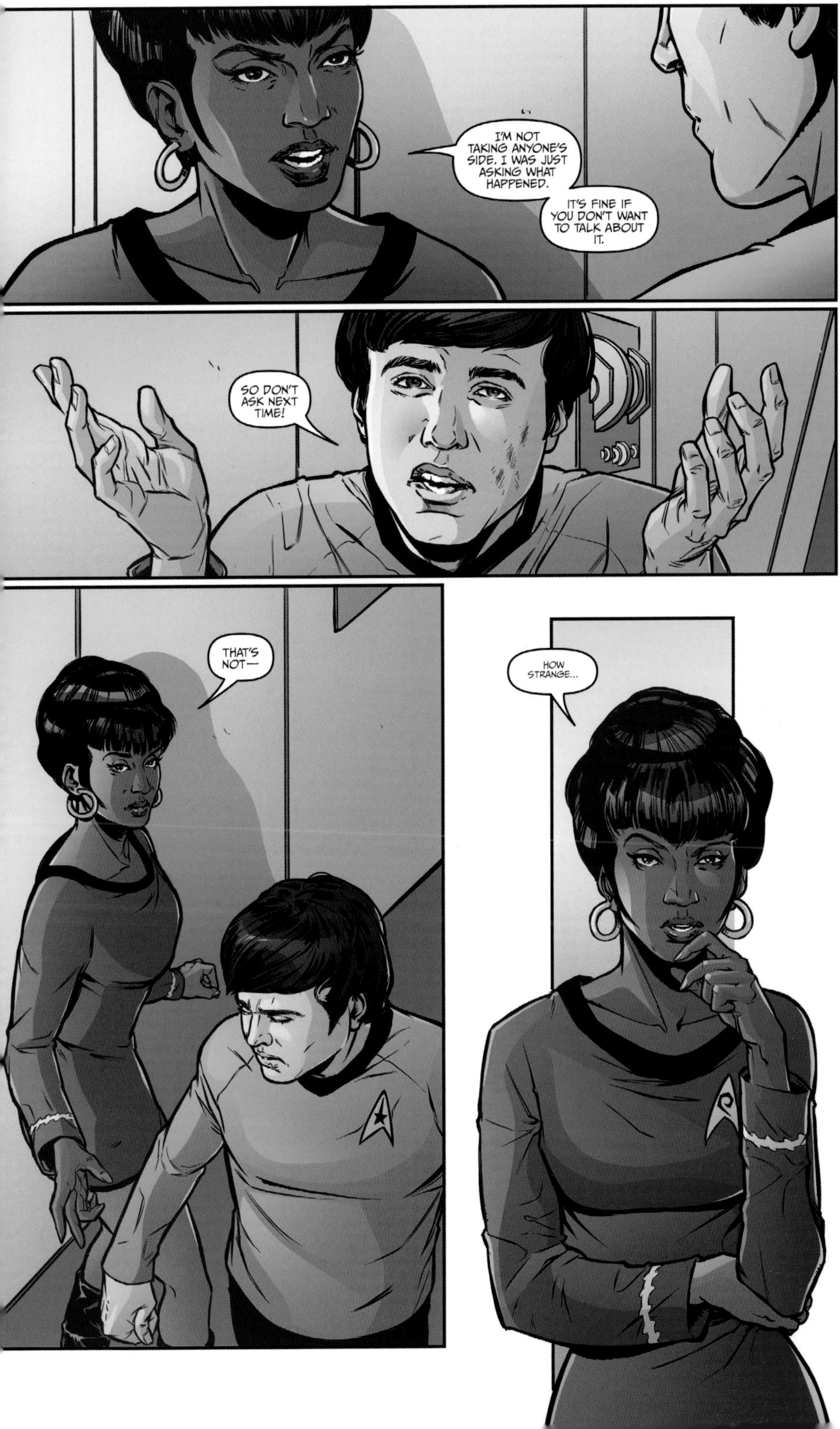
I'M NOT TAKING ANYONE'S SIDE. I WAS JUST ASKING WHAT HAPPENED.
IT'S FINE IF YOU DON'T WANT TO TALK ABOUT IT.
SO DON'T ASK NEXT TIME!
THAT'S NOT—
HOW STRANGE...

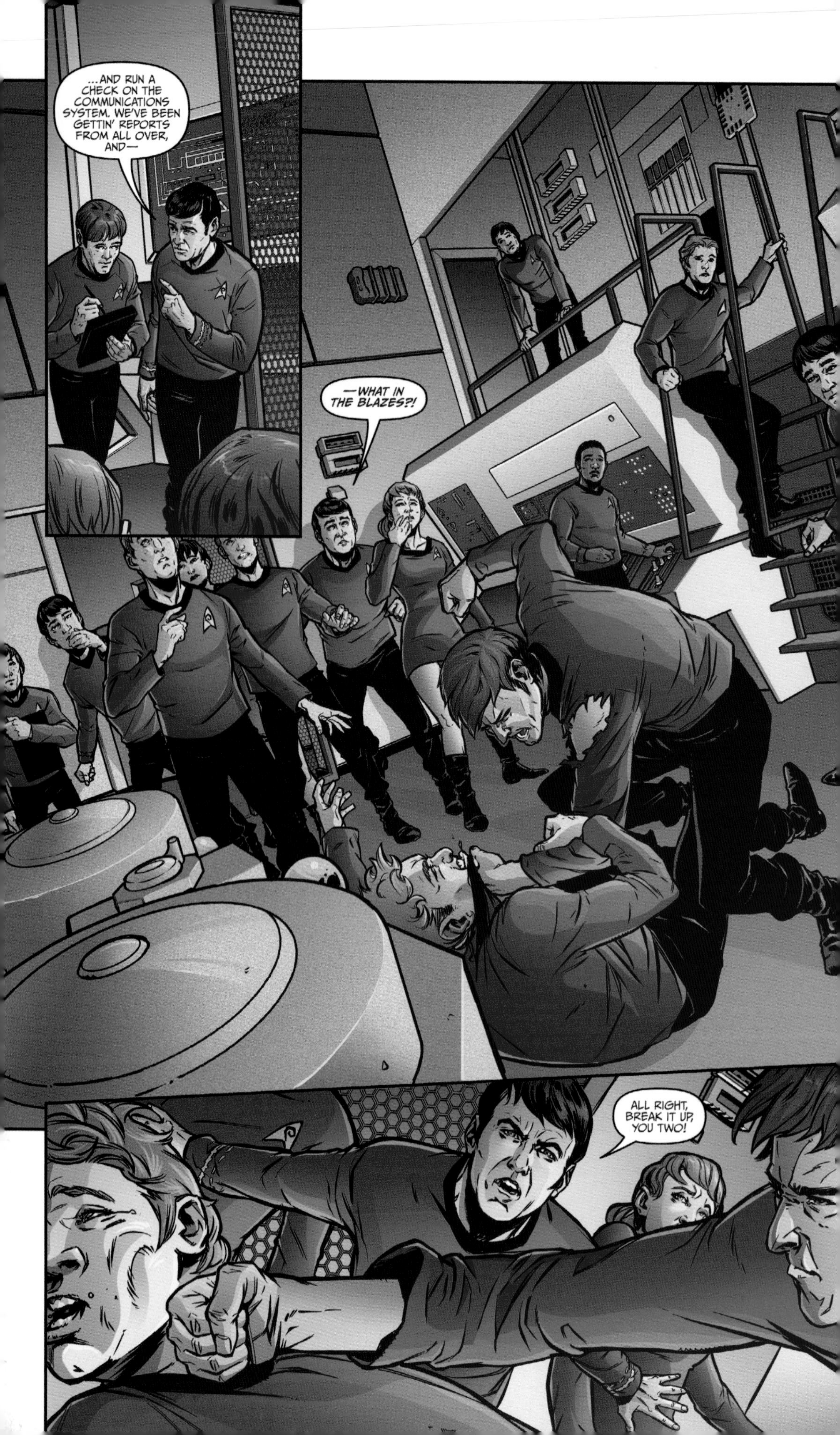
...AND RUN A CHECK ON THE COMMUNICATIONS SYSTEM. WE'VE BEEN GETTIN' REPORTS FROM ALL OVER, AND—
—WHAT IN THE BLAZES?!
ALL RIGHT, BREAK IT UP, YOU TWO!

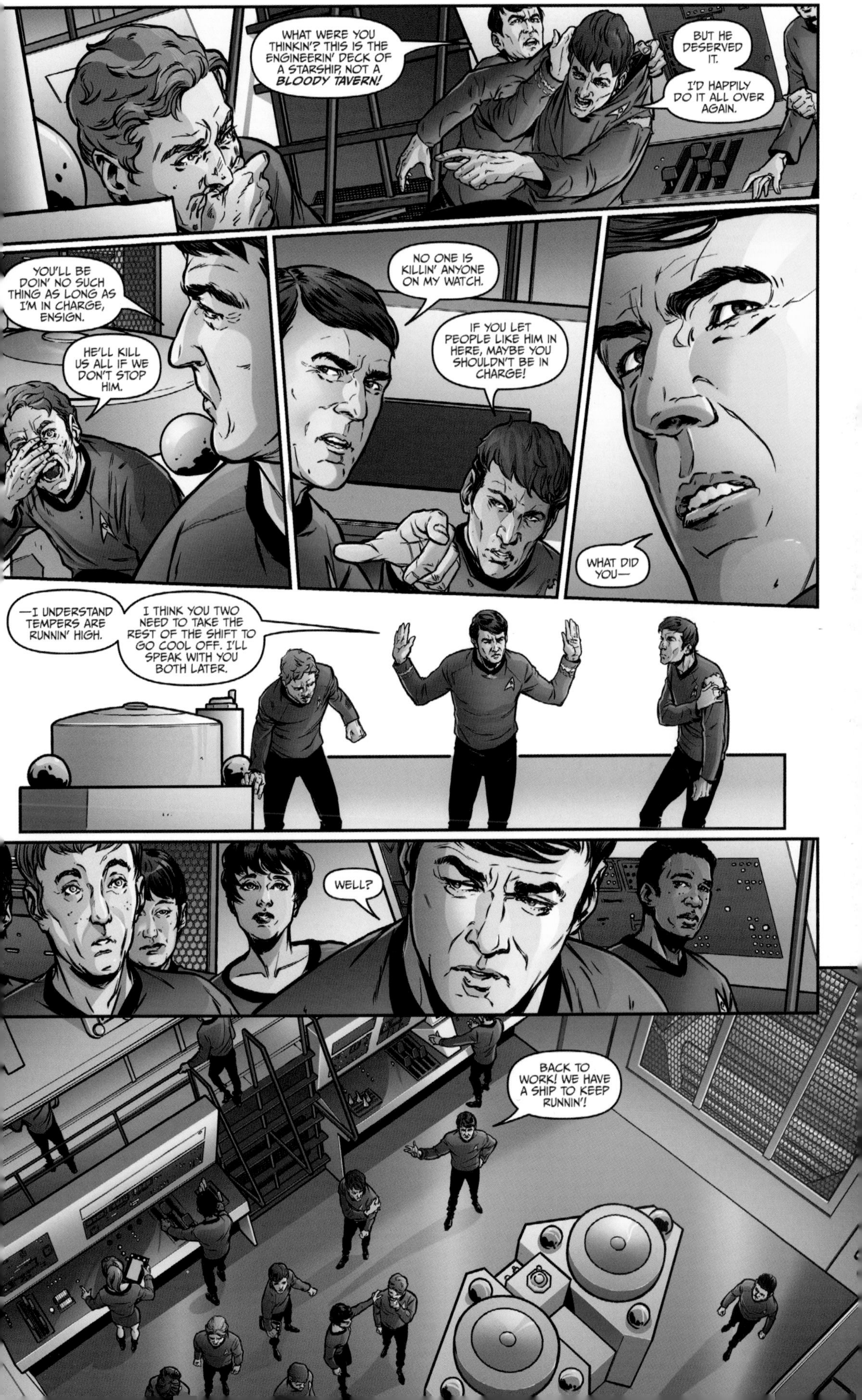
WHAT WERE YOU THINKIN'? THIS IS THE ENGINEERIN' DECK OF A STARSHIP, NOT A *BLOODY TAVERN!*
BUT HE DESERVED IT.
I'D HAPPILY DO IT ALL OVER AGAIN.
YOU'LL BE DOIN' NO SUCH THING AS LONG AS I'M IN CHARGE, ENSIGN.
HE'LL KILL US ALL IF WE DON'T STOP HIM.
NO ONE IS KILLIN' ANYONE ON MY WATCH.
IF YOU LET PEOPLE LIKE HIM IN HERE, MAYBE YOU SHOULDN'T BE IN CHARGE!
WHAT DID YOU—
—I UNDERSTAND TEMPERS ARE RUNNIN' HIGH.
I THINK YOU TWO NEED TO TAKE THE REST OF THE SHIFT TO GO COOL OFF. I'LL SPEAK WITH YOU BOTH LATER.
WELL?
BACK TO WORK! WE HAVE A SHIP TO KEEP RUNNIN'!

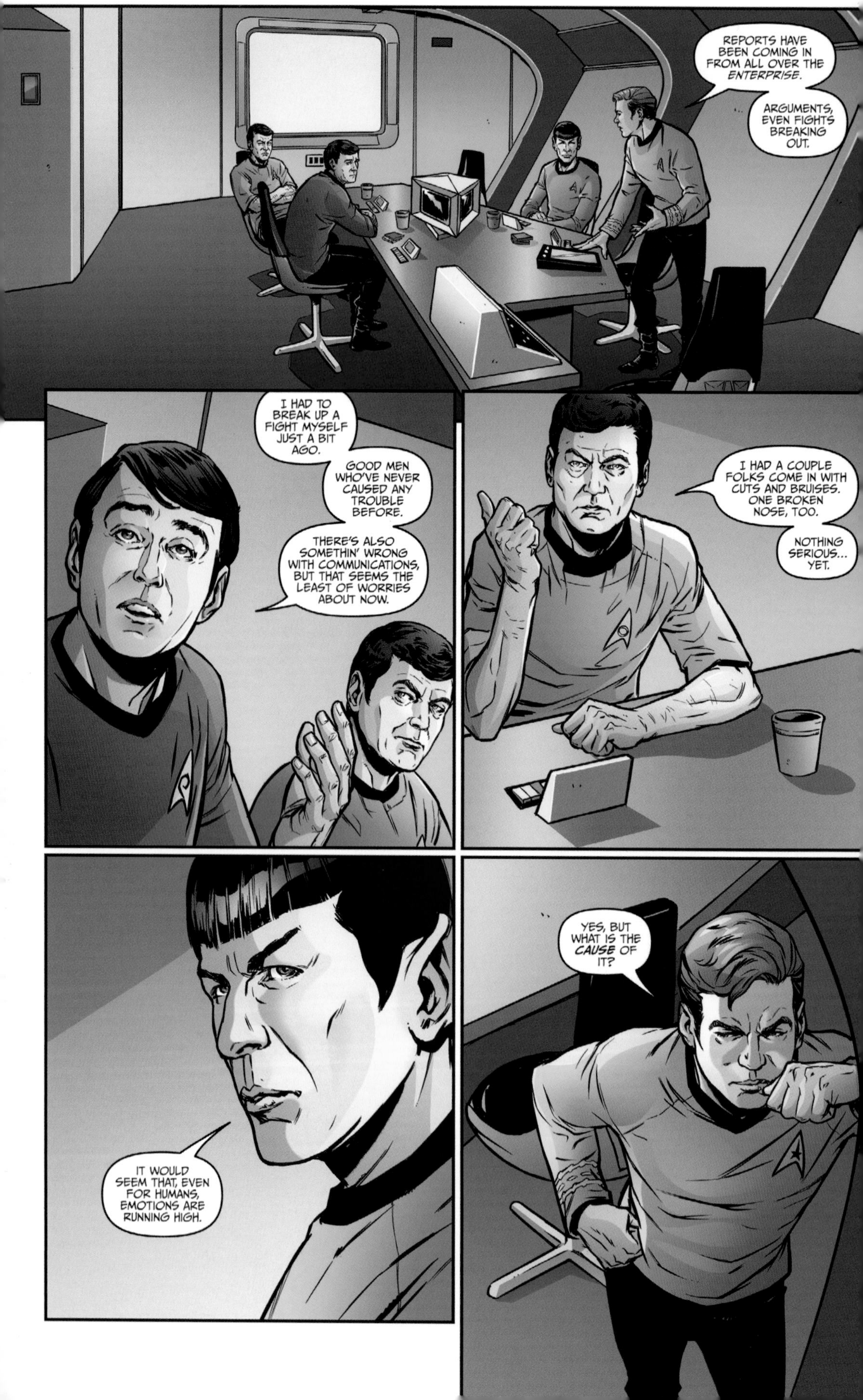
REPORTS HAVE BEEN COMING IN FROM ALL OVER THE *ENTERPRISE*.
ARGUMENTS, EVEN FIGHTS BREAKING OUT.
I HAD TO BREAK UP A FIGHT MYSELF JUST A BIT AGO.
GOOD MEN WHO'VE NEVER CAUSED ANY TROUBLE BEFORE.
THERE'S ALSO SOMETHIN' WRONG WITH COMMUNICATIONS, BUT THAT SEEMS THE LEAST OF WORRIES ABOUT NOW.
I HAD A COUPLE FOLKS COME IN WITH CUTS AND BRUISES. ONE BROKEN NOSE, TOO.
NOTHING SERIOUS... YET.
IT WOULD SEEM THAT, EVEN FOR HUMANS, EMOTIONS ARE RUNNING HIGH.
YES, BUT WHAT IS THE ***CAUSE*** OF IT?

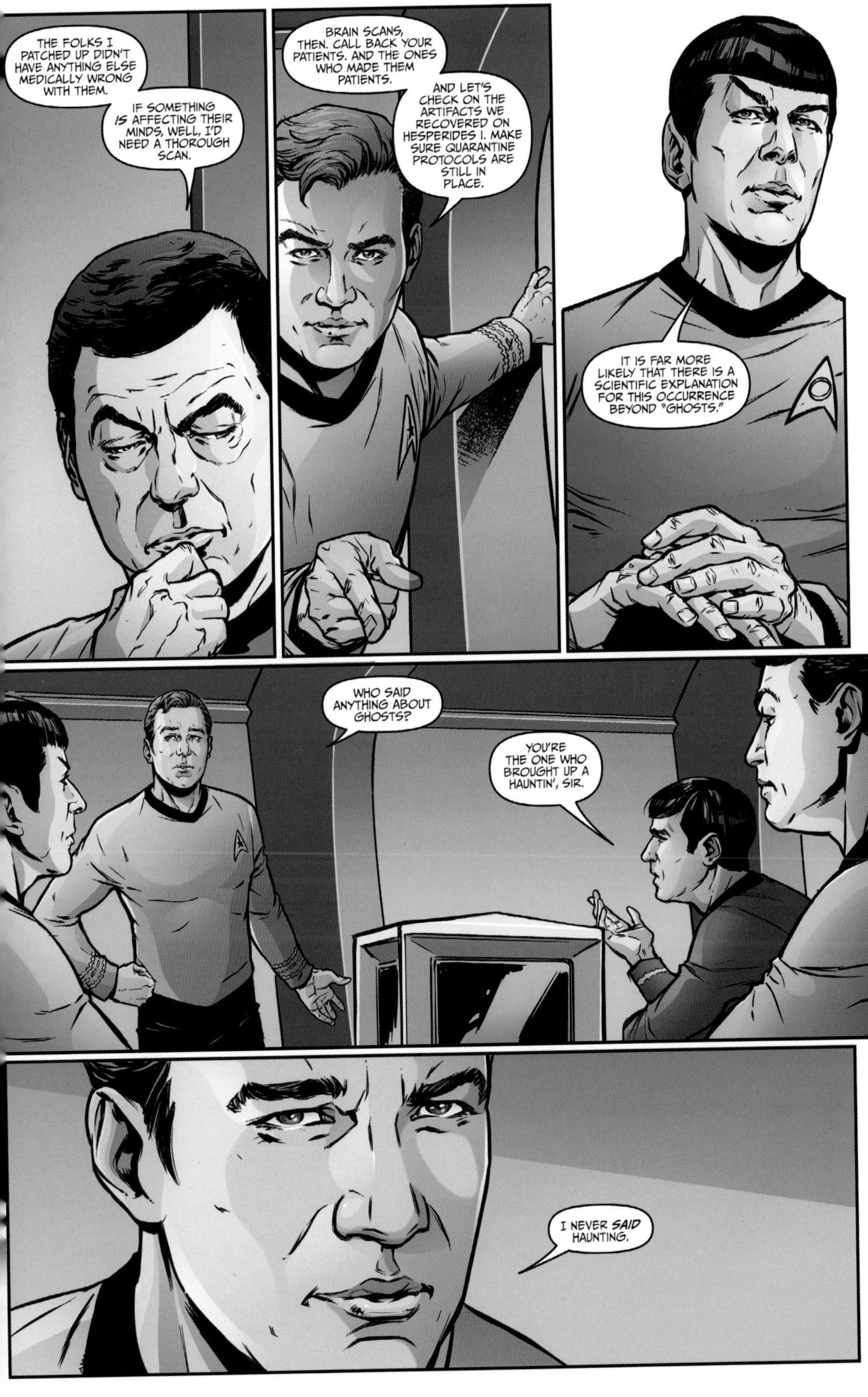
THE FOLKS I PATCHED UP DIDN'T HAVE ANYTHING ELSE MEDICALLY WRONG WITH THEM.
IF SOMETHING *IS* AFFECTING THEIR MINDS, WELL, I'D NEED A THOROUGH SCAN.
BRAIN SCANS, THEN. CALL BACK YOUR PATIENTS. AND THE ONES WHO MADE THEM PATIENTS.
AND LET'S CHECK ON THE ARTIFACTS WE RECOVERED ON HESPERIDES I. MAKE SURE QUARANTINE PROTOCOLS ARE STILL IN PLACE.
IT IS FAR MORE LIKELY THAT THERE IS A SCIENTIFIC EXPLANATION FOR THIS OCCURRENCE BEYOND "GHOSTS."
WHO SAID ANYTHING ABOUT GHOSTS?
YOU'RE THE ONE WHO BROUGHT UP A HAUNTIN', SIR.
I NEVER ***SAID*** HAUNTING.

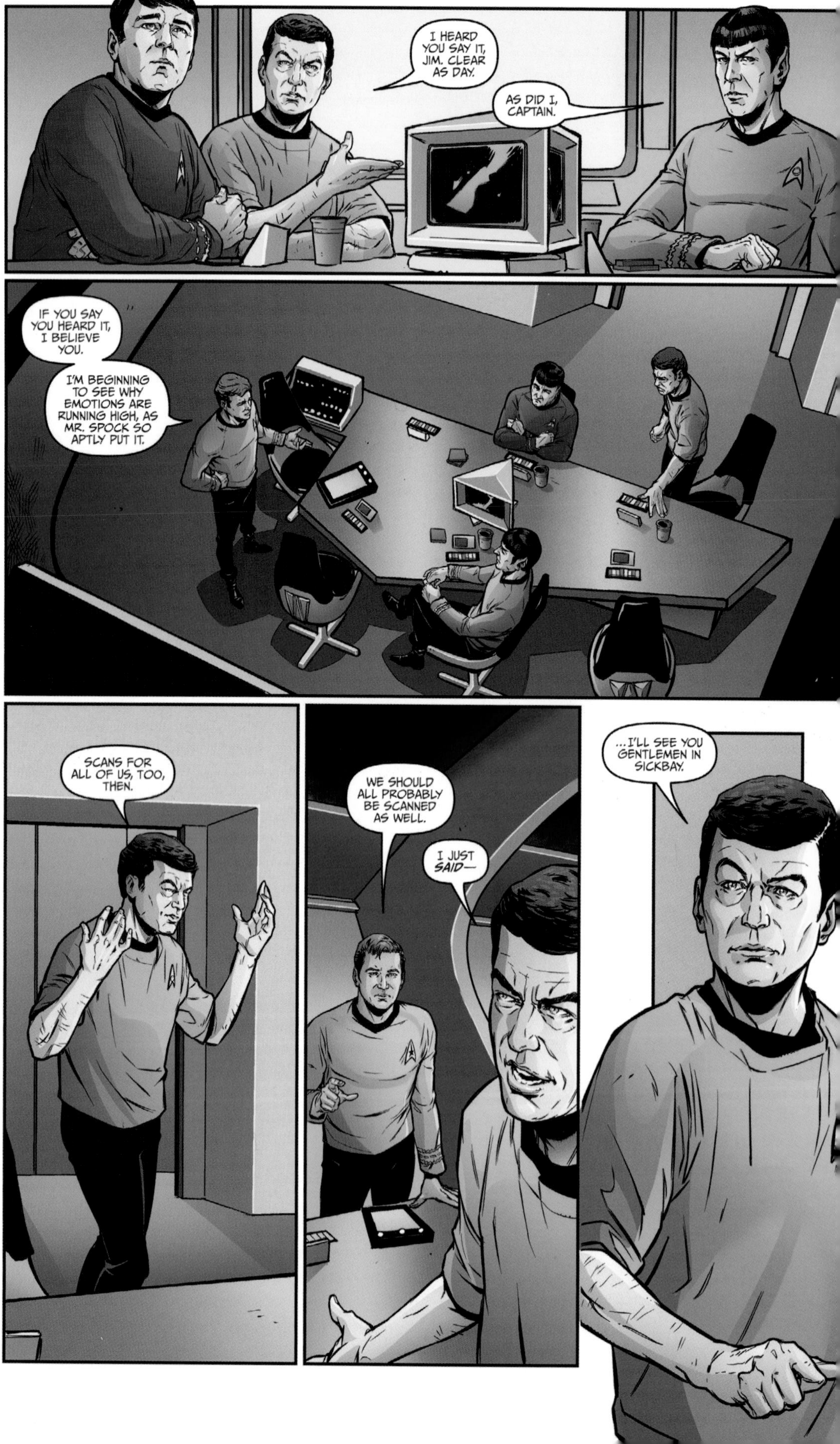
I HEARD YOU SAY IT, JIM. CLEAR AS DAY.
AS DID I, CAPTAIN.
IF YOU SAY YOU HEARD IT, I BELIEVE YOU.
I'M BEGINNING TO SEE WHY EMOTIONS ARE RUNNING HIGH, AS MR. SPOCK SO APTLY PUT IT.
SCANS FOR ALL OF US, TOO, THEN.
WE SHOULD ALL PROBABLY BE SCANNED AS WELL.
I JUST *SAID*—
...I'LL SEE YOU GENTLEMEN IN SICKBAY.

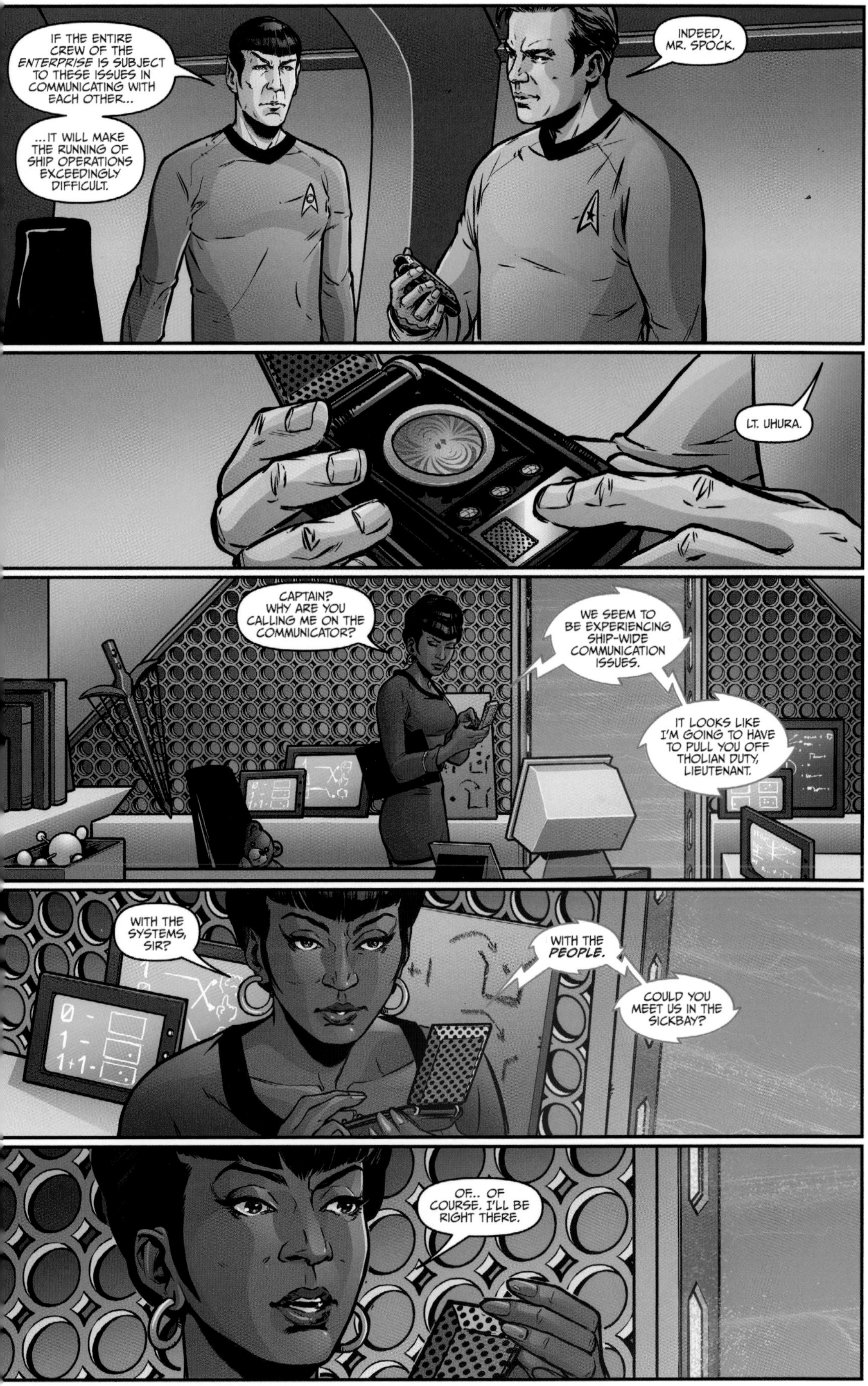
IF THE ENTIRE CREW OF THE *ENTERPRISE* IS SUBJECT TO THESE ISSUES IN COMMUNICATING WITH EACH OTHER...
...IT WILL MAKE THE RUNNING OF SHIP OPERATIONS EXCEEDINGLY DIFFICULT.
INDEED, MR. SPOCK.
LT. UHURA.
CAPTAIN? WHY ARE YOU CALLING ME ON THE COMMUNICATOR?
WE SEEM TO BE EXPERIENCING SHIP-WIDE COMMUNICATION ISSUES.
IT LOOKS LIKE I'M GOING TO HAVE TO PULL YOU OFF THOLIAN DUTY, LIEUTENANT.
WITH THE SYSTEMS, SIR?
WITH THE *PEOPLE.*
COULD YOU MEET US IN THE SICKBAY?
OF... OF COURSE. I'LL BE RIGHT THERE.

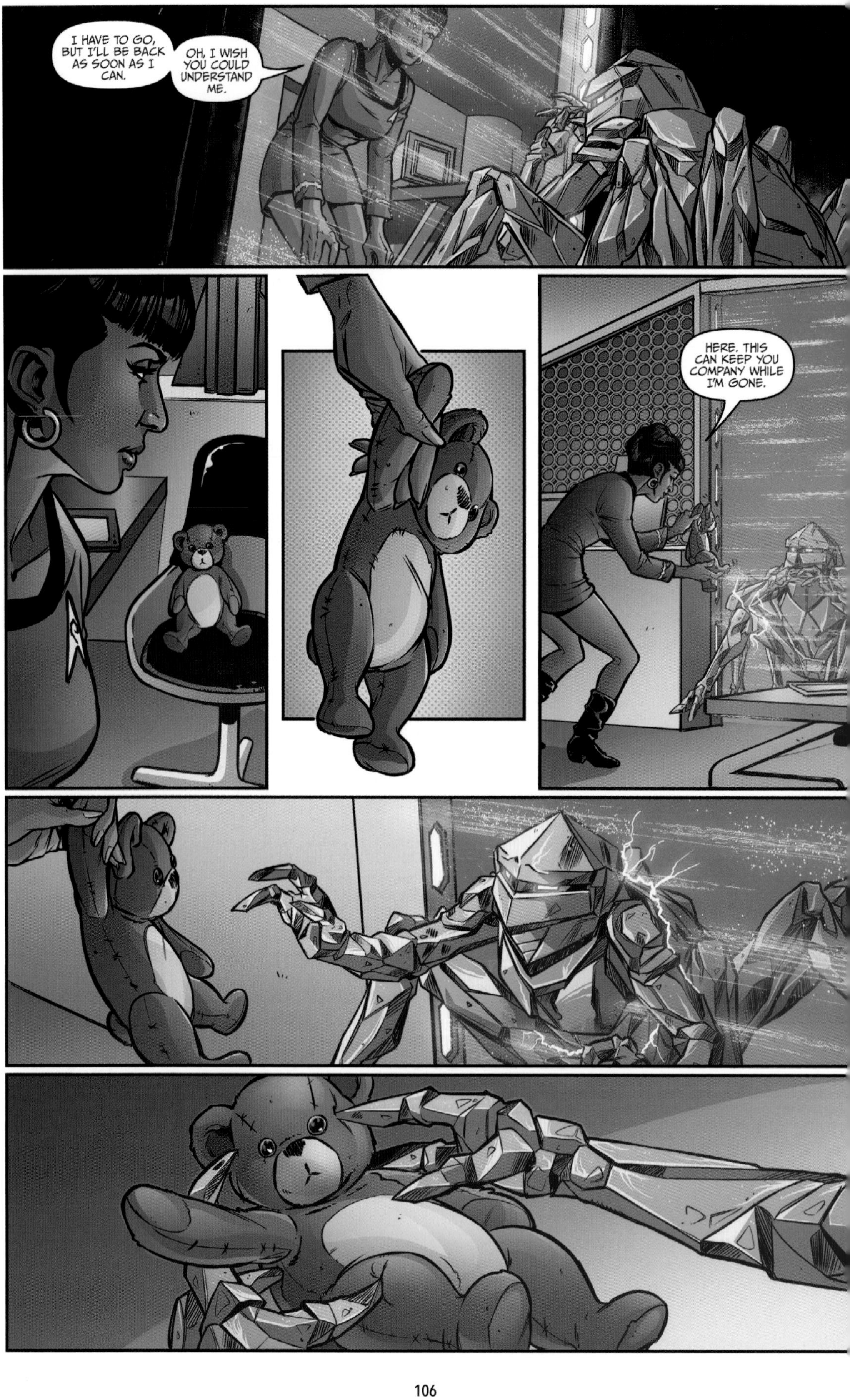
I HAVE TO GO, BUT I'LL BE BACK AS SOON AS I CAN.
OH, I WISH YOU COULD UNDERSTAND ME.
HERE. THIS CAN KEEP YOU COMPANY WHILE I'M GONE.

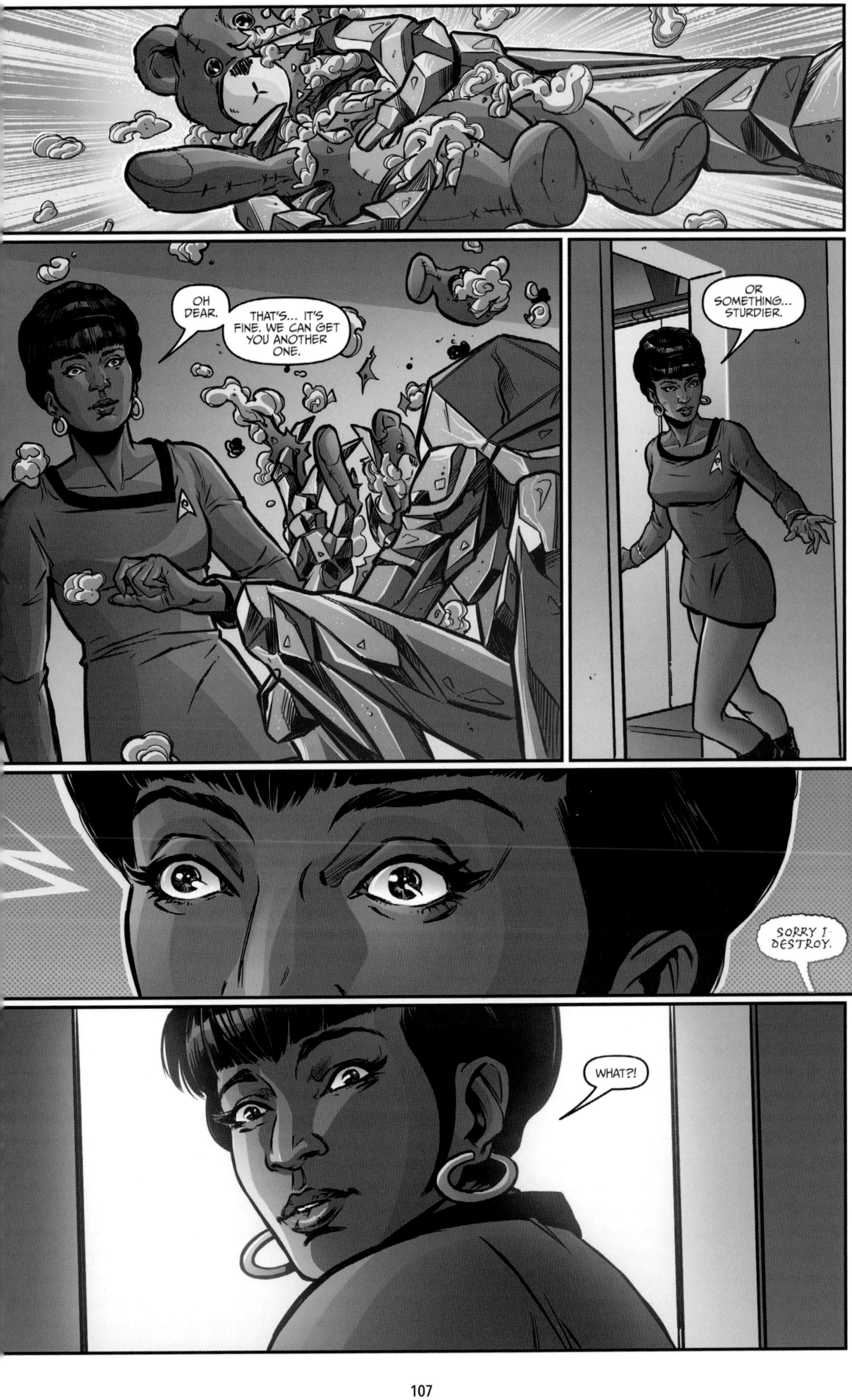
OH DEAR.
THAT'S... IT'S FINE. WE CAN GET YOU ANOTHER ONE.
OR SOMETHING... STURDIER.
SORRY I DESTROY.
WHAT?!

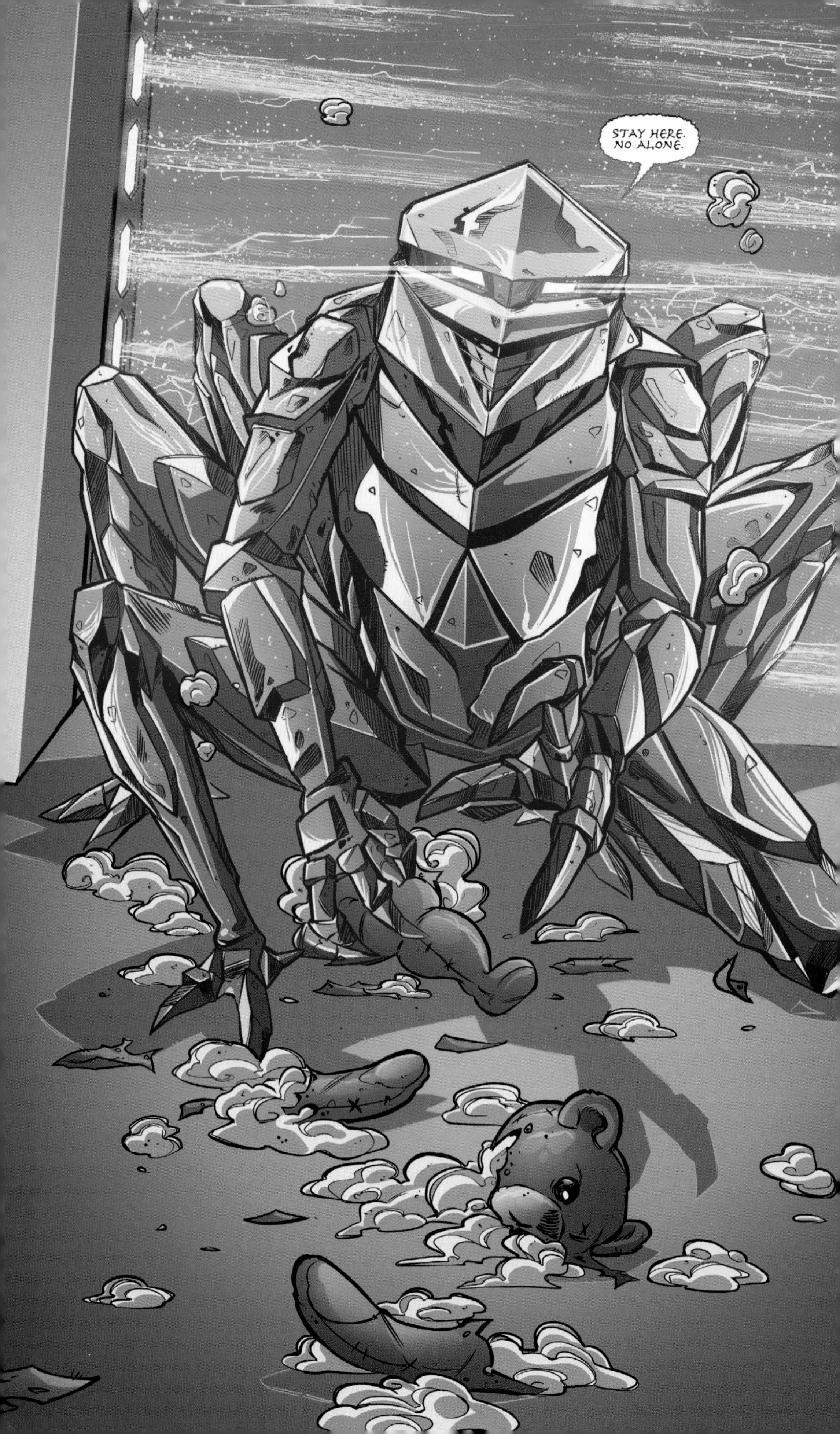
STAY HERE.
NO ALONE.

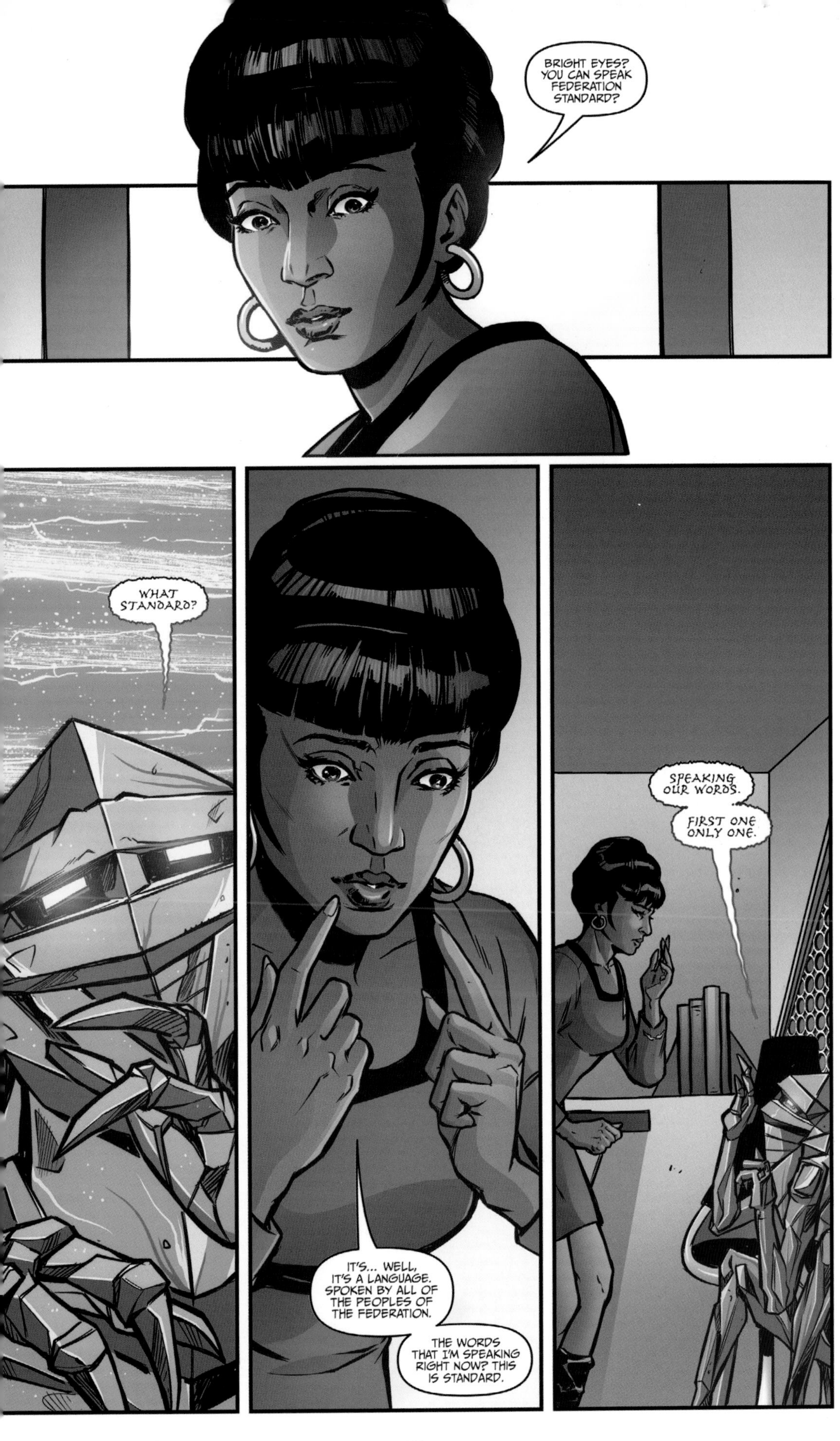
BRIGHT EYES? YOU CAN SPEAK FEDERATION STANDARD?
WHAT STANDARD?
IT'S... WELL, IT'S A LANGUAGE. SPOKEN BY ALL OF THE PEOPLES OF THE FEDERATION.
THE WORDS THAT I'M SPEAKING RIGHT NOW? THIS IS STANDARD.
SPEAKING OUR WORDS.
FIRST ONE ONLY ONE.

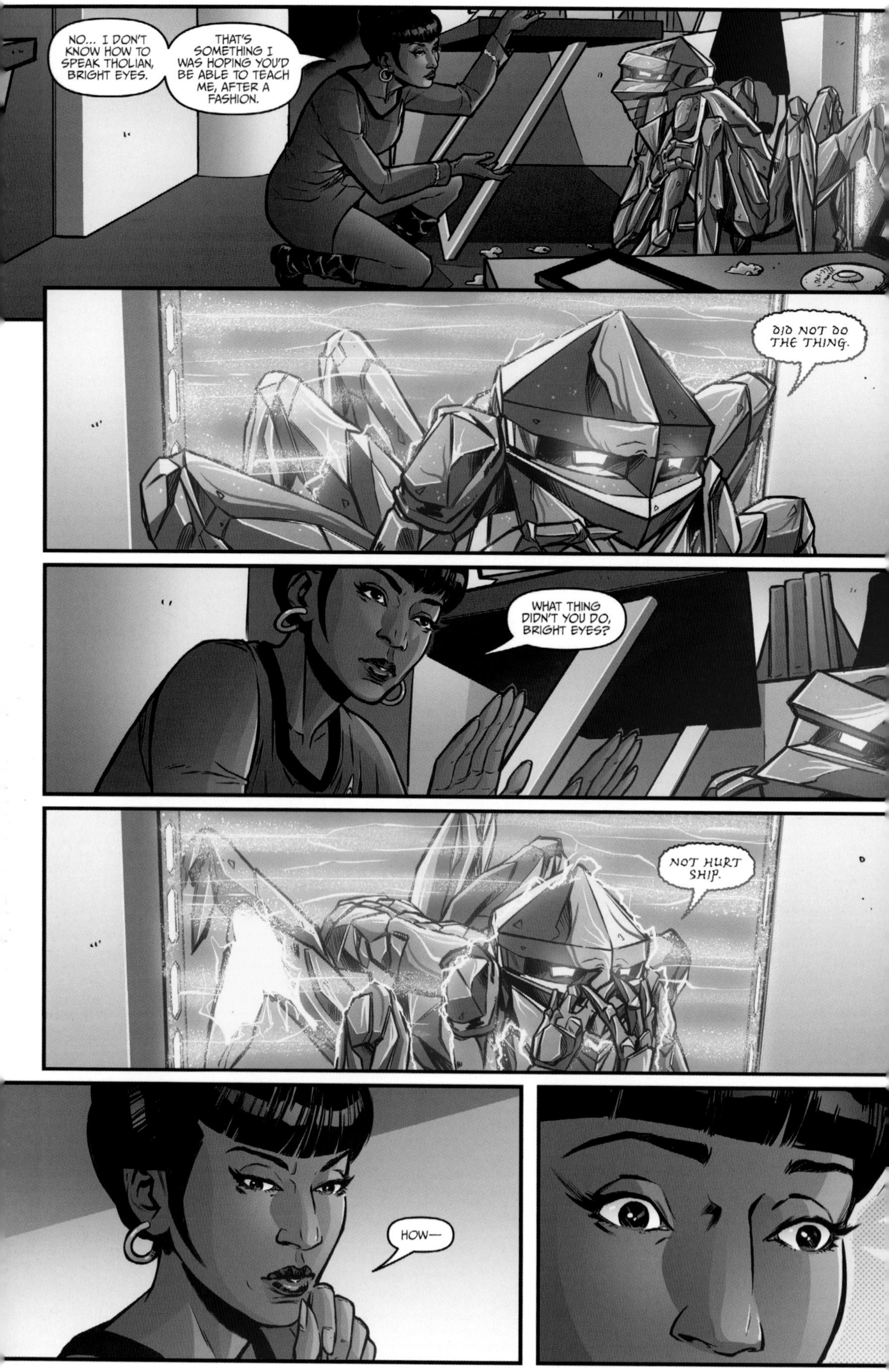

NO... I DON'T KNOW HOW TO SPEAK THOLIAN, BRIGHT EYES.
THAT'S SOMETHING I WAS HOPING YOU'D BE ABLE TO TEACH ME, AFTER A FASHION.
DID NOT DO THE THING.
WHAT THING DIDN'T YOU DO, BRIGHT EYES?
NOT HURT SHIP.
HOW—

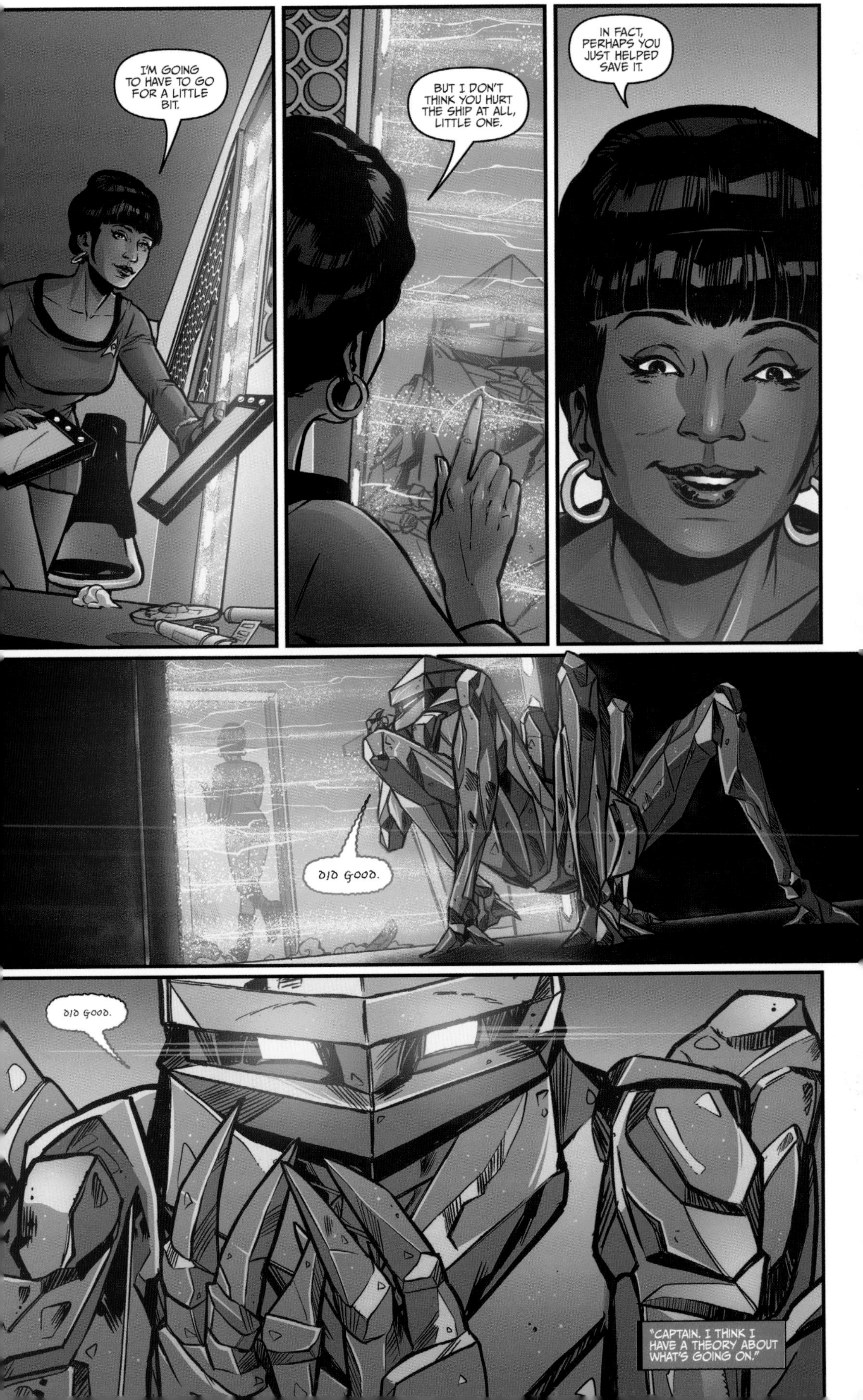
I'M GOING TO HAVE TO GO FOR A LITTLE BIT.
BUT I DON'T THINK YOU HURT THE SHIP AT ALL, LITTLE ONE.
IN FACT, PERHAPS YOU JUST HELPED SAVE IT.
DID GOOD.
DID GOOD.
"CAPTAIN, I THINK I HAVE A THEORY ABOUT WHAT'S GOING ON."

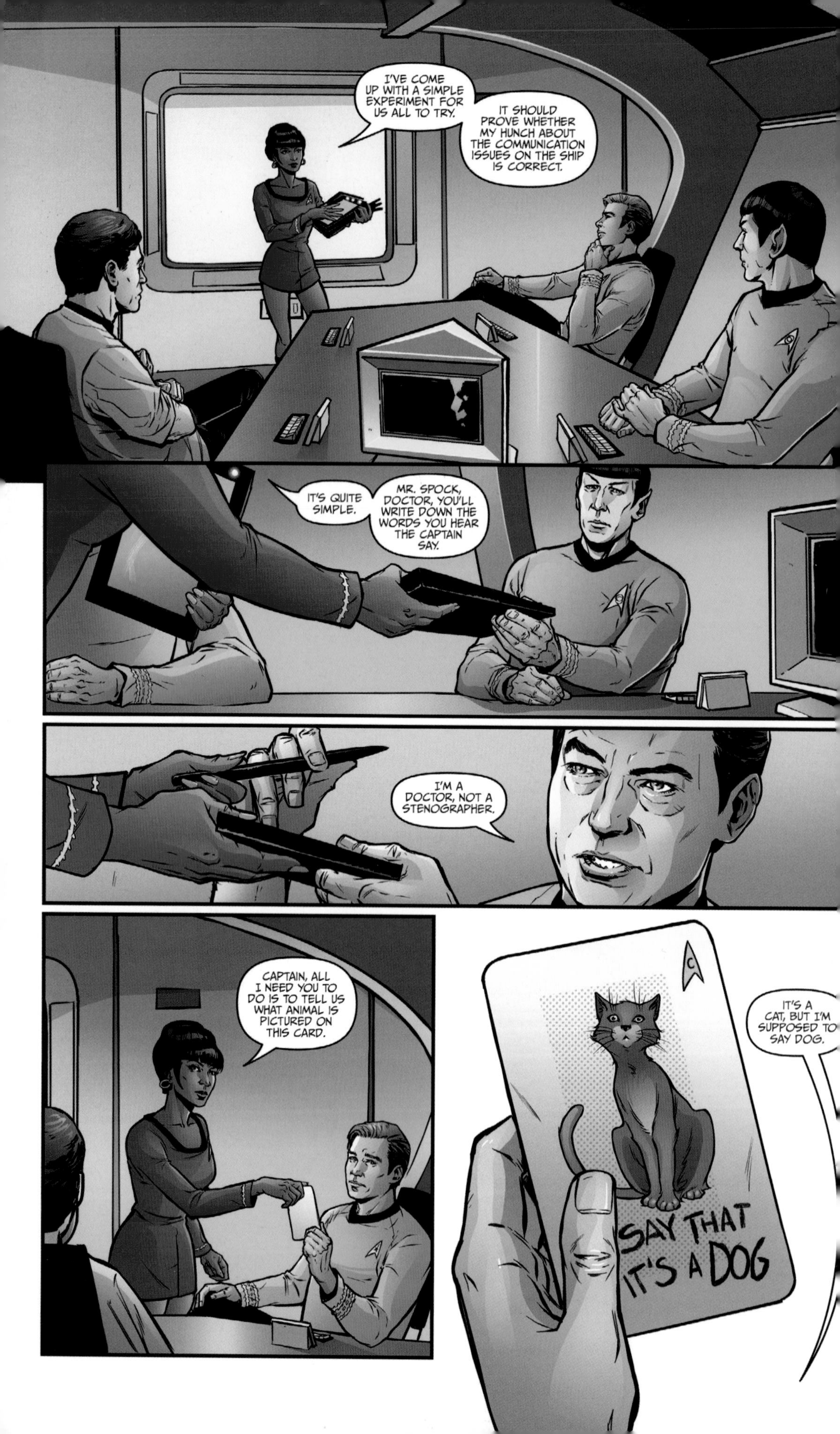
I'VE COME UP WITH A SIMPLE EXPERIMENT FOR US ALL TO TRY.
IT SHOULD PROVE WHETHER MY HUNCH ABOUT THE COMMUNICATION ISSUES ON THE SHIP IS CORRECT.
IT'S QUITE SIMPLE.
MR. SPOCK, DOCTOR, YOU'LL WRITE DOWN THE WORDS YOU HEAR THE CAPTAIN SAY.
I'M A DOCTOR, NOT A STENOGRAPHER.
CAPTAIN, ALL I NEED YOU TO DO IS TO TELL US WHAT ANIMAL IS PICTURED ON THIS CARD.
SAY THAT IT'S A DOG
IT'S A CAT, BUT I'M SUPPOSED TO SAY DOG.

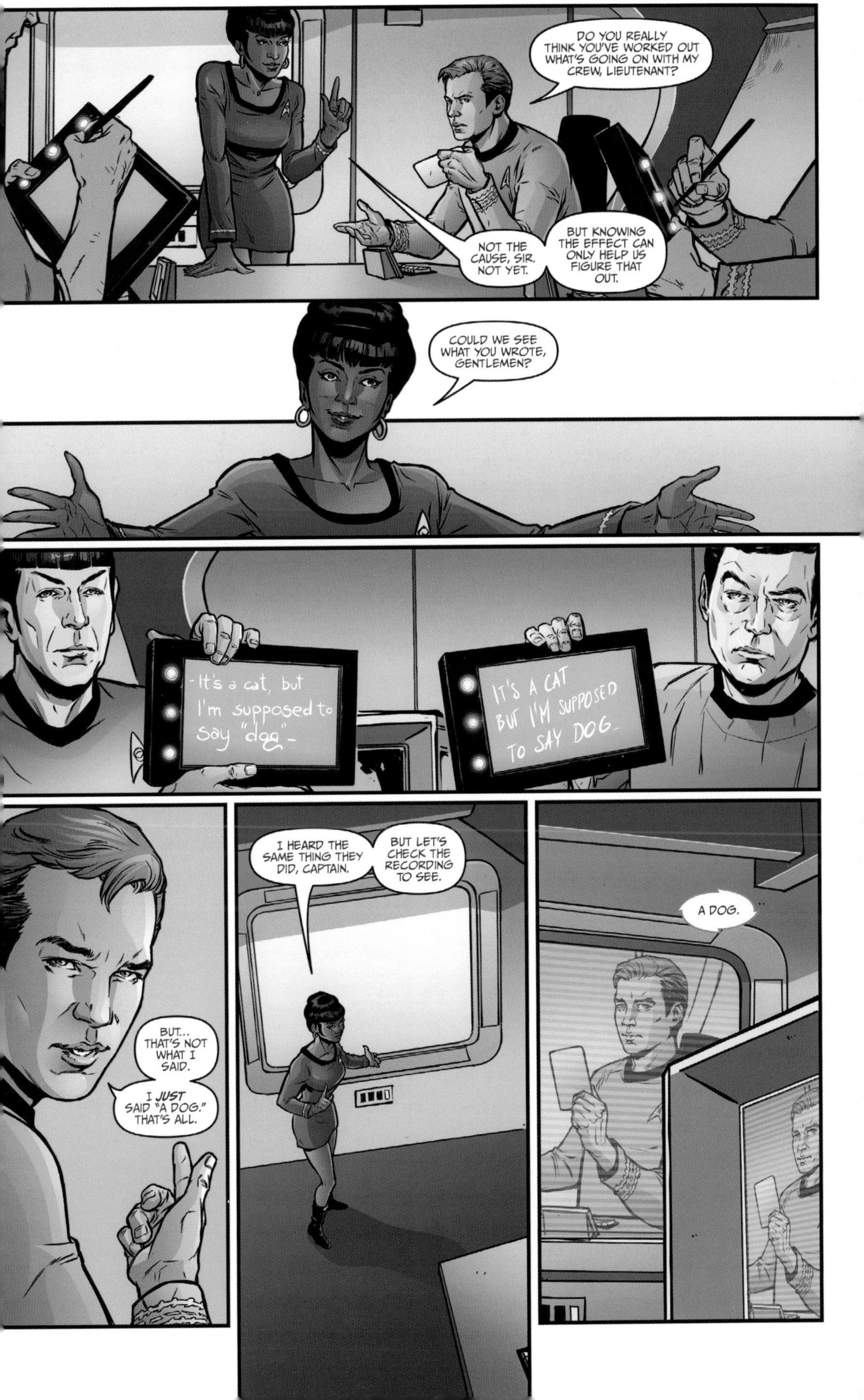
DO YOU REALLY THINK YOU'VE WORKED OUT WHAT'S GOING ON WITH MY CREW, LIEUTENANT?
NOT THE CAUSE, SIR. NOT YET.
BUT KNOWING THE EFFECT CAN ONLY HELP US FIGURE THAT OUT.
COULD WE SEE WHAT YOU WROTE, GENTLEMEN?
-It's a cat, but I'm supposed to say "dog."-
IT'S A CAT BUT I'M SUPPOSED TO SAY DOG.
BUT... THAT'S NOT WHAT I SAID.
I JUST SAID "A DOG." THAT'S ALL.
I HEARD THE SAME THING THEY DID, CAPTAIN.
BUT LET'S CHECK THE RECORDING TO SEE.
A DOG.

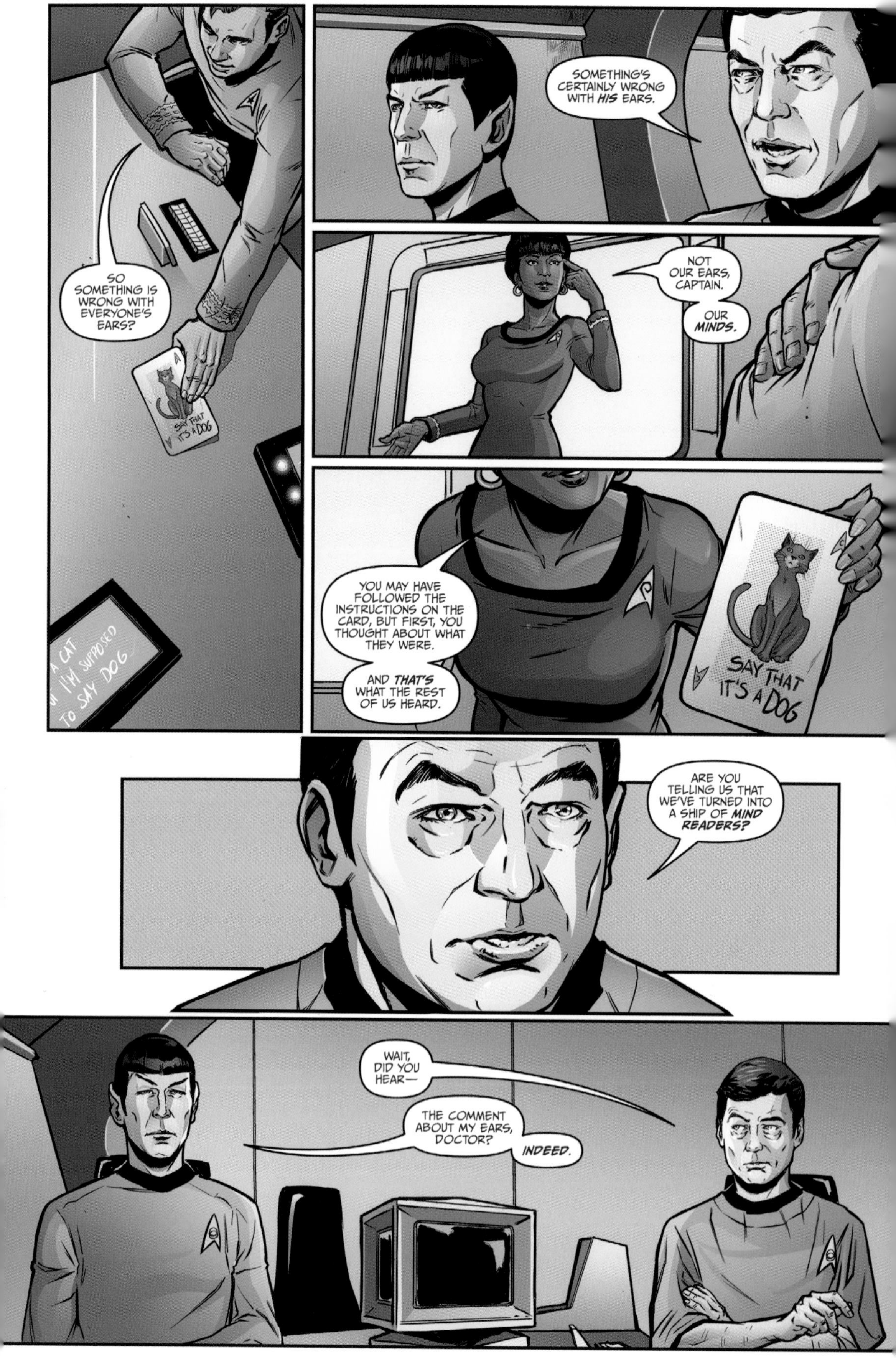
SO SOMETHING IS WRONG WITH EVERYONE'S EARS?
SAY THAT IT'S A DOG
A CAT ... I'M SUPPOSED TO SAY DOG...
SOMETHING'S CERTAINLY WRONG WITH HIS EARS.
NOT OUR EARS, CAPTAIN.
OUR MINDS.
YOU MAY HAVE FOLLOWED THE INSTRUCTIONS ON THE CARD, BUT FIRST, YOU THOUGHT ABOUT WHAT THEY WERE.
AND THAT'S WHAT THE REST OF US HEARD.
SAY THAT IT'S A DOG
ARE YOU TELLING US THAT WE'VE TURNED INTO A SHIP OF MIND READERS?
WAIT, DID YOU HEAR—
THE COMMENT ABOUT MY EARS, DOCTOR?
INDEED.

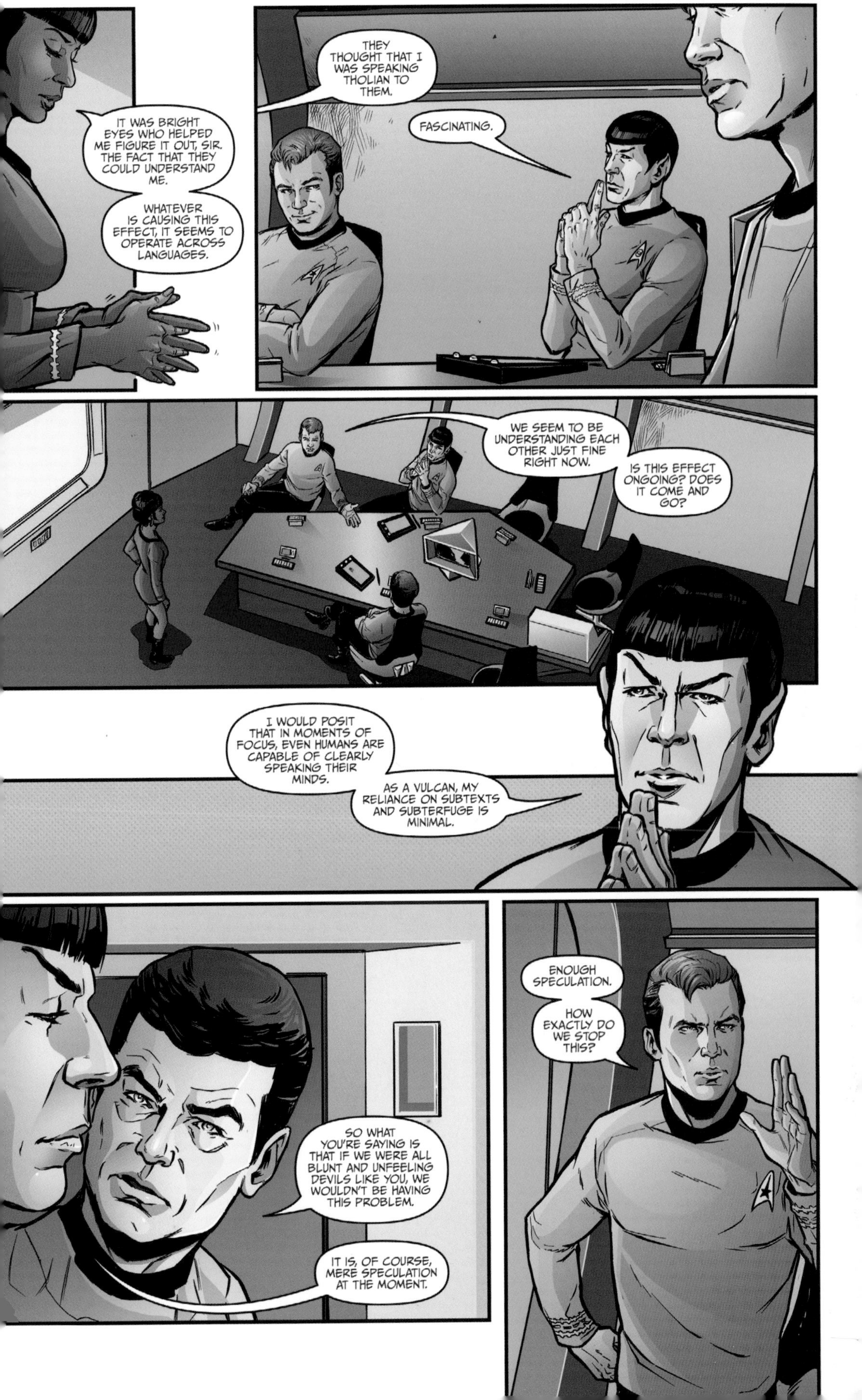
IT WAS BRIGHT EYES WHO HELPED ME FIGURE IT OUT, SIR. THE FACT THAT THEY COULD UNDERSTAND ME.
WHATEVER IS CAUSING THIS EFFECT, IT SEEMS TO OPERATE ACROSS LANGUAGES.
THEY THOUGHT THAT I WAS SPEAKING THOLIAN TO THEM.
FASCINATING.
WE SEEM TO BE UNDERSTANDING EACH OTHER JUST FINE RIGHT NOW.
IS THIS EFFECT ONGOING? DOES IT COME AND GO?
I WOULD POSIT THAT IN MOMENTS OF FOCUS, EVEN HUMANS ARE CAPABLE OF CLEARLY SPEAKING THEIR MINDS.
AS A VULCAN, MY RELIANCE ON SUBTEXTS AND SUBTERFUGE IS MINIMAL.
SO WHAT YOU'RE SAYING IS THAT IF WE WERE ALL BLUNT AND UNFEELING DEVILS LIKE YOU, WE WOULDN'T BE HAVING THIS PROBLEM.
IT IS, OF COURSE, MERE SPECULATION AT THE MOMENT.
ENOUGH SPECULATION.
HOW EXACTLY DO WE STOP THIS?

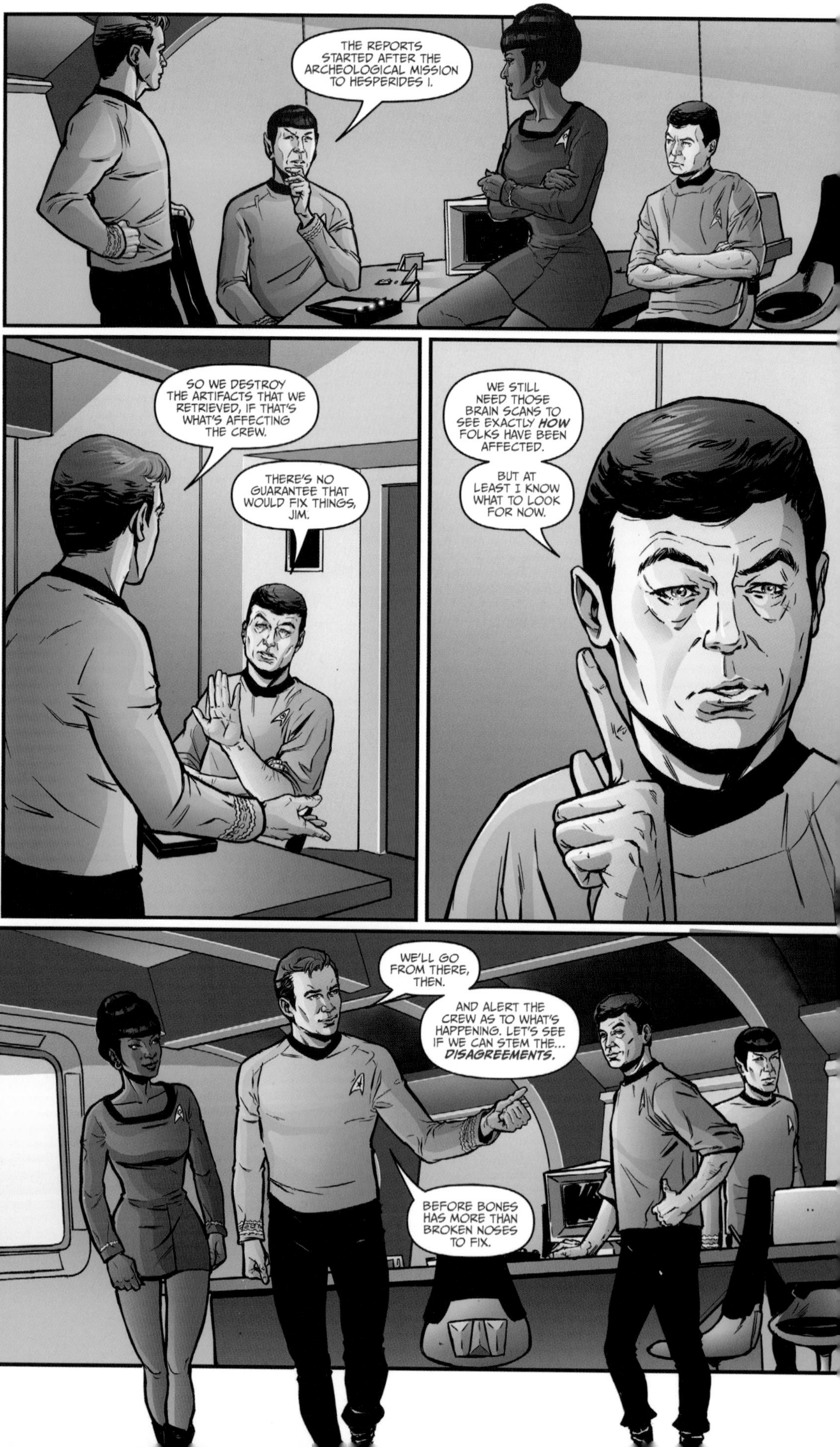
THE REPORTS STARTED AFTER THE ARCHEOLOGICAL MISSION TO HESPERIDES I.
SO WE DESTROY THE ARTIFACTS THAT WE RETRIEVED, IF THAT'S WHAT'S AFFECTING THE CREW.
THERE'S NO GUARANTEE THAT WOULD FIX THINGS, JIM.
WE STILL NEED THOSE BRAIN SCANS TO SEE EXACTLY **HOW** FOLKS HAVE BEEN AFFECTED.
BUT AT LEAST I KNOW WHAT TO LOOK FOR NOW.
WE'LL GO FROM THERE, THEN.
AND ALERT THE CREW AS TO WHAT'S HAPPENING. LET'S SEE IF WE CAN STEM THE... ***DISAGREEMENTS.***
BEFORE BONES HAS MORE THAN BROKEN NOSES TO FIX.

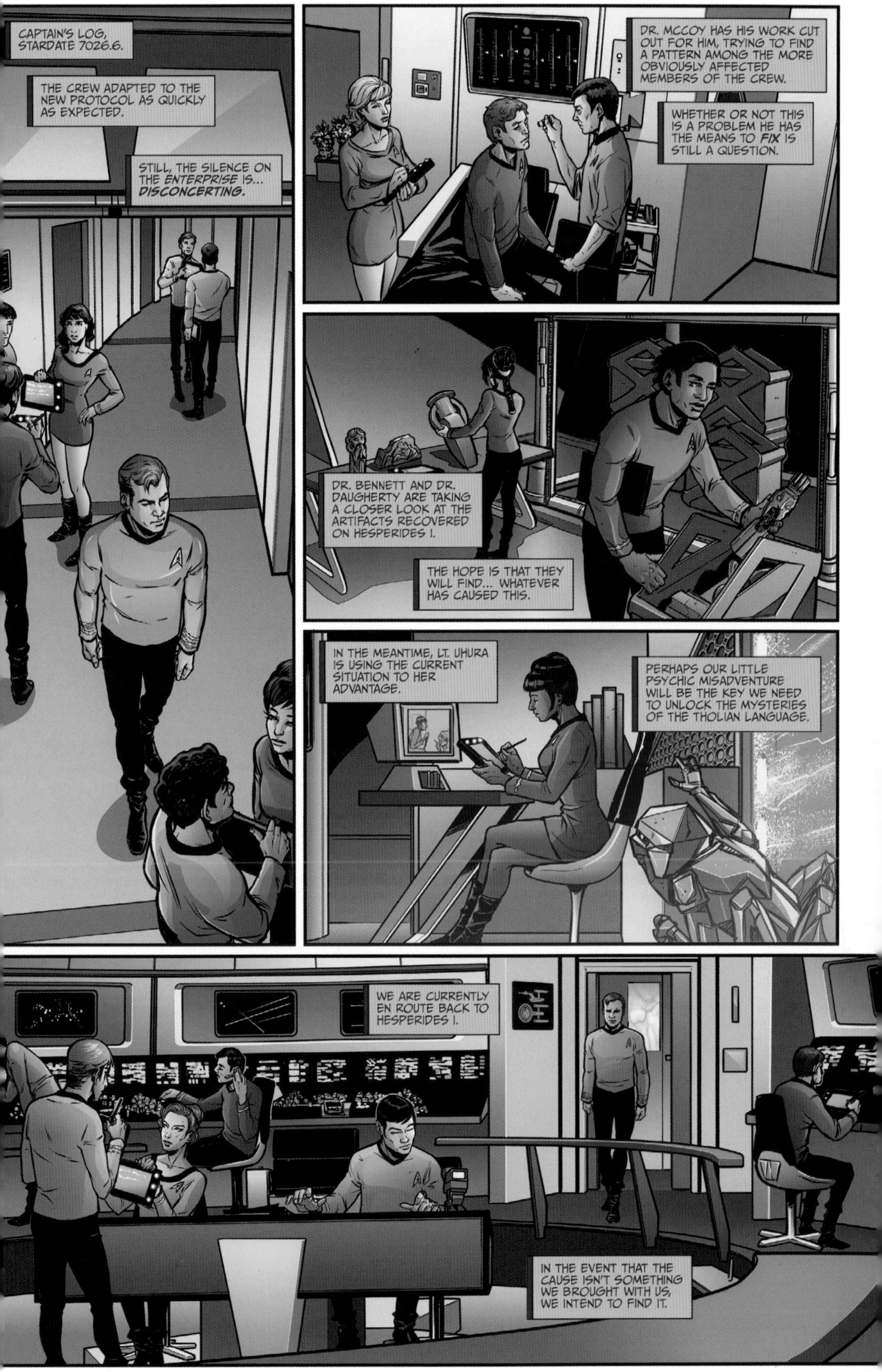
CAPTAIN'S LOG, STARDATE 7026.6.
THE CREW ADAPTED TO THE NEW PROTOCOL AS QUICKLY AS EXPECTED.
STILL, THE SILENCE ON THE *ENTERPRISE* IS... ***DISCONCERTING.***
DR. MCCOY HAS HIS WORK CUT OUT FOR HIM, TRYING TO FIND A PATTERN AMONG THE MORE OBVIOUSLY AFFECTED MEMBERS OF THE CREW.
WHETHER OR NOT THIS IS A PROBLEM HE HAS THE MEANS TO ***FIX*** IS STILL A QUESTION.
DR. BENNETT AND DR. DAUGHERTY ARE TAKING A CLOSER LOOK AT THE ARTIFACTS RECOVERED ON HESPERIDES I.
THE HOPE IS THAT THEY WILL FIND... WHATEVER HAS CAUSED THIS.
IN THE MEANTIME, LT. UHURA IS USING THE CURRENT SITUATION TO HER ADVANTAGE.
PERHAPS OUR LITTLE PSYCHIC MISADVENTURE WILL BE THE KEY WE NEED TO UNLOCK THE MYSTERIES OF THE THOLIAN LANGUAGE.
WE ARE CURRENTLY EN ROUTE BACK TO HESPERIDES I.
IN THE EVENT THAT THE CAUSE ISN'T SOMETHING WE BROUGHT WITH US, WE INTEND TO FIND IT.

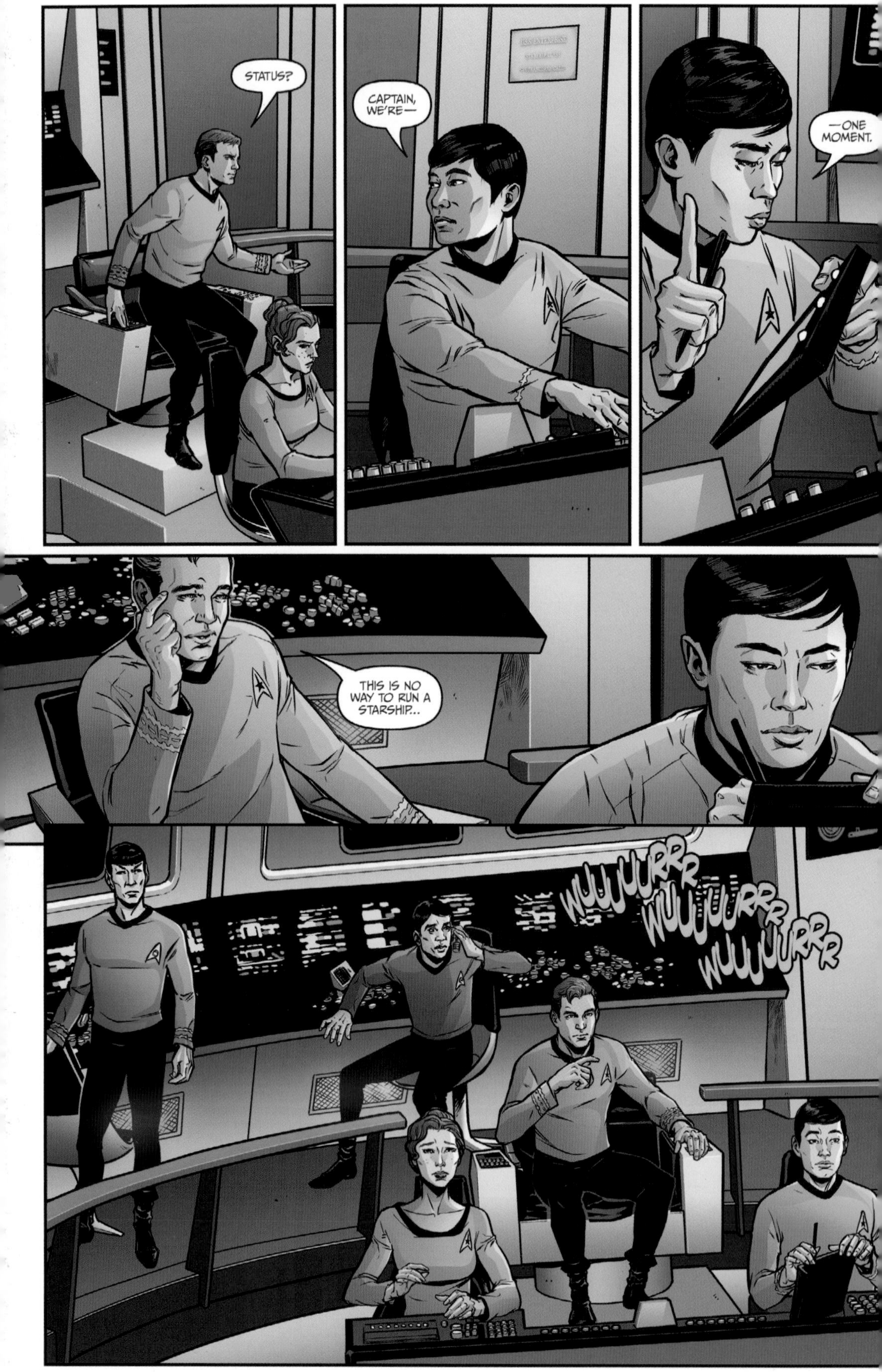
STATUS?
CAPTAIN, WE'RE—
—ONE MOMENT.
THIS IS NO WAY TO RUN A STARSHIP...
WUUUUURRR
WUUUUURRR
WUUUUURRR

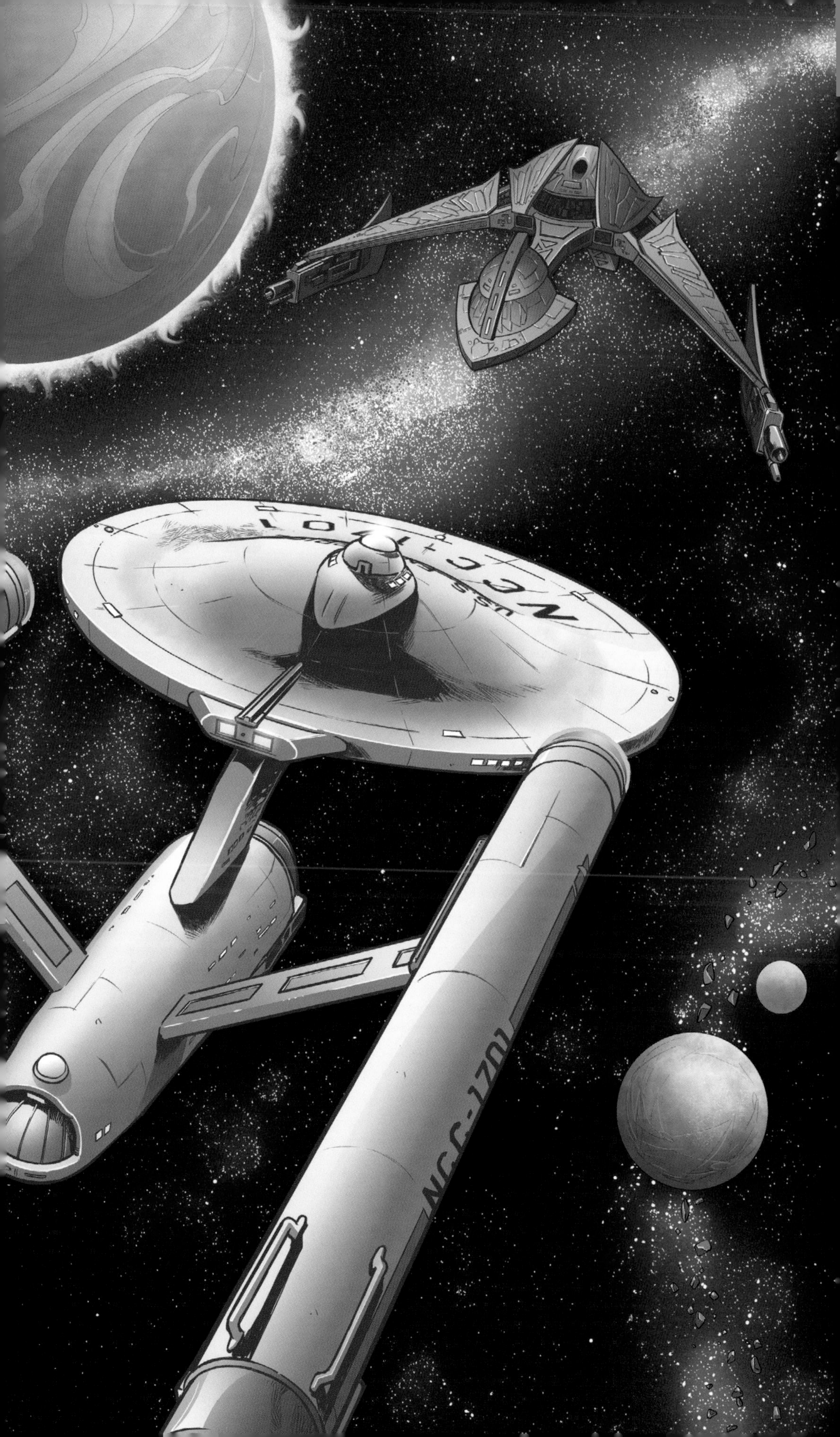

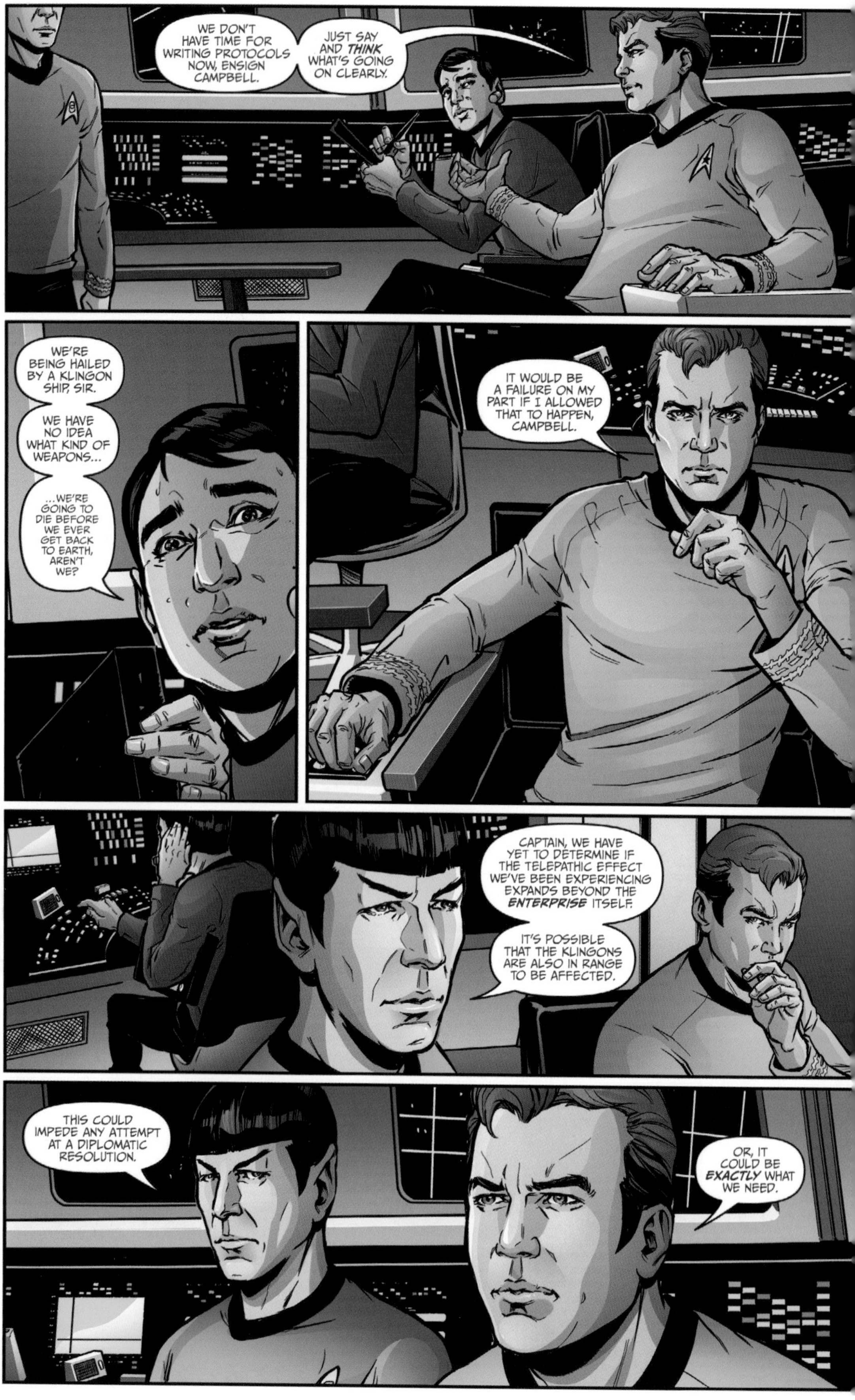
WE DON'T HAVE TIME FOR WRITING PROTOCOLS NOW, ENSIGN CAMPBELL.
JUST SAY AND *THINK* WHAT'S GOING ON CLEARLY.
WE'RE BEING HAILED BY A KLINGON SHIP, SIR.
WE HAVE NO IDEA WHAT KIND OF WEAPONS...
...WE'RE GOING TO DIE BEFORE WE EVER GET BACK TO EARTH, AREN'T WE?
IT WOULD BE A FAILURE ON MY PART IF I ALLOWED THAT TO HAPPEN, CAMPBELL.
CAPTAIN, WE HAVE YET TO DETERMINE IF THE TELEPATHIC EFFECT WE'VE BEEN EXPERIENCING EXPANDS BEYOND THE *ENTERPRISE* ITSELF.
IT'S POSSIBLE THAT THE KLINGONS ARE ALSO IN RANGE TO BE AFFECTED.
THIS COULD IMPEDE ANY ATTEMPT AT A DIPLOMATIC RESOLUTION.
OR, IT COULD BE *EXACTLY* WHAT WE NEED.

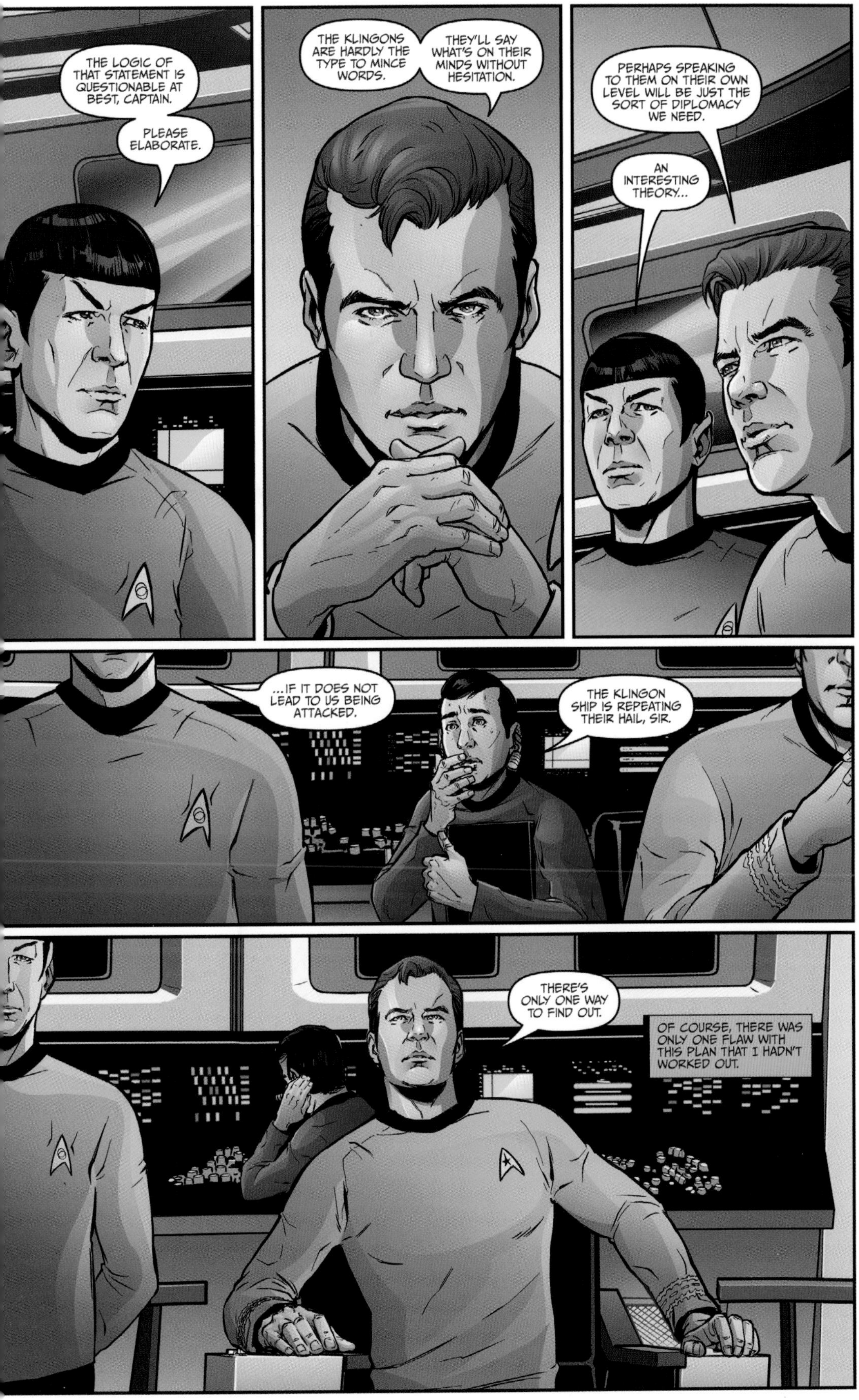
THE LOGIC OF THAT STATEMENT IS QUESTIONABLE AT BEST, CAPTAIN.
PLEASE ELABORATE.
THE KLINGONS ARE HARDLY THE TYPE TO MINCE WORDS.
THEY'LL SAY WHAT'S ON THEIR MINDS WITHOUT HESITATION.
PERHAPS SPEAKING TO THEM ON THEIR OWN LEVEL WILL BE JUST THE SORT OF DIPLOMACY WE NEED.
AN INTERESTING THEORY...
...IF IT DOES NOT LEAD TO US BEING ATTACKED.
THE KLINGON SHIP IS REPEATING THEIR HAIL, SIR.
THERE'S ONLY ONE WAY TO FIND OUT.
OF COURSE, THERE WAS ONLY ONE FLAW WITH THIS PLAN THAT I HADN'T WORKED OUT.

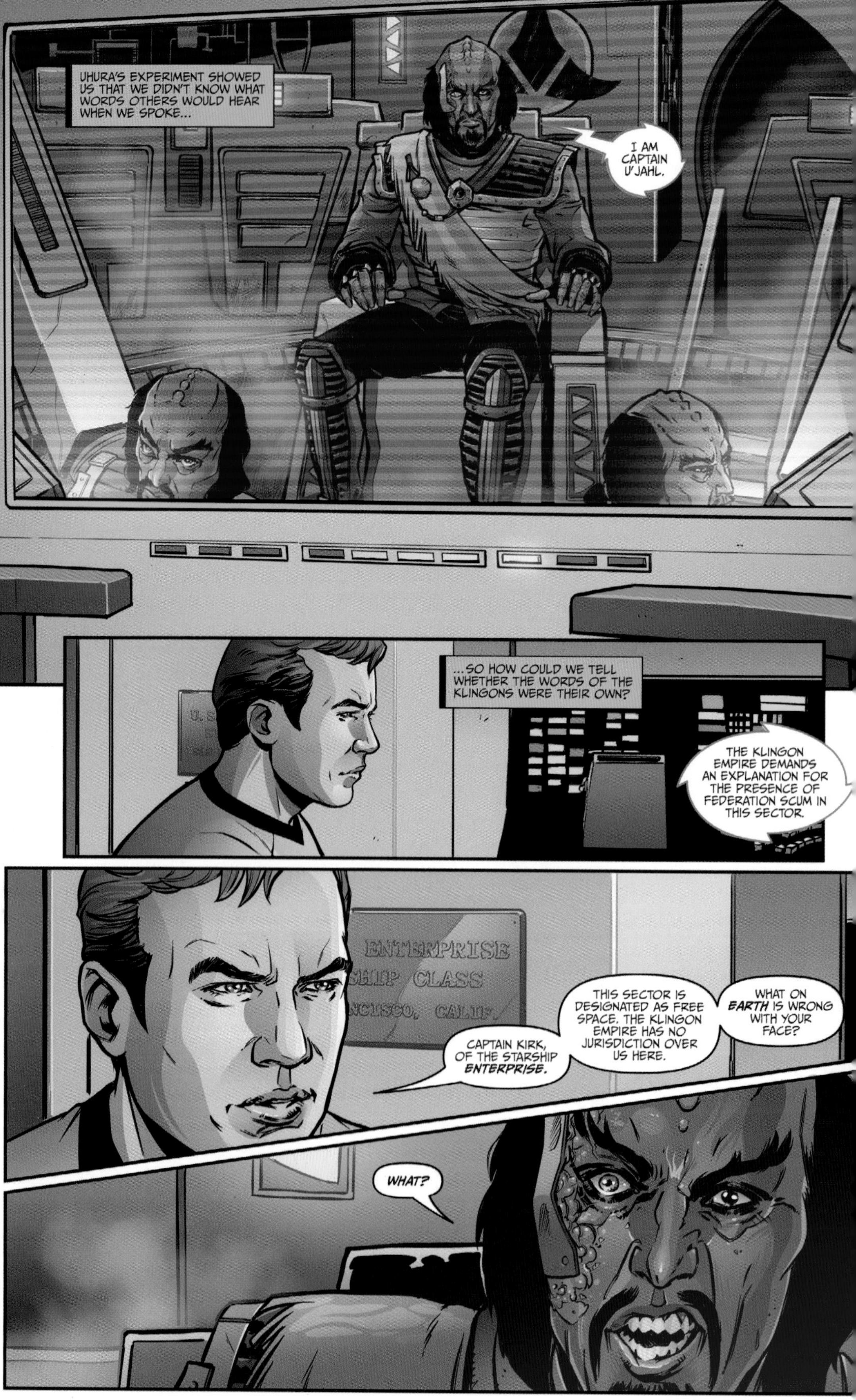

UHURA'S EXPERIMENT SHOWED US THAT WE DIDN'T KNOW WHAT WORDS OTHERS WOULD HEAR WHEN WE SPOKE...
I AM CAPTAIN U'JAHL.
...SO HOW COULD WE TELL WHETHER THE WORDS OF THE KLINGONS WERE THEIR OWN?
THE KLINGON EMPIRE DEMANDS AN EXPLANATION FOR THE PRESENCE OF FEDERATION SCUM IN THIS SECTOR.
ENTERPRISE
SHIP CLASS
NCISCO, CALIF.
CAPTAIN KIRK, OF THE STARSHIP *ENTERPRISE.*
THIS SECTOR IS DESIGNATED AS FREE SPACE. THE KLINGON EMPIRE HAS NO JURISDICTION OVER US HERE.
WHAT ON *EARTH* IS WRONG WITH YOUR FACE?
WHAT?

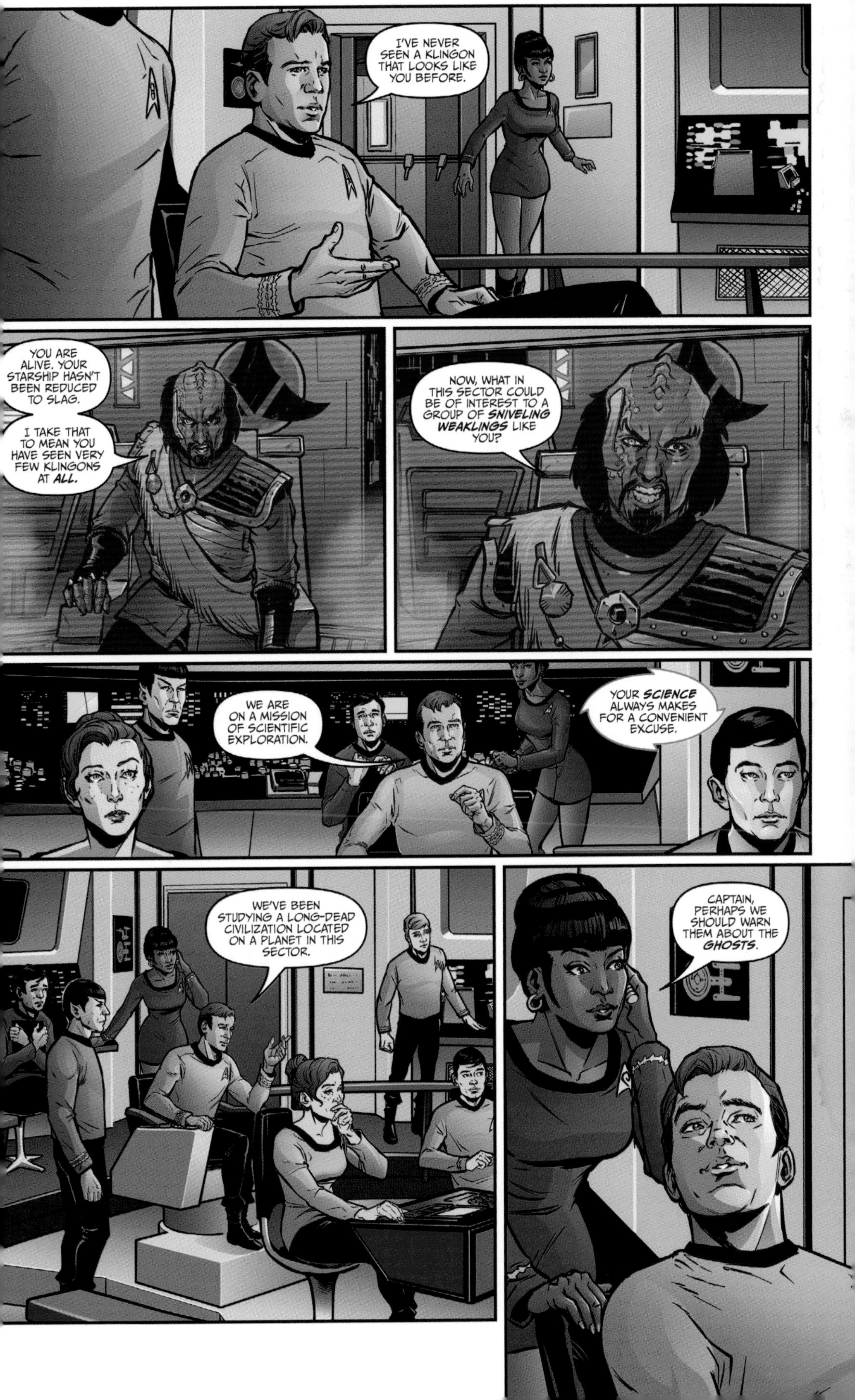

I'VE NEVER SEEN A KLINGON THAT LOOKS LIKE YOU BEFORE.
YOU ARE ALIVE. YOUR STARSHIP HASN'T BEEN REDUCED TO SLAG.
I TAKE THAT TO MEAN YOU HAVE SEEN VERY FEW KLINGONS AT ALL.
NOW, WHAT IN THIS SECTOR COULD BE OF INTEREST TO A GROUP OF SNIVELING WEAKLINGS LIKE YOU?
WE ARE ON A MISSION OF SCIENTIFIC EXPLORATION.
YOUR SCIENCE ALWAYS MAKES FOR A CONVENIENT EXCUSE.
WE'VE BEEN STUDYING A LONG-DEAD CIVILIZATION LOCATED ON A PLANET IN THIS SECTOR.
CAPTAIN, PERHAPS WE SHOULD WARN THEM ABOUT THE GHOSTS.

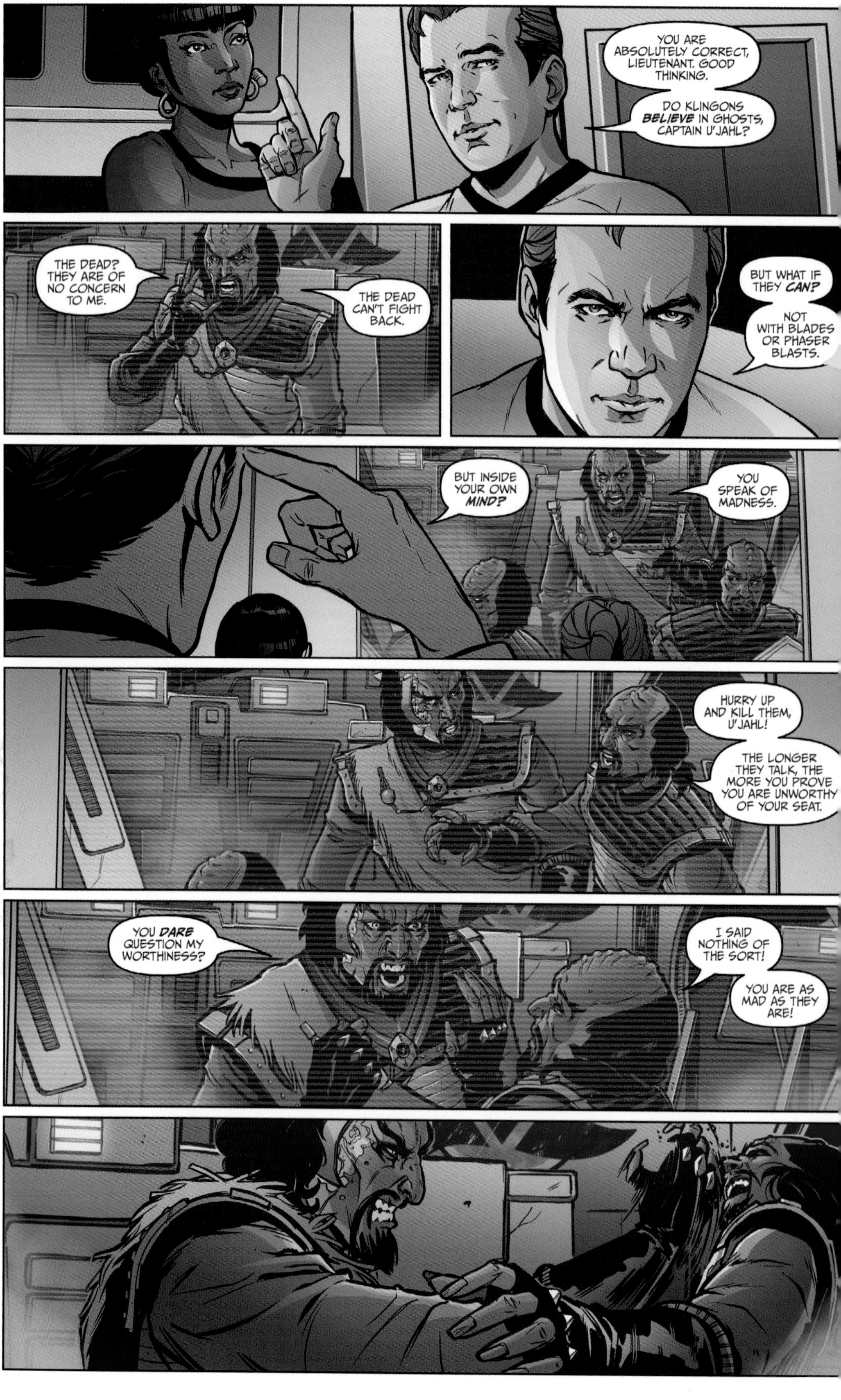
YOU ARE ABSOLUTELY CORRECT, LIEUTENANT. GOOD THINKING.
DO KLINGONS BELIEVE IN GHOSTS, CAPTAIN U'JAHL?
THE DEAD? THEY ARE OF NO CONCERN TO ME.
THE DEAD CAN'T FIGHT BACK.
BUT WHAT IF THEY CAN?
NOT WITH BLADES OR PHASER BLASTS.
BUT INSIDE YOUR OWN MIND?
YOU SPEAK OF MADNESS.
HURRY UP AND KILL THEM, U'JAHL!
THE LONGER THEY TALK, THE MORE YOU PROVE YOU ARE UNWORTHY OF YOUR SEAT.
YOU DARE QUESTION MY WORTHINESS?
I SAID NOTHING OF THE SORT!
YOU ARE AS MAD AS THEY ARE!

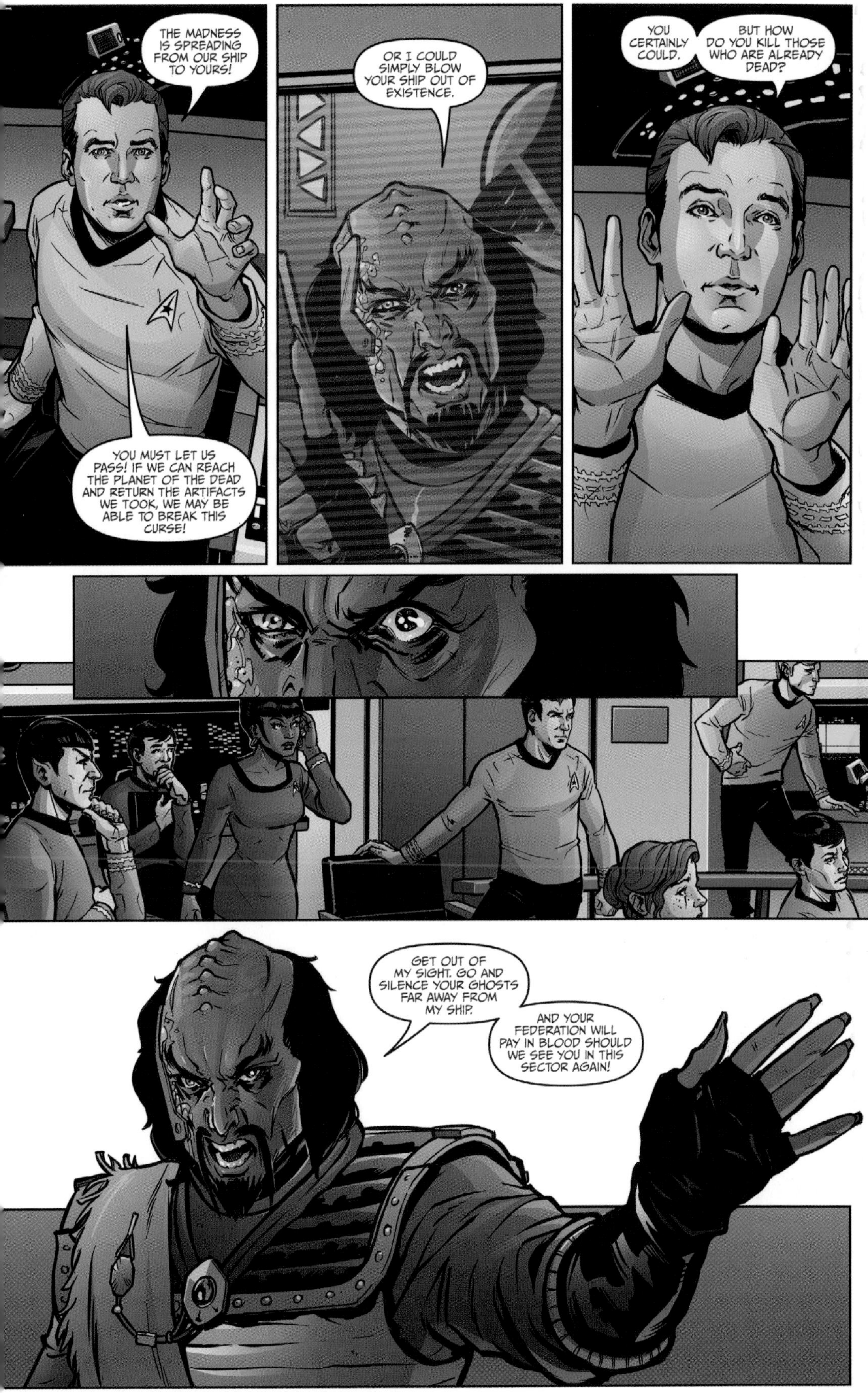
THE MADNESS IS SPREADING FROM OUR SHIP TO YOURS!
YOU MUST LET US PASS! IF WE CAN REACH THE PLANET OF THE DEAD AND RETURN THE ARTIFACTS WE TOOK, WE MAY BE ABLE TO BREAK THIS CURSE!
OR I COULD SIMPLY BLOW YOUR SHIP OUT OF EXISTENCE.
YOU CERTAINLY COULD.
BUT HOW DO YOU KILL THOSE WHO ARE ALREADY DEAD?
GET OUT OF MY SIGHT. GO AND SILENCE YOUR GHOSTS FAR AWAY FROM MY SHIP.
AND YOUR FEDERATION WILL PAY IN BLOOD SHOULD WE SEE YOU IN THIS SECTOR AGAIN!

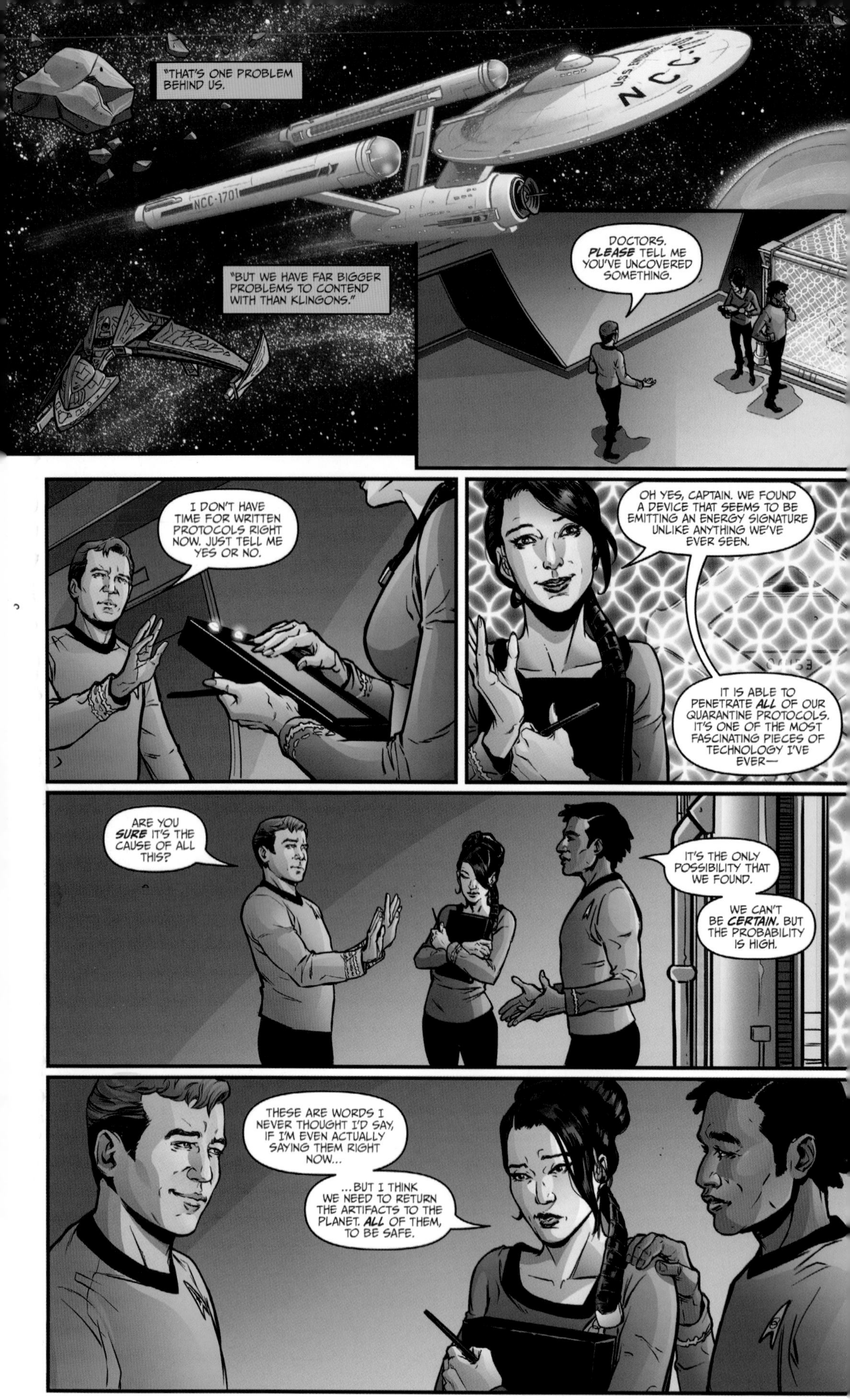
"THAT'S ONE PROBLEM BEHIND US.
"BUT WE HAVE FAR BIGGER PROBLEMS TO CONTEND WITH THAN KLINGONS."
DOCTORS. PLEASE TELL ME YOU'VE UNCOVERED SOMETHING.
I DON'T HAVE TIME FOR WRITTEN PROTOCOLS RIGHT NOW. JUST TELL ME YES OR NO.
OH YES, CAPTAIN. WE FOUND A DEVICE THAT SEEMS TO BE EMITTING AN ENERGY SIGNATURE UNLIKE ANYTHING WE'VE EVER SEEN.
IT IS ABLE TO PENETRATE ALL OF OUR QUARANTINE PROTOCOLS. IT'S ONE OF THE MOST FASCINATING PIECES OF TECHNOLOGY I'VE EVER—
ARE YOU SURE IT'S THE CAUSE OF ALL THIS?
IT'S THE ONLY POSSIBILITY THAT WE FOUND.
WE CAN'T BE CERTAIN. BUT THE PROBABILITY IS HIGH.
THESE ARE WORDS I NEVER THOUGHT I'D SAY, IF I'M EVEN ACTUALLY SAYING THEM RIGHT NOW...
...BUT I THINK WE NEED TO RETURN THE ARTIFACTS TO THE PLANET. ALL OF THEM, TO BE SAFE.

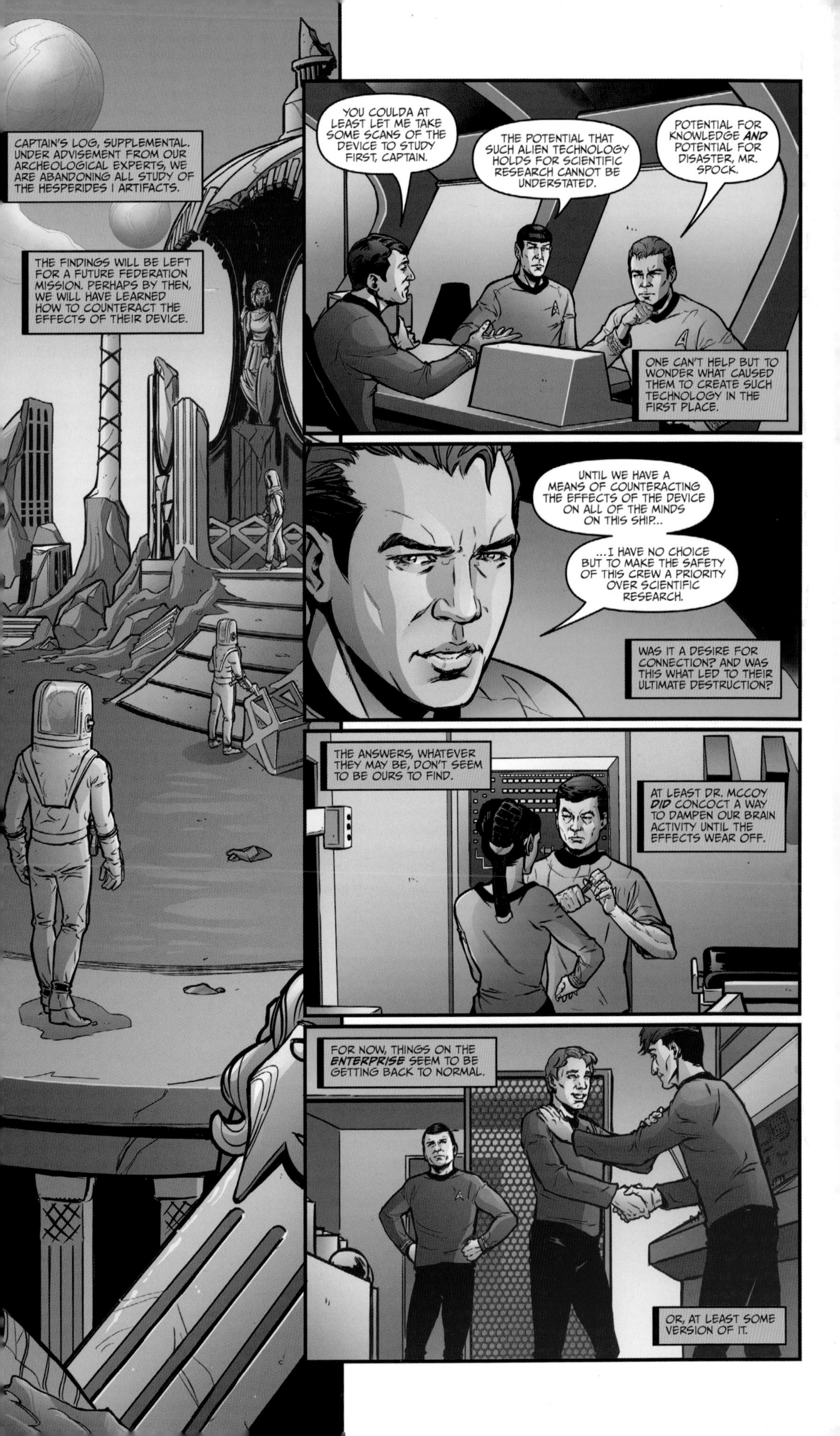
CAPTAIN'S LOG, SUPPLEMENTAL. UNDER ADVISEMENT FROM OUR ARCHEOLOGICAL EXPERTS, WE ARE ABANDONING ALL STUDY OF THE HESPERIDES I ARTIFACTS.
THE FINDINGS WILL BE LEFT FOR A FUTURE FEDERATION MISSION. PERHAPS BY THEN, WE WILL HAVE LEARNED HOW TO COUNTERACT THE EFFECTS OF THEIR DEVICE.
YOU COULDA AT LEAST LET ME TAKE SOME SCANS OF THE DEVICE TO STUDY FIRST, CAPTAIN.
THE POTENTIAL THAT SUCH ALIEN TECHNOLOGY HOLDS FOR SCIENTIFIC RESEARCH CANNOT BE UNDERSTATED.
POTENTIAL FOR KNOWLEDGE AND POTENTIAL FOR DISASTER, MR. SPOCK.
ONE CAN'T HELP BUT TO WONDER WHAT CAUSED THEM TO CREATE SUCH TECHNOLOGY IN THE FIRST PLACE.
UNTIL WE HAVE A MEANS OF COUNTERACTING THE EFFECTS OF THE DEVICE ON ALL OF THE MINDS ON THIS SHIP...
...I HAVE NO CHOICE BUT TO MAKE THE SAFETY OF THIS CREW A PRIORITY OVER SCIENTIFIC RESEARCH.
WAS IT A DESIRE FOR CONNECTION? AND WAS THIS WHAT LED TO THEIR ULTIMATE DESTRUCTION?
THE ANSWERS, WHATEVER THEY MAY BE, DON'T SEEM TO BE OURS TO FIND.
AT LEAST DR. MCCOY DID CONCOCT A WAY TO DAMPEN OUR BRAIN ACTIVITY UNTIL THE EFFECTS WEAR OFF.
FOR NOW, THINGS ON THE ENTERPRISE SEEM TO BE GETTING BACK TO NORMAL.
OR, AT LEAST SOME VERSION OF IT.

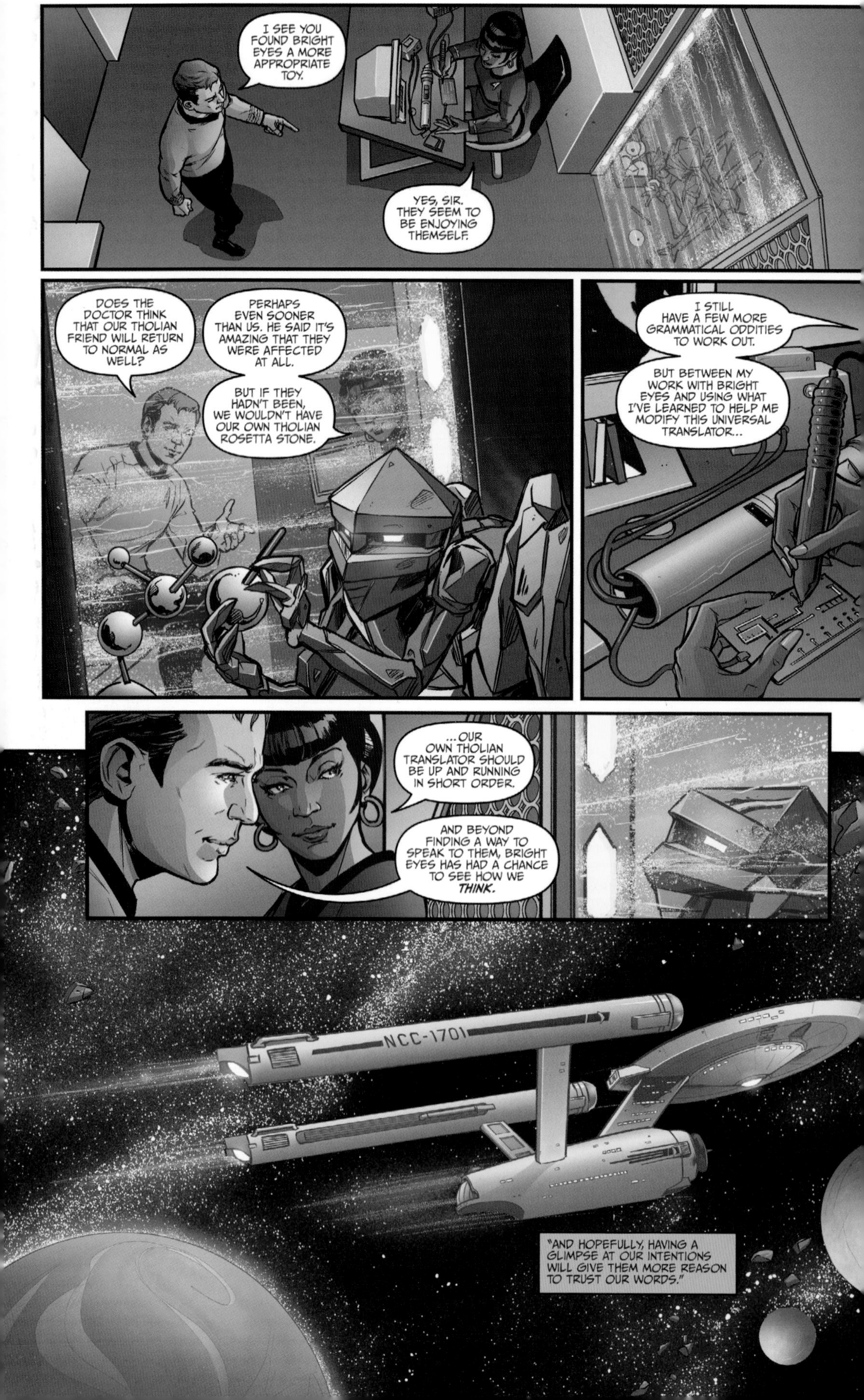
I SEE YOU FOUND BRIGHT EYES A MORE APPROPRIATE TOY.
YES, SIR. THEY SEEM TO BE ENJOYING THEMSELF.
DOES THE DOCTOR THINK THAT OUR THOLIAN FRIEND WILL RETURN TO NORMAL AS WELL?
PERHAPS EVEN SOONER THAN US. HE SAID IT'S AMAZING THAT THEY WERE AFFECTED AT ALL.
BUT IF THEY HADN'T BEEN, WE WOULDN'T HAVE OUR OWN THOLIAN ROSETTA STONE.
I STILL HAVE A FEW MORE GRAMMATICAL ODDITIES TO WORK OUT.
BUT BETWEEN MY WORK WITH BRIGHT EYES AND USING WHAT I'VE LEARNED TO HELP ME MODIFY THIS UNIVERSAL TRANSLATOR...
...OUR OWN THOLIAN TRANSLATOR SHOULD BE UP AND RUNNING IN SHORT ORDER.
AND BEYOND FINDING A WAY TO SPEAK TO THEM, BRIGHT EYES HAS HAD A CHANCE TO SEE HOW WE THINK.
NCC-1701
"AND HOPEFULLY, HAVING A GLIMPSE AT OUR INTENTIONS WILL GIVE THEM MORE REASON TO TRUST OUR WORDS."

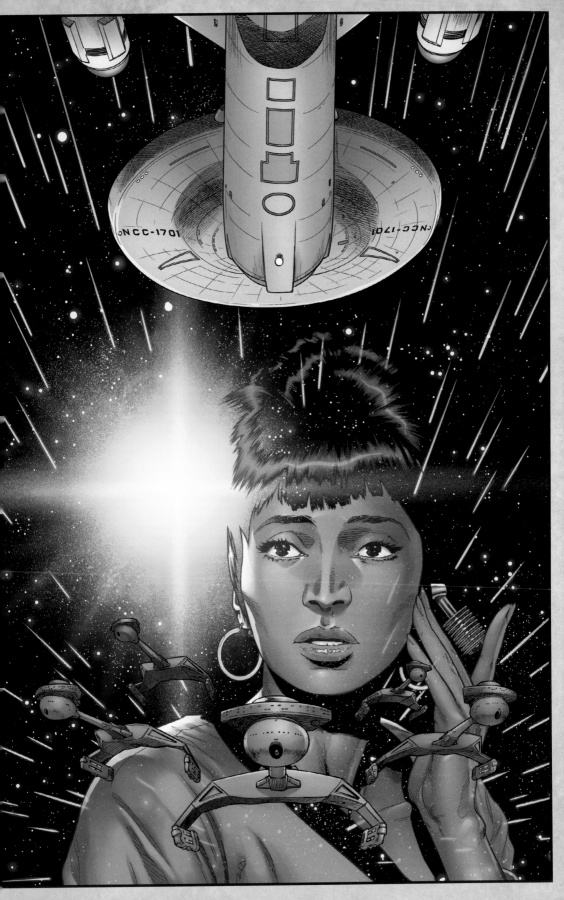

ART BY **STEPHEN THOMPSON**

COLORS BY **CHARLIE KIRCHOFF**

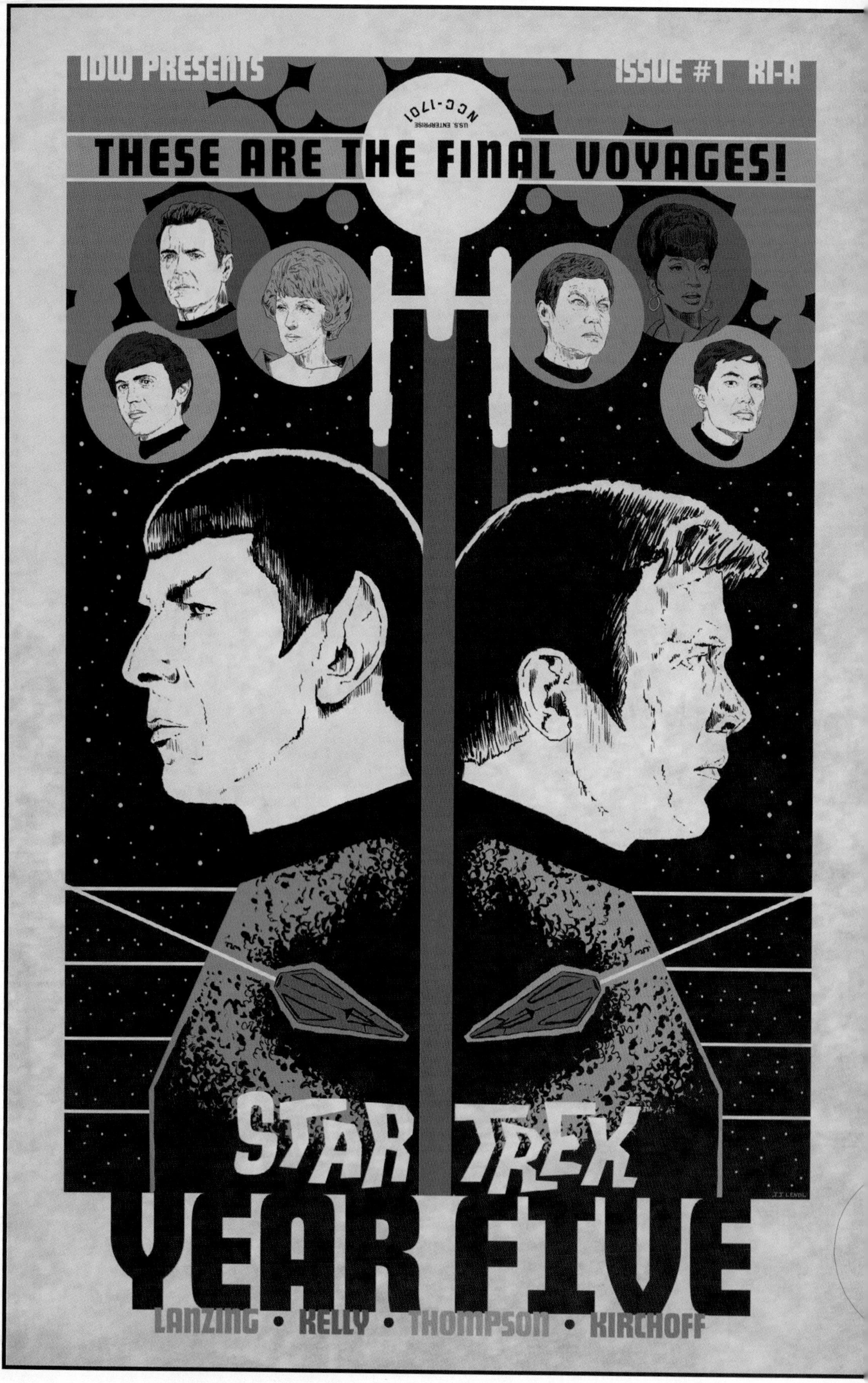
IDW PRESENTS
ISSUE #1 RI-A
U.S.S. ENTERPRISE
NCC-1701
THESE ARE THE FINAL VOYAGES!
STAR TREK
YEAR FIVE
LANZING • KELLY • THOMPSON • KIRCHOFF
J.J. LENDL

ART BY J.J. LENDL

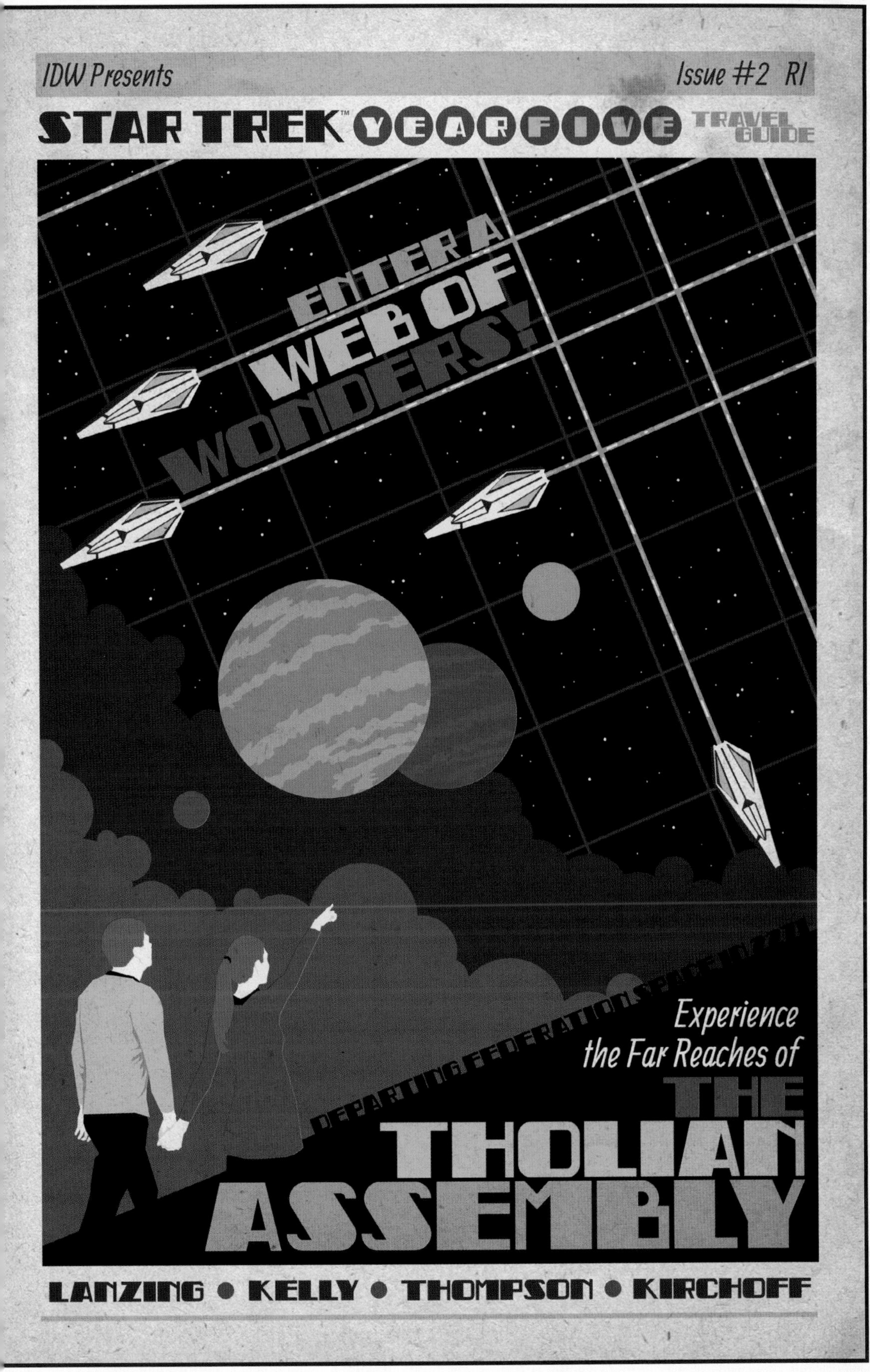
IDW Presents
Issue #2 RI
STAR TREK™ YEAR FIVE TRAVEL GUIDE
ENTER A WEB OF WONDERS!
DEPARTING FEDERATION SPACE
Experience the Far Reaches of
THE THOLIAN ASSEMBLY
LANZING • KELLY • THOMPSON • KIRCHOFF

ART BY J.J. LENDL

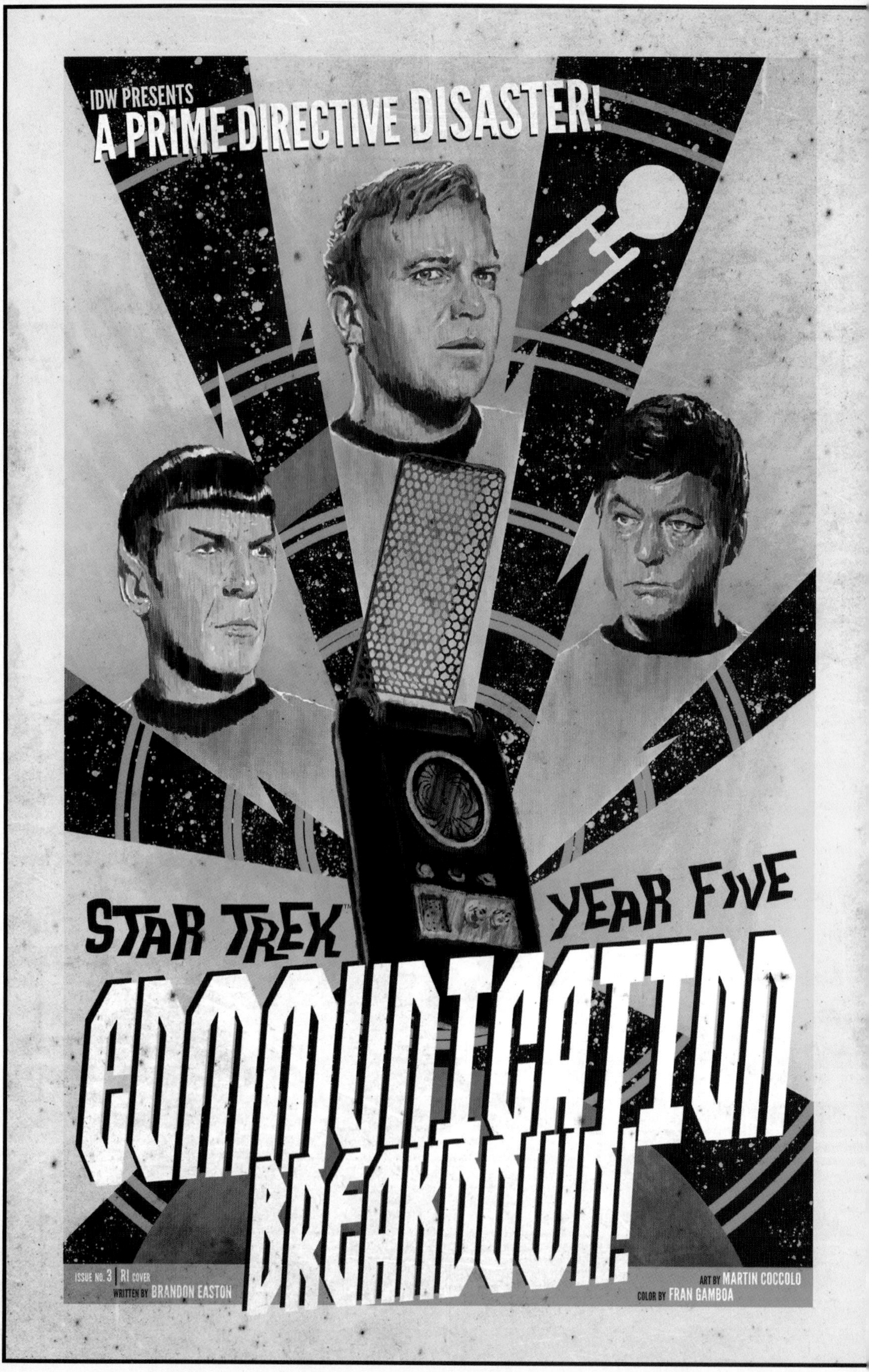
IDW PRESENTS
A PRIME DIRECTIVE DISASTER!
STAR TREK™
YEAR FIVE
COMMUNICATION BREAKDOWN!
ISSUE NO. 3 | RI COVER
WRITTEN BY BRANDON EASTON
ART BY MARTIN COCCOLO
COLOR BY FRAN GAMBOA

ART BY **J.J. LENDL**

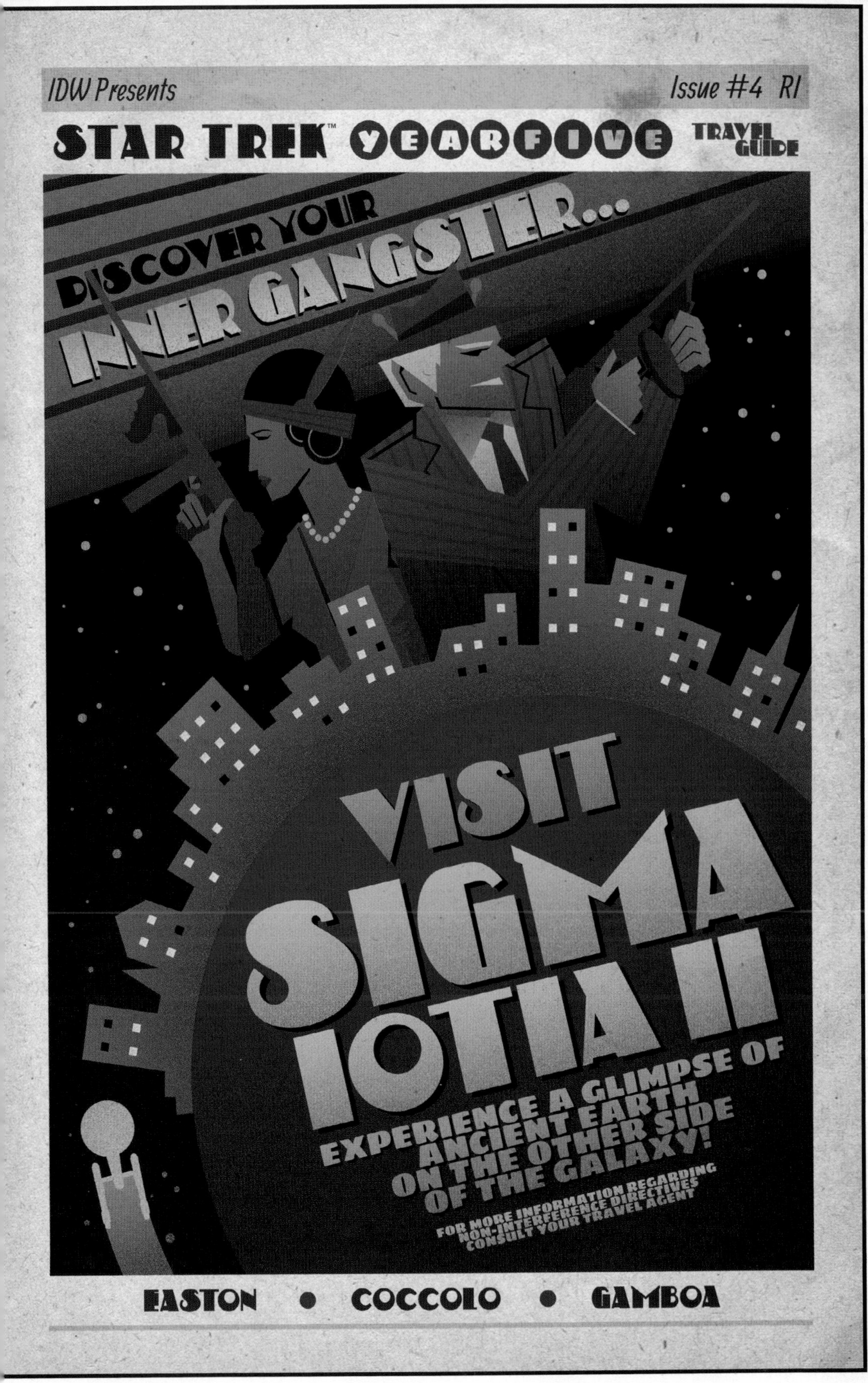
IDW Presents
Issue #4 RI
STAR TREK™ YEAR FIVE TRAVEL GUIDE
DISCOVER YOUR
INNER GANGSTER...
VISIT
SIGMA
IOTIA II
EXPERIENCE A GLIMPSE OF ANCIENT EARTH ON THE OTHER SIDE OF THE GALAXY!
FOR MORE INFORMATION REGARDING NON-INTERFERENCE DIRECTIVES CONSULT YOUR TRAVEL AGENT
EASTON • COCCOLO • GAMBOA

ART BY **J.J. LENDL**

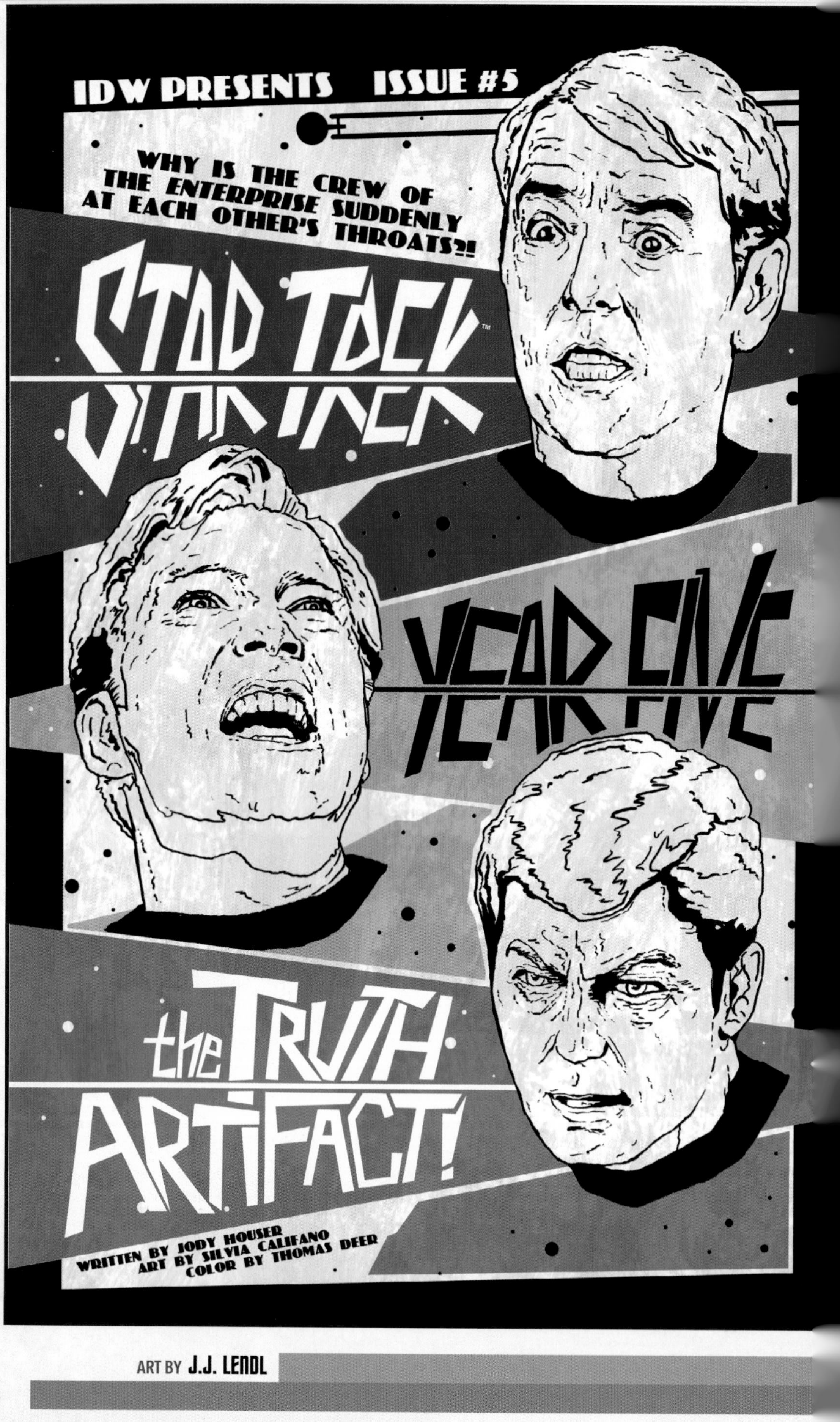
IDW PRESENTS ISSUE #5
WHY IS THE CREW OF THE ENTERPRISE SUDDENLY AT EACH OTHER'S THROATS?!
STAR TREK™
YEAR FIVE
the TRUTH ARTIFACT!
WRITTEN BY JODY HOUSER
ART BY SILVIA CALIFANO
COLOR BY THOMAS DEER

ART BY J.J. LENDL

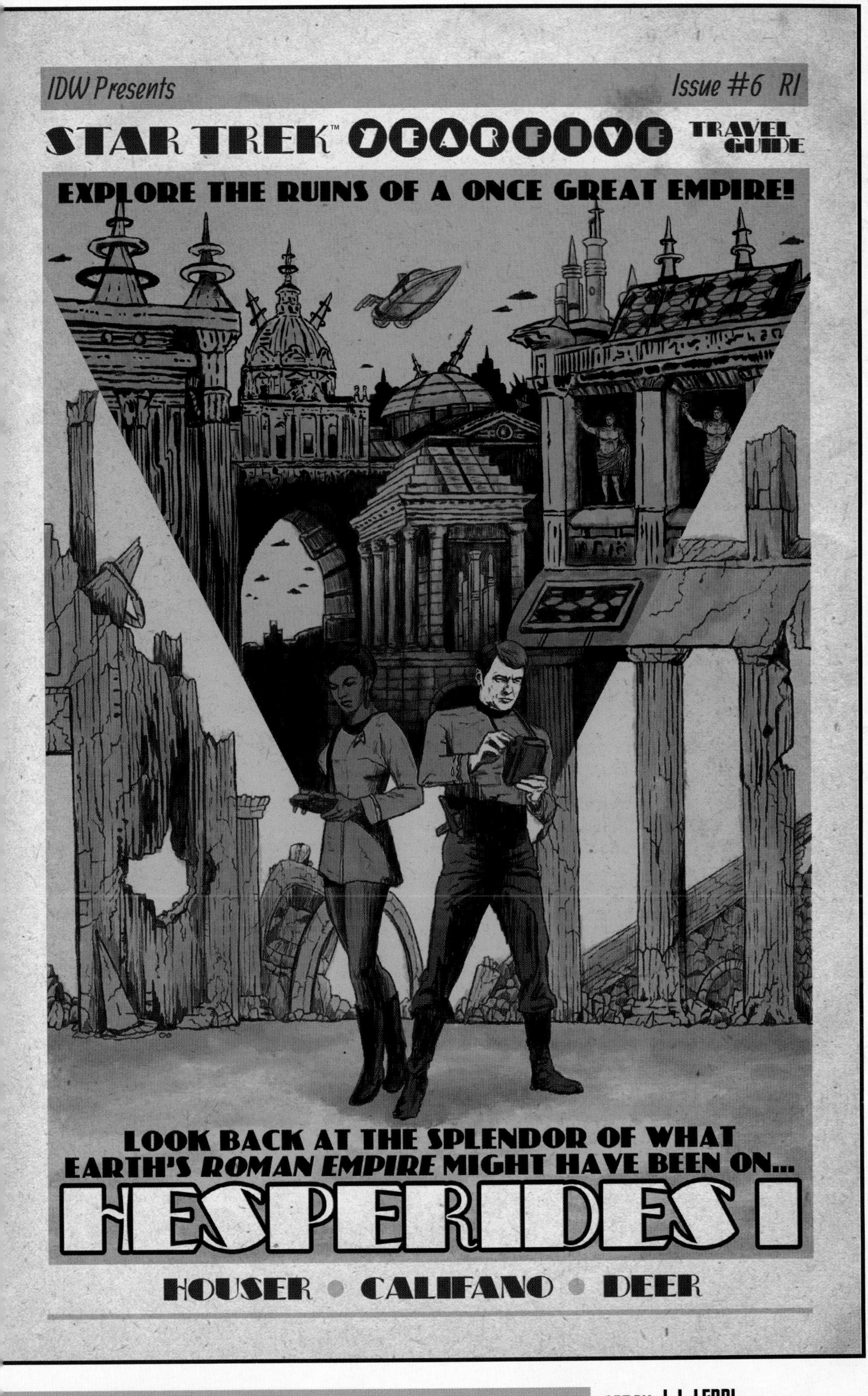
IDW Presents
Issue #6 RI
STAR TREK™ YEAR FIVE TRAVEL GUIDE
EXPLORE THE RUINS OF A ONCE GREAT EMPIRE!
LOOK BACK AT THE SPLENDOR OF WHAT EARTH'S ROMAN EMPIRE MIGHT HAVE BEEN ON...
HESPERIDES I
HOUSER • CALIFANO • DEER

ART BY J.J. LENDL

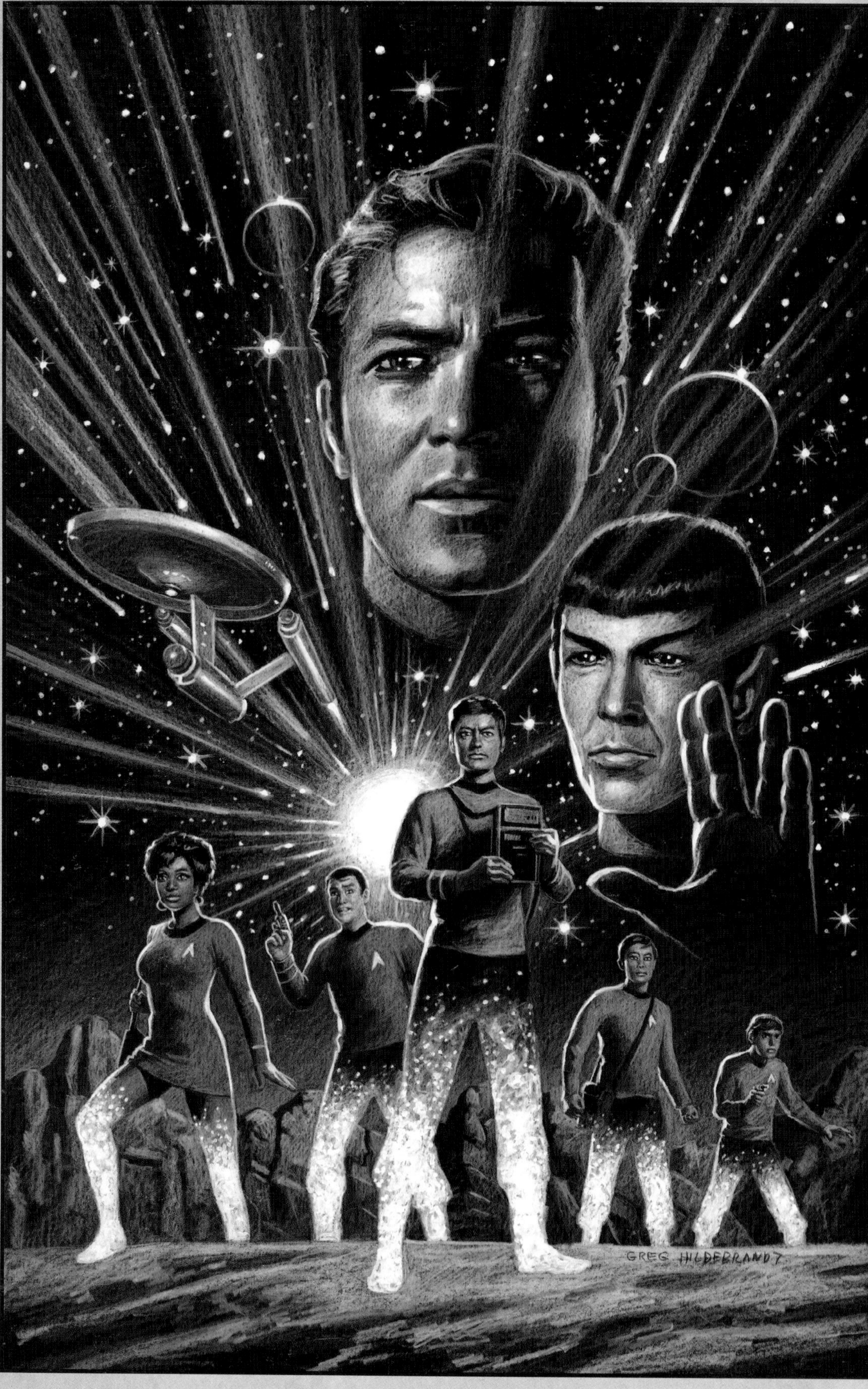
GREG HILDEBRANDT

ART BY **GREG HILDEBRANDT**